# DAUGHTER OF
# DEATHS

## THE SCYTHE WIELDER'S SECRET: BOOK 3

## Christopher Mannino

MuseItUp Publishing
Canada

Daughter of Deaths© 2016 by Christopher Mannino

MuseItUp Publishing
https://museituppublishing.com

Cover Art © 2016 by Eerilyfair Design
Layout and Book Production by Lea Schizas
Print ISBN: 978-1-77127-831-7
eBook ISBN: 978-1-77127-830-0
First eBook Edition *September 2016

### School of Deaths

*"With strong characters, a fairly fast moving plot, and snappy dialogue, this novel should keep readers engaged from the beginning to the end. Five Stars."*
—Book Breeze Magazine

*"This YA fantasy book was too good to put down. I devoured it in two days."*
—Joan Curtis, Author of *A Jenna Scali Novel* series

*"If you like Harry Potter, you'll love School of Deaths!"*
—A Book Utopia BookTube Review

### Sword of Deaths

*"As a HUGE fan of reaper stories this series is one of the best I have read. I can't wait to read the next one! Five stars!"*
—NerdGirl Reviews

*"This one seemed to be more suspenseful than the first, holding me in its clutches until I finished, and left me begging for more."*
—Amanda Gillepsie

*"I love, love this series! Suzie really grows up in this one and it's great to see. 5/5 stars!"*
—AnjelineReads BookTube Review

*To my first two fans: Mom and Dad*

# Alone

$S$he lay on a soft bed, under a blanket. Rolling, she grimaced at the pain in her limbs.

"You'll need food and water," said a voice. "Drink this."

Susan opened her eyes.

Sindril stood above her, holding a pitcher. The man she'd fought last year. The man who'd brought her to this world, and tried to kill her. The Death who'd betrayed them all.

"Sindril."

"Welcome, Susan."

She reached for Grym.

*Help me.*

Nothing. She couldn't sense the First Scythe.

"It's no use struggling." Sindril smiled. "You are mine." He reached forward, stroking her hair. She shrank back, repulsed.

"Rest." He grinned like a serpent. Rising, he walked out of the room. The door clicked and locked.

Susan sat up, staring at the walls of her cell. A single, narrow window let a chill wind through the rocky chamber. Her fingers ran over the filmy webbing covering her right wrist.

*"The College of Deaths gives a special welcome to Susan Sarnio, the first female Death in a million years."*

It'd been nearly two years since Sindril made the speech. In an instant, her life had been thrown into chaos. She'd been a kid in Maryland, a normal girl, forced into the World of Deaths reaping souls.

She stood and walked to the window.

"Will!" She screamed into the air, but the wind whipped her voice back into her face. She looked out at craggy snow-covered mountains. Dragons flew in the distance.

Hurrying to one of the walls she called again, "Will? Are you there? Can you hear me?"

No one answered.

*He's alive. If he'd been killed, I wouldn't even remember his name.*

She ran her fingers over her wrist again. *Grym? What have they done to you?*

Grym may have murdered innocent people through her arm, yet she wished the First Scythe would respond. She sat on the mattress again, staring at the ground.

*It's over. Sindril won.*

With a shudder she remembered Sarmarin shedding his human skin. The massive Dragon grabbed her in his talons, while another beast captured Will.

*Will.*

The first boy she'd kissed, the first friend she'd made in the College, and one of her closest allies in this strange, inhospitable world.

"Will?" she called again. Silence answered.

*Where are you?*

Tears welled in her eyes. Tears for the girl torn from her home; tears for the isolation she'd suffered as the only female in a world of men; tears for the doubts circling her heart.

*I am alone.*

# PART ONE

THROUGH FIRE

# The Vow

*Where are they? It's been weeks.*

None of the teachers knew. His friends were alive, else he'd never realize they were missing. In the World of Deaths, if a Death was killed they vanished from memory, *erased*. If Susan and Will died, he wouldn't even remember their names. He suspected Hann knew something, yet the Headmaster avoided him whenever he approached.

Frank yawned, half-listening to Professor Stevens.

"Few realize how important Reaping is to society." Stevens looked as old as the history he taught. "Unreaped souls linger, lost forever in the cruel world. Why do you think stories of ghosts persist there? All stories derive from a foundation of truth."

Frank looked out the window, gazing across the mounds of the College.

"Only Deaths can bring souls to the Hereafter." Stevens tapped his bony finger on the desk. "Without us, the living would never find solace. Sometimes events in the Mortal World push us to the brink of our abilities. During the Second World War, an extra seven hundred young Deaths were summoned to aid with the Reapings. By the time they were fully trained, the war ended. Who knows what this group of Deaths became?"

*Susan would know. She's the only one of us who actually studied. Heck, she spent all her free time in the Library.*

The class droned on around him. Frank couldn't focus.

*Why am I here? I came back for Susan and Will, but they're gone. I'm not a Death. I have no business pretending anymore. After what they did…*

Behind his mind, the chimera stirred.

For a terrible moment he saw his mother's face, while she melted into the glowing lake. *Murdered.*

An itch on his neck told him Michi was tapping her feet.

With a deep sigh, he forced his power back into the recesses of his subconscious.

Stevens signaled the end of class. Frank rose from his seat and scratched his collar. Michi crawled near his neck as a tiny beetle. Her legs tickled, but her presence reassured him. He'd lost control of his power, and had hurt her. He wouldn't let that happen again.

Walking through the stone labyrinth of the College he gazed up at West Tower.

*I can't use my power to search for them. I have to trust that they're all right.*

Red clouds hung behind the mountain of stone. The giant tower loomed in the sky like a dark finger, pointing to the heavens.

*"Frank!"*

The voice called into his mind, like a whisper from far away.

*Susan?*

*"Help us!"*

The voice faded into wind. Had he imagined it?

No, something was wrong.

"Michi, Susan just called to me." He glanced around.

The beetle flew into the air, growing larger. Its legs expanded downward and its head and neck blurred. A cloud enveloped the shifting form, until only a sallow-faced seventeen-year-old girl with straggly auburn hair and piercing black eyes remained. Michi dusted off her clothes and coughed, before peering into the sky.

"Do you see anything?" He touched her shoulder.

She gazed into the west, her arms extended. Frank guessed she was asking other insects for help in spotting the voice he'd heard riding the wind.

"My friends tell me she's been captured by Dragons. A black Dragon held Susan in its claws, and a white Dragon carried Will. Both Deaths appeared unconscious." Michi clutched her chest, breathing hard. Frank put his arm around her. The cost of an Elemental's power was a sliver of their soul. Whether she'd paid with her own, or one of her insect friends, she'd paid dearly.

"We have to go after them." Frank's fingers tightened into a fist.

"You barely fought off one Dragon last time. You want to go chasing a group of them? Those two are probably flying back to their country, where there could be hundreds or thousands of Dragons."

"We have to do something. Our friends need us."

He spun around, his heart racing. Susan was in mortal danger, yet as long as he remembered her name, she lived, and there was a chance he could save her. He ran through the canyons of the College, with Michi trailing behind.

Mounds of stone snaked away in every direction, forming a labyrinth of rock beneath the massive towers. East and West Tower writhed above the stony maze like two gnarled mountains, each over a hundred stories high. Deaths young and old milled about the campus, coming and going from classes or Reapings. Some shouted at him as he sped past. Still, his mind remained fixed on Susan. He stopped at the base of East Tower. Its walls shot toward the clouds, forming a massive column of twisted rock.

"Frank, what are you doing? They think you're a Death. How will you explain what you heard?"

Frank's pride welled. He'd hidden his identity from the College so that he could remain and help the integration of Elementals and Deaths. Yet, what did it matter? His mother lay murdered, and he still didn't know whether Deaths or Dragons killed her. Was he really going to ask the Deaths for help? No, there were only two Deaths he trusted, and they were far away, in terrible danger.

"You're right," he whispered. "Deaths can't be trusted."

Michi put her hand on his arm. "Listen to me. You're still upset over Kasumir. If we want to help Susan, we should tell the Deaths, but be careful what you reveal. How would they react if they learn you've spent two years lying about your identity?"

She glanced around, and her features melted and dissolved. Michi became a tiny beetle, which landed on Frank's neck.

The massive doorway in front of them opened, and a chubby older Death with a gold necklace staggered out. Frank recognized him as one of Susan's favorite teachers, the one she'd saved by failing her first year test.

"He-he-hello." When Cronk started past them, something in Frank's conscious caught. They did need help, and this was someone Susan cared for and trusted. Even if a Death attacked his mother, it couldn't be Cronk, the Death was too much of a bumbling idiot.

"Susan's in trouble." Frank frowned.

Cronk nodded, his face creasing into furrows. "She's b-b-been m-m-m-missing my classes."

"Come with us to see Hann," said Frank.

Michi tapped her tiny feet against his neck, perhaps puzzled.

Cronk followed Frank into East Tower. They boarded an elevator and rose to the hundredth floor, where Headmaster Hann's office watched over the campus.

"Yes?" called the Headmaster, when Frank rapped the skull-shaped knocker.

"We need to talk to you. It's about Susan Sarnio and Will Black."

A moment later, Hann pulled the door open, scowling. The thin, goateed Death frowned. "Susan and Will are on special assignment."

"They've been captured." Frank walked to the desk, staring at the Headmaster. *Could he be involved in mother's murder?*

Hann's frown deepened.

"C-c-captured?" Cronk scowled.

"Sit." Hann ushered them toward a pair of chairs near the large mahogany desk. A circular window behind it overlooked the College below. Hann walked to the window, his back toward the others, who remained standing.

"Susan and Will are prisoners of the Dragons." Frank paused. "We need to send a rescue party."

"Tell me what you know, and *how* you know it." Hann didn't turn.

"An Elemental saw them." Michi buzzed on his neck, but remained hidden. "They were too frightened to approach you directly. They told me they saw Susan and Will, each in a Dragon's talons, flying west."

"An Elemental?"

"Yes. She told the first Death she encountered." If Hann had any hand in Kasumir's murder, Frank couldn't reveal himself.

"Is it t-t-t-true?"

"If they've been captured, they are gone." Hann turned to face them. "War is coming, and this news is a terrible blow. Our greatest hope is lost. All we can do is fortify the College and prepare for the onslaught."

"Where were they?" Frank scowled. "What did you send them to do?"

Sinking into his chair, Hann frowned. "Very well, since you are their friend I'll tell you, but this remains in this room. Both of you must swear to secrecy."

Frank and Cronk mumbled their assent.

"Susan and Will went with a group of Deaths to explore a new source of mortamant. With our shipments under attack, we needed to replenish our stores."

"You sent two kids from the Junior College?" Frank waved his hand in surprise.

"Everyone else is busy preparing for the conflict," snapped Hann. "Those not on Reapings have been replenishing the mortamant within the Ring of Scythes, and have been readying the College. The Dragons want this war; there's no avoiding it."

"So you send Susan and Will on a fool's errand, and now that it's failed, you abandon them to our enemy?"

Hann slammed his fist on the table and stood. "Who do you think you are? I am the Headmaster of this College. I decide—"

"You're abandoning two of your own." Frank stepped forward, his fingers balled into tight fists. "Two Deaths who were captured because of you."

Hann stared at him, his eyes glistening with anger.

"L-l-let's settle d-d-d-down." Cronk raised his hands.

"I'm going after her. I'll find them."

"You are a Death, and the College needs everyone now."

Frank's power watched from behind his eyes, the chimera clawed forward ready to scream.

*I'm not a Death!*

A blur of motion sped away from Frank, ballooning into a gray blur. Michi transformed into her normal form.

"Who are you?"

"I'm the Elemental who saw Susan and Will. I snuck into this room, to ensure you'd help them. They are my friends."

Michi raised her hand before he could interrupt. "Please, sir. You need help and information on the Dragons, right? If Frank wants to search for his friends, he'll become a distraction. Let him go. If he succeeds, Will and Susan might help you learn the Dragons' plan. If he fails, you'll only have lost a distraction."

"I w-w-w-want to help t-too."

"You?" laughed Hann. "You want to h-h-help?"

Cronk bristled, nodding.

"This is insane." Hann tugged his goatee. "Still, I don't have the time to stop you. Go, if you must. You three are on your own. I have no way to communicate with you, and no one will follow to offer support."

"When we return, I expect an apology." Frank raised an eyebrow.

Hann laughed again. "If you come back with information that helps in this effort, I'll grant each of you one request, anything you want. You could even have this office."

The chimera of Frank's power started to growl behind his thoughts. *He's confident we'll all be killed. He doesn't even mask his ridicule.*

"Put it in writing." Frank's words were half-speak, half-snarl.

Hann pulled out a sheet of parchment, and scrawled his promise, signing his name and adding a wax seal. His expression sobered.

"I don't think you will succeed. However, I hope I'm wrong. Will and Susan are two of the finest Deaths here. Frank, you're impressive too. I need you. I need *all* of you here."

"We will return." Frank slipped Hann's letter into his pocket.

Hann turned to Michi. "I don't know what abilities you possess, but help them. The power of a 'Mental might just save their lives."

She nodded.

Hann rose and walked to a closet. He withdrew a scythe, handing it to Cronk. "I only have one scythe to spare. The shortage of mortamant prevents me from giving you more. However, there is one other weapon I can provide." He reached further into his closet, pulling out a large bundle. He opened it, revealing a boskery blade.

"I thought they were melted down after the finals." Frank's eyebrow rose.

"We spared this one. It's no different from any other boskery blade; its blade will paralyze an enemy. Although far weaker than a traditional scythe, given your skill on the boskery field, I'm sure you'll think of something."

"Thank you." Frank took the double-bladed scythe from Hann. "We'll need gorgers and other supplies too."

Hann scribbled an order on a slip of paper, handing it to Cronk. "Take what you need from the kitchens. Leave soon, and don't tell anyone where you're going. Unless you return, this conversation never happened."

Frank, Michi, and Cronk rode the elevator down in silence.

"We'll meet at the western gate at midnight." Frank shook his head. "Once we leave this campus, we're not returning without Susan and Will."

CHAPTER TWO—SUSAN

# Flight

Susan stared at the locked door. Her stomach knotted in revulsion. Gripping the edge of her bed, she exhaled slowly, willing her heart to stop pounding.

*"You are mine."* Sindril's statement echoed in her mind.

*I will kill you, Sindril*, she promised.

She surveyed the tiny chamber. A flower nearby grew brighter, radiating a gentle white glow which filled the small room. Unadorned beige stone walls stretched from ceiling to floor all around. Aside from the bed, she had a table, chair, and chamber pot. She walked to a hole in the wall, no larger than her hand. The glassless portal extended through the foot-thick rock, offering her a view outside.

She gazed down the side of a mountain. Across the valley, another mountain extended, followed by hundreds of other enormous peaks. The mountain range seemed deserted, though she heard the flutter of wings and scraping of claws below. A single green Dragon flew in the dim light, circling toward a cave in the opposite cliffs. A chill breeze blew through the open window, whistling against the rocks. The air smelled of snow and pine, mixed with the pungent odors of sulfur and smoke.

Susan glanced at the door, and walked to it. She pushed against the handle-less entryway with all her might. The door didn't move. Though somewhat comfortable, the room was still a prison.

*Grym? Can you hear me?*

The First Scythe didn't answer. Grym, also known as Caladbolg, the First Scythe. She'd discovered him last year, and for a time he'd shown her flashes of the ancient past, when the first Deaths battled Dragons. After Sindril's attack, they'd fused somehow. The ancient weapon now lay trapped beneath the Dragon's coating. He couldn't help her.

She paced the chamber, walking to the window again. Her view of the mountains offered no clue for her friend's location or condition.

*Not her friend. No, Will is far more than a friend.*

She remembered his drooping body, while the Dragons carried them across the continent.

*Please, God, let Will live. Let him escape and find me.*

She hadn't prayed since elementary school, back in Maryland. A smile crept across her lips when she pictured the nine-year-old girl with pigtails saying her evening prayers after Grandma's funeral. Would that child even recognize the woman trapped in a Dragon's prison? How would a child who loved pizza and playing on her cell phone understand the girl who Reaped souls and used a scythe? She'd been alive for fourteen and half years, yet she was a fully-grown woman now.

Sindril did that. He'd robbed her of four years.

Yet her physical changes only shadowed the changes her heart had undergone. Grym murdered two women in front of her. Their deaths gnawed at her soul.

*I freed the monster. It was my hand.*

*I killed them.*

No. She couldn't let herself dwell on mistakes of the past. She'd find a way out of this prison.

The door opened, and Susan jumped to her feet, startled.

A pale, scrawny man with stubble across his chin entered the chamber with a tray. His head was shaved clean, and the bald dome caught the glowing reflection of the flower lights. He set the tray down, walked to the chamber pot and glanced inside. The bald man left, closing the door behind him. Susan stared at the door a moment, rose and slammed her full weight against it. It didn't budge.

She walked to the tray, which held a small loaf of bread and a cup of water.

Though her stomach growled in hunger, she kicked the food with all her might. The bread smashed against a wall and fell to the rocky floor. The water spilled.

*That was dumb. I need my strength.*

She studied the copper cup and bronze tray; nothing breakable. She walked to the chamber pot. It was ceramic.

Without waiting, she threw the pot against the wall. It bounced off, and she threw it a second time. This time, the pot shattered. She clutched at a shard of pottery, and sat on the bed waiting.

An hour or more passed before the door opened again. She forced herself to remain attentive, staring at the entryway, her body tense.

The same scrawny bald guard entered the room.

Susan didn't wait. Leaping off the bed, she threw herself at the man, slashing at his throat with the shard. He knocked it aside with a bemused expression.

"You will not escape," he growled in a deep, thunderous voice.

Twisting her arms behind her, the man dragged Susan into the passage.

She saw a gash on his throat, and a lump of loose skin fell onto the stones. Beneath the skin, crimson scales flashed. With a shudder, the man's hand sloughed off, and a large claw emerged, clamping around Susan's waist like a vice. He dragged her through a winding corridor, pushing her into a large chamber. In front of them, icy air from the mountains blew into Susan's eyes. The chamber opened onto a large deck, like the entrance to a cave. Three Dragons watched them.

"Please," she gasped.

"You want to escape?" the Dragon snarled. "Allow me to help."

The guard's body writhed into a shiver of falling skin. He cast the human-looking body aside, and spread his wings. The red Dragon was far smaller than the Dragons who'd captured her and Will; each wing stretched a mere six feet from his body. His claw tightened as he flew to the open air.

The ground tilted to one side when he lifted Susan. He glided through the open wall and into the frigid air outside.

The mountains stretched for thousands of feet above and below her. She couldn't make out the ground, and the crests of mountain peaks lay hidden behind veils of clouds. The red Dragon soared upwards, beating his wings furiously against the wind. Susan struggled to breathe. The air grew thin, and her head spun.

A blue Dragon circled below them, spinning away. The stench of sulfur rose, choking Susan's struggling lungs.

"A little taste of freedom," snarled the red Dragon. "Lest you desire escape again."

His claws opened.

For a moment, Susan felt relief. Without his grip, her lungs opened. She struggled to breathe in the thin air.

A scream escaped her lips, before her breath stopped.

Wind howled against her, whipping her face and skin.

She plummeted.

Down, down, down she fell, every second an eternity.

*This is my end. I'll never have existed.*

The mountains around her blurred, and the boulder-strewn ground below came into startling focus, approaching with terrifying speed.

*Goodbye, Will.*

She jerked backward in agony. A red wing flapped beside her. Her arm yanked upwards, caught in the Dragon's claws. With a snap, the bones dislocated.

She tried to yell, yet no sound escaped.

The Dragon extended a second claw around her waist, and carried her back toward the mountain.

She hung, her body limp and in searing pain. The air scorched her lungs like fire, and every breath burned.

The red Dragon circled up the mountainside, his bat-like crimson wings pulsing with a steady rhythm.

"There." He snorted. "There is your room." They flew past a tiny hole. "Try anything again, and I won't catch you."

Susan said nothing.

An enormous cave approached, twenty feet above her window hole. Susan now noticed many other openings across the mountains, where other Dragons waited. The red Dragon dropped her on the floor.

"Keirash," shouted the red Dragon. "Return Susan to her room. I need a new skin."

A dark-skinned woman in a yellow dress approached and touched Susan's arm. The young Death yelled.

"The arm's broken." The woman's human-looking face betrayed no emotion at all. "I'll have someone tend to her."

The red Dragon snorted again. Spreading his wings, he flew into the valley.

"Come with me." The woman smiled, her reptilian eyes glinting in the light.

*Not a woman,* thought Susan. *A Dragon.*

She hobbled in pain as the creature led her back to the prison.

CHAPTER THREE—FRANK

# Departure

**H**igh in the star-dabbled sky, a cloud passed over the moon's thin silver crescent. West Tower rose behind them in a column of shadow, its gnarled sides peppered with tiny flower lights. A raven cawed in the distance. A warm March breeze swept through the Ring of Scythes, carrying scents of pollen and dew.

Frank tightened his pack. Michi and Cronk walked in silence behind him, also carrying packs full of gorgers. The boskery blade bounced against its ropes on his sack behind him. He'd wrapped cloths around the two blades so a stray bounce wouldn't leave him paralyzed.

Cronk carried their one proper scythe like a walking stick, leaning on the snath as they trudged away from the College. Frank glanced back at the chubby Death accompanying them.

"Are you sure you want to come?" asked Frank. "If you give me the scythe and turn around, no one will think less of you."

"She s-s-saved my l-l-life. I w-w-w-want to help."

"You'd better not slow us down. Michi and I could do this alone."

"You're j-j-just k-kids. I n-n-need to c-c-come."

Frank snorted. Cronk might be older, however, he certainly wasn't in charge. He suspected Susan's teacher would turn around before dawn.

Michi stepped beside him, carrying a lantern. Within the glass frame, a cluster of white flowers cast a bright glow.

"Step carefully." She touched his arm with a soft caress. "We should've waited for daybreak." She smiled, and Frank's heart fluttered.

*Michi.* A flood of thoughts crowded his mind. *Michi.* His first crush, and his oldest friend. For a year, she'd watched him pine after Susan. What a fool he'd been. When he'd faced issues with his power, it was

Michi, not Susan, who stood by him. Besides, Susan's heart was set on Will. That was clear.

He looked into her smiling face, remembering the mischievous girl who used to throw insects at him in the woods. *Times have changed.*

"I don't want the College to see us leave." Frank pushed a branch aside.

"Do you trust him?" whispered Michi. Cronk walked several steps behind them.

"We don't have much choice," Frank whispered back. "Susan liked him, and that's a good sign. Still, keep your eyes open."

Their path veered to the left before plunging into the Southern Forest. Trees barred their way, forming a wall of twisted darkness. Michi paused, raising the lamp.

"This road continues through the woods. Go slowly, there's a lot of overgrowth."

"How long will we have a path?" Frank surveyed the dense, shadowy foliage.

"This continues three miles, before veering south. We'll need to make our own way after that."

"Let's go." Frank envied her insect eyes. "We make camp once the College is out of sight."

Something scurried away into the undergrowth. Cricket noises grew around them, and Frank wondered if any were talking to Michi.

"I'm glad you're here, with me."

"My insects will help, Frank, but no one's journeyed from the College of Deaths to the land of Dragons. We know they live somewhere to the west, however that's pretty vague. How do you intend to find them?"

Frank didn't respond.

"Great," murmured Michi. "I hoped you had some idea."

Pushing his way forward, Frank shoved a branch aside, holding his lantern higher. Trees closed in on every side. They continued in silence for ten minutes.

"This should be far enough." Frank pulled off his sack. "Cronk, you and I will gather branches for a small fire. We camp here for the night. Michi, set up the tent. We'll take shifts watching, and at dawn we leave."

Cronk mumbled something and lifted a stick, carrying it to the path. Frank stepped into the overgrowth. He walked a few feet before he tripped on a root, dropping his lantern. The flower light went out.

Cursing under his breath, Frank grasped for the lantern.

"Are you all right?" called Michi.

"Fine. Just dropped my light."

Something above him moved, darting across the branches. Frank froze, staring up. His hand reached for the lantern, grasping at empty air.

A shadow fluttered across his vision, and then another.

A flurry of darkness spun around him.

"Who's there," he called out.

Four red eyes stared at him, growling.

"Who are you?"

The shape moved closer. Two wolf heads, a monstrous body, and an eagle's wings.

*My power.*

Frank had seen the chimera only once before, however he knew his power intimately. It was always with him. Always watching. *Always threatening.*

The beast stepped forward, fangs bared.

With a pang, Frank's heart emptied. He was worthless, a fool on a fool's errand.

*"It's your fault,"* snarled the power. *"Kasumir's dead, and Susan's lost."*

*I'll set things right.*

The monster laughed.

"Frank?" Michi called from far away, yet his eyes remained fixed on the creature before him.

Cronk burst from the woods, waving at something invisible.

The chimera blurred and vanished.

Frank turned and froze. Terror shot through his soul.

A darkness, blacker than a starless night, enveloped the forest, snaking toward them in anger. Frank saw Kasumir reaching toward him.

*Mother!*

Stretching out a hand, his fingers slipped through her, and she fell into the glowing lake.

*"You killed me."* Her dark eyes bored into him.

*No!*

The image faded again, and Frank grasped fallen leaves and brambles. He'd fallen down. Michi's hand rested on his back, reassuring him.

"It's okay." She stared ahead. "We won't hurt you."

Frank gasped for air. He'd never felt so afraid.

The world slipped back into focus. A shadow lurked in the middle of a dense clump of trees.

Michi smiled, her lips pulled tight across her teeth. "We're friends. I'm an Elemental, just like you. You can come out."

A scrawny girl, perhaps seven years old, emerged from the darkness. Her clothes were disheveled, her face pale, and her eyes shone bright red. A mane of long, tangled raven black hair trailed behind her, reaching to her knees. Her face was scarred and dirty, and she clutched a doll in one hand.

*"What do you want?"*

The voice screamed in his mind, ringing with dread.

"You're a Fearmonger." Frank struggled to form the words, and a bead of sweat trickled off his forehead.

*"Go away!"*

The trees started to move, their trunks rising and becoming serpents. Frank's fears returned. He'd known Fearmongers, even trained with a small group of them, yet he'd never felt fear like this. The girl's abilities far outstripped anything he'd dreamed.

"What is your name?" Michi's voice echoed in the distance, hidden behind the veil of surrounding terror.

Cronk shuddered against a tree on the other side of the path. "W-w-what's h-h-happening?"

"Please." Michi raised her palms, smiling. "We're friends."

*"Why aren't you afraid?"*

The voice screamed in his soul. Frank wanted to run and cry. He heard Cronk sobbing. Yet, Michi stood her ground. She walked to the disheveled girl with outstretched arms, embracing her.

The strange girl broke into tears.

Frank rose to his feet, grateful again for Michi. For a moment, he waited to see what the girls would do. Forcing his legs to move, he grabbed two branches, laying them beside the tent. Michi and the girl followed.

"It's okay." He forced a smile at Cronk. "She didn't mean to harm us."

Frank started a small fire, and the four faced the dancing sparks.

The girl stared at the tiny blaze, entranced. The group sat in silence, watching flickers dance across the kindling.

"Why are you alone in the forest?" Michi reached for the child's hand.

*"I ran away. They all fear me, even the Fearmongers. My powers are too great."*

Frank shuddered. For all their open-mindedness, Elementals could be cruel. At times he hated being the only 'Mental in a world of Deaths. This girl had suffered even greater solitude; even the other Fearmongers ostracized her.

"I'm Michi. I'm an arthromorph, and control insects. Frank is a seer."

Cronk looked up, startled. Frank hadn't told the older Death his secret, yet it didn't matter now. He nodded as the girl stared at him.

*"My name is Agmundria. Please don't tell anyone where I live."*

Every word she uttered stabbed at Frank's confidence like a veiled threat. This child looked so small, yet was a terrifying being. He doubted the entire band of Fearmonger soldiers could face this creature and survive. Only Michi seemed unperturbed by her words.

"How long have you been here alone?" Michi raised an eyebrow.

*"When I was five, there was...an accident."* She paused, looking away.

"It's okay. What happened?"

*"We were near Vyr. Three Elemental children were playing. I just wanted to join them, to have fun. I didn't mean to frighten them."* Every word pierced his soul with fresh waves of terror.

"Your powers developed that young?" asked Frank.

*"I didn't know. They leaked out. One of the children became so terrified she ran, and ended up falling over a ledge. She survived, but*

the *'Mentals of Vyr never forgave me. I left the city, wandering the forests. For a time, I stayed near the College, stealing food from Weston. I've lived in the forests here for months now, maybe years."* Her frightening words trailed off, and the child turned away. She didn't speak like a child, but this wasn't just an Elemental, she was a Fearmonger.

"Come with us, Agmundria." Michi grinned. "We're journeying to find the Dragons. Two of our friends were taken prisoners. We could use your help, and perhaps Frank and I can help you control your powers."

A shiver ran down Frank's spine. Travel with this girl? By the look on his face, Cronk shared his doubts. And yet, Michi always knew what to do. Ever since Kasumir's death, his feelings for her had shifted. She cared about him, of course. Frank now realized the deep feelings he'd once held toward Michi had never vanished. They'd lingered behind his thoughts, much like his power lingered within his soul. *If she thinks we should take this girl, I agree.*

*"I would frighten you too much on your journey. No, I will stay here."*

"Nonsense." Michi shook her head. "I'm just as scared as the others. I'm not immune. Yet, you're only a child. You've been alone in the wild far too long. We will face our fears, and be stronger for it."

The chimera of Frank's power growled behind his thoughts. At first, he thought it another of Agmundria's visions, until he realized the power wasn't angry or afraid, it agreed with Michi.

"Gather your things." Frank forced his voice not to quaver. "You're coming with us. We leave at daybreak."

*"I will return at dawn. If you intend to sleep, I will keep my distance."*

Facing their waking fears was a difficult struggle; he trembled at the nightmares Agmundria might cause without meaning to.

"Very well. If you're not here at dawn, we leave without you."

The disheveled child smiled, spinning around. Her wild raven hair vanished into the forest behind her.

"What have we done?" asked Frank.

"She's a child," admonished Michi. "Besides, you expect to go into the country of Dragons. Will you refuse help? This is an omen. Fate is on our side."

"She is t-t-terrifying. D-d-does she h-have to c-c-ome?"

"Michi's right." Frank took a deep breath. "If we stay calm, and remember the fear isn't real, she will help us."

*Or drive us all mad.*

CHAPTER FOUR—WILL

# Keirash

The first thing Will noticed was the pain. Even before opening his eyes, he screamed. The noise sounded weak and stifled. The scream faltered, becoming a series of labored coughs. His wrists and ankles seared like fire, and his ribs pressed against his skin at wrong angles.

*At least I'm alive.*

His eyelids opened, revealing a dim rocky chamber. Breaths came with more pain, every gasp a struggle.

*They took us. The Dragons.*

*Susan!*

He rolled his head to the side, every vertebra colliding in agony. Wincing, he scanned the cell.

Polished obsidian stone surrounded him on all sides. The chamber was tiny, no more than six feet on each side. He lay on the floor, with metal chains around his ankles and wrists. Through the iron grate he saw a large darkened hallway.

"Susan," he whispered. "Susan? Are you there?"

He tried again, calling louder. No one answered.

For a time, Will lay still, waiting. Soon, the tears fell. One by one they left his eyes, dropping down his sore cheek. His vision blurred as he wept.

*What do they want? Why am I here?*

An image crept into his thoughts. The picture of his mother in the Mortal World. They'd never gotten along well. Nevertheless, Will wondered where she was now, and if she even missed him.

*She never wanted me when I was there. If I die here, she'll never know I existed.*

I'll c*ease.*

The notion of *ceasing* terrified him. To be erased from all existence. Only one thing frightened him more.

*What are they doing to Susan?*

Something stirred in the corridor outside his cell. He blinked his tears away.

A dark hand grasped the iron grate, and two yellow eyes glowed above.

"Are you done crying?" asked a woman. She seemed human, yet Will knew better. The Dragon smiled, her white teeth gleaming against her dark face.

The grate swung open, creaking against the stones. The woman wore tan sandals beneath an embroidered yellow and brown dress. Her black toes ended in red painted toenails, which sharpened, almost like claws. She carried a hunk of bread and a flask.

"You've been asleep for two days. This is water. Drink."

She knelt, holding the flask to Will's mouth, and poured liquid onto his sore, parched lips.

"What do you want? Where's Susan?"

"Susan is fine." The woman's voice was emotionless, but something passed over her face, a strange expression that vanished a moment later. "Eat." She broke a piece of bread and held it by Will's lips.

He tried to chew. After three failed bites, the woman poured water on the bread to moisten it, and placed pieces in his mouth. She held his head up. Will's eyes watered again, frustrated at his own helplessness.

"Your guard will arrive soon," whispered the woman. "I'll return in an hour. Whatever they say, don't believe them."

"What?" Will started, confused. *Isn't she my guard?*

"Don't ask now." She stood, taking the bread and flask. Will's head sank to the cold floor. The iron bars slammed closed, and footsteps vanished into the corridor.

Will labored to take deep breaths. With food and water, his pain only intensified. His limbs chafed against the chains, and his stomach grumbled for further sustenance.

Someone approached again. The grate swung open, and a scowling man appeared. His body seemed almost human, until Will's gaze drifted up. Half of the man's face was missing, revealing bright silver scales around gleaming violet eyes.

"Are you awake?"

The Dragon strode forward and kicked Will in the chest. The blow sent searing agony coursing through his body. Will screamed, writhing against his chains, while the Dragon laughed.

"My first pet Death." The Dragon grinned. He reached forward, grasping Will by the neck. Blood rose in Will's throat. The creature's breath stank of rotten eggs and smoke.

"P-please." The Death's vision blurred.

The Dragon slapped him across the face, sending him back to the floor. A trickle of red crept into his vision, his own blood staining the cold, polished stone.

"You speak when I give you permission. If you obey, I'll let you live. If you disobey, I'll kill you, and won't even remember you wasting my time."

Will said nothing, staring at the Dragon's leather boots. The creature leaned down. His human skin didn't fit his features. The nose was deflated, bulging against silver scales.

"I wouldn't mind a new face." The beast bared rows of fangs. "I hate wearing human skin. Maybe I'd look better with yours."

The guard rose and laughed again. "Here." A chunk of rotten meat landed next to Will's mouth. It stank, and was covered in squirming maggots. "Eat up."

The guard strode to the grate, and left. Will could just reach the meat with his mouth, yet didn't want to. A handful of maggots squirmed off the disgusting offering and wriggled onto his face. One started up his nose.

He tried to breathe out, struggling to exhale as the creature burrowed higher. Its slimy skin tickled and choked him. A second worm wriggled by his mouth, forcing its way in.

One by one, the tiny tormentors worked their way over his broken body. Unable to resist, he no longer cared.

*Let it end. Let me die.*

A maggot wriggled into his windpipe, burning like fire.

Will lay in pain and misery, unable to move. The grate opened again. He saw red claw-like toenails on brown toes, beneath a yellow dress.

"Are you all right?" asked the woman. She kicked the rotten meat to the side, and picked maggots off his face. Then she made a strange, low musical sound. A wave of warmth swept over his body, and somehow he knew the worms were gone.

"Help me," he whispered.

"That's why I'm here," replied the Dragon woman. "We need your help even more than you need ours."

Will's vision blurred again. He felt cool water falling to his lips.

"Wyren will return soon, and I'm afraid you'll have to endure his *methods* a few more times. We need longer to prepare."

A moan escaped Will's lips.

"I cannot stop the pain, however, I can dull it." She sang again, and a second wave of energy spread over his body. His breaths no longer pained him, though his wrists and ankles still chafed.

The woman leaned next to his upturned ear. He smelled the same sulfur and smoke he'd noticed on Wyren.

"My name is Keirash. You have friends here, Will. You are not alone."

She rose again, and left without another word. Will stared at the grate and the empty corridor. As minutes turned to hours, the tears fell again.

## CHAPTER FIVE—FRANK

# The Soul Snatcher

**D**awn crept through the overhead trees, casting dim rays onto the forest below. The air smelled sweet, and droplets of morning dew clung to Frank's brow when he opened his eyes.

Agmundria sat across from him, her disheveled hair hung loose around the seven-year-old's lean face. Her eyes followed him as he rose.

"You came back," he muttered.

*"There is nowhere else for me,"* replied a voice within his head. While trying to sound cheerful, a jolt of pure terror accompanied the words. Frank shuddered, pulled out a gorger, and broke it in half.

"Think of a food you like before you eat." He tossed half to the young fearmonger, and then tapped Cronk on the shoulder.

"M-m-morning all r-ready?"

Frank nodded, handing him the other gorger half. He glanced around the glen. Dirt covered their fire and the equipment was packed. Michi approached from behind a tree.

"Good morning." He blushed, thinking of the dream he'd woken from. In the dream, Michi gave birth to their child.

"There's something in the forest ahead." Her eyes narrowed.

"What?"

"I don't know. After my insects reach a certain point, they vanish from my senses. There's a power at work I don't understand."

"Another 'Mental?" asked Frank. Agmundria's eyes flashed with an expression of curiosity, yet the girl remained silent.

"If so, they're unlike any 'Mental I've encountered before."

"L-l-let's g-go around." Cronk's chubby face scrunched.

"I've sent beetles along every westward path. I see no way to circumvent whatever's there."

"Agmundria." Frank turned to her. "You live here. What's in the forest to the west?"

The girl shook her head, shrugging. *"Wolves, deer, mice. Nothing unusual."*

"Let's be cautious," urged Michi.

They set off. With every step, the forest grew more dense. Branches closed in every side; their gnarled trunks cold and menacing. Moss and lichen covered weathered trunks, and the air thickened. Patches of sunlight became scarce, soon vanishing altogether.

Frank scrambled over a tangled patch of roots, forcing his way through brambles and thorns. Nettles scratched at his skin, and every vine he pushed aside was replaced by two more.

"Are you sure there isn't an easier path?" he asked.

*"This shouldn't be here."* Agmundria's words made the hairs on his neck stand on end. *"The road continues for miles before turning. This isn't natural forest."*

Frank turned, watching the way behind vanish. Trees surrounded them, growing closer with every breath. A thorn-covered vine shot up from the ground, wrapping around his ankle in a sudden, piercing grip.

"Something's got me," Michi yelled, struggling. Agmundria and Cronk squirmed in pain, also snagged by the vines. Thorns burrowed through Frank's trousers, pushing their way into his skin.

Everything went dark.

* * * *

Frank opened his eyes, waiting for his surroundings to fade into focus. The air stank of rancid meat and spoiled fruits. Leaves larger than his chest hung from twisted jungle trees above. Branches shot in every direction, casting long tendrils into the earth like the banyan trees he'd seen during a Reaping in India. Glancing to the left, he saw Michi hanging from a tree. Thick cords of white webbing held her arms above her head and wrapped around her ankles below.

"Michi," he called. Panic coursed through his veins, tightening in his neck. She didn't open her eyes. Behind her, Agmundria rustled against similar webs. The cords covered most of the young girl's body, suspending her mid-air. Frank didn't see Cronk, yet sensed the older Death's presence behind him. Something bound Frank's hands behind his head. Thick trunks wrapped around his legs, extending into the jungle trees. He struggled, desperate to free himself.

Clumps of large leaves rustled and parted. A single bristled leg, like a spider's only much larger, poked through the foliage. The trees drew their tendrils back into the branches, hurrying away from the leg.

Fear knotted in Frank's throat. A second leg clawed out, wrapping around the trunk of a tree before snapping it in half.

The creature moved forward. Eight enormous spider legs, each wider than his waist and over twenty feet tall stood before him. Between the arachnid limbs, he saw no body. A cloud of vapor hung between the legs, shimmering yet invisible. He stared at the void, and warmth surrounded him. The world turned to gold.

*"Thanks so much for rescuing me,"* said a clear voice.

*Susan?*

*"It's all right,"* she replied. *"Just let go, and come up here. I've been waiting for you."*

While Frank tried to concentrate, his thoughts spiraled away from him. This was wrong, yet *Susan is calling me.*

He gazed into the swirling void more deeply. Susan stood on a cloud, holding a boskery blade. Her smile shone down through a golden halo.

*Susan, how did you…*

*"I'm here, Frank. Just relax and let go. Come join me."*

She reached out and Frank took her hand. The tree around him slipped away as she lifted him into the sky.

*Michi smiled, running toward him on the boskery field.*

*"Hey guys, what are you hanging around for? The game's about to begin."*

*Susan smiled beside him.*

*We waited. She was waiting for me. What am I waiting for?*

*If I grab the blade, I know I'd win.*

"Frank!"

*Don't yell at me, Michi, it's part of the game.*

Something bit his cheek. Frank cringed, blinking his eyes.

"FRANK! Keep your eyes closed!"

Michi yelled again. Four beetles dislodged from his face and fluttered away.

Frank snapped his eyes shut. He felt a muscular, hairy leg wrapped around his waist, holding him in the air.

"What's going on?" he asked.

"She's trying to devour us," said Michi. "I think she needs you to look at her."

*"Frank, don't turn away."* Susan's voice pleaded. *"I need you."*

"Did you hear that?" Frank squirmed.

"Hear what?" answered Michi.

*"Frank, open your eyes. Take my hand."*

He struggled to keep his eyes shut.

"Help me," he called.

Wind whipped by his face as the leg shook him in violent convulsions. He lifted into the air again. A branch slapped against a cheek, yet he kept his eyes closed tight.

"The insects die or vanish if they get too close to that thing," warned Michi.

"W-w-what's ha-ha-happening?" stammered Cronk's voice.

"Cronk, don't open your eyes," said Michi.

The leg around Frank stiffened and swayed. The creature scurried forward, carrying him. His body slammed against a tree. His eyes parted for a moment. Blood dripped on the throbbing spider leg around his waist. He squeezed his eyes shut again. The leg could crush him in a second if it wanted, why did it need him to be looking?

"Y-y-yes," said a nearby voice. "I'm c-c-coming."

"It's going for Cronk," screamed Michi.

*"What's happening?"* asked the fear-laden voice of Agmundria.

*"Keep your eyes shut,"* he yelled in his mind. *"The creature has me. Be careful, Michi thinks it needs us to see it to attack."*

The leg shifted again. Struggling against a powerful creature was difficult, yet doing so without sight was impossible. If Michi could use her power, however, perhaps he could as well.

Frank stilled his thoughts, ignoring the doubts and fears that plagued every breath. He sank into the recesses of his soul, where his power lurked.

"*I need your help,*" he told the two-headed chimera. The monster's serpent tail flicked in annoyance. It bared its teeth.

"*You can't even open your eyes,*" it replied with a snarl. "*What do you expect me to do?*"

"*If I open them for only an instant, perhaps you could attack. We have no choice, it's going to devour Cronk.*"

The beast smiled with both wolf faces. Its body started to glow, until the white-hot light seared into the backs of his pupils.

"*Do it now,*" said the chimera.

Frank opened his eyes.

At first, he couldn't tell where the ground was. He saw Cronk, held by another of the creature's enormous spider legs. The Death stared at an empty void with a wide grin on his face. The beast's leg rose, pulling Cronk toward the gap.

Frank's power roared, quivering through his entire being. He felt the leg around him explode outwards in a mass of blood, hair, and muscle. Shards of the creature's skin scratched at his face, shattering like glass.

It turned. The void appeared before him.

With a swift, terrible certainty, Frank *understood* the beast.

He fell to the ground.

The monster shrieked. The shrill sound pierced the heavens, and Frank held his hands to his ears. Cronk fell in the distance.

With surprising speed, the legs vanished into the trees.

"Frank, you did it," called Michi. "You did it."

Frank sat up, stupefied. Tears streamed down his cheeks.

"*Is it over?*" asked Agmundria.

Frank stood in silence, clutching at his heart. He'd never felt so empty in his life.

"*It was the only way,*" he murmured to himself. "*It feeds on souls. It would've taken us, otherwise.*"

"Frank?" asked Michi, putting her hand on his back.

"It's gone." He stared ahead in disbelief.

"What did you do?"

"My power is gone."

CHAPTER SIX—SUSAN

# Throne of Shadows

Caladbolg flew through the air, riding on the back of a magnificent Dragon. Clouds whizzed past, each casting a damp blanket around his clammy skin. Beneath the black scales and enormous leather wings, the rippled waves of the ocean extended to every horizon. Cold, salty air filled his lungs.

He stroked his beard, enjoying the shimmer of sunlight on his armor. His legs ached against the glassy scales, each harder than stone. A soft warmth emanated through the scales, pulsing with every breath the Dragon took.

*"Are you ready, my friend?"* asked Caladbolg.

*"I am not your friend,"* replied Karos. His deep, thunderous voice echoed in Caladbolg's mind. *"Let us finish this."*

A point emerged before them, followed by another. Soon, a range of white-capped mountains rose from the waves in the distance. The miniscule peaks grew as they soared swiftly toward the landmass.

Donkar.

*"I wish we didn't need them,"* thought Caladbolg. *"Yet, you saw what the Shadows have become."*

Karos snorted in derisive disdain. *"If you release me, I will kill you."*

*"You're no more a Shadow than I am, Karos. Not anymore. Slay me, and they'll slay you."*

*"You think these creatures can help?"*

*"I do,"* replied Caladbolg. *"I feel drawn to them, like a wave to the beach. I am meant to guide them."*

Karos angled his enormous wings and tilted into the wind. They swooped lower and lower. Rocks and snow riddled the land before them. A gravel beach arced toward a long headland. Two enormous stone arches extended into the ocean, where great boulder stacks sat nestled against the icy surf. On the headland, patches of dirt speckled the thin snowdrifts.

Karos roared, bellowing into the heavens. His breath stank of sulfur, pungent even from the Dragon's back. His scales stiffened and quivered as he touched down. Caladbolg absorbed the shock, leaped up and slid down one of Karos's legs. His feet crunched against the snow-blanketed gravel.

"*There*." The Dragon beckoned with his head, folding his wings behind him.

A group of ragged-looking men stood clustered fifty feet away, holding wooden clubs and loose stones.

"I mean you no harm." Caladbolg strode forward with outstretched arms and a wide smile.

The men made no sound or movement, keeping their eyes fixed on Karos.

"This was once a Shadow Dragon. Yet, I have tamed him. Now we come for your help. Join us, and we will show you that the Shadows are not all-powerful."

Karos shifted, remaining silent. The men raised their clubs higher.

"I need men, and you need guidance. Karos, build me a castle. Let us show the Donkari their future." He doubted they understood him, still, time was essential.

The Dragon opened his mouth and sang. Dark and brooding notes crept like fog around them. The Donkari yelled and jumped as mists seeped around them, spreading toward the cliff face. The ground shook.

In a blur of smoke, sound, and shadow, a ten-story palace of marble emerged around the Donkari. Karos jumped to the top of a wall, looking down at them in the wide open courtyard.

One by one, the Donkari fell to their knees before him.

"I am your king now." Caladbolg grinned. "Come, Karos, let's have some more light. Perhaps bonfires or great lanterns—"

"*No,*" snapped the Dragon. "*Not fire. Never fire. You do not want them involved. Find plants beneath the snow, and I shall fill them with light.*"

\* \* \* \*

Susan opened her eyes.

The dream lingered in her memory. She'd watched Grym build a castle with a Dragon's help. Grym, the ancient king once known as Caladbolg.

*I saw through his eyes. Those were ancient memories, from millennia ago. What is it he's trying to show me?*

She shuddered, remembering where she was. Sitting upright, she ran her fingers over her right hand. A thin webbing still stretched across her skin.

*Grym?*

She felt nothing from the First Scythe. His power was severed from her. Yet, in the dream, she'd flown atop *his* Dragon, and felt the icy wind blow across *his* face. It wasn't a dream. No, it was a memory. *Did my injury re-awaken his power?*

A glimmer of hope sprang into her heart. Grym was trapped, and his power inaccessible, however he wasn't cut off from her completely. She'd seen into his past, and perhaps she'd be able to reach him again.

She sighed, pulling the covers off the bed. Reaching under the pillow, she lifted a shard of the smashed chamber pot and scratched the wall, counting the marks.

*I've been here for eight days,* she thought.

Sindril visited her once a day, always with a wry smile. He'd refused to discuss Will, and hadn't even told her what they wanted with her. He simply asked if she was comfortable, and made small talk, pretending he wasn't the reason she'd been captured and held in the Dragon's prison.

*What does he want?*

The mountain air blew in through the window, making her shiver. For a moment, she saw herself tumbling toward the ground, the wind slamming into her face. She climbed under the covers.

*The Dragons want war with the Deaths. They kidnapped Will and me, and wanted me for a long time. If Sindril's spies rode the boat, ready to snatch us, why cast the curse?*

Running her hand over her face, Susan tried to remember her visage in the mirror. It had been over a week, and the image faded in her memory. Strange to think her face, her very *life*, had shifted with Sindril's words.

*He stole four years of my life. I shall never forgive him.*

Staring at the ceiling, she waited.

It was the only thing she could do.

CHAPTER SEVEN—FRANK

# The Loss

*W*hat am I?

Frank stared at the trees around him. Roots and branches receded, following the monster away from the glen. The entire forest opened. The twisted jungle dissipated like a dream.

"*Thank you.*" Agmundria touched his arm, looking up with sad, hollow eyes. The eyes of a child, and the eyes of a 'Mental.

*What am I?* He wondered again.

All his life, Frank's identity was linked to his power. His power was a manifestation of his soul, his essence as an Elemental. It was gone now, torn from him like a severed limb or a cleaved heart.

*I am nothing.*

"We'll follow the creature." Michi glanced behind. "We'll get your power back."

Frank watched the changing forest. Vines unwrapped from trunks, and roots lifted from the ground. A bird cried out, trying to land on a branch that curled away like a clenching finger.

*I am nothing.*

"Frank?" Michi grasped his hand. "We can't just stand here. The path is easy enough to follow—" *She's right, she's always right. She cares for me. But she's wrong now. No, the emptiness is too great.*

"Follow the creature?" He shook his head. "That thing is far more powerful than we are. Before we reach it, the beast will devour my... my...it will feast. We'll be powerless when it's done. No, we came for Susan, and we need to keep going. Let's get out of here while we can."

"Are you sure?"

"I'm still alive. I'm not even hurt, not physically. No, let's get out of here."

"That thing has a part of you." Her eyes grew wide, pleading. "We should at least try."

"*I don't understand.*" Agmundria walked over. "*What happened?*"

"It's g-g-gone." Cronk joined them. "Let's g-g-go."

Frank looked away, staring into the forest. He took the opposite direction from the still-retreating vines and tropical foliage.

"Come on," he murmured.

They followed him through the woods. With each step, the forest grew more sparse, until they emerged onto a wide open field. Clouds littered the sky above, which grew dark with the oncoming evening. The soul snatcher must've held them for longer than he'd thought. They continued toward a copse of beech and pine. The sound of water rushed in the distance.

"The Acheron," said Michi. "We must be getting close."

The others moved over a ridge, yet Frank sank next to a tree.

"Frank?"

"Go on," he said. "The River continues into the mountains. It should take you all the way to the Dragons."

"You're coming with us." Michi's fingers wrapped around his.

Frank turned. How could he explain? This was the farthest he could go. He felt the *stretch*, like a rope pulled taut deep within him.

"*Frank?*" Agmundria knelt beside him.

"It's pulling me back. There's part of my soul still in here. I can't explain any better."

"If you still have part of your soul, perhaps your power isn't gone," suggested Michi. "It grows from childhood. Yours might need to form over again."

The empty shell of his body leaned against the tree. *I need to go back.*

"You said we could follow it." He gazed at the distant forest.

"I thought you wanted to press on." Michi's eyes narrowed.

"I did. I don't know. Maybe I need to follow the creature by myself."

He stood. A cord of tension pulled from his chest back toward the forest. Reaching his hand out, he waved it through the open air, however nothing tangible pulled him. Staring blindly at nothing, he staggered forward.

"*We have to stop him*," said a distant voice in his mind.

"The s-s-scythe." Something flashed before his eyes and the tension vanished. He fell to the ground, untethered from the intangible chains emanating from the forest. Lifting his eyes, he saw Cronk holding the scythe.

"What did you do?" He breathed hard.

"S-s-something was h-h-holding you. I s-swung."

"I'll kill you." Frank jumped to his feet, blood pounding in his ears. He ran forward and tackled Cronk, knocking the scythe to the ground. The chubby Death gaped in surprise. Frank balled his fist and slammed it into Cronk's face.

"Stop it!" screamed Michi.

A sudden terror swept over Frank, and his muscles paralyzed. Agmundria hurried over, her palms outstretched.

"Let go of me," Frank struggled to say.

Blood flowed freely from Cronk's nose.

"What's wrong with you," demanded Michi.

"Don't you see what he's done?" Frank's lips moved, yet his other muscles remained stiff. Agmundria's powers were even greater than he'd suspected.

"You walked in a trance, heading back the way we'd come." Michi pointed. "You grasped the air in front of you like a rope."

"I th-thought it w-was the c-creature."

"You severed my only hope of re-uniting with my power. My last chance of connecting with my soul." Frank stopped fighting, and his arms relaxed. He collapsed beside Cronk, who crawled away. "I offered to go after the creature."

"Chasing it wouldn't help—you could've been killed. All of you. No, I needed to go alone." Frank's voice wavered and tears welled. "It's too late now."

Cronk sat warily. He wiped the blood from his nose. "I-I'm sorry."

"You didn't do anything wrong," said Michi. "Frank's not himself."

"I'm nothing." Frank shook his head. "Nothing."

Michi crouched in front of him. Her eyes bored into his. He tried to look away, unable to break from her stare.

"Frank." Her voice was soft, yet firm.

Running the back of his hand across his mouth, he tasted the salt from his own tears.

"We'll get through this." She placed her fingers on his shoulder.

"Get me out of here," he whispered. "Before I change my mind."

She helped him rise, and they hobbled down the ridge. At the edge of the horizon, the setting sun cast auburn and golden ripples across the silver surface of the Acheron River. It flowed past without a care. He watched the water swimming by, and tried not to think.

## CHAPTER EIGHT—WILL

# White Claw

"**W**ake up." Keirash spoke in a soft voice, with a note of urgency.

Will opened his eyes, instantly aware of the acrid stench. A stone dug into his back, and his head ached against the icy floor. The taste of his own blood filled Will's mouth. With each gasped breath, the room came into greater focus. He lay on the ground, and started spitting. His stomach throbbed with sharp piercing convulsions.

"Stay quiet," whispered the Dragon. Keirash knelt beside him, running her claws across his manacled wrists. Her reptilian eyes glinted yellow in the dim light. Even in the shadows, he knew she wasn't wearing any human skin.

"What do you want?" he asked.

"I'm here to help."

"Take me to Susan. Just let us go."

"Don't respond, just listen. I can't let you see Susan yet, and it's not yet time to plan an escape. It's late, and I've been studying your schedule. They won't check on you or feed you for two days. You're in a period of isolation, intended to make you more compliant."

Will tried to sit up, straining against the chains around his wrists. Keirash swept around his head and clicked both manacles. The shackles fell to the ground.

"What do you want?" He winced, pushing himself to a sitting position.

"I only want to show you the truth."

"What truth?"

"Nothing that's happened is an accident. You've been a pawn in their game since Susan arrived in our world."

Will struggled to kneel. His head spun and he slumped to one side. Keirash stepped forward, catching him before he collapsed.

"Easy," she warned. She hummed, holding her palm to his cheek. His pain ebbed away, and strength flowed into his body. "Eat this." She took a small chunk of bread from somewhere. "It will help clear your mind. We have a great distance to travel."

Will didn't trust the strange Dragon, however he saw no alternative. His stomach growled in anticipation. He grabbed the food and took eager bite after bite.

Keirash watched him eat. The Dragon's eyes continued to glint golden-yellow in the dim light. He suspected she was smaller than the enormous Dragon who'd carried him to this prison. The smell of burnt sulfur lingered around her.

He finished the bread and looked up.

"Can you walk?" she asked.

"I think so." He staggered to one foot, and then the other. A firm claw grasped his arm, helping to support his weight. Something slithered against his leg and he recoiled, before realizing it was Keirash's scaly tail. She pushed him toward the narrow entrance of the cell.

No lights shone in the corridor. The chill air made him shiver.

"This way," whispered Keirash. He followed the lumbering shadow of the strange Dragon as she led him through widening dark passageways. He soon lost all sense of direction. They turned and walked, then turned again. Every passage looked identical, and with no lights or markings, Will wondered how she knew their direction at all.

After seeming hours of trudging in the dark, a faint light emerged in the distance. They continued to the end of a long tunnel. A bitter wind whipped past them. As the pallid gleam grew closer, Will discerned the silhouette of Keirah's wings on either side.

At the end of the tunnel, they reached a ledge. Thousands of tiny stars shone like glistening pearls above the ominous shadows of enormous mountains. A pale half-moon glowed between two craggy peaks before them. The dim moonlight reflected off a circular mirror at the tunnel's entrance.

"Now we fly." In the open air, Will saw scales of deep mahogany. Razor-sharp fangs lined the Dragon's mouth. Her golden eyes pierced the night sky like daggers of light. Keirash knelt, and gestured with her head. "Climb on my back."

"If I don't?"

"You'll be discovered here and killed. Unless you think you can find your way back to the cell, you have no choice."

Will walked over. The wind cut through his thin clothes like an icy knife. He wrapped his weak arms around Keirash's neck, and leaned forward.

Without another warning, the Dragon leaped into the air. Her wings spread, gliding on the mountain breezes with no effort. Keirash's scales chafed against his arms and legs, and they pulsed with every shift in the wind. She soared downward, coasting across the frigid winds.

"Hold on tighter."

He clutched his arms tighter as the Dragon tilted to the left, flapping hard. With each beat of her leathery wings, they climbed higher. A dark, snow-capped mountain swept beneath them.

"Stay low."

A second Dragon passed beneath them. With violet wings five times longer than Keirash's, its scales glistened in the starlight. Will shrank closer to Keirash's body. He sensed that she didn't want him seen.

Keirash climbed again, clawing her way over a second mountain. She veered to the right, diving toward the ground. Will started to slide forward, yet she tossed her head back, holding him in place.

With a flurry of wings, the Dragon scrambled to land. She knelt again, and Will rolled off, falling hard on the snowy ground. Tall trees fingered the sky around them, their leafless branches grasping into the wintry night sky. Keirash shuddered from head to tail, shaking herself like a dog after rain.

"We're close." The Dragon's words wisped out of her fangs with curls of dissipating steam.

"Where are we going?"

"To a meeting." She started forward; her feet left deep claw patterns in the snow, which vanished into snow drifts a moment later. The wind blasted Will's face hard. He hurried after her.

She stepped to a barren tree, pushing a claw into its trunk. With a rustle, the snow in front of Will sprang upward. A hatch opened in the gray ground, revealing a hidden corridor.

"Jump in." She gestured with a claw.

"Excuse me?"

"Before someone sees us. It's too narrow for me to fly you, now jump."

"But, I—"

Will's words disappeared into the night air. Keirash shoved him from behind and he plunged down, down into darkness.

Sulfur-tinged smoke whipped past his face as he plummeted down through the passageway. Mid-air, talons gripped his ribs, wrapping around his sides.

"Almost there," Keirash whispered with hot, sulfuric breath.

The shaft widened, and he lurched backward as she flapped her wings twice, pulling him higher. Her claws tightened, and she changed directions, veering to the right.

*These passages must extend for miles. We're far beneath the mountains.*

Faint light shone ahead, and the Dragon continued to fly, alighting on the banks of a pool of water. Under its tranquil surface, Will saw clumps of glowing flower lights. The glowing pond cast a pallid light into a wide chamber. Long stalactites hung over the glowing water, dripping onto the pool, each sending slow ripples outward.

Keirash set Will down. He dropped to the dusty floor. The cavern stank of rotten eggs and charred meat. Squinting, he allowed the shadows to focus. On the far side of the pool, a pair of wings unfolded.

"How long before the human is missed?" asked a gravelly voice.

"Two days," replied Keirash.

The other Dragon snorted. Its wings flashed green in the pale, tremulous light.

"May we enter?" asked Keirash.

"You were not seen?"

"I'm no hatchling, Brandr. Open the gate."

Brandr snorted again; plumes of white smoke billowed from his nostrils. His glowing yellow eyes narrowed, yet he nodded. The wall behind the strange Dragon rumbled. Keirash turned, and walked around the glowing pool.

"Keep quiet when we get inside," she whispered. Will followed, watching Keirash's tail snap the dust-covered floor.

When they reached the far side of the pond, Brandr vanished into a separate passage. Will and Keirash crossed into a side-chamber. The new room was enormous. Stalactites and stalagmites joined, forming gnarled columns of limestone, which reminded Will of the writhing Towers of the College. Small pools of light, similar to the large pond outside, dotted the cavern floor, each filled with glowing flowers. More flower lights hung in viny clumps from the ceiling high above.

Around the chamber, twelve massive megaliths stood in a circle: twelve great stones, each carved into a pillar over fifty feet tall, supporting the ceiling high above. Dragons sat at the base of all save one column. Keirash strode to the empty place and took a seat, wrapping her tail around her mahogany scales. Brandr sat to her right, his green skin smooth like a lizard's. The other Dragons ranged from behemoths five times larger than Keirash, to a small golden creature only a foot long.

"Welcome, William Black." The tiny gold Dragon spoke with a gentle, authoritative air. "My name is Samas. The twelve of us represent White Claw."

"White Claw?" asked Will.

"Not all Dragons seek the destruction of Deaths," said Brandr.

Samas shot the green Dragon a look, arched his back, and continued. "The Dragons have had one king for a long time. The Nameless King is eternal, yet not all-knowing. For generations we existed in happiness. Now, all of that is threatened. The King's path will destroy all. He must be stopped."

"Why are you telling me this? Why am I here?"

"For only the second time in a million years, a female Death has entered our world," said Samas. "Her presence places us in danger once more."

"Susan?" Will's eyes narrowed. "Why does it matter that she's here."

"I told you he wouldn't understand." An enormous white Dragon with bright sapphire eyes hissed, running a crimson tongue across his fangs. A row of black spikes ran down the Dragon's back. Will gasped, recognizing the creature who'd carried him to the mountains.

"Elkanah?"

"If Elkanah hadn't captured you," continued Samas, "there would be no hope for this world or the Mortal World. Everything would be lost. White Claw has operatives in the highest positions, working to prevent that. We convinced the King to bring you, as an alternate option."

"What are you talking about?" Will walked to the center of the ring of Dragons, glaring at their scaled faces.

"Silence, human." Brandr's fangs bared in a snarl. "Let Samas speak."

"Will, I know you don't trust us." Keirash clawed the ground with a talon. "Why should you? Yet, you must believe me, they'd have killed you if we hadn't intervened. Elkanah saved your life. Susan is all that matters to them."

"Why is she so important?"

"What makes females different from males in your species?" Samas cocked his head.

"Is this a game to you? I'm not here to discuss anatomy."

"For five generations, my family has watched over White Claw. I was born for this moment, Will. This is no game." He paused.

Will's eyes circled the dim cavern. Tremulous light glimmered in each flower-filled pool, and the sulfuric air burned his lungs and tongue. Elkanah watched him with piercing blue eyes. He turned back to Samas. The tiny golden Dragon spread its wings, and then flexed them again.

"Female humans bear young." Samas glanced up. "This is a world shaped by Dragonsong. From its heart, Elementals take their powers, scythes gain their hunger, and souls find rest. A child born here, born of Mortal blood, is what the King has hoped for. For generations, he manipulated us all. Now, his plan comes to fruition. Susan is a descendant of an Elemental; her soul already contains traces of Dragonsong. Her child will be the strongest Dragon Key ever dreamt of, the Key he needs."

"Wait, did you say Dragon Key?" Will's mind jarred back to days spent pouring over ancient texts in Susan's hidden library. She'd been obsessed with discovering the meaning of the strange secret. Kasumir claimed it was a myth during their first year together. However, when Grym awoke, Susan's doubts rekindled.

"We cannot allow a second Dragon Key to be forged." Brandr clawed the ground.

"Indeed," added Samas, "That is why we have called you, Will. Do you love Susan?"

"I—"

"Do you love her?"

"I don't know if—"

"You must protect her." The gold Dragon curled into a ball, raising his head. "Our operatives have convinced the Royal Council that Susan's fragile state will produce a weak child. A weak child could limit the power of the Dragon Key. However, it's only a matter of time. The King's puppet Sindril will impregnate her soon."

"*What!*" Will leaped up.

"He does care," said Brandr.

"I won't let that monster touch her!"

"If he succeeds," said Samas, "he will create a potent Dragon Key. A Dragon Key born in hate would tear apart the two worlds."

"There won't be any damn Key. Take me to Susan. Take me there now!"

"Patience, young Death. The King has waited a million years for a second Dragon Key. Do you believe he'd give her up now? Even if every member of White Claw helped you, we'd be slaughtered in minutes. For every Dragon loyal to us, there are a thousand loyal to the King. Most Dragons don't realize his true goal. The Nameless King spent millennia spreading lies. He convinced my kind that a Dragon Key will bring prosperity. Most Dragons believe a Key would restore Dragons as the reapers of souls, and bring all Dragonkind to a glorious future. White Claw alone knows the terrible truth. To reach his prosperity, he'll destroy us. He needs only the Key."

Will frowned. "No. I don't care about grand prophecies or a dispute among Dragons. I won't let Sindril rape Susan."

"She won't be touched." Keirash shook her scaled head. "That's why you're here now, and why we're working together to free you both."

Samas nodded. "Will, you must understand that the Dragon Key is the greatest secret in this world. Susan is a Death, and our seers foresee a child in her future. Any child born to her could be used to fashion a Dragon Key."

"What is a Dragon Key? We never learned what it means."

"A Dragon Key is the physical manifestation of blood and Dragonsong. We made sure Deaths were not born here, and since our powers created Elementals, they pose no direct threat. Now, for only the second time in history, a Dragon Key is possible." Samas paused, scratching at long white whiskers hanging from his nose. "Do you know how the Dragons began?"

"You mean the Earth Dragons and the Shadow Dragons?"

"How did you hear those names?" Elkanah's head raised, his eyes glowing.

Will clamped his lips together. *Grym*. He'd almost forgotten. Susan still wore the First Scythe; she might be protected. Should he betray the one advantage they held?

"It is interesting that Susan should learn those words." Samas grinned. "Perhaps a remnant of Lovethar awakened upon your friend's arrival. She is correct, once two mighty species shaped the worlds: the Earth Dragons and the Shadow Dragons. The Earth Queen and Shadow King reigned over creation. For eons the two lived in harmony, overseeing the dawn of the two worlds: the World of Light and the Shadow World. The Earth Dragons loved the Shadow Dragons, and for three and a half billion years there was peace and harmony.

"The Earth Dragons sang life into existence, and their counterparts the Shadow Dragons built a home for the dead, devouring souls and building a world to house them. Life grew more complex in both worlds, until the Earth Dragons fashioned humans."

"Humans evolved," interrupted Will. "There were no Dragons."

"That's what they wanted you to think. Why are there images of Dragons in every one of your ancient cultures, even long after the last Earth Dragon perished?"

"This is ridiculous." Will glanced around the strange chamber in disbelief.

"Believe it or not, this is how our worlds started," continued Samas. "However, after the first humans found their way here, something happened."

"What do you mean humans found a way here?"

"An ancient race of humans called the Donkari discovered the Shadow World, perhaps with a Dragon's claw. Some speculate that the Earth Dragons fashioned the Donkari even before your last ice age, and it was their demise that spun your world backward. Whatever the reason, when the Donkari came, the Earth Queen died. How she died remains a mystery. However, that is when the chaos began."

"The Shadow King went mad." Brandr's eyes glinted in the dim light. "The Shadows fought the Earth Dragons, until the last Earth Dragons sealed the barrier between worlds."

"Wait." Will's fingers flexed. "One of my 'Mental friends mentioned this. She said the final act of the Earth Dragons was to create the Elementals."

"That is correct." Samas nodded. "They sacrificed themselves to create beings filled with their power. It was a final attempt to quell the King's rage. It failed. After the barriers raised, the Shadow Dragons turned their anger to the Donkari. By that point, the Donkari called themselves Deaths, bringing souls to a realm beyond this world."

"The Hereafter."

"Yes. A young Death named Lovethar came along, the first female Death. The Shadow King wasted no time. When she gave birth to a son, Gesayn, the King stole the child. Lovethar and her Elemental lover rescued the boy, yet the King severed one of Gesayn's hands. It wasn't powerful enough to create the Dragon Key he wanted, so he used the weaker Dragon Key to give himself immortality. He vowed to never rest until he fashioned a second Key, one that would grant him his wish."

"And what is that?"

"He wants to bring the Earth Queen back."

Will paused, his mind a blur. "Let me get this straight. An ancient immortal Dragon King wants to bring a dead queen back to life, and he thinks a child of Susan's would let him do so?"

"A child born of hate would do just that. However, you don't realize *how* he will bring the Queen back. The King wants to reverse time, to go to a moment before humans, Donkari, or Deaths. He wants to erase the two worlds, and start anew. Everything and everyone you know will cease to exist, *if* he succeeds. You Deaths dread being killed for fear of *ceasing*. Now, imagine *all of civilization* ceasing. Countless billions never even born."

"No," whispered Will.

"There's more." Samas propped himself on tiny arms, leaning in. "I told you that our seers foresee a child. Will, she *must* have a child born of love. However, *any* child Susan bears can still become a Dragon Key. The King is mad, he will hunt down Susan and her children until he achieves his goal. He will murder her children and forge a hundred Keys if he thinks one will work. Remember, most Dragons have no idea what a Dragon Key actually does. They only know it will bring us glory. They follow his madness blindly, with a fury that will destroy all creation."

"No." Will's gaze swept the room, his fingers balled in tight fists. "We have to stop this."

He stared at Samas, before turning to the other eleven Dragons. Even among such powerful creatures, he felt helpless. Elkanah tapped a claw into one of the pools of water, and the dim cavern light trembled.

"Tell him the plan," said Brandr.

CHAPTER NINE—FRANK

# Eternal Song

Frank staggered forward. Each step seemed hollow and more meaningless than the step before. They paralleled the Acheron for mile after mile. At first, distance helped take Frank's mind off his missing power. Yet, the emptiness continued.

The river flowed past without end. Its swift silver water slipped away toward the west, the College, and the distant sea. Frank and the others walked east, toward the growing towers of the Dragonspine Mountains. The snow-covered peaks stretched across the horizon, vanishing into clouds above. The nearest mountain loomed closer every day.

On the second day after the creature robbed him of his soul, Frank saw a Dragon flying over the forest. The following day, the entire group huddled under a clump of trees when two Dragons soared by.

Today, the noon sun emerged from the towering mountains before them. The four travelers trudged in a weary silence. Michi led the group, her fingers ever-moving in an intricate pattern. Flies buzzed to her hands, danced through her fingertips, and then flitted into the air again. Cronk and Agmundria walked behind her. The older Death broke the silence with occasional stuttered observations about the weather, yet Agmundria kept to herself. Frank walked behind the group. He held his boskery blade in his right hand, swinging it with each step.

Michi stopped and turned. She raised her hand.

"W-w-what is it?" asked Cronk.

"The insects are excited. There's something close."

"*Another creature?*" Agmundria's arms rose in defense.

"I don't know. Let's proceed with caution."

"Let's go." Frank nodded. "The only way to see what's there is to keep moving."

They rounded a bend in the river, and came to a grove of enormous birches. Their narrow trunks climbed far higher than any trees Frank had seen before. The dense grove hummed with life.

"*I don't like this place. Let's go around.*"

"What's not to like?" Frank started forward. "It's beautiful."

"Frank, be careful." Michi held up her palm in warning.

He continued. The trees stretched to impossible heights inside the grove, which seemed far larger than a moment ago. The sky vanished in a blur of silver trunks. A narrow path wormed through the trunks. Something called him forward. For the first time since encountering the soul snatcher, a glimmer of hope flitted into his heart.

"Frank, wait," called a voice behind him. He turned, seeing only forest. Birches shot up all around him in every direction. The path he'd entered through was gone.

He spun again, fearless. Perhaps it was for the best. The creature had returned, and now would consume what small scraps remained of his soul. He passed into the heart of the soaring forest.

Around him, a hum started. Frank paused, listening. It began as a single note: a vibrant, resonant tone echoing through the wood. He couldn't help smiling. Walking deeper into the towering thicket, he ran his fingers along the papery trunks. Each tree vibrated with the same pulsing sound.

Passing a low-hanging branch, a second note formed in the recess of his mind. The two hums blended in a simple, beautiful way, growing stronger with every step. Soon more notes added to the sound, until the entire forest rang with perfect harmony. The sounds buzzed through his skin, causing his heart to beat in strange new rhythms. His steps quickened, breaking into an eager run.

The birches grew both taller and brighter. Their trunks glowed and brightened. At the forest's heart, they shone with a ferocious brilliance. The light pulsed in tempo to the music all around him. He stopped, staring. A strange colored shape: a cloud with wings, danced and twirled in the center of the shining, singing trees.

The shape took no notice of him. However, the notes sharpened, deepening into words. The song was more beautiful than any sound he'd ever dreamed. Yet, it was also dark and sad. The words poured all around him, pulling tears to his eyes.

*Can you hear me, oh my love?*
*As ever sunsets drift away,*
*Where is the joy we sang to life?*
*Where are our souls*
*This fading day?*

*Spin the broken wheel of fate,*
*Fold your wings and war no more.*
*Return to me, your once-bound wife.*
*Steer anger beyond death;*
*As once we swore.*

*Can you hear me, oh my king?*
*Recall again our dying plea,*
*The embers of our faded song.*
*Fold your wings and war no more.*
*Return to me.*

The words filled Frank with an intense longing. An emptiness settled over the glowing forest, and the dancing shape within. The words faded, yet the sounds remained. The hum pulsed into strong chords; an ancient harmony and heartfelt loneliness.

"Who left you?" asked Frank.

The dancing form paused, and its colors drifted in mid-air. Then the hum shifted, the light refocused, and a new chorus sang.

*I called you here, oh soul-less child,*
*Who journeys to the heart of pain.*
*Sing the ancient promise new,*
*Find love again.*

A new cloud of amber light lifted from the glowing forest floor, wisping around the swaying form of the creature. Luminous clouds flowed into and around each other, and rainbow wings pulsed with excitement. The light danced into a blur, sweeping straight at Frank.

"What's happening?" he whispered.

His skin pricked, pierced by a thousand shards of light. They crawled inside him, filling his body with warmth. Something *grew* deep in the recess of his mind, where his power once lay. Frank's body lightened, and the trees around him spun.

He floated in and out of consciousness.

*Dancing colors.*
*Ancient promises.*
*Broken dreams.*

Thought danced around him, followed by the song. It pounded through every fiber of his being, emanating from his heart.

*Spin the broken wheel of fate,*
*Fold your wings and war no more.*
*Return to me, your once-bound wife.*
*Steer anger beyond death;*
*As once we swore.*

*Journey to the heart of pain.*
*Sing the ancient promise new.*
*Find love again,*
*Find love again.*

Something tugged on Frank's back. He flew away from the light, pushed out of the forest.

In a haze, he watched the enormous birches from high above. They stretched in a vast circle, with a pulsing light in the forest's heart. The trees bent and swayed, lowering toward the center light. Deeper and deeper they bent, until the entire forest swallowed itself into the dancing colors. A single note hummed through the air, and the forest vanished.

*Remember...*

\* \* \* \*

"W-w-what is it?" asked Cronk.

Frank blinked in confusion. The river flowed to their left. The noon sun shone bright between mountains ahead. There were no trees in sight.

"The insects are excited. There's something close."

"*Another creature?*" Agmundria's arms rose in defense.

"I don't know. Let's proceed with caution," said Michi.

They started forward, and the Elemental paused again, flies swirling around her outstretched fingers.

"Whatever I sensed is gone."

Something nagged at the back of Frank's mind. Out of habit, he reached for his power. It was gone. Yet, he didn't feel empty.

*Remember...*

CHAPTER TEN—SUSAN

# Promises

*S*usan sat in a dark room.

*The walls vanished, and she plummeted. Down, down she fell, speeding past thousands of Dragons.*

*Clouds and mist parted. The image faded.*

*She felt herself watching a different Dragon, an ancient creature who once belonged to Grym.*

*Little by little, Susan receded.*

*I am Grym.*

*I am Caladbolg, the First Scythe.*

Karos bellowed into the night: a deep booming roar, load enough to shake the heavens. Stars vanished and reappeared, as the black Dragon paced the frosty air. A cloud of sulfur caught the moonlight. For a moment, rows of fangs appeared, before vanishing into the darkness again.

"I know you're unhappy." Caladbolg looked up, stroking the Dragon's warm scales.

"*He's coming*," warned the Dragon. "*His voice rides the wind.*"

Caladbolg strained his ears. Far in the distance, thunder roared.

"We are strong. We have the Donkari."

Karos laughed. His deep, bellowing voice made the ground tremble. A shadow moved against the darkness, and two glowing eyes appeared before Caladbolg.

"*You forget who fashioned you.*"

"I remember, and she's gone. He thinks it's my fault."

*"You did not know the Earth Queen. The Shadow King shall never forget. You embody all he hates. You are betrayal personified, the promise that was broken. He will not rest until you are destroyed."*

"We shall see. Every shadow fades into day. I believe the time of Dragons nears an end."

Karos snorted, his bright eyes narrowing.

Caladbolg turned his gaze toward the distant stars. A cloud moved across the tiny dots, blotting them out one by one. The cloud grew larger, breaking into shadowy winged forms. Thunder roared, and Karos answered with a bellow of his own.

Wind whipped past Caladbolg's face as three enormous Dragons landed in front of them. Their shadowed forms stood tall against the dim, clouded sky. Piercing, venomous eyes glared from faces covered in crimson scales. *The Blood Guard.*

*"Karos,"* screamed an angry voice in his mind. *"We have no quarrel with you. Leave the traitor, and step away."*

Caladbolg felt the Dragon's scales tense, however he remained still.

*"This is your final chance."* One of the crimson shadows pawed the ground. *"You were a great Dragon once."*

*"Begone. I made my choice long ago."*

Caladbolg smiled, touched at the Dragon's loyalty. The three Dragons growled and lifted above the ground, their wings beat frigid air against his face. The sky above them trembled, and a darkness wider than a mountain hovered overhead.

*"I will ask once."* The thunderous sound roared with a deafening blast, echoing out of the heavens. *"Displease me, and I will return in daylight, slaying you in front of your pathetic subjects."*

"You know my answer." Caladbolg held his head high.

*"Where is she?"* demanded the Nameless King.

"As I've said before, I have no idea."

A column of fire shot down from the Dragon, lighting the world for a terrifying instant. The beast's wings stretched from horizon to horizon. Shadow black scales, flecked with spots of brown and ashen gray, covered its hide. Caladbolg stepped back, shielding himself from the heat.

"*My lord,*" said one of the Blood Guard. "*Urgent news from the West. The Towers near completion.*"

The Shadow King snorted with the power of a thunderclap. The sky wheeled as the massive dragon spun with startling speed. Wind battered Caladbolg and Karos, until the stars re-emerged.

"*I shall return.*" The voice echoed through the heavens.

"He doesn't believe me, yet it's true." He stroked Karos's scales. "I wish I knew."

"*He used fire,*" warned the Dragon. "*The Nameless King is out of options. He will return soon, and we will not survive.*"

"I have an idea."

\* \* \* \*

Susan awoke in a sweat. Her dreams of Grym grew more frequent, and more vivid.

*What are you trying to tell me?*

The sword remained silent in the waking hours, trapped deep beneath the Dragon's spell. She sat on the edge of the bed, waiting. However, the dreams grew more frequent. She watched visions of the ancient past, and a strange image of flames between the towers of the College.

After a time, the boredom returned. She rose and walked to the narrow window, shivering in the cold air. Outside, a lone silver-scaled Dragon glided to the opposing mountain. Behind her, Susan heard the door open.

"How are you feeling?" asked an all-too-familiar voice.

She turned and stared at Sindril. "What do you want with me? Why am I here?"

"You won't be harmed," he replied. "If you co-operate, your stay might even be pleasant."

"Pleasant? I'm a prisoner."

"Don't be difficult."

He walked forward and touched her shoulder. She shrank back, but he grabbed her wrist.

"If I wanted your death, it would've happened long ago," he whispered.

He released her, and she staggered back to the bed. Sindril smirked and walked to the window, gazing out.

Susan's gaze darted to the door. It stood open, and the hall looked empty beyond. However, where would she go?

"Thinking of leaving?"

She hated him. Every fiber in her body cried out to attack Sindril, however, she remained rooted to the floor.

"What do you want?" she asked again.

"The same as you, I imagine."

"What do you mean?"

"I want to leave, Susan. It's all I've wanted since I came to this forsaken world."

"So leave. You manipulated my final test. You can leave whenever you want."

Sindril smiled and chuckled. "If only it were that simple. The laws that bind Deaths keep me here as well. I'm trapped. To return, I need to bend the rules."

"So you work with Dragons?"

"Our interests in this matter coincide."

"Why would Dragons care if you go back to the Mortal World?"

Sindril flexed his fingers, looking down at the ground. "How is your hand?"

"It's fine." Susan's skin tensed beneath the silk webbing binding her palm and wrist.

"A 'Mental trick, no doubt. Still, I'm impressed that they imbued your wrist with such abilities."

*He doesn't know it's Grym.* The realization filled her with new hope. Even if the First Scythe's power was blocked, it was a valuable secret.

"At any rate, I'm not here to threaten you, Susan." He smiled. "I'm here to reassure you."

It was Susan's turn to laugh.

"I know you don't trust me," he continued. "In time, you'll adapt. You and I need each other."

"I don't need you."

"Oh, but you do. The Dragons wanted things done more…*quickly*. I convinced them to take some time; to make you comfortable. I'm not your enemy, Susan."

She laughed, forcing the sound out.

"You need a friend here. I alone can protect you from these beasts."

"I don't want your *protection* or your help."

"You'll change your mind soon. I promise you won't be harmed, *if* you cooperate."

He walked to the door. "Come with me."

She stared without moving.

"Very well, I will return soon. Should you change your mind, tell one of the guards."

He closed the door, and his footsteps receded down the hallway.

Susan took a deep breath before sitting on the bed. She pulled out her shard and marked the wall. Another day in prison.

CHAPTER ELEVEN—FRANK

# The Guide

Frank took the water bottle from Michi, glad for a drink. The afternoon sun glittered off the Acheron's gentle waves. A chill air blew from snow-capped mountains crowding the horizon.

"This is the first day we haven't seen a Dragon." Michi glanced skyward. "I wonder if we've strayed too far south. Perhaps we should leave the river and head into the mountains."

"This is the right way."

"What makes you say that?" asked Michi.

Frank paused, unsure himself. "I don't know, yet we need to follow the Acheron."

Agmundria gave him a haunted, questioning look. Cronk stared at his scythe, before biting a gorger.

"Perhaps your power's started to return." Michi brushed a strand of hair from her face. "That sounded like a Seer's advice."

"I hope you're right." He forced a smile. "I feel stronger, but still empty. It's like some other presence guides me."

Michi's eyes narrowed with concern. She touched his face.

"It's nothing bad. I know what you're thinking, however, the soul snatcher didn't leave anything foreign behind. It just stole. No, this is different. I don't think it's my power, I think...I think it's my mother."

"Kasumir? She—"

"I know." He paused, meeting her eyes with silence. "Do we really know what happens to Elementals after death? Perhaps she's with us now, guiding our steps toward Susan."

Agmundria frowned. "*You think your dead mother is here with us now?*"

"It's possible." Frank shrugged, ignoring the terror that edged with each of Agmundria's words. Cronk shifted in unease. Only Michi seemed tolerant of the fearmonger's power.

"Whether it's Kasumir or your latent power returning, let's continue following the river." Michi gave him a strange look. *Trust? Worry?* She turned to the others. "Frank's family are among the most powerful Elementals."

"H-how much f-f-further d-do you think w-w-we'll go?"

"I don't know, Cronk." Frank shook his head. "The mountains are close, but the Dragons might be weeks away."

They finished their lunch in silence, watching the river swim past them. Its water flowed back toward the east, back beyond the soul snatcher, back through the forests south of the College, back toward the distant sea.

*Susan and Will sailed across the ocean before their capture. How far did the Dragons drag them through the air? They'd been gone for two weeks, perhaps more. How much longer will the Dragons let them live?*

No, the Dragons wouldn't have captured his friends only to kill them. He'd find them alive, and he'd save them.

Frank rose and adjusted his pack. He lifted the boskery blade. Its double blades quivered with an unseen hunger.

The four travelers walked for an hour, until Michi stopped.

"What is it?" Frank raised the blade.

"Something flashed in the woods over there."

"A Dragon?" He peered into the forest, without seeing anything.

"I'm not sure."

"*We should avoid it,*" warned Agmundria. "*It could be another soul-snatcher.*"

"L-L-look." Cronk pointed in the opposite direction. "A b-b-bridge."

Frank spun. A thin, wooden bridge spanned the Acheron just a few feet away.

"I didn't see that before." Michi frowned. "Where did it come from?"

"*Why would there be a bridge here? There's nothing for miles.*"

"I don't like it." Michi shook her head.

"What should we do?" Frank shrugged. "Go into the woods and risk Dragons, or cross the river?"

"Neither. We continue straight, ignoring both." Michi paused, pointing. "Let's stay away from the banks."

Frank nodded, and they continued. He kept both hands tight on the boskery blade. Cronk held his scythe in front of him. Michi stretched both hands, flies and beetles surrounding each finger. Even Agmundria walked with caution. The others walked first, and he took up the rear.

The bridge approached on their left. Michi glanced right again.

"I saw it again," she said. "A flash of light in the forest, like a spark."

Frank spun, sprinting to the bridge. Something deep within his heart pulled him there. He ran before realizing his legs were moving.

"Frank? What are you doing?" shouted Michi.

"We have to go this way."

"Why? We agreed to avoid the bridge. Are you all right?"

A beetle buzzed next to his ear, and landed on his forehead. He knew Michi was sensing him, trying to see if he was in control.

*Am I in control?*

He took a step onto the bridge.

"Frank! Get back here, now." Michi walked to the edge of the bridge.

"W-w-what's w-wrong?"

"*Frank? Why are you backing up like that?*" added Agmundria.

He took another step backward. Something pulled him into the center of the bridge.

"Help me," he whispered, unsure of anything.

Michi and Agmundria ran onto the bridge, however, he staggered away, reaching the center of the span. Wooden planks creaked under his boots, and he grasped the knotted rope railing. Cronk followed the two young women, using his scythe like a staff.

"Close your eyes. The soul snatcher might still be controlling you. Take a deep breath and come with us." Michi reached out. Agmundria smiled beside her and also held out a hand.

Frank stretched his fingers to meet his friends. He inhaled and took a cautious step. The bridge shook.

"Look out!" shouted Michi.

His eyes popped open to see Cronk tumbling toward them. The ends of the bridge curled away from the river banks, and the wooden planks trembled as the entire bridge rose high above the river. Cronk slammed into Agmundria and Michi, who fell into Frank.

The four collapsed in the center of the rising jumble of floating planks and twisting cord. The ends of the bridge snaked around them, forming a single tangled mass around their trapped bodies. Something flashed in the woods, and Frank's foot warmed.

A flicker of flame inched upward along the tangle of bridge and travelers. With a sudden burst, the mass erupted in fire.

Michi screamed, and Agmundria struggled to break free. Cronk pushed planks away with his scythe, yet the cords re-wrapped around, holding him still.

Frank tried to scream. The sound never came.

"Relax. Don't fight it." With astonishment, he heard those words slip from his own mouth.

The air grew heavy with smoke, yet the fire didn't cause pain. Tongues of orange and gold danced along his cheek, flitting past his eyes. Frank's mouth opened, and a stranger's voice sounded:

*"It is I, the formless song*
*Remember my joy, and forgive my wrongs."*

The voice sang in a mellifluent melody, both familiar and unknown. Michi's eyes widened in panic. Flames moved in pulse to the stranger's song. The fiery tongues brightened, and the mass of wood, ropes, and flame fell into the Acheron.

Icy waves rushed at them, and then parted. The mass of flame, bodies, wood, and smoke tumbled through an opening within the river. Water rose on all sides around their astonished eyes, soaring into the sky like the reverse waterfall of the Door.

As his eyes closed, Frank thought he saw two hands clasping: one hand covered in rainbow scales, and one hand made of fire.

All went black.

CHAPTER TWELVE—WILL

# Night Hunters

**W**ill and Keirash climbed a ridge and the trees parted. Stars shone bright above, and the moon's pale light swept over a vast open plain. Snow lingered in patches across the opening space, seeming to collect and spin.

"Wait," whispered Keirash.

From the corner of his eye, Will watched an enormous winged shadow descend onto the plains. It snatched something, and a drift of snow shot through its talons. The creature bellowed, flying to another spot on the plains.

"We're in luck," said Keirash. "Just a few nocturns."

"Nocturns?"

"Night hunters. Most Dragons hunt in the day, when we can see our prey more easily."

"Prey?"

Another shadow swept across the stars, blocking each out for a moment. It turned, diving to the shadowy plain.

"Look closer at the field before you."

The shadow sped across the field. Will squinted, spying no animals. Ghostlike threads of white hovered and bunched. Clumps of snow caught the moonlight, glowing with a faint, weary light. The nocturn sped to a glowing clump and ripped it apart with its jaws. The snow burst into clouds of white, which fell back to the plain.

"Dragons eat snow?" asked Will.

"That's not snow, you fool. Have you ever wondered what happens to souls you Deaths don't reach in time?"

"In time for what? All souls get Reaped."

"Do they?"

Will watched another nocturn, closer to them. It dove across the plain with outstretched leathery wings. Its silver scales caught the light of the moon. The Dragon flew toward two glowing shapes below.

*Not snow?*

For a terrible moment, Will thought he saw an outstretched ethereal arm, waving in terror. The nocturn sank its teeth into the apparition, and it dissolved into wisps of white cloud. White powder fell to the ground.

"It's ash." Keirash's eyes glinted in the dim light. "We're standing in the same ash now."

"Ash?"

"Keep your voice down."

"What are they eating?"

"When a soul dies, it lingers by its body for a short time. Deaths come and Reap many of the souls, guiding them to their little Door. Yet, many go unclaimed. Hundreds of souls each day sink away from their bodies, with no one to guide them. Over time they slip into this world. We call them *shades*. We collect shades in places like this. That plain is, well, think of it like a *magnet* for un-Reaped souls."

"You eat *souls*?"

"Is it really strange? You Deaths eat bread, manipulated with Elemental powers to taste like the animals you ate in the Mortal World. I find that far more repugnant."

"You find *that*—"

"Enough," said Keirash. "I haven't brought you here to discuss food. We must continue around the hunting field. We have one more stop before I bring you back to the cell."

She started through the white powder. Could it really be ash from devoured *souls*? The idea repulsed Will. His stomach knotted as he stepped through the ash, hurrying behind Keirash.

"Come on." The Dragon walked on. Will held his breath. Each time a shadow darted over the plain he fought between the urge to warn the souls, and the desire to stay hidden. He doubted the night hunters would be friendlier than Keirash.

CHAPTER THIRTEEN—FRANK

# The Swarm

**W**armth surrounded him, pulsing like a beating heart. The air stank of fire and smoke.

Frank opened his eyes.

"Where are we?" murmured Michi beside him.

"W-w-we're in H-hell."

Frank's fingers flexed. The ground was soft and powdery.

"*Ash. It's all fire and ash.*" Agmundria's voice quivered with fear. Somehow, sensing the young Fearmonger's terror made their plight even worse.

Tongues of flame flickered around them. Farther away, an enormous wall of fire ringed them, stretching twenty feet high. The air was filled with hot smoke. Although it stank, Frank breathed without choking. Apart from flames, ash, and smoke, he saw nothing else. There was no river, no sign of the destroyed bridge. No land. No sky. Only fire, ash, and desolation.

"You led us here." Michi turned to Frank, rising to her feet. "Do you know what's going on?"

"Something pulled me to the bridge." He stood up. The cinders underfoot sank beneath his weight like sand, until he stood ankle-deep in ash. "It's gone now. I don't know where we are or why we've been brought."

"*We've been captured. We're all dead.*" Agmundria wept.

"No, we're not dead." Frank extended his hand to help her up. He pulled the young girl into an embrace. "If Cronk died, he'd *cease*. We'd never know he existed. He's here with us. We're alive, and we're going to get out of here."

"W-w-where ar-ar-are we?" Cronk rose, bending into the embers around them, sifting through the smoking ash. He pulled out the scythe.

Frank bent, feeling through the cinders until he touched something sharp. He drew back, yet the boskery blade hadn't paralyzed him. He probed again, and this time pulled the weapon out by the blade.

Michi raised her hands, frowning. "My insects are gone. I have no power here."

"The boskery blade didn't paralyze me," added Frank. "Wherever we are, this place nullifies Elemental abilities."

"*So no one will fear me here?*" asked Agmundria.

"Seems that way." Michi shook her head.

A slight smile crept to the young girl's lips: the first smile Frank had seen on her in some time.

A pile of ash in front of Michi started to glow, reddening and brightening until it shone white-hot. She backed away. Two tongues of flame flickered upwards, dancing around each other. They pulsed together, one flame brightening while the other dimmed, and then switching. The pulsing reminded Frank of a beating heart.

"Who are you?" ventured Frank.

"It's fire," said Michi. "It won't answer."

"WHO ARE YOU?"

Frank and the others staggered back. A thousand voices screamed the words back at him: voices young and old, male and female. Voices poured through the flames, echoing from the hellish inferno around them, pulsing with a single beating heart.

"*What was that?*" asked Agmundria.

"It echoed your question." Michi's hands rose, warding off some unseen threat.

"WHO ARE YOU?" The chorus screamed the words again, louder. Their voices bristled with anger and fiery rage.

"It's not just echoing." Frank's fingers tightened around the boskery blade. He stared into the pulsating flames. Tiny golden sparks danced around their fringes, vanishing into the smoky air.

"I am Plamen, son of Kasumir and Giri. I am an Elemental. Some call me Frank. These are my friends: Michi and Agmundria, also Elementals; and this is Cronk, a Death."

"WHERE IS SHE?"

Frank turned to Michi, who shrugged.

"THE SONG CALLED. WHERE IS SHE?"

The ring of flame surrounding them leaped forward, penning them tighter. Jets of golden fire extended from the blazing wall, like hands grasping toward them. Burning tendrils wrapped around Cronk's waist, and then a second burst of fire brought pulsing flames around Agmundria and Michi.

"WHERE IS SHE?" The flames screamed; their deafening chorus filled the hot air with anger. The flames receded from the others, and a thin tongue of fire wrapped around Frank's arm. The blaze didn't burn; it throbbed with a gentle, probing warmth.

A sudden burst of flames shot toward Frank from every direction. His entire body vanished beneath a conflagration.

"Frank!" shouted Michi.

"I'm all right." Smoke filled his lungs and he coughed. He closed his eyes, however, the searing light shone through his eyelids. After a moment, the flames receded.

"WE UNDERSTAND," said the chorus.

"Who are you?" Frank squinted in the ashy air.

"WE SEE ALL."

The outer ring swept back away, and the pulsing pillars before him brightened, blooming into a single tendril of flame. It turned in mid-air, writhing like an uncoiling serpent. Fire leaped forward, jabbing Frank in the forehead. Through the corner of his eyes, he watched similar jets of fire snake into the foreheads of each of his companions.

A searing pain shot through his skull. Opening his mouth to scream, only smoke escaped from his lips. Warmth blanketed him. His sight blurred into gilded swirls of auburn, orange, white, and blue. He rode a cascade of images and emotions.

*His hands flickered and flared.*

*He was flame.*

*He was fire.*

His sight bounced up and down through a dim corridor. He sat atop a dripping wax candle. The image settled on a table. An elderly man stepped away.

"Do you see it?" Frank heard Michi's voice.

"W-what's h-happening?" asked Cronk.

The image faded and re-formed. A billion eyes watched from the walls of a house. One by one, the perspective jumped from eye to eye. Smoke hovered above, billowing from Frank.

*They are fire, or at least live in it.*

A fire truck pulled up and a jet of water sped toward the picture. It shifted again. A black disk covered much of the view. It rose, held by a hand, and Frank saw it was a pot. The image blurred, and an enormous mountain range came into focus. A Dragon bellowed, releasing a burst of flame. The image changed, falling away from the Dragon's mouth, speeding to a tree.

Frank fell through the air, racing downward as he sped on the backs of the rippling fames. "Fire. They see through fire."

"WE SEE ALL." The chorus of shrill voices swarmed around them.

"Any fire?" asked Michi.

"Those were images of the Mortal World, and then of a Dragon's flame. Whatever these creatures are, they see through flames."

"FLAME. FIRE. WINDOWS."

Everything around him faded to gray. Smoke wisped past his nose, and a new heat engulfed him. Frank gasped as he watched Susan plummeting through the air. A mahogany Dragon swooped down, grabbing her.

"PAST."

The image changed, and Frank watched himself pushing Will under a table. His mind sped forward on the flames, ramming into a wall. *The Elemental attack from last year.* The image blurred and he saw a young Death in a field, preparing a picnic. The picture raced downward, riding flames. The boy put out his hand, and vanished. *Who was that?* The image blurred again, and Frank watched two enormous Dragons flying over snow, away from a burning boat. One Dragon was white, and the other black. In their claws, the beasts held bodies.

"Will and Susan." Michi's voice echoed across an unseen void. "That must be their capture. These are images from the past."

"W-we use f-f-flower l-lights," said Cronk.

"Instead of candles," added Frank. "Now we know why."

"WE SEE ALL. PRESENT." The swarm of fiery voices echoed through his consciousness, like flickering sparks dancing around a conflagration.

Around Frank, grays blurred into clouded smoke, refocusing into white-hot light. An enormous mountain capped in snow stood before him. A dozen small Dragons flew around the massive peak. Something in Frank's chest stirred. The mountain shuddered. The world blurred again.

Smoke drifted from a boat. On the shoreline, Mors burned. A Dragon hovered over the city, beating its wings. Bolts of lightning shot up from the city. The beast dodged them. A second Dragon flew into sight, opening its mouth. Frank's mind jumped into the Dragon's flame, thundering down to the ground. Sight blurred as a group of Deaths and Elementals ran for cover.

"The war's started." Worry crept into Michi's words. "Mors is under attack."

"WE SEE ALL. FUTURE."

For a moment, Frank stood on the pile of ash again. He felt the tongue of flame burning into his forehead. Michi, Agmundria, and Cronk stared ahead with vacant expressions. Slender fingers of fire shot from each of their foreheads to the pulsating ring of hellfire around them. He struggled to break free, however, the flames refocused. The world faded into clouds of blurred smoke.

Susan sat in a dim cavern. The light around her flickered, perhaps from a cooking fire. She held a baby in her arms. Her hair was disheveled, and a trail of blood dripped from one cheek. Sindril strode into sight with a scythe. He lifted the blade to her neck. Tears streamed down her face. Sindril pulled the blade, and Susan's head fell to the cavern floor. Sindril lifted the child, smiling. The picture blurred again.

"No," said Frank. "That's not going to happen."

"POSSIBILITIES. FUTURE." The myriad of voices echoed in cacophony. "WE SEE ALL. FUTURE. POSSIBILITIES."

A new image took form. Clouds raced past, and the ground sped by below. Frank circled, lowering. Sindril and the baby stood at the center of a barren plain. The former Headmaster held the child high above his head like a trophy. The image descended, and a talon shot forward, skewering

Sindril through the heart. The Death vanished. The baby tumbled down. A second talon clawed forward, impaling the baby. The image filled with white-hot light. It flared, and the bulging flames dispersed.

"The future isn't set in stone!" he heard Michi yell.

"They said possibilities," said Frank. "They're showing us why we must succeed."

Smoke obfuscated everything around, until dim threads of light took form. Once again, he became aware of standing in ash. The fire receded from their heads, coiling back to the ring beyond. Frank rubbed his forehead; though warm, it was unburned.

The flaming columns resumed their heartbeat pattern.

*"Why did you bring us here?"* asked Agmundria.

*Why indeed,* thought Frank. "You've shown us what you see. What can you *do*? If you inhabit fire, you are strong."

"STRONG. FIRE. STRONG." The swarm of infinite voices swelled around him, growing louder by the minute. Michi and Agmundria held their hands over their ears. Cronk's grip tightened on his scythe. "STRONG. FIRE. STRONG."

"Will you help us?"

For a moment the outer ring shuddered. The pulsing pillars of flame paused, brightening until their white-hot light became unbearable to look at.

"Will you help us?" Frank repeated.

"YES."

CHAPTER FOURTEEN—SUSAN

# Whispers in the Night

Caladbolg stared into the roaring bonfire. A log fell, and a wave of sparks leaped into the air, dancing into vanishing smoke.

"You think this will work?"

"*They were our greatest allies once.*" The Dragon's breath warmed his back, filling the room with a sulfur stench.

"That was long ago," replied the King of Donkar.

"*The Nameless King promised your death. If you wish destruction, do nothing. You've made it so a human death results in complete erasure. If he kills you, no one will know you ever existed.*"

"I will not *cease*," said Caladbolg.

"*Then call them.*" Koros snorted.

Caladbolg took a deep breath, plunging his hands into the flame. Pain coursed through his fingers, searing into his skin. "*Help me!*"

A tongue of fire snaked toward his forehead.

As the blaze touched him, the room vanished into billows of smoke.

*The smoke faded.*

*Time slipped away.*

Suzie stood at the back of Grandma's wake. Dad held Mom in his arms, she was weeping. Joe stepped up to the open coffin, placing a rose on Grandma's chest. When he turned back to the aisle, Suzie saw tears in her brother's eyes. Uncle Steve patted her on the shoulder, and guided her forward.

She walked with somber steps. Grown-ups on either side of the aisle gave her pitied smiles or nods of encouragement. Suzie reached the coffin, and looked down. She'd never seen a dead person before. Grandma looked asleep. Her face, covered in immaculate makeup, sat in surreal stillness beneath pristine hair. Suzie reached out and touched Grandma's hand. It was cold and lifeless.

"Say goodbye," said Uncle Steve.

"Why?" Suzie glanced up.

"It's polite." Her uncle nodded.

"Bye, Grandma."

She turned away and returned to the back of the room. There was a seat up front, yet she ignored it, uncomfortable. Suzie didn't like this place. Too many crying people. Uncle Steve patted her shoulder, and turned to talk to a crowd of people she didn't know.

She sat in a chair in the corner, wishing Mom would let her have a cell phone. They thought she was too young, but Amber got her own phone when she turned seven. That was two years ago.

"Are you sad?" An older man took the seat beside her.

"Yes." Suzie brushed a strand of hair away from her eyes. "She was my Grandma."

"You don't seem sad."

She stared at the man. A thick white beard hung from his chin, and wisps of long silver hair poked from beneath a black hat. Wrinkles lined the man's face. She'd never seen him before, however he looked familiar somehow.

"I don't know you." Her leg bounced against the chair.

"My name is Caladbolg. You can call me Grym, if that's easier."

"That's a weird name."

"I didn't choose it. Most people don't pick their own names. Did you pick yours?"

"No. I mean my parents named me Susan. Everyone calls me Suzie."

"I see." He stared at her a moment in awkward silence.

"I *am* sad. At least I think I am. I don't know what to feel."

"That's all right, Susan. Sometimes answers come to us when we least expect them. Life and death have a way of sorting themselves out. What we need is hope."

"Hope?"

"That we'll have the courage to face death with dignity when it comes." He laughed, and stood, reaching a hand to her. "It was nice to meet you, Susan."

She frowned, shaking his hand.

The strange old man leaned down and whispered in her ear. "Have hope. Ignite the Eye of Donkar."

He grabbed her right wrist, and an intense pain shot through it.

"Ignite the Eye." He stared at her. "Don't lose hope."

The wake vanished into billows of smoke, and a single tongue of flame darted toward her forehead.

\* \* \* \*

Susan awoke with a start, her right arm burning and throbbing in pain. She ran her fingers across the gauzy webbing that encased her wrist, trapping Grym. Her mind raced between nightmares. She often dreamed of Grym, however, one of the dreams bothered her. She'd seen him at Grandma's funeral.

*It felt like a memory. It can't be real, though. Grym was trapped until I freed him.*

No, she remembered the funeral. There'd been no old man; no wizened stranger filling her with confusion. *He inserted himself into my memory. Why?* He'd said something about an eye. *What eye? What does it mean?*

Susan shook her head. She was going mad. The monotony of her prison cell, the constant sound of Dragon wings in the distance, and the ever-present fear of death. Maybe the dreams weren't Grym at all, but the delusions of her despairing mind.

*Will I ever be free from this hell?*

The familiar sounds of footsteps echoed in the hallway, growing nearer. She rose from the bed. The door opened, and Sindril entered, holding a scythe. He closed the door, and leaned his blade against it. Turning, he smiled.

"Hello, Susan."

"What do you want?"

He stepped closer. The stink of sulfur and ash wafted from his clothes. His eyes bored into hers with malice. "I want what you want, my dear, to go home."

"I can't help you."

"I think you can." He walked to the bed, reaching his fingers toward her cheek.

"Don't touch me." She recoiled.

"I know you've heard of the Dragon Key. Don't deny it. Susan, lying will bring you no comfort here."

"What of it?"

"You are a daughter of three worlds, Susan. You are a human born in the Mortal World. Now you live in the World of Deaths, with traces of ancient Elemental blood flowing in your veins. A child of yours could become a Dragon Key. With a single act, you and I both gain our freedom."

"You're not—"

"I know it's not what you expected, but I will treat the child with respect. When our child becomes a Dragon Key, I will overthrow the Deaths. Help me welcome a new era of peace, one where humans are never brought to this world. Dragons will usher souls as they did long ago. Change will come to all creation, and you and I will return to our homes in the Mortal World."

"I'd *never*—" She tried to run past him. He grabbed her wrist, twisting it back, and forced her to the bed.

"This is about necessity. I *need* your child, and you need my help. Once the child fulfills its purpose, you will never see me again."

"You're disgusting."

He slapped her across the face, and she fell hard into the mattress.

"This can be easy or hard, it's up to you. Your friend Billy will die soon. We caught him this morning, trying to escape."

"No!"

"There is no other path for you to choose. One night with me, and you shall have the freedom you desire."

Tears welled in her eyes; she tried to blink them back. A knot of revulsion tightened in her throat.

"I will return in two nights. The Dragon Key will be stronger if unforced, yet I *will* force one if I need to."

He stood abruptly, strode to the door and lifted the scythe.

"A bonus." He raised his eyebrows. "If you cooperate, I'll set Billy free. We'll return him to the Mortal World with you, if you wish."

"No, never, I—" Her voice dropped to a whisper. "*Never.*"

"See you soon. Sleep well, and choose wisely."

The door closed and echoing footsteps receded into the hallway. Suzie collapsed into tears, clutching her arms tight around her body.

CHAPTER FIFTEEN—FRANK

# Temple of Fangs

Frank hit the ground hard, rolling onto his side. Smoke wafted away from him, fading into the open sky above. He pulled himself up and walked to Michi, helping her rise.

"What do you think they were?" Michi wiped a line of soot from her cheek.

"Either something that lives in fire, or fire itself." Frank shook his head. "They're old. Maybe fire's always been alive."

They stood at the feet of the Dragonspine Mountains. High above them, blankets of cloud hid the peaks of the massive stony range. Dark shadows flew through the distant haze, far too large to be birds.

"We rode down a Dragon's flame." Michi stared at the sky. "Every time a Dragon breathes, or there is flame at all, those *things* see?"

"Or perhaps they *are* the flame itself. Either way, they're a powerful ally."

"They said they'd help, and here we are." She gestured. "Perhaps bringing us to the feet of the mountains is how they intend to help."

"*They frightened me.*"

"A fearmonger afraid of fire?" Frank's eyebrow rose.

"I d-d-don't t-t-trust them. W-we use f-f-flowers so they c-can't see us."

"Deaths fear anything from this world that they didn't bring." Frank put a hand on Cronk's shoulder. "That doesn't mean the Swarm was evil. I think they'll continue supporting us."

"We still don't know what's happened to you, Frank." Michi stepped toward him, her tone cautious.

She said no more, however Frank frowned. She was right. Something brought him to that bridge. Something grew within him, in the empty space where his power once lurked. He sensed it deep behind his thoughts, slowly taking form. Every time he turned his attention toward it, the mystery receded from thought, like a distant dream vanishing from memory. Yet, he knew the mystery was there, waiting for something.

"We should move." He'd worry later. "We don't want to be seen."

"C-c-can we r-r-rest? It's l-l-like w-we've been b-b-burned alive."

"There's a copse of trees." Frank pointed. "It'll give us a little cover. We can rest when we're in the thicket."

They shouldered their packs. The scythe and boskery blade lay to the side of where they'd fallen. Frank glanced around, looking for fire. Seeing no sign of the strange beings who'd brought them there, he shrugged, leading the others toward the trees.

An hour later, they forced their way through the dense overgrowth surrounding the thicket. Dragon shadows grew more numerous with every step. Frank pulled out a gorger and split it into four. Their supplies ran low; the trip had taken longer than he'd planned.

"What now?" Michi pulled out a water bottle. "We're at the doorstep of the Dragons' domain, yet still have no idea where Suzie is, or what to do when we find her."

"*This wasn't a well-planned rescue.*"

"I had to do something." Frank frowned. "The Deaths would've abandoned her."

"I'll send my insects to search the area. Perhaps there's a path through the mountains that won't get us captured or killed."

"*You don't sound optimistic.*" The raven-haired child sat on a log.

Michi extended her fingers, and a cluster of fireflies, beetles, and flying ants emerged from the trees and brush. The tiny scouts hovered around her hands until she pointed to the mountains. One by one, the bugs scattered, and Michi leaned on her hands, breathing hard.

"Don't push yourself, Michi. You only just got your abilities back." Frank rested a hand on her back, and then unslung his pack. "Are you okay to keep watch?"

"I'll be fine. Thanks for asking. You're sounding more like your old self every day."

"Through fire and back," he murmured. "Cronk, take a break. You too, Agmundria. The fire Swarm drained you both, yet I'm wide awake. Michi and I will keep watch in case any Dragons get too close."

Cronk grunted, stretching his legs. He gestured for Frank to approach, and handed him the scythe. Frank nodded, smiling.

After Agmundria and Cronk closed their eyes, he ran his hands over the snath, thinking.

"Scythes transport us through space. Couldn't we use one to bring us to Susan?"

"Try it if you like." Michi cocked her head. "Didn't they teach you anything about scythes or Dragons while you pretended to be a Death? The Dragons' power is greater than the Elemental power saturating the mortamant. The Great Scythes around the College help repel Dragons, yet even they wouldn't be able to bring you within the mountain kingdom."

He paused, gazing into her face. "I don't have a crush on her anymore, you know. That's not why we're here."

She smiled. "I know, Frank. She's my friend too. Both of them are. You're right to try and rescue them."

For a moment both lapsed into silence. Michi smiled, and Frank felt his cheeks grow warm.

"You haven't heard from any of your bugs yet?"

"Not yet."

Pretending to look at the scythe in his hands, Frank kept glancing at Michi.

"Since I have the scythe, why don't you take the boskery blade?"

"I'll be fine. If a Dragon attacks, my insects are more likely to help than a toy blade."

"It's not—"

"Frank, I'll be all right. What about you? What's going on with your power?"

He sighed. "I don't know. That's the truth."

"Your power will grow back. The soul isn't a stagnant thing. It grows and changes over time."

"You don't know that."

She sighed. "It's true. What you're experiencing could be Kasumir's influence. Or it might be something else. Either way, I'm worried about you."

"Now it's my turn to say I'll be fine."

She held up a hand, her expression changing.

"What is it?"

"Someone's returned already; they've found something." A firefly glowed, flitting toward Michi's ear. She frowned, nodding.

"Well?" he asked.

"There's a structure an hour's walk away. It's too small for Dragons; the insects think it guards an entrance to the mountains."

"What sort of structure?"

"A building. It looks like Deaths walking outside it."

"Deaths *here*?" Frank shook his head. "That can't be right. Deaths and Dragons are enemies."

"Sindril worked with them, didn't he?"

"And was chased out of the College when his connection to Dragons was discovered."

"I looked through the insect's eyes." As she spoke, the firefly dimmed, collapsing dead on the ground. *The price of her power.* "Whatever's living in that building, they're *human*."

"Let's wake the others; it sounds promising."

"Frank, if these *are* Deaths, they're working with Sindril."

"*I say we find out.*" Agmundria's eyes popped open.

"What do you propose?" Michi walked to the girl.

"*If they're human, they'll scare easily.*" Agmundria winked. "*Fear is my specialty.*"

Frank tapped Cronk on the shoulder. "Time to wake up."

"W-w-what is it?"

"We've got some plans to discuss."

\* \* \* \*

Frank pushed aside a clump of thick cattails. A wide muddy plain stretched below him, crossed with tiny rivulets that snaked toward the Acheron. The river veered southwest, fading to the horizon. Towering peaks of snow-capped craggy rock shouldered the sky on both sides of the silver water. He lay in thick grass, chest-down on a ridge. Directly across from him, a two story structure stood between the mud and the mountain.

Bone-white walls climbed to jagged points, which ran across the building's roof. Four men in white cloaks stood outside the building. Frank started to rise when a thunderous bell clanged. Two doors opened, and six more cloaked men strode forth, carrying a bundle draped in red cloth. All eight figures processed to the center of the mud, where they lay the bundle down, removing the cloth. With a quick glance at the sky, they hurried back to the building.

Frank stared. A young boy, maybe thirteen, lay on his back. His hands and wrists were bound, and a gag covered his mouth. He lay motionless, either unconscious or dead.

A beetle fluttered beside Frank's cheek. "We need to put our plans on hold," he whispered to the insect. "That boy needs our—"

Before he could finish, a monstrous roar bellowed from above. Breaking out of the cloud cover, a Dragon plunged toward the plain. Its copper scales gleamed in the sun and its ferocious red eyes burned like hot coals. The Dragon raced to the boy, and swallowed him in a single bite.

For a moment, Frank couldn't remember why he was staring ahead. A copper Dragon sped into the sky, vanishing from sight. A spot on the ground looked red with blood.

*Did the Dragon kill someone?*

Eight men stood in front of the building, their white cloaks billowing in the breeze. Each man lifted his hands and face skyward. A distant sound echoed across the bog.

*They're singing.*

"*We're moving ahead.*" Michi spoke through the beetle beside him.

Frank nodded, trying to clear his mind.

Ten yards to his right, Agmundria climbed out of the rushes, and started downhill. The men seemed not to notice, until she stepped onto the mud. Their song halted and the men shouted. Two ran forward, however Agmundria held up her hands.

The two men closest to her collapsed face first, trembling. They crawled away as the other figures turned and fled into the fang-covered building.

Michi and Cronk ran out from their hiding places, with Frank close behind. Cronk slipped in the mud, yet they kept running and staggering toward the structure. The doors slammed closed before them. Frank stumbled in the mud, catching himself with his hands. He rose and continued forward.

The building stood ten feet away. Sharp points jutted out from every wall. *Fangs. The walls are formed from hundreds of teeth, probably Dragon fangs by their size.* Fangs pointed outward from each of the closed doors, arranged like enormous knives of bone warding off intruders.

Agmundria raised her arms again, waving her hand in a convoluted pattern. The massive doors shuddered, and swung open a crack. Frank shook his head in disbelief. The child was amazing.

A single white robed man staggered out of the building, waving away some unseen menace. Cronk ran forward, pressing the scythe blade to his neck. The man's eyes cleared, focusing on the group staring at him.

"Who are you? How dare you defile this temple?"

"What is this place?" Frank pointed. "Are you Deaths?"

The man swung his beady eyes to Frank before spinning around. "We're under attack. Stop the Elementals!" he shouted.

Michi frowned, a swarm of insects buzzing around her. Cronk pushed the scythe blade tight on the man's neck.

A stream of men ran out of the structure. Each wore a small, shiny medallion.

"Release him." One of the strange men strode forward. "We have you surrounded."

Agmundria waved her arms. Only the man captured by Cronk flinched.

"Your powers won't work on us, 'Mental freak. These are special Dragon scales, which reject your abilities." Six of the men held long lances with scythe blades at the end. They pointed the lances into the center of their circle, stepping closer.

"I'll k-k-kill him." Cronk pressed the blade close.

"If you harm him, all of you die."

The two groups stared at each other. Frank moved first, lowering his boskery blade to the ground. Cronk let the scythe fall away from the man's throat.

"Tie their hands," shouted the same man who'd addressed them. "Take them into the temple. We'll question them before they are sacrificed."

CHAPTER SIXTEEN—WILL

# Blood Oath

Keirash and Will paused on the opposite edge of the hunting fields. Three Dragons swept out of the skies, and grabbed glowing souls in the wasteland. Will crouched behind an outcropping of rock to avoid detection.

"You think the plan will work?" he asked.

"It's the only way to get you two together and alone. If we free you from Sindril and the other Dragons, escaping the mountains undetected becomes a distinct possibility."

"I just wait in my cell? If they come to torture me again, what if I say too much? If the other Dragons discover what we've—"

She silenced him with a glance. The mahogany scales around her eyes pulsed. The Dragon bared her fangs. "You talk too much as it is, human. That is why we're taking a detour first."

"Forgive me. I want this to work, even more than you do."

"We *all* pray for success. Climb on; we fly from here."

Keirash lowered her body to the ground. Will struggled onto her back, wrapping his arms around her neck. She shifted her enormous weight beneath him. Each scale was harder than iron, and yet the warm plates flexed and bent with every twist of the Dragon's body. She spread her thin brown wings, flapped once, and leaped above the hunting field.

Tiny shimmering souls dotted the desolation below. Poor un-reaped lives that the Dragons now claimed for food.

Keirash banked heavy to her right, and Will slipped to the side. His fingers unclasped and he cried out, flailing. The Dragon maneuvered again, catching him on her back.

"Stay *quiet.*"

Wind whipped against his face, and Will clamped his mouth shut. Keirash undulated beneath him, riding gusts of wind, gliding between mountain peaks. The cold air stank of sulfur and ash. She flew higher, circling a snow-capped pinnacle. On the other side, the Dragon flattened her wings, speeding toward the mountainside. Will's grip tightened as the Dragon dove down.

"Look out!" he shouted.

Keirash passed through the rocks, and flapped her wings. The inside of the mountain was a hollow cone. A single shaft of sunlight fell from above, lighting a large white boulder on the center of a sandy floor. The mountain wall that they'd flown through looked solid, though they'd passed through it like cloud.

Samas lay curled on the top of the boulder, in the center of the light. The rest of the cavern was empty. Keirash flew to the dusty floor, blowing billows of sand and ash into the chamber. She lowered her body, and Will climbed off.

"You are the first human to see this holy space." The tiny golden dragon lifted into the air and hovered above the boulder.

"Another hidden chamber?" asked Will. "Couldn't you tell me in the last one?"

Samas snapped his tail back; its gilded scales caught the shaft of light. "This space is secret even from most members of White Claw."

"This is the Tomb of the Severed." Keirash spoke in a low and reverent voice.

"The King knows of White Claw," said Samas. "He knows of me, at least. Yet, he has no idea how widespread our influence has become. This tomb helped ensure our survival."

"Who is buried here?" Will stared around the chamber.

"Those members of White Claw with knowledge that he'd find useful. I told you the World of Deaths is formed from Dragonsong. All Dragons are connected, for we all come from a single source. This place, which took generations to form, conceals our true power: our past."

The small creature flapped down to the floor, and laid his talons on the boulder. The cavern shuddered, and the stone rose, climbing up the shaft of light. Beneath the boulder, a hollow pillar emerged, filled with large shelves. Upon each shelf, a lump of flesh rested.

"When a Dragon dies, their body is burned." Keirash nodded in a strange, reverent bow. "They become ash and memory."

"In this place, we save a portion of each Dragon's flesh." Samas gestured. "The ash in this cavern protects these noble creatures: my ancestors." He lifted a piece of flesh, and flapped back to Will.

"This was part of a great Dragon called Firidyn. Within these cells, I can feel his memories, his desires, his *blood*."

Will stared at the lump of lifeless, putrid meat.

"Extend your hand, Will."

"What?"

"Do it," urged Keirash.

Will reached forward. Samas held the meat above his open palm, and tore the hunk in two. Three drops of fluid fell onto Will's fingers.

"Dragon blood." Samas's head flicked to one side. "It never leaves our bodies, even after death. Dragon blood is one of the most potent forces in this world. Will, the sole way we can ensure our safety is for you to swear a blood oath. Clear your heart, your mind, and your doubts."

Will's mind raced, struggling to focus. The Dragon blood on his hand burned his skin, yet he made no move to wipe it off.

"Repeat after me," continued the golden Dragon. "I swear to keep White Claw secret. I swear to never betray any secrets they have told me, and to tell no one of their plans involving Susan. I swear to keep their sites secret, and I will never betray the names of any Dragon I know to be involved."

Will nodded and repeated the words.

Samas paused, adding, "Swear also that should they torture you, you will lie to protect our plans, and our secrets. Swear that our interests are your interests."

"I swear to protect your plans, at any cost. I swear that your secrets are my secrets, and your interests are my interests."

While he swore, for a moment he felt a strange bond between the three creatures. He sensed Keirash's sadness, and her deep longing for something. *For what?* He felt Samas's concern and anticipation. He felt something stirring deep within his heart: his own worries. He looked through three sets of eyes, tethered to the past and the future.

Samas made him pledge a second time before he smiled, baring tiny fangs. The Dragon flew to the top of the pillar, calmly replacing the lumps of flesh on the top shelf. With a tremor, the pillar sank beneath the ashy floor once more, until only the boulder was visible. The Dragon blood droplets smoked and vanished.

"You will not betray us." The golden Dragon's eyes widened. "An oath sworn on Dragon blood can never be broken. No matter how they torture you, you won't reveal anything. You'll die before you utter a single word against us."

Will flexed his palm, turning to Keirash. "We need to get back. I understand what I have to do."

"Good luck, William Black." Samas lowered his tiny head in a curt bow. "When next we meet, the stakes shall be high indeed."

"I'm ready." He climbed onto Keirash, and she flapped her wings, circling the shaft of light. Speeding through the mountain wall, she emerged into the chill air. She banked to the left, gliding fast over the peaks.

*I hope Susan understands.*

CHAPTER SEVENTEEN—FRANK

# Riddle of the Priests

Frank peered down at the open pit extending in every direction. Sharpened fangs lined the top walls, jutting toward them like waiting daggers. Their suspended cage swung gently, moving with every shift in gravity. Frank gripped the chiseled bone bars. Michi clung to the bars on the opposite side. Agmundria and Cronk sat on the floor of their hanging cell.

A door opened and three white-robed men walked out. They stood on a ledge overlooking the pit. High above them, the floor of the temple clamored with hurried footsteps. Large clumps of glowing flower lights hung from the walls above the abyss, creating a chasm of darkness beneath the cage.

The man in the center spoke. "I am Senchion, Head Priest of this temple—"

"Don't talk to them." A shorter man with beady eyes clutched his robe. "They're outsiders."

"Quiet, Vestru," said the third man, whose face was half-hidden beneath long, wavy hair.

Senchion frowned, stepping forward. "Who are you?"

"No one." Frank forced his voice to remain calm.

"Of course." Senchion smiled. "I haven't used the bone cellar in years. This was once my favorite place to worry Sacrifices before their time."

"Let us out." Frank grabbed the bony bars.

"In time, all Sacrifices find honor." He paused, cocking his head to the side. "Now tell me, why are you here? Three Elementals and a Death, lost in the wilds at the base of the Dragonspine Mountains."

"They are spies." Vestru's beady eyes darted from side to side. "The war's begun."

"They are fools." The wavy-haired priest glanced at his hand. "Whatever brought them here is no concern of ours. Let us begin their processing."

"Silence, both of you," whispered Senchion. The other priests composed themselves, glaring at the prisoners. "My friends don't know what to make of you. You're something of a riddle to us. Why would three Elementals and a Death approach our temple, and why would one of you attack us?"

"We seek passage into the mountains." Frank forced a smile. "We frightened you, yet meant no harm. We weren't sure who you are."

"As I recall, you held one of my priests hostage with a scythe blade on his neck."

"You're a riddle to us as well." Frank leaned forward against the bars. "A group of Deaths at the feet of the mountains. Who are you? Why are you here?"

Senchion chuckled. "My friend, it is not I swinging from the bone cellar. You are in no position to ask anything." He paused, pulling a thin purple vial from his robe. "They say Dragon's blood is the most powerful substance ever imagined." He fingered the vial, grinning. "Feren, man the pulleys. Let's see what they know."

"*They're going to drug us,*" whispered a voice in Frank's ear. He felt a buzzing flicker, and knew an insect perched inside.

"*What can we do?*" He tried to aim the thought at Michi. Without his power, he wasn't sure she understood.

"*Stall them. Agmundria and I are working on a plan.*"

The cage shuddered, knocking him down. One of his feet slipped out of the bony cage and his ankle twisted. The suspended cell dropped two feet, before easing toward the rim. As they edged closer to the pit he saw fangs of every color and size: thousands of Dragon teeth sharper than razors, pointing upward like spears. He slipped his foot into the cage before it hit the rim. Vestru pulled the bones onto the ledge.

On closer inspection, the three men were no more than boys. Senchion was the oldest; he looked eighteen or nineteen. The other two couldn't be much older than thirteen. *They'd be first year Deaths back at the College.*

"Hold the cage." Senchion pointed. "Let's find the answer to our riddle."

He pulled a syringe from another pocket in his robe, and stabbed the top of the vial. The tube filled with purple fluid. The others backed away from the walls of the skeletal cage.

"Try the little girl first." Feren tossed his wavy hair back.

"She's a 'Mental, you fool." Vestru scowled. "Inject the Death; he'll be most susceptible."

"I'll take it." Frank grasped the bars again. "I am both a 'Mental and a Death. I have nothing to hide."

"So be it." Senchion walked to Frank's hand, which he held through the bony bars. He stabbed the needle into Frank's wrist.

The pain was instantaneous. The blood flowed into Frank like lava, burning through his veins. His vision blurred and the room spun.

Something welled within his soul; a distant song called to him.

"Who are you?" demanded Senchion.

"Plamen, son of Kasumir and Giri, also known as Frank."

"Do you know who we are?"

"No."

"He's lying." Feren yawned. "His 'Mental blood is resisting."

"You claimed to be a 'Mental *and* a Death." Senchion stepped closer. "What does that mean?"

Frank struggled to fight his own mouth. The fire burned through him, and the agonizing pain compelled his tongue to move.

"I pretended to be a Death to meet Susan Sarnio, who I'd hoped would change our world, and she has. I remained a Death to bridge the gap between our cultures."

"Susan? The female Death?"

"Yes."

Senchion's lips parted in a massive grin. "The answer to our riddle isn't as strange as I'd imagined. You've come to rescue Susan, haven't you?"

"Yes."

"You would interfere with the work of God?"

"I don't understand," said Frank.

"I told you they're spies." Vestru's lip curled.

"These scales were gifts from God, as was this temple." Senchion held one of the shiny medallions they'd seen when captured. "We are his servants. If he holds the female, it is his right. He grants us powers no other humans in this world will ever know. We are the only souls who *remember* when a Death is killed. Do you even know what happened before you attacked us?"

"A Dragon swept down." Frank stared ahead in dull compliance.

"A minister of God accepted his Sacrifice, as another minister will soon do for you. I tire of this chat, we have our answers, and their oblation is accepted. Feren, pull them back."

The cage shuddered. Agmundria sat upright, stretching her arms. A wave of disbelief came onto Senchion's face.

"No, my lord, how could you—" he muttered, waving his hands over his eyes. Stumbling, he fell into the pit of fangs, impaling himself. A second scream rang out as Feren jumped into the teeth behind him.

Vestru pulled out his medallion, clutching it in front of his face like a shield. "I know this is a trick. I know the girl is doing this."

"*You cannot fight me.*" Agmundria's voice thundered loud enough to fill the cabin. "*Michi's insects have burrowed deep beneath your skin, and I am channeling my powers through each of them. Let us out, and lead us into the mountains, or I will crush your heart with a single thought.*"

"Even if you escape the temple, the Dragons will find you. They'll know. God is always watching."

"*Show us the way.*" The thin, seven-year-old girl clutched the bars of the cage and Frank's heart quailed in terror. Cronk shuffled away from her, and even Michi seemed troubled. Vestru's beady eyes darted between them, dollops of sweat visible on his forehead. He ran to the cage, opened it, and then turned, fleeing along the ledge.

Frank's body responded with agonizing slowness, he pushed one leg and then another.

The strange feeling welled again in his chest, and he leaned over the pit, vomiting purple blood.

"Come on," shouted Michi.

Cronk helped him rise, and they hurried after Vestru.

"*Wait.*" Agmundria raised a hand. Vestru's chest and face heaved and trembled; he looked ready to explode. "*Our things, including our weapons.*"

Vestru vanished into a side room, and emerged with their sacks. He handed the scythe and boskery blade to Frank. "Let me go," he whimpered. "Please. Follow this corridor to the silver door. No one will be there at this hour. The door leads straight to the mountains."

Agmundria stared at him, raised a hand, and then lowered it again. He collapsed on the ground, weeping.

"Bring him," said Michi. "He might be useful. If we leave him, he'll just tell the others where we went."

Cronk helped the boy up, holding his scythe in warning.

"He'll be more trouble than he's worth." Frank shook his head, dizzy.

"If he knows how to enter the mountains, it's worth it." Michi glanced behind.

"*You know a path leading to Dragons, don't you?*" Agmundria's voice filled with menace again.

Vestru nodded, crying.

"*Bring us.*"

He nodded, rose and led them to the door.

They ran away from the temple, and with every step Frank felt his strength returning. Whatever force was guiding him settled down behind his consciousness again.

## CHAPTER EIGHTEEN—SUSAN

# Change of Plans

Susan's dreams passed in a blur of fire and smoke. She stood atop a mountain, defying the gods to strike her down. She rode a Dragon. Waving her arm, the world split open.

A face emerged, wreathed in flame.

*You may wield the scythe, but you don't yet grasp its secret.*

Susan stared at her own face.

The image shattered, and she awoke with a start. Footsteps approached, and the door lock clicked.

"Have you decided?" asked Sindril, leaning his scythe against the wall.

Even after the dreams, this nightmare was real. This disgusting man wanted to…no, it was too terrible to even consider.

"Don't touch me."

"Such a pity." His leer oozed with malice. "The King feared that a child by force might not be as strong a Dragon Key. We will find out."

He lifted the scythe and held the blade toward her neck. She remained on the bed, clutching her fingers on the sheet so tightly that she almost cried out in pain.

"Ever since the spell, you've become something of a beauty. It wasn't my intent, but the result is wonderful. The shy child is gone, replaced by a brave woman: a brave, beautiful and sexy young woman." He touched her skin with the blade. She felt the familiar *hunger* of the scythe. This was no partial-mortamant blade like they'd used during the shortage, this was a pure scythe: evil and eager.

"You misunderstand." She willed her voice not to tremble. "I can't sleep with you."

"You can, and you will."

"All you want is a child. I'm already pregnant."

"What?" He pulled the scythe back, frowning. "You're lying."

"You aged me. Your spell robbed me of my youth, and stole four years of my life. What you didn't consider is our location when the spell struck."

"The ship?"

"Alone on a ship with Will, my boyfriend. I matured in minutes, and he couldn't stop looking at me. Before we reached Donkar, he and I made love."

"Are you telling me the truth?"

"I have nothing to lose. You've captured us both, and threatened to kill him."

Sindril shook his head. "Pregnant?"

"Let me talk to Will."

Sindril laughed.

"It's not a joke. I know we don't have a chance. I know there's no way out for us, unless…"

"I'm listening."

"Let me see Will. We had one night together: a mistake. I'll convince him the one path to freedom is to sacrifice our child. I may look eighteen, yet I've only lived fourteen years. I don't want a baby. Let us leave together, and we'll give the child to you."

Susan felt the strain of deceit in her throat. Would he believe this plan?

"You'd have to remain until the child was born. Still, many of the King's advisors have urged this very thing. They suggested a child born of love would be far more powerful than any other Dragon Key."

"You'll have it. A child born of love."

Sindril stared at the wall, lost in thought. "Their suggestion doesn't seem so preposterous now." He snorted.

"What suggestion?"

"One group of the King's advisors think it's not enough for the child to be conceived in love. They think the child gains power within the womb, and should be in the most comfortable environment possible.

We have no way to know of course, there's only been one other Key before, and that was ages ago."

"So you'll let us go?"

"Let you go? Don't be ridiculous. No, but I will discuss the situation with the council. They may have another plan."

She stood, walking toward him. When he raised the scythe, she pushed it away.

"Sindril, I hate you. You've manipulated me since I arrived, and have already violated me once, robbing four years from my soul. You disgust me." She paused, breathing hard, and put a hand to her belly. "I *am* pregnant. Believe me, I'd rather see all the Dragons burn in hell than see any child of mine raised by you. However, I'm also no fool. I have no choice. If Will leaves, he and I will never see each other again. If I stay with you, I'm worse than dead. If he and I tried to raise a child together, we'd be lost; neither of us is ready for that. However, if you let us leave together, and if you take the child, we *all* get something we want."

The older Death frowned, and shifted on his feet.

Susan clenched her fist. "You need my child to go home? This is the way."

"I admit, the idea of forcing myself was not entirely pleasant." She was surprised to hear a hint of relief in his voice. "This is a serious matter, I cannot decide alone."

"Of course."

"The King shall decide your fate."

"I understand."

"Why did you say nothing of this earlier? Why did you never speak of being pregnant?"

"At first I wasn't sure, after what you did to me." She sat on the bed, slipping her hands beneath the sheet to hide their shaking. "Once I knew, why would I tell you? One of your Dragon friends almost killed me, and I shudder to imagine what you've done to Will. I didn't know what you wanted, and thought you'd kill me."

"Susan…I want you to know, it was never personal." He took a step backward. "You are the only girl, the sole opportunity. I…I'm not a monster."

"No one's born a monster. Some people choose to become one."

Sindril nodded and turned away. "You've made an adult decision. I'll discuss this with the Dragons. Perhaps things will improve for you in this light. We can make your lives *comfortable*."

"Don't think this is easy for me. It's the only way."

"What of the boy? You think he'll give up his claim on the child?"

"He has no choice, and neither do I."

He turned again, a strange glint in his eye. "Revile me if you like. I don't have to leave, you know. I could *ensure* that a child is coming."

"You said yourself that you're not a monster."

Sindril grimaced. "So be it." He opened the door and walked out.

Susan waited until his footsteps faded from earshot before allowing herself to cry.

CHAPTER NINETEEN—FRANK

# Into the Mountains

"Let's rest here." Michi sighed, leaning against a boulder.

Frank pulled off his sack, eager for the break. They'd run without pause for two hours. The sun vanished behind the peaks before them, and the air was frigid. A chill wind whipped through barren trees. The temple had long since vanished from sight, and now even the gentle sound of the Acheron was gone. The forest was devoid of birds or animals. Only the occasional distant flap of Dragon wings broke the silence.

"I-I'm st-starving." Cronk frowned.

"We have three gorgers left." Frank took one out and broke a small piece off, tossing it to the Death.

"I'm hungry too," said Vestru.

"Is there a place to get food?" Michi raised an eyebrow. "The Dragons must eat."

"They accept our sacrifices, that's all I know."

"Cronk, watch him." Frank pointed. "If he moves, cut his neck. I'm going to gather some wood for a fire."

"No." Vestru's beady eyes widened. "Don't draw their attention. Don't start fires here."

"I thought they were your gods. Wouldn't you like to meet them?"

"We worship them out of fear." Frank was again struck by the boy's youth.

"How did you get here?" Michi stared at the boy. "You're human. Were you a Death?"

Frank sat on tree stump, and tossed Vestru a small piece of gorger. "Go on, tell us. I doubt the priests will take you back now."

"I was a Death for two days."

"Two days?" Frank laughed.

"It's no joke. I signed my contract, and then Senchion came. He spoke of a great purpose, of God watching from within the mountains."

"You don't sound like a believer." Michi smirked.

"*He fears the Dragons.*" Agmundria's voice sounded tired, and had lost some of its fearsome edge. "*The one they call God is the Dragon King.*"

"He's more than that," Vestru protested. "He created this world, your College, the humans in the Mortal World, everything. He *is* God. I would lay down my life for Him."

"You've seen him, this Dragon God of yours?" Frank cocked his head to the side.

"No one has seen him, not for thousands of years. He sends gifts to us, and sometimes speaks to the temple Himself. He told us when he'd captured Susan."

"What?" Frank jumped to his feet.

"She's important to him for some reason."

"Sit down, Frank." Michi raised a hand. "We need to rest for a few minutes. I doubt we'll do any good storming into a horde of Dragons if we're too tired to stand."

"*Where did the Temple come from? I doubt Dragons formed it from their own bones.*"

"Men of an ancient place called Donkar served as the first priests. Other Donkari joined what became your College, however, some worshipped the Dragons for what they are: the gods of this world. They built the Temple from the bones of the unholy."

"Unholy?" Frank paused, confused.

"Not all Dragons follow God. Some seek to defy him."

"I don't understand."

"Perhaps the Dragons aren't as unified as we imagined." Michi shot him a glance.

"Or perhaps the ones who resisted all ended up as walls of a temple a million years ago," added Frank. "Now there could be none who resist the Dragon King."

"He is all powerful." Vestru shook his young head. "I will lead you to His kingdom, so that he might judge you Himself. However, I will not step foot inside. No amount of fear can compel me."

"L-l-let's keep m-m-moving. I d-don't trust th-th-their k-king."

"All right." Michi stood, yawning.

Vestru muttered about the cold and his weariness, and Frank shot him a dark look. "Don't make us frighten you further," he warned. "Lead on."

They continued into the twilight, moving slow over the rocky, rising ground. They walked in silence. Cronk and Vestru led the group. Frank crept behind the two women, feeling his way. Agmundria stumbled in the dark, and he helped her up.

"Let's rest here for the night." Michi paused, breathing hard.

"We should keep going." Determination gripped Frank's heart. "We're close, and Susan needs us."

"No. We need to rest. We'll get ourselves killed stumbling in the—"

She broke off as something rustled above them. A silver Dragon, twenty feet wide soared overhead.

"Help me!" shouted Vestru.

Frank ran to the boy and clamped his hand over the priest's mouth. It was too late. The Dragon spun, circling lower.

Its hot coal eyes burned with hatred. Smoke billowed from its jaws.

"Run!" shouted Frank.

They fled down the hillside, with the Dragon sweeping overhead. It opened its mouth, baring rows of razor-sharp jaws. A jet of flame emerged, striking the stones where they'd rested a moment before. Sparks sizzled, fading into the night air.

The creature circled twice before continuing into the mountains, vanishing behind a peak.

"It spared us when he saw me." Vestru nodded, his eyes half-glazed in terror.

"He was in a hurry to get somewhere else." Frank watched the sky. "We don't matter enough to waste its time."

"I'm not sticking around until he comes back." Michi took a deep breath. "I will lead. We move slow, and follow me. There are no insects here to call on, yet I can transform my eyes." She blinked, revealing thick black insect eyes with no white at all. Frank hadn't realized she could partially transform herself, it was a gift many Elementals found impossible. She stared at him, and for a moment all he could see was Kasumir. His mother's eyes had often looked back at him, two pools of absolute darkness. This was Michi, not Kasumir. This was his closest friend, and more.

"Ewww." Vestru backed away. "What happened to your eyes?"

"I have taken the eyes of a moth. I will see better in the darkness like this."

They hurried away from the open hill, following paths beneath the trees. The Dragon did not return. For hours they wound their way higher and higher. The air chilled and wind whistled. Dragon wings flapped in the distance. The slope steepened, and the group soon crawled on all fours, pulling themselves up the face of a cliff.

Frank grabbed a handhold before helping Agmundria find one for herself. The boskery blade hung behind him with his sack. All five clamored over the lip of the cliff, and stood in a clearing. In the distance, the stars faded into a pre-dawn grey.

"This is the only way?" asked Michi, breathing hard.

"*They're Dragons.*" Agmundria's tiny fingers trembled, clutching the ground, as she sank to her knees. She struggled to catch her breath. "*I doubt they'd need to walk.*"

"D-d-dawn's c-c-coming."

"We need to rest." Frank wiped his forehead. "That looks like a cave."

"It could be a Dragon cave," warned Michi.

"We've got to risk it." Frank shook his head. "We're exhausted. We've been walking all night." He reached for the water bottle, but found it bone dry. "We have no water, and are almost out of food. We make for the cave."

He stumbled toward the opening. The cave widened as he approached, until he saw that the opening formed a fissure, a gap between two enormous peaks.

"Do you hear that?" asked Michi, turning to him with wide moth eyes.

"Water," gasped Frank.

He forced one foot to move, and then the other. Half stumbling, half walking, the group of weary travelers entered the crevice. At its base, a tiny stream ran, collecting water from the snowy mountains around it. Frank plunged his face into the cold water and drank. The others followed his example.

After drinking, he walked to an isolated outcropping of rock to relieve his bladder. Exhausted, Frank lay on his back, watching the dawning sky. The mountains behind him stood like a granite wall, facing the golden sunrise. The Acheron snaked through dense forests below, vanishing into the horizon.

"We made it." Michi's eyes faded and blurred, becoming beautiful again.

"Almost." Frank nodded. "We're *almost* there."

As he spoke, a dozen roars broke the silence. A host of Dragons swooped overhead. They roared again, and Frank froze.

## CHAPTER TWENTY—WILL

# Torture

Sindril slammed the door behind him. He stormed into the tiny cell, followed by two Dragons. Each Dragon pulled Will up, clutching him in their talons.

"Come, let's have a chat." Sindril grinned.

They dragged Will through a wide corridor filled with crimson flower lights. At the end of the red passageway, they shoved him down a flight of stairs and into a dark room. They pulled his arms above his head, and something slithered from the ceiling, coiling his wrists together.

Will screamed as the creature above slithered down his suspended arm, sinking its teeth into his shoulder. Its body tightened, pulling him upright so his toes just grazed the ground. With a pop he heard something dislocate, and his arms felt ready to tear off his body.

The two Dragons backed up to the rear wall of the room, and Sindril strolled forward. He held a small sickle with a curved blade, like a miniature scythe. Water dripped from the ceiling above. The serpentine creature above gnawed on his shoulder, tightening the coiled muscles around his wrists.

"It's called a vika." Sindril's eyes glinted in the faint light. "Nasty little creatures, almost extinct. There are only a handful left."

Will struggled for breath, gasping between agonizing waves of pain. Tears filled his eyes, and a whimpering sound escaped his lips. He'd never dreamed of such pain.

"They were bred for the war, long ago." Sindril ran a finger down the handle of his dagger. "The King keeps a few as pets."

"Why?" It was the one word he could manage to say.

"I won't kill you, I just need some information. This doesn't have to be painful." He gestured to one of the Dragons. The beast shot a jet of flame onto the ceiling. In the light, Will saw that the vika filled the room. Beads of water poured off the creature's coiled body like sweat. The vika stretched into hundreds, or perhaps thousands of purple coils. In the center of the room, the snake slithered down, wrapping around his arms. In the flame, the vika relaxed its grip, allowing Will to stand on the floor. Its fangs remained planted beneath his skin. The flame stopped, and the room faded into eerie darkness again. Two crimson flowers in the corner cast the only light.

"I don't know anything," gasped Will. Numbness spread from the vika's fangs. It swept across the agony of his arms and down his back, blanketing him in a dull paralysis. Was it poisoning him?

"Do you love Susan?"

"Yes." His mind swam, and his vision blurred. He struggled to breathe.

"You were alone with her on the boat?"

"Yes." The vika's coils tightened around his wrists.

"Did you sleep with her? Were you intimate?"

"I…"

"Answer me."

Tightness and pain welled from his chest, arms, and entire body.

"Yes. Oh God, it hurts."

"Answer me."

"We, we made love."

The vika's fangs sank deeper into his skin, and the slimy creature pulled his wrists higher. He stood on the tips of his toes.

"You're children." Sindril stepped closer. "Why would you do that?"

"She was…older," he gasped. "She aged."

Sindril waved to the Dragon who released a second burst of flame at the ceiling. The vika hissed, releasing its grip on his shoulder. It climbed up Will's arms. Will sank back to the floor, his arms still held high, tangled in the serpent's coils.

"She claims she's pregnant."

"What?" Despite the pain, the shock was real.

"You didn't know?"

The vika sank its fangs into his arm. He screamed.

"No, I didn't think…aggh, please, make it stop."

Through squinting eyes, Will saw a bright blaze of fire coat the ceiling. The vika hissed and unwound from his arms, releasing its hold on him. Will collapsed to the ground. The ceiling above him writhed and squirmed in a blend of serpent coils and Dragon flame.

The other Dragon grabbed him, and carried Will to Sindril's feet.

"I don't know anything else." He stared up, pleading.

Sindril knelt, holding the edge of his sickle to Will's throat. "The child is ours. You and Susan will swear it in front of the King. You both shall pledge the blood within her womb to us. Do you understand?"

"No…We'll never—"

Sindril pressed the blade into Will's neck. He felt the warmth of his own blood. His arms and body continued to cry out in anguish and pain.

"You will give the child to us, or I will kill you, and claim the child is my own. She won't even remember you existed."

Will wept. He couldn't hold back the tears. They fell from his eyes, mixing with blood, sweat, and vika venom on his neck and arms.

"Do you agree to the terms?"

"Yes." The hoarse whisper caught in his throat.

Sindril kept the blade on his neck. Kneeling, he stared into Will's eyes. His goatee was unkempt, and tiny scars littered his face. His dark pupils watched Will without compassion. His breath reeked of ash and burnt meat.

"I have another question. On the ship, Susan *aged*. That was not the spell we cast. What prevented us from taking her then? What power does she hide?"

He couldn't lie, couldn't think. His heart pounded against his ribs, and each breath just brought fresh pain. "Grym." Will shook his head, beaten. "Grym."

"Who is grim?" The words ran together, and the room spun.

"Grym," he murmured.

All faded into darkness.

CHAPTER TWENTY-ONE—FRANK

# Flight from the Fields

$F$rank froze, listening to the chorus of Dragon song thundering overhead. He shrank back into the narrow crevice in the mountainside. In the dawning sky above he watched dozens of Dragons. They sped over the gap without pause.

Michi touched his shoulder, waving him closer. They edged away from the open promontory. Creeping deeper into the narrow ravine, they waded into the shallow stream that cleaved the ridges.

All five huddled in silence, staring up. Frank hoped the shadows in the enormous fissure would shield them from sight. Even Vestru refrained from calling out.

The cacophony faded as the Dragons continued flying west. Letting out a slow breath, Frank shook his head. "That was close."

"I know this place." Vestru turned from side to side. "I've seen it painted in the temple. This ravine is called Tribulation Pass. The first priests used this passage to visit the gods."

"Lead on." Frank gestured. "Just keep quiet."

Vestru nodded, following the direction the Dragons flew. The gorge seemed thousands of feet deep, yet a mere dozen feet wide. At times, they walked single file, squeezing through the narrow fissure. A thin band of sky overhead brightened. Water trickled beneath their feet, bringing a gentle murmur to the chasm.

"*It's amazing that this stream carved these mountains.*" Agmundria's voice still made him tense, yet no longer terrified.

"I see why priests would use this." Michi waved to the walls. "It's better than being out in the open."

*We'll be in the open with Dragons soon enough*, mused Frank.

They continued through the ravine for over two hours. Frank heard sounds of hunger coming from all of their stomachs, including his own. Jagged rocks jutted out of the stream, bruising their damp feet. Agmundria followed Vestru, keeping an eye on the boy.

As they struggled through the crevice, the two leaders vanished behind curves of rock. Cronk hurried to catch up, leaving Frank and Michi behind.

"We're following two children into a den of Dragons." Frank helped Michi climb through a curve in the gorge beside an enormous boulder.

"Fun, isn't it?" She smiled. "Just like chasing each other when we were kids."

"Yeah, right." He returned the smile. "I'm glad you came, Michi. On this whole rescue mission, I mean. We wouldn't have been able to get this far without you."

"You think I'd let you run off to the mountains alone?" She winked.

"I'm serious. You're my oldest friend. With all that's happened, and with all we're going to face, sometimes I worry that you don't know how I—"

"I know, Frank." She touched his hand. "We'll get through this."

"If anything should happen to us when we meet the Dragons—"

"It won't. I won't let it. I care about you too much."

Frank paused, and the two looked at each other. There was so much more to say, so much more he wanted to tell her.

"Are you al-al-all right?" Cronk's voice called back to them.

"We're coming," answered Michi.

They rounded the boulder, and the gorge widened. Agmundria, Vestru, and Cronk sat on a stone ledge, waiting. The entire chamber stank of sulfur and ash. Water trickled near their feet. The floor sloped upwards, toward the end of the ravine. A column of daylight met the open sky above.

"This is it." Vestru paused, biting his finger.

"Lead on." Frank pointed. "We're not turning back now."

The ravine opened onto a large plain, blanketed in ash. Mountains ringed the barren wasteland.

"This is where the Dragons live?" whispered Frank as they stepped onto the edge of the empty expanse. "Where are they?"

"Something's glowing on the plain." Vestru's fingers moved in a ritualized hand sign. "It must be a signal from God."

"Wait." Michi raised a hand in warning. The priest ignored her, darting forward into the open desert.

"*Should I stop him?*" Agmundria turned.

A terrible roar broke the silence. A Dragon with emerald scales soared from the clouds, tearing through the air at impossible speeds. Vestru's back was turned; he stared at a glowing form in the wasteland. The boy spun, looking up.

The Dragon opened his jaws, snapping up both the glow and Vestru. Rows of razor-sharp fangs closed over the priest's writhing body. Blood fell to the ground.

*Don't forget him,* willed Frank. *They're not Deaths, perhaps they won't cease.*

The Dragon spread his wings and flew back to the clouds. There seemed to be blood on the ground, where he'd landed.

For a moment, the memory tugged at his mind. The strange boy-priest lingered at the edge of thought, vanishing like dissipating smoke. Frank stared at the blood pool.

*Blood from where? Did that glow create blood?*

"They're souls," whispered Michi. "This is a feeding ground, or some sort of slaughterhouse."

A second Dragon opened his wings and flew down, devouring another glow, farther way.

"What do we do?" asked Frank.

"If we stay on the outside of the plain, walking the rim, we might be able to get around it. We still don't know where Susan or Will are. I'm guessing the main kingdom's farther in."

"Th-th-this is s-s-suicide."

"I won't ask any of you to continue if you don't wish to." Frank backed against the ledge.

"*I do not fear them.*"

Cronk frowned. "I-I'm n-not staying here al-al-alone."

"Then it's settled." Michi pointed, her face set with determination. "We skirt the plain, trying not to draw attention. If a Dragon comes, run and pray."

A silver scaled Dragon coasted overhead, gliding to a glowing soul. It snatched it up, snorted, and flew away. Thick bands of knotted clouds stretched across the sky. *How many Dragons are lurking up there, waiting to pounce?*

"Are you ready?"

"Michi, maybe you and the others should turn back. I don't want you to get hurt."

"Then you'd better catch up." She turned and sprinted downhill. Cursing under his breath, Frank followed with Cronk and Agmundria close behind. He kept a tight grip on his boskery blade.

They ran to a narrow ledge, circling the massive wasteland. The barren depression of ash and slate extended for miles. At the ledge, all four slowed, keeping their backs against the cliff sides behind them. Michi walked first. Frank kept half his attention on her, and the other half on the glowing souls and the empty desert before him.

Suddenly, Michi stumbled. The ledge beneath her collapsed, and an avalanche of stones tumbled down. She slipped and Frank ran after her, jumping over falling rock.

"My ankle's caught."

He pulled on the fallen rock, and Cronk came to help him. They dislodged it, and she struggled out, pointing to the sky.

An enormous Dragon with smooth green skin and bright yellow eyes bellowed in rage. It landed behind them, jumping when the rocks slid again. Waving its wings, it hovered a foot off the ground.

Agmundria lifted her hands. For a moment, the creature paused.

"Run!" shouted Michi. Agmundria swayed, falling to her knees unconscious. Frank lifted her, carrying the young girl in both arms. Michi staggered to her feet and they sprinted onto the plain.

A monstrous black Dragon thirty feet wide landed in front of them. Cronk raised his scythe, yet the creature batted Cronk to the side. The Death flew through the air like a ragdoll, landing hard. Michi took Agmundria. Frank raised his boskery blade. He whirled the double scythe, slamming its blade into the Dragon's hide. It bounced off, its metal quivering.

"Get out of there," yelled Michi.

A burst of hot flame swept over him. Frank rolled to his left, coughing in the stench of sulfur and smoke. The ground below warmed, kicking off a cloud of ash. The Dragon screamed. Cronk wedged his scythe under the creature's tail. Frank wasted no time watching. He grabbed the fallen boskery blade and jumped onto the Dragon's foot. The creature's head spun around, and Frank slashed the blade into its eye.

The Dragon bellowed, lifting off. Frank jumped down just in time, ripping the boskery blade free. He landed hard, and for a second the world blurred.

"Are you all right?" Michi ran up.

"We have to get out of here."

Cronk hurried to catch up to them, yet the green Dragon wrapped its tail around the Death. He called out for help.

Agmundria woke up. "*What's happening?*"

"We need your help." Michi lowered the girl to the ground.

The green Dragon spun around again, before shooting a bolt of flame skyward. He lunged forward, grabbing Michi and Agmundria in one taloned claw, and Frank in the other. Cronk hung like a listless doll from his coiled tail.

"No!" Frank screamed. "*No!*"

The Dragon reared onto his hind legs and soared into the sky.

*We failed you, Susan.*

He tried to see Michi, or any of the others. The wind pounded his face, while the creature's talons tightened around his belly. The wasteland below passed, and they flew into the mountains.

<u>CHAPTER TWENTY-TWO—SUSAN</u>

# Wedding Deaths

"**Y**ou look beautiful."

Susan smiled in the mirror. An ivory dress fell in graceful curves over her slender body. A circlet of flowers sat over her brow. Her long black hair was tied with ribbons and flowers. The dress was sleeveless and cut low enough in the front to show her curves. A slit ran up her right leg, lined on either side with beads. The dress extended to a very short train behind. Despite the outfit, she couldn't feel more ridiculous. *They've dressed me for their charade.*

"Beautiful." Keirash grinned. "For a Death, I mean." The mahogany Dragon stood beside her, wearing human skin.

"You look nice as well." Though forced, the words were true. The Dragon's hair was pulled in tight curls, and she wore a long lavender dress.

"Sindril asked me to wear this skin, to put you at ease. I alone shall attend in *this* form. Sindril hated the idea of a wedding, but in the end, *we* convinced the Dragon King." She raised an eyebrow. Susan knew she meant White Claw. "A wedding and a honeymoon, following the customs of the humans. Those traditions would pacify the child within, and strengthen the Dragon Key. The Key is all they care about."

*Mom and Dad, I doubt you imagined my wedding would be anything like this.* Susan trembled and sat. *This isn't right.* Keirash placed a hand on her shoulder. It was appreciated, however, Keirash was no friend, she wasn't even human. *I'm a puppet in their million-year-old game. I'm just another piece on a board I can't even see.*

"Let's get this over with." Susan's stomach knotted with apprehension.

Keirash nodded, leading her out of the room. Every passage beyond her cell was deserted. They passed through corridor after corridor in slow succession. Carved hallways gave way to barren caves. The caves continued until they reached a wide platform with an open wall, looking over the valley and the mountains.

Sindril stood on the platform, glowering.

"It's about time. Get on, we're running late."

Susan and Keirash joined him on the terrace. Golden railings surrounded the thin ledge on three sides. Sindril grasped the railings and Keirash motioned Susan to do the same.

With an enormous shudder, the platform rose and dislodged from the cliff face behind it. Two massive Dragons beneath them rose into view, tethering the terrace between them, forming a strange chariot.

Her new dress rippled around her legs as they glided over the snowy mountains. A bank of gray fog drifted by. Above them, the sun winked in-between bands of tightly knotted clouds. The Dragons to her right and left pulled the sky chariot with gentle, undulating pulses of their wings. They flew to the heart of the mountain range, where craggy peaks pierced the sky in every direction. Jagged fields of rock and snow parted to reveal a wide plain of solid black.

Circles of black hillside, shorter than the snowy pinnacles around it, ringed a thin pillar of stone. The hills formed perfect bands around the pillar. Each hillside stretched a mile across, and wrapped for dozens of miles in their strange concentric pattern around the tower in the center.

Around and on the hills, Dragons waited. Thousands upon thousands of Dragons of every size and color ringed the stone column, watching and waiting. When the sky chariot swept lower, they roared as one, filling the sky with so much noise that Susan clasped her hands to her ears.

The stench of sulfur and ash choked her, stinging her eyes. The chariot lowered beside the central pillar, which had a flat top, like a butte or mesa. Three Dragons stood waiting. One moved as their chariot touched the ground.

"Will." She half-whispered, half-screamed his name.

He nodded to her, remaining where he stood.

Will's face was haggard. His hair had been combed back, a look that fit him somehow. He wore a gray suit. At his nod, Susan thought she glimpsed bruises on his neck. She wanted to run to him, to embrace him, yet most of all to apologize for what they were about to do. She nodded back to him.

Sindril grasped her arm, leading her to the center of the narrow stone spire. The tiny point of land was no more than ten yards wide. With the chariot behind them, Sindril walked to the edge of the spire. He turned toward the sea of Dragons, waving his arms in a strange salute.

"My friends." Some strange power gave strength to the words. They echoed across the black hillsides, casting sound to the towering mountains on every horizon. The sun vanished behind a cloud, and shadow blanketed them. The stench of sulfur intensified as the Dragons shouted their approval. Susan risked a glance at Will. He stared in silence at Sindril.

"We gather as one, Dragons and Deaths, to witness a union and a pledge. In the name of the Shadow King, he who rules all, I welcome you here."

The crowd roared its approval.

"At the behest of the King and the Dragon Council, today we abandon the traditions of Dragons, and adopt the traditions of humans. For the sake of the child within, the babe who will become the Dragon Key, we allot this ceremony in the custom its parents know. According to the Council's wisdom, their union, and their *comfort,* shall strengthen the Dragon Key immeasurably."

The Dragons roared again. Jets of raw flame burst from jaws all around them, soaring skyward into fountains of fire. The four Dragons on the stone tower stepped closer, including Keirash.

"William Albert Black, step forward."

He shifted closer to Sindril. His hands fumbled with his pockets, and he avoided her eyes.

"William, do you swear to take Susan as your wife; to love and protect her in sickness and in health, until you both *pass* or *cease*, and are parted as Deaths?"

"I do," he said.

"Take her hand."

He turned, and she held her hand out. Their fingers met, and tears welled in her eyes. She blinked them away, swallowing.

"Do you, William, swear that your child belongs to us? Do you swear that the King of Dragons *owns* the fruit of Susan womb, and that you renounce all pledges to this offspring?"

Will met her eyes. His face revealed nothing of what he must be feeling. She tried to read past his determined stare, yet he turned and looked at Sindril.

"I swear. The child...shall belong to the Dragon King."

"Susan Elizabeth Sarnio."

She stared at the former Headmaster. This was it, there was no turning back. Looking past him, she saw thousands of Dragons leaning in, watching her. Sunlight emerged from the cloudbanks above, glinting off countless Dragon scales: beasts of every color glared at her with fierce reptilian eyes. The sea of gold, emerald, black, silver, whites, and every other hue imaginable swam around the periphery of her vision. A taste of charred ash and bitter smoke lingered on her tongue. Sweat beaded on her forehead.

"Susan, do you swear to take William as your husband; to love and protect him in sickness and in health until you both *pass* or *cease*, and you are parted as Deaths?"

For a moment, the world was still. A light breeze rustled her dress, and she brushed the hair out of her eyes. A Dragon behind them growled with impatience.

"Well?" Sindril frowned.

She turned to Will. This was wrong, but it was the only way.

"I repeat. Susan, do you take William as your husband until you are parted as Deaths?"

Looking at him standing there in the sunlight, she remembered how much she cared. It didn't matter if Sindril was watching, or trying to pull their strings. Was it really wrong? *I do love him, after all.*

"I do."

Sindril's shoulders relaxed.

Susan's fingers tightened around Will's. Sweat lined each of their palms.

"Good. And do you, Susan, swear that your child belongs to us? Do you swear that the King of Dragons *owns* the fruit of your womb, and that you renounce all pledges to this offspring?"

She swallowed hard. There was no choice. "I swear. The child growing in my womb." She took a deep breath. "Our child belongs to the Dragon King."

"Swear again. The child belongs to us."

The Dragons behind Sindril roared, bellowing fountains of flame skyward. The sun retreated behind cloud, and the world dimmed.

Susan squeezed Will's hand, and they spoke as one. "We swear."

"For the sake of the child's comfort, I pronounce you man and wife." Sindril smiled. "May you live together as Deaths in peace. You will remain guests of honor, here in the Dragonspine Mountains until you give birth. Once the child is in our hands, you both shall be free to return to the College or even the Mortal World should you wish."

Sindril spun around. "This child will usher in a golden age for all Dragons. It shall restore Dragons as the reapers of souls, and the masters of this world."

Every Dragon clamored, stomping their claws and roaring. Flames jumped into the air in bursts, leaping out of fanged mouths and vanishing into puffs of smoke. So much noise filled the air, Susan and Will released each others' hands, covering their ears.

Beneath them, the stone spire trembled. Susan thought it was more celebration, until she saw shock spread across Sindril's face. Wings flapped, and Dragons on the rings of black hillsides rose, hovering.

All noise ceased. The sudden, swift silence following the tumult of seconds before startled Susan. The Dragons hovered in silence, colored scales glinting in the shafted sunrays.

The stone tower trembled again, shaking violently. Susan fell to her knees, and Will tried to help her up, losing his own balance in the process.

"God rises," whispered a Dragon behind her.

The rings of black hillside convulsed, swelling like waves on an ocean. A voice rang out, louder than any sound she'd ever heard. It pealed like thunder, and every syllable rocked the ground.

"SHE WILL TAKE THE BLOOD OATH."

"My lord." Sindril knelt. "They have already sworn the child to you."

The hills billowed, surging higher. They rose like a tidal wave of black behind Sindril. Dragons sped away, flying to the distant mountains. A bulge of shadows and darkness broadened, stretching miles across. Two circles of bright red opened, squinting.

"SHE WILL TAKE THE BLOOD OATH," repeated the voice, casting a gale of smoky wind across the top of the spire. Susan and Will fell back, coughing in the acrid stench.

The form rose higher, revealing a row of white pillars, sharpened into fangs.

"The Dragon King," whispered Keirash behind them.

Susan stared, terrified.

The King's scales reflected no light. They seemed formed from shadow itself, sucking light inside with no escape. The beast's eyes sat a mile apart, and each fang stood a hundred feet tall. The rings of hills rose: the King's body unwrapped from the spire.

"Of course, my lord." Sindril nodded. "Eronen, come here."

"Let me." Keirash stepped forward. "It would be an honor."

Susan saw something pass over Will's face. Concern?

"Fine." Sindril scowled. "Even in that form, your blood will suffice."

Keirash walked to him. Her dress billowed in the smoky air.

"Goodbye, Susan and Will." Her voice choked with emotion. "Good luck to you both."

The other three Dragons stepped forward. She held her arms out, palms open, face to the sky.

One Dragon grabbed Keirash's head and snapped it off. Susan screamed. Human skin fell off mahogany Dragon scales. Violet blood spurted out of her neck, running over her body. Another Dragon plunged his talons into her stomach, ripping out pink organs, drenched in purple blood. They tossed Keirash's head to the ground, where lifeless eyes stared out. She still wore a smile.

"Dip your hands in the blood," commanded Sindril.

"I won't." Susan stared, horrified.

Sindril nodded to the Dragons, who lifted her, tossing her body into Keirash's corpse.

"Swear the child belongs to us."

"I already did, you bastard."

"Say it."

"I swear."

*Fear. Lies. Pain.*

*Loss. Red. Blood.*

A torrent of emotion swept through her, and the gossamer covering her wrist steamed, growing hot. She saw through a thousand eyes, through a thousand years, and knew a thousand souls.

The world vanished, and she stood before the Shadow Dragon King. Grym stood beside her. The three looked at each other, surrounded by seas of blood.

With a clap of thunder, Susan snapped back to the present.

"SHE LIES!"

The King bellowed, blowing white-hot smoke across the trembling stone spire. Something grabbed her from above, digging talons into her shoulders.

Jets of fire raced across her vision, darting from side to side. She couldn't tell what was happening.

"Will?" she cried out.

A white Dragon with black spikes held Will in his claws, lifting off the tower, which crumbled into debris. Sindril was nowhere to be seen.

The red Dragon clutching Susan shot a bolt of flames to their right, setting a smaller Dragon aflame. Dragons everywhere clawed at each other, battling each other for life and death. A silver Dragon leaped up, grabbing the red Dragon's chest in its fangs. The red Dragon spun, throwing Susan to a turquoise scaled Dragon.

The Shadow King rose from the ground, thousands of times larger than any other creature around. The Dragon holding her dove around a craggy peak, soaring so fast that the wind slammed into her face, knocking her breath away.

They sped around a bend, diving into a pass.

"GET THEM!" the King screamed, sending shockwaves through the air. "THE GIRL! GET THE GIRL!"

Jets of flame arced all around them, as Susan and the turquoise Dragon darted around bends, sweeping over ravines and darting past peaks. The world raced by in a blur.

The white Dragon holding Will re-emerged below them. She tried to cry out, yet things sped by too fast. It vanished again into the melee of fangs and flame.

Darkness flooded the sky. The Shadow Dragon soared above, filling the expanse between every horizon. Susan trembled in the Dragon's talons. The beast dove, plunging down in a furious race. Wind slammed against her face, and Susan's vision blurred.

The Dragon jerked up at the last moment, throwing Susan out of its claws. She fell into a tiny cave. Her dress tore on stone, and her leg opened in a gash where she skidded over the rocks. She panted for breath, searching around in desperation. A dim light came from the entrance. The cave was little more than a nook, it ended a few feet away in walls of solid granite.

The dim light vanished into shadow, as the blue-green Dragon appeared outside, opening its jaws. Susan backed away. Heat streamed outward from its jaws.

The world vanished in a blaze of fire.

# PART TWO

## THROUGH BLOOD

## CHAPTER TWENTY-THREE—WILL

# Love

**W**ill awoke in Hell.

His last memories crowded in a jumble, pounding against his temples.

*I'm dead.*

White Claw interrupted the wedding. Dragons fighting everywhere, a tumultuous ride through cloud and flame, and Susan's screams in the distance.

*We failed.*

The taste of blood lay thick on his tongue. His eyes blinked in the harsh light, and he struggled to crawl. He opened his mouth and vomited.

*It was a doomed plan.*

He couldn't escape the talons, or the mountain rocks speeding closer. He remembered calling out when Susan sped by, only to have his voice knocked back into his face by the racing wind.

*I'm dead.*

The King. That's why they failed. Samas hadn't guessed the King would demand a blood oath. Poor Keirash.

Will forced his eyes to focus, and struggled to rise. The world spun around him. He stood on an endless plateau of ash, littered with occasional pockets of fire. The sky was an empty void of smoke and darkness. A ring of solid flames surrounded him in the distance.

*So much for Deaths ceasing. I'm in Hell.*

He stood, and started trudging through the ash.

*What now?*

Walking across the barren wasteland, he avoided the small fires until he saw a mound in the distance, moving. He paused, deciding to approach it.

A pile of ash fell to the side, and Susan emerged, turning her wide eyes toward him. Her wedding dress was singed and tattered, and her face was blackened. Still, she looked beautiful.

"Susan! What are you doing here?"

"Where are we?"

"I think it's Hell. We must have died. This is where people go beyond the Door—"

"Don't be ridiculous," she retorted. "We're not dead. When Deaths die they *cease*."

"What does that mean for them? Maybe we've stopped existing to the rest of the world, and are trapped here now."

"I don't think we died."

"Well it's not the ideal honeymoon." He helped her stand in the ash.

"Is that a joke? We're not even married."

"We had the ceremony, we said the vows."

"Keirash told me the plan. Those White Claw Dragons were supposed to wait until we were alone together, and then they'd help us escape. The wedding was a ruse, just like the supposed pregnancy."

"Susan, I know we were young, but since we're dead I might as well tell you. Of course there was no child, since we've never been…you know…together." He paused, unsure of how to explain. "I'd forced myself to lie when Sindril tortured me, and that wasn't easy. The wedding, on the other hand, well, some of it was true. The emotions were real. I love you."

"What's that?" She pointed. Will's heart caught in his throat. Had she even heard him? He turned, following her outstretched finger. A section of the fiery wall bent and brightened, convulsing into a jet of flame. The fire struck a patch of ash, and a group of figures appeared.

"Come on." Susan hurried to the people rising out of the cinders. "Frank!" She threw her arms around him. Michi and even the art teacher, Cronk, appeared beside him. A sallow-faced child of maybe seven or eight with scraggly black hair stood next. More ash shifted, and Samas appeared, uncoiling his tiny wings.

"You're all safe," said the Dragon. "One ordeal is over, although your trials have just begun."

"Who are you?" asked Susan.

"My name is Samas, and I am a leader of White Claw."

"We're not dead?" Will stared at the tiny creature.

"No. The plan didn't go quite as we'd planned, yet it succeeded nonetheless."

"I've been here before." Frank surveyed the fires and ash around them. One hand grasped a boskery blade, which he tossed into the ash. "This is the Swarm, isn't it?"

"They offered to help." Samas nodded. "It was unprecedented, and their assistance proved invaluable."

"Someone please tell me what's going on?" demanded Susan.

"I must return soon." The small golden dragon twitched his white whiskers, and coiled into a ball, sinking onto a mound of ash. "I will explain what I can.

"Susan, long before you became a Death, a faction of Dragons dissented from the Shadow King. We disagreed with his goals and his obsessions. This group became White Claw, as I'm sure Keirash explained. The plan was simple. You were to lie, claiming you were pregnant. My Dragons convinced the King to hold a wedding. We even copied your human customs to put you at ease, insisting that a wedding and child of love would strengthen the Dragon Key. Sindril would avoid touching you, and you and Will would be brought together. The Dragons would've kept you prisoners until a child was born. While they waited, White Claw would help you escape. The wedding was meant to scare Sindril away, and was the only excuse to bring you two together. Their sole care is the Dragon Key. If they knew you weren't pregnant, you'd never have been brought to Will."

"Keirash told me." Susan glanced at Will. "What went wrong?"

"The Shadow King must have suspected our hand. He demanded a blood oath, which cannot be broken. Keirash volunteered because she is a member of the Resistance, so is removed from the King. She hoped her blood would weaken the connection between you two. Yet, it seems the bond was enough for the King to see our lie."

"When I touched the blood…" Susan paused, looking at her wrist. "Grym. The First Scythe. He was there beside me, and we stood before the King. I felt hollow, as if they looked through me."

One of the Dragon's eyebrows twitched, and he raised a claw to his beard, stroking it. "The seal on your arm protects Caladbolg? This is a surprise. It's possible that the power of the First Scythe countered the blood oath, however also strengthened the bond of understanding between the oath maker and the King.

"At any rate," he continued, "White Claw had no choice. Once the Nameless King realized your deception, his plan altered. He hoped to slay Will, and force Sindril and you to mate. He would've enslaved you until you bore a Dragon Key. Nothing else matters to him. He is blind to the world—blind to everything except his own desires.

"Frank, we didn't realize you and your friends were on a rescue mission of your own, until you appeared in the hunting fields. If Brandr hadn't discovered you, we might all be lost now. Brandr told me of your pact with the Swarm, seconds before the chaos erupted."

"They claimed they'd help." Frank shook his head. "I hardly call that a pact. You didn't know we'd end up here, did you? It was a gamble."

"I admit, the chances were slim." The golden Dragon's tiny head flicked to one side. "Yet, if we failed and Susan ceased, the King would need a new plan. Either way would've resulted in victory for us."

"You would sacrifice Susan and me?" Will's head ached, and he knelt to the ground. He wanted to scream at them all to shut up and stop talking. The ashy ground was hot, and his eyes teared from smoke in the air.

"Yes. I'd do it again without hesitation. However, you are safe, so this argument is pointless. I must return to the other Dragons, I fear our numbers shall suffer greatly. Before I go, I must warn you. The King knows you survived. If you'd been killed in the fire blast, he'd forget you ever existed. He knows this. However, I also believe he will stop pursuing you for a time."

"Why?" demanded Will.

"Susan shall give birth at some point; every seer in this world has foreseen it. I don't know when, or with whom, yet it must happen. The Nameless King has waited a million years for this opportunity. He'll hunt you down in time. White Claw's convinced him that a child of love will be more powerful. He might wait for an actual pregnancy now."

"I don't want a child." Susan shook her head. "I want to be free from this whole situation."

"You will never be free." Samas's tail flicked. "As long as you live, you feed the Shadow King's hope. By entering this world, you've shown him possibilities he can't ignore. He's woken up from millennia of slumber. Your fate is sealed."

"What am I supposed to do then?" She grabbed the golden Dragon by the neck, pulling him up. "What do you want from me?" Samas writhed in anger, clawing his way out of her fingers. Snarling, he turned to the ring of flames. "I want you to be careful. Stay away from Dragons, and stay safe. The *Swarm*, your friend called them, they will protect you."

"We'll protect you as well, Susan. We've traveled miles to rescue you."

"Thank you, Frank."

Samas spread his small wings, and gestured to the flames around them. "Return me. I've been away too long."

A thin flaming jet snaked out of the ash, wrapping around the golden Dragon. White light flashed, and he vanished into a cloud of fading smoke.

Will reached for Susan's hand, wrapping his fingers around hers. "We're all here for you, Susan."

"We have a lot of catching up to do. Who's your friend, Frank?"

"*My name is Agmundria.*" The child's voice echoed in the back of his mind, making his skin crawl. Will backed away.

"You're a fearmonger?" asked Susan.

"*Yes.*"

"It-it-it's g-good to s-see you again." Cronk's pockmarked, chubby face stretched into a wide grin.

For several minutes, everyone embraced. Will's eyes dampened with tears. Frank, Will, Michi, and Susan found themselves in a single group hug, laughing at nothing and everything.

"You wouldn't believe the things we've seen," said Frank.

"I've got stories of my own." Will shook his head, the memory of tortures and conspiring Dragons still fresh. "We all do."

The ashy ground beneath them trembled and they looked around.

"The Swarm." Frank raised his hands. "Don't worry, they're friends."

"*We think*," added Agmundria, notes of terror lingering on the edge of every syllable.

Will's feet sank into the ash like quicksand. A wall of solid fire swept around their group, ringing them into a clump. He took Susan's hand again, holding tight.

The flames bounced and danced closer. A thin blazing tendril of fire snaked out, touching Susan's forehead. She froze, staring.

"Hey!" shouted Will. A second jet of flame snaked to his forehead, and the world burned and faded from sight.

Swirls of smoke. Waves of heat.

Fire roiled over him, through him, within him.

*Fire.*

He rode atop a flicker, a tiny candle in a window, looking out into an empty room. His body bounced up and down on the small wick, bending in the slight breeze. A woman entered, holding a picture.

*Mom?*

She put the picture down beside him. His own image, from years ago, stared back from the frame.

"Forgive me, Billy," she whispered. "I should've been a better mother."

She leaned forward and extinguished his flame.

Smoke swirled. Orange and red light danced.

*Fire.*

*I am fire.*

Rocks surrounded his vision. Tiny embers danced out of him, fading into a cave above. Susan stood in front of him, holding a baby in her arms.

She leaned into the fire. Sweat and worry lined her face.

Will found himself standing on ash again. The flaming arm touching Susan's head quivered with excitement.

"THE SCYTHE!" Voices thundered all around them. Voices young and old, male and female, poured out through the flames.

"THE SCYTHE!"

"They know Grym." Susan's eyes glazed beneath the flaming tendril tethered to her forehead.

"YOU ARE THE SCYTHE WIELDER!" screamed the Swarm.

Tongues of fire darted from the ground, slithering around Susan's arm. They encased the area where Caladbolg lay sealed.

"SCYTHE WIELDER! SCYTHE WIELDER!" The Swarm danced around them, their voices flaring with enthusiasm. Heat boiled from the flames, rolling away from Susan in waves.

"Are you all right?" Will tried to move forward, however, his feet remained still in the ash.

"It doesn't hurt." Susan's voice echoed from a great distance. "They're trying to free Grym."

More flames joined the first jets. Each blaze turned white-hot. Will continued to clutch Susan's other hand, even as the heat burned him. She shifted in discomfort, and the flames backed away.

"Something's wrong." She winced. "They can't undo the seal."

"Grym's sealed away?" Frank stood in ash several feet away, watching them.

"The Dragons did something." Susan grimaced when a fresh wave of fire washed over her again. "He shows me things in dreams. However, I can't reach him or his power when I'm awake."

"DRAGONS!" shouted the Swarm. "DID SOMETHING." They pulled their tongues of flame off Susan, and turned as one, to Will.

"What're they doing?" He raised his hands, shielding his eyes from the glare.

Flames darted forward, piercing his forearm.

*Smoke and fire.*

*Waves of heat.*

*I am flame.*

Will rode a jet of fire up toward the seething violet coils of the vika. It released its hold on a man's arm. *My arm.*

"DRAGONS. DID SOMETHING." The Swarm repeated their chant, shouting at him.

"They think there's something in your arm." Frank pointed.

*Smoke and fire.*

*Waves of heat.*

*I am flame.*

Will struggled to get his bearings. He felt something pull out of his arm. The flames became fingers and claws, pulling, ripping, probing.

They extracted a small black pebble, and it sizzled into ash. A second sear of light pulled another dot from his shoulder.

"The flames say there were eggs beneath your skin." Frank's fingers hovered above a tongue of flame, moving in time to its flicker. "I hear their thoughts. They've pulled the eggs out."

"The vika." Will panted, gasping in air. "Sindril tortured me."

"He must've planned to follow it somehow." Frank took a step forward.

"Vikas lay eggs through their fangs." Susan spoke in a distant voice. "They wanted to track you." She paused. "Frank, I'm guessing your power lets you communicate with the Swarm. Even though I can't reach Grym, I also hear them. The flames scream in my mind."

"Grym's still alive in you." Frank nodded. "He's helping, even if you can't reach him directly. As for my power, it's gone. I don't know how I understand the Swarm."

"What do you mean, your power's gone?"

"We have a lot more catching up to do."

"REST!" shouted the Swarm. The flames receded from each person, and the wall of fire backed away. Below the ash, Will sensed something letting go of his feet.

"Have a seat," said Frank. "We'll be here a while."

* * * *

Will watched his mother lean toward the photo frame. His eyes danced up with each bend of the flickering light, of *his* flickering light. He spat heat onto the tiny wax pillar beneath him.

Wrinkles lined her unsmiling lips. Her hair was pulled back in a tight ponytail. One eye glistened, its unshed tear lingered in the candlelight.

She turned, and blew out the flame.

Swirling smoke and fire blended into ripples of fading light.

A searing hot tendril of fire withdrew from his forehead, and Will stood on the barren ash desert once more.

"It won't change." Frank's head shook from side to side. Gray ash matted his unkempt hair. "They're showing you the same moment in time."

"I don't understand. When I skipped my final test, all ties to the Mortal World were erased. No one there should remember me."

A flicker of fire leaped from the ash and touched his arm. A single word screamed in his mind.

"LIES!"

"The Deaths didn't want it known that your memories live on after you remain in the World of Deaths." Frank shook his head, an expression of disgust clear on his face.

"They lied to us. My mother, a woman who barely noticed me when I was alive, still thinks about me now."

"Are you sure the memory's current? Besides, what good is it to dwell on those issues?"

Will ignored the questions. "Each time I watch, I feel closer to her. It comforts me."

"Third time this week." Frank wiped soot from his cheek. "You'll never see her again."

"At least I know she cared for me," snapped Will. "What do you care? There's nothing else to do here." He kicked a pile of ash.

"We should leave." Michi walked over. "We're getting irritated." She put her hand on Frank's shoulder. Will turned and walked away.

Two arms of flame twisted up from the ash, expanding and growing brighter. They vanished into dissipating smoke, and an unburned piece of cake on a plate floated in mid-air.

"I'm not hungry." He brushed the food away.

He walked to Susan, who sat on a pile of ash. Her black hair hung in wild disarray down her back, matted with soot. A thin braid of fire snaked from her forehead, arcing into the ground. Will knelt behind her, and gently stroked her hair, pulling ash out.

The blazing filament recoiled into the ground, and Susan turned. The wedding dress was gone, she'd demanded the Swarm give her different clothes. She wore dark blue jeans and a black tee-shirt.

"They've showed me so much, Will. The Swarm is somehow connected to all fire throughout the ages and across the worlds. I used to wonder if Lovethar really lived a million years ago. A million years seems so long, it's almost surreal. Yet, they were there. When early humans first discovered fire, the Swarm brought an entire group called Donkari to this world." She sighed, standing.

"They've watched me all this time, always sure I'd come. Flower lights prevent much of their sight, but there are still flames, especially now with the world at war." She shook her head.

"Mors is lost, Will. The Dragons leveled most of the city, and the few Deaths and 'Mentals left are hiding." She frowned. "That's what they show me, at any rate."

"You still don't trust them?"

"I think the Swarm means well."

He sat in the ash, facing her. "We've been married for a week now." His lips parted in an awkward grin.

"We're not married, Will. You're my boyfriend, and I care about you. I love you."

For a moment the words hung there. Will grinned from ear to ear, filled with warmth. "I love you too."

Susan's mouth widened into a smile, and she brushed her hair out of her face. "Understand, if we ever marry, *we* will make the choice, not Sindril, not Dragons, and not anyone else."

"If we ever marry, can we honeymoon somewhere nicer? This place is getting to me."

Susan laughed. Even in that hellish landscape, the sound of her laughter rang like angelic music. A shiver ran down Will's spine. He rubbed his fingers over scabs where the vika bit him. *If we ever marry.* He looked back at Susan's smiling face, and changed the topic.

"The Deaths lied to us. We were told that ties to the Mortal World ended after our first year in the World of Deaths. I keep seeing my mom through the flames. It's a recent vision, I know. The Swarm even said the Deaths lied about our families forgetting us."

Susan sighed. "Half of what I learned when I first got to the College was a lie. They made such a big deal about Lovethar being evil and being burned as a traitor. They feared girls and said Grym was just a legend. None of those things were true." She turned away. "I haven't thought about my family back there for a long time. I never imagined they'd still remember me."

"I'm sure they remember you." Will frowned, looking around. "We should leave this place. Let the Swarm bring us somewhere safe. Frank and I fight every day now, there's nothing to do, and soon we'll all go mad."

She nodded. "I agree. We can't hide here forever. This isn't living." She waved the others over. Frank and Michi walked hand-in-hand. Cronk and Agmundria followed behind them.

"W-w-what's h-h-happening?"

"We're leaving."

"You can't." Frank straightened, frowning. "The Dragons are after you, Susan."

"We can't stay." She looked at each of them in turn. "This week was tortuous, and I'm sick of being tortured. How long do we hide in the Swarm's flames, watching a war we're in the center of, but can't affect? If the visions I saw today are true, Mors was destroyed. They've already stopped the mortamant shipments and leveled the capital. There's only one other place left. The Dragons will attack the College."

"Th-there's a-a-another r-reason to l-l-leave. I t-t-too h-have b-b-been w-watching—"

"Oh, spit it out." Frank turned to the older Death with an irritated expression.

*"Be kind."* The fearmonger's voice made Will's hair stand on end. *"We're all impatient here."*

"R-R-Rayn. H-h-he's a D-D-Dragon."

"Rayn?" Frank dropped Michi's hand.

"The Death appointed to help 'Mental relations?" Susan's eyes widened. "Will and I saw him in the tunnel beneath East Tower, the day we left the College."

"He visited Kasumir before she died." Michi looked down, her brow knit.

"He killed her." Frank's fingers clenched, and his voice dropped to a whisper. "That bastard sent me there at the beginning of the year. That dagger he gave me; I wonder if he tracked it."

"Giri suspected it might have been Rayn." Michi put her hand on Frank's shoulder. He shrugged it off.

*"This man is a teacher in the Death College?"* The fear laced in Agmundria's voice seeped into Will's stomach. A Dragon disguised as a Death, within the walls of the College. *"If he's inside, and the Dragons are planning an attack, the College won't survive."*

"This explains why Rayn was in the tunnel." Will's head spun. "Dragons can't cross the Ring of Scythes."

"So he went under it." Frank looked ready to scream.

"I w-w-want t-t-to w-w-warn the C-College."

"I'm going with him." Frank's body trembled. "I want to make Rayn suffer."

"What about us?" Will kicked a pile of ash. "Susan's the key to the entire conflict. The Dragons want her more than they want the College."

"Frank and I will stay and protect Susan." Michi spoke in a calm, determined voice.

"Since when do you—"

"You came to find Susan and rescue her. Well, we didn't exactly rescue her in the end, but we're here now. It took all of our strength and effort to get this far. Now we'll keep her safe. She needs us, Frank. Besides, we still don't know what's happened with your power. Until we understand the changes you're going through, I won't send you into the heart of conflict. Rayn will kill you even faster than he killed Kasumir."

Frank grimaced.

"Please, Frank." She lowered her voice. *"I* need you, and I'm not abandoning Susan."

*"Someone has to warn the College."*

"I w-w-will g-go." Cronk handed the scythe to Will. "T-t-take this."

*"I've never been to the College, but as a fearmonger, I'm sure I'll be helpful. I'll go with him."*

"Be careful." Susan embraced Agmundria, and then wrapped her arms around Cronk. "You were the first Death I met. I saved your life once, now you're helping to save mine. This won't be the last time we see each other."

Cronk wiped his eyes, blushing. "I'll b-b-be ok."

Susan nodded. "All right, Swarm, take Agmundria and Cronk to the College."

Tongues of flame leaped out of the ash, coiling around the chubby Death and the scrawny child.

"There might be other Dragons in disguise," warned Will. "Many of them take human form."

The fire tightened, snaking higher on their bodies.

"Make a fire, and tell us what's happening." Susan stepped back, taking Will's hand. "We'll use the Swarm to communicate."

Cronk nodded, and the fire blazed brighter, searing their eyes with scorching white heat. The flames vanished, along with Cronk and Agmundria.

"That leaves us." Displeasure echoed in Frank's voice. "You still want to leave?"

"Yes." Susan turned to the open air around them. "You've been helpful and kind. We shall continue to rely on your eyes, your wisdom, and your help."

"SCYTHE WIELDER!" screamed the chorus of unseen voices.

"Now, use your power, and send myself and the rest of my friends to a place of safety. Somewhere in the World of Deaths where Dragons will not find us, and where neither Deaths nor 'Mentals go."

"SCYTHE WIELDER!"

Will's feet sank into the ash. He took Susan's hand, wrapping his fingers around hers. The world around them vanished into flame.

* * * *

Will sat on a large rock, peering through the trees overhead. Between the highest branches, tiny dots of perfect white light gleamed amid the dark canopy. The smell of pine and moss lingered in the air. Beneath his hands, the stone was cool and damp.

"Can I join you?" whispered a voice behind him, scarcely louder than the chirping crickets in the shadows.

Turning, he helped Susan climb the boulder. At the top, she unslung a satchel from her shoulder, tossed her hair, and leaned back.

For a timeless moment, perhaps seconds, perhaps minutes, they sat in stillness. Will half-watched the stars above. However, he found his gaze drifting to Susan's long hair, which fell like a blanket of shadow across his leg; or her shoulders that bobbed with every gentle breath.

"Any word from Cronk?"

She shook her head before turning to face him.

He stared deep into her eyes. Their pupils flicked back and forth, trying to maintain contact. She looked away.

"What happens now?" he whispered.

She shrugged. Leaning forward, she kissed him. It was an unexpected gesture, and their first intimate contact since their forced wedding and escape. Will let her lips press against his before opening his mouth. She held his face with tender fingers, pulling him closer. Their tongues met and danced around and around. With each second the kiss grew more passionate, more intense, until at last Susan pulled away.

They stared at each other again.

"Shouldn't stay out here too long," she warned.

"We've been in these mountains for a week, and haven't seen a single Dragon."

"Doesn't mean they're not nearby. Come on, let's go back to the cave."

Nodding, he propped himself up on the boulder. He eased down the rock, before helping Susan climb down. Her dirt-covered jeans slid against the stone, and her worn t-shirt smelled of overuse. At the base of the boulder, Will drew her close, wrapping his arms around her.

Their mouths met again, and their lips parted at once. With every soft probe of her tongue their bodies crept closer. He pushed his fingers into her hair, stroking it away from her neck and down her back.

They separated, breathing hard.

Susan stood before him, a creature of perfect beauty: younger than Will in age, yet older in body. His girlfriend. No, his *wife*. It hadn't been a real wedding to her, but it changed things. It had to.

"I love you, Susan."

She looked away. "I know, Will."

Taking her chin in his fingers, he turned her to face him again. "What's wrong?"

Her shoulders heaved, and she leaned against his chest. "We're trapped in a game we can't control. If I allow myself to love you fully, Sindril wins. If I don't, you get hurt. We're hiding in the shadows, too afraid to venture more than a mile from a cave, in the middle of God-only-knows where. Cronk and our other friends are fighting a war we're at the center of, yet can't even see."

"What else can we do? We can't risk getting caught again."

"I had a thought, but I'm—" She pushed her hair away from her face.

"What?"

"Never mind. Let's get back to the cave."

She slipped her hand into his. They walked downhill, making their way slowly through the night forest. Roots and branches clawed at them from all sides, yet Will led them without hesitation through the winding path between two rocky ledges. Shafts of moonlight spilled down from the dense canopy overhead. A bullfrog croaked in protest as they passed.

"I love you too, Will."

He squeezed her fingers in response.

They made their way through the forest. On one side of the mountain range, a white birch stump stood, stripped of its branches and bark. Eyeing it, Will calculated the distance below. Reaching into a crevice between shadows, he found the nook marking their cave's entrance.

The two exchanged a silent smile. Will crawled through the narrow opening. Cold, slick moisture lined the stones inside. Around a bend, lights quivered and swayed on the walls. He stood in the large central cave. Michi and Frank sat around the embers of the bonfire.

"Where were you two?" Frank held the boskery blade on his arm, weighing the balance. He rose, setting it against the wall. "We shouldn't be outside for long. We could be seen."

"There aren't any Dragons here," countered Will. "We'd have seen them by now."

"We've only been here a week. Don't get stupid."

Will's shoulders tightened, however Susan's hand on his back relaxed the tension.

"At any rate, Cronk made contact." Frank sat again, flicking a twig into the fire.

Michi rose, shadows and light gamboled across her features in a shifting pattern. "They're at the College. Things are worse than we feared. Rayn, Erebus, and Eshue started a campaign to convince the Deaths that there is no war, no threat at all."

"They hope to catch the College unprepared." With firelight dancing off her brow, Susan looked even more beautiful.

"What about Hann?" asked Will.

"Missing. He went to Mors to help the fight, and no one's seen him since."

"He's still alive." Michi placed a hand on Frank's shoulder. "We know that much."

The four stared at the empty flames in silence. Tiny sparks leaped into the dense shadows above. Fragrant and warm wood smoke drifted toward the cave's entrance.

Will's stomach growled. "What do we have to eat?"

"There's a little venison leftover from this morning." Frank tossed a hunk of burnt flesh over.

"I'll hunt tomorrow." Will bit into the tough meat.

"I want to find a pool or lake." Susan ran a hand through her hair again. "The spring is fine for drinking, but I'm tired of feeling filthy."

"This isn't a vacation, or a *honeymoon*." Frank spat the last word.

"What is your problem?"

"Will, settle down." Susan's fingers clasped his arm. "We're all testy."

"He's been antagonizing us since we got here. If you didn't want to stay, why didn't you go with Cronk?"

"Someone has to protect Susan. It's not like *you* can."

Will's fist rammed into Frank's face. The 'Mental rolled toward the fire. He screamed, and Michi pulled him out of the way just in time.

"Stop it, both of you!" Susan ran forward, arms outstretched, as a trickle of blood crawled out of Frank's nose.

"We only have each other." Michi's voice sounded hollow. She stood. Flickering firelight gleamed off her wide eyes. "Two weeks ago, we thought we'd never see each other. Now here we are fighting. Our job is to survive, that's it. You two are best friends. We all are. There's no reason to squabble."

Frank grunted, shoving his way past Will, and hurried out of the cave.

Will sat down, watching the stares of the two women. He took an awkward bite of meat.

Susan shook her head.

\* \* \* \*

Will bobbed atop the flame, watching.

A scaled hand grabbed Samas, throwing him across the chamber. Three Dragons stepped forward, their eyes fierce with rage.

"A child born of *love*," snarled a green Dragon. "What other lies have you spread?"

Samas crawled along the floor, struggling to rise. A wall burst open, rocks collapsed in a shower of shattered stone.

Elkanah burst through, spraying fire in every direction.

The three Dragons lunged forward. One sank its teeth into Elkanah's neck. Another slashed at her chest with its talons.

Elkanah screamed, arching her bag and convulsing. A burst of fire erupted, and Will's view jumped to the roaring blast. He slammed into the wall, vanishing in a cloud of smoke.

The image refocused and he saw an enormous white tiger, snarling.

A tremor of fear caused Will's heart to skip a beat.

*Fire.*

Will awoke to a gentle hand on his face. Susan sat beside him. The dreams faded like dissipating fog.

"What day is it?"

She laughed. "We've been in the cave for over a month. Other than that, I have no idea."

"I meant is it our turn to hunt?"

"It is, and that's why I woke you."

"I thought you just wanted to see me."

"We see each other every day, Will."

"And that's the best part of every day." Will rolled onto his side, picking up his shirt. He used it as a pillow on the rough stone of the cave. Pulling his arms through each sleeve, he smiled at Susan.

Frank sauntered into the cavern, tossing a log onto the fire. "I contacted my father, Giri."

"And?" Will walked to the trickle of falling water on the cave's wall and leaned his head in for a drink.

"The Dragons bide their time. They've set up a nest or something in Mors, and are waiting."

"Waiting for what?"

Frank shrugged, walked to a stone, and sharpened his knife. He spun the crude weapon around. "Here. Happy hunting."

Will grasped the knife. It was a sharpened piece of obsidian, which they'd found in the cave.

"Oh, one more thing," added Frank, with a slight laugh. "It's May Thirtieth."

Susan's hands went to her mouth, and her eyes widened.

"Happy birthday." Frank sat down beside the fire, pulling off his shoes.

"Happy birthday, Susan." Will gave her a kiss on the cheek.

"Let's go." She spun, darting out of the cave.

"Susan, wait." Slipping the knife in his belt, he hurried after her, crawling out of the cave and emerging into the forest. High above the canopy, sunlight blanketed the mountains, slipping between the dense trees. He glanced around and saw her running downhill.

"Susan, what's wrong?"

She sped through the woods, ignoring his calls. He tried to keep pace, but she darted over roots and around boulders. Will almost crashed when she stopped abruptly.

"Susan? What's going on?"

Without responding, she fell into his arms, shaking. He wrapped his arms around her trembling body.

"It's okay, I'm here." He stroked her hair.

"This is all wrong."

"Is this about your birthday?"

"Will, I don't even know how old I am. I was born fifteen years ago, yet Sindril robbed four years of my life. Am I nineteen or fifteen? There's a spirit trapped inside my wrist, bonded to my soul, who's a million years old. I hear his thoughts, and see through his eyes every time I sleep. It's like Grym's becoming more a part of me each day, even though he's sealed. He wants me to ignite something called the Eye of Donkar."

"What's that?"

"I have no idea. I see more and more memories, and he keeps insisting that I ignite the Eye and have hope."

She pulled back, wiping tears away. "How can I have any hope? Who, and *what* am I? I don't belong in this world, and I can't return to the Living World, or even to the College of Deaths. I'm no one, trapped nowhere."

"You're Susan, the girl I love. I don't care how old you are, or what's been done to you. You belong with me." His lips parted in a faltering smile.

"Don't waste your life on me, Will. I'm nothing."

"Stop it. You're being ridiculous. Look at things a different way. Sure, we're waiting for things to calm down, but what a beautiful place. The air's fresh in these mountains, no sulfur smell or dank prison pits. Frank and Michi are with us, and even if we don't always get along, having our friends nearby is a blessing. We have game to hunt and eat, fresh water in the cave, and the Swarm keeps us informed of the world outside. We have each other, Susan, and we're free. Is this so bad?"

"You'll hate me for saying this. At times I almost wish for a Dragon overhead. I'm tired of being useless."

"We're not going to the College. The Dragons are after *you*. Susan, what if the Dragons *never* find us? I'd be happy spending the rest of my life here, with you. We'd grow old together, and the war won't even matter. We could build a house out here, and let the Dragons and Deaths sort out their own problems."

She sat on a boulder, brushing her hair out of her eyes, and gazed up at the leaves overhead. "I wish it was that simple."

"Why can't it be?"

With shaking shoulders, Susan doubled over, clutching her arm.

"What's wrong?" He jumped to her side.

"It's nothing. I get pains sometimes."

"What kinds of pain? Is it your wrist? It's Grym, isn't it?"

"When I'm tense, something happens. I can't explain. It's like he's seeping into me. Like we're merging somehow, even more than before."

"Have you told Frank or Michi?"

"No, and I don't want you to either."

"Why not?"

"It's nothing." She turned away. "I'll tell them if it gets worse."

"If you say so. I worry, Susan. You're unhappy, and I want to help."

Her fingers rubbed the gauzy covering on her wrist. "I'll be fine."

Frowning, Will stood beside her in silence.

* * * *

The summer heat sizzled off the tops of the rocks, shimmering in the air. Will wiped the sweat from his forehead. Susan emerged from the cave carrying two bows.

"We'll need to haft more arrowheads."

"Frank carved some new heads last night," he replied. "I've got a load of shafts and plenty of sinew; figured we'd get them ready en route."

She embraced him, parting her lips and joining a tender kiss.

"You won't catch any food that way." Michi pushed aside the flap covering the cave's entrance. "Will, can I speak to you a moment inside?"

"Sure."

He dropped the bag of arrow parts, and followed her, bending low at the cave's entrance. A pile of neatly stacked split logs stood against one wall. Three crude spears stood against the opposite side of the cave. A small circle of stones ringed a large pile of ashes. Frank lay on a pile of deer skins, his back to Will, perhaps asleep.

"She was screaming in her sleep again." Michi leaned against the wall. A spider crawled across her face.

"I know."

"Will, I'm worried. Whatever's happening to Susan isn't normal. We've been living here for over four months. Nothing's changed outside, yet she's changing from within."

"What can I do? She insists she's fine."

Michi put a hand on Will's arm and opened her wide eyes. Brushing her disheveled hair away, she grinned. "Of the four of us, you transitioned to this lifestyle the easiest. You were the first to realize we could be happy here. Help Susan remember we're here for *her*. If something's wrong, we want to help."

"I'll try."

He slipped back under the flap and embraced Susan.

"What was that about?" Smiling, she pulled back, her dark eyes catching his.

"Michi recommended a new hunting spot."

"Well let's get going."

They walked through the dense foliage, passing across the foothills of the mountains they'd started calling Reaper Ridge. The peaks sat far lower than the enormous snow-capped peaks of the Dragonspine. Hunched above the thick leafy forest, the boulder-covered mounds and rims of Reaper Ridge watched their hunting forays with indifference, yet warning. Even with four months of peace, Will's eyes scanned the open sky beyond the rocks with trepidation, searching for leathery wings.

Picking their way through the underbrush without cutting a path, Will and Susan followed landmarks.

"So where's this new hunting area?"

"We'll head east at Scythe Point," lied Will. There were many areas unexplored around the forests. With abundant deer and scarce predators, finding a new hunting field should be simple.

"Let's pause here to ready the arrows." Susan sat on a moss-covered granite slab poking out of the hillside. Will put his bag down by a rotting ant-covered tree stump. Michi's insects had separated the deer's tendons, before she'd dried and pounded them. Now he pulled a clump of white fibrous sinew from the bag and popped it in his mouth, letting his saliva soften the cord. He placed an arrowhead onto a shaft and started wrapping, tying loops at the end to hold it tight.

Susan took an arrowhead. "I don't think we'd have survived without the Swarm. Michi's the only one with working powers. I'm glad they showed us what to do."

"Fire teaches man how to hunt." Will laughed. "There's some mixed-up evolution."

"Pass me some of the sinew." She smiled, extending her hand.

"Remember when Michi suggested we survive off of moss and mushrooms?"

"That first week was awful. I'm glad we figured things out."

"This time, let's not forget to check the garden when we come back."

They hafted arrowheads until they each held a full quiver. Grabbing a mouthful of dried jerky before setting off, they left the grove. They continued through Reaper Ridge, passing a long stone outcropping shaped like a crescent. Will led Susan farther east, walking on the balls of his feet through the dense forest.

He paused, hiding behind a trunk, and motioned her to circle to the right. Two bucks stood ten feet ahead, grazing. The sun vanished behind a cloud, and the forest fell into shadow. Will nocked an arrow and drew the string taut. He waited until the deer lifted his head before loosing. Susan shot the other buck at the same time. Her arrow missed, and the deer sprinted away. His target struggled before falling limp to the ground.

They carved the carcass on the spot, dividing it into smaller chunks to carry. They placed the largest chunks of flesh in the bag, and left the rest of the kill on the forest for predators to finish off.

"I need to wash off." Susan held up her hands, red with blood. "No matter how many times we do this, I still hate taking life."

"We need to eat."

"We have a garden now."

"For how long? The steaks we're drying and storing might make the difference between life and death when winter comes."

"Will, how long do you think we'll be living like this? It's late summer, and we've been here four months. What are the Dragons waiting for?"

"Does it matter? We're safe, for now."

She frowned, and he led her away from the bloody body on the ground. "Come on, we'll go to the pool."

"I'm sorry, Will. It's not the hunting, it's the reminder. You remember the first time I killed. It still haunts me." She stared at her blood-covered hands.

"If you mean the movie set, it was Grym, not you." He wrapped his gentle fingers around hers, ignoring the blood and the smell.

"It was my fault." Susan's hands trembled, and her lips quivered.

"Susan, you're not responsible for what he did. Besides, that thing is sealed."

"Is it?" Pulling her hands back, she spun, pushing a branch out of the way. They climbed a small hill. For several minutes they walked in silence before she whispered, "I'm living his life every night. I'm me when awake, however I'm Caladbolg when I dream."

"You've been screaming in your sleep again. We're all worried. How can we help?"

"There's nothing to do."

"Maybe we should ask the Swarm?"

"I'm sure they've seen me. We've kindled fires at night. They don't know what to do either."

"How can I help, at least?" He reached out, touching her back, and she turned. "Susan, I love you."

The sun emerged from the clouds high above the canopy. The forest warmed in gentle green-gold light. A soft breeze rustled the leaves, catching stray strands of her straggled hair. Susan's eyes glistened with unshed tears. "I love you too."

They walked in silence back along Reaper Ridge, turning north at a point where two rocky hills met. At the base of the stony mountains, a small pool of crystalline water glinted in the sunlight. The pool was one of the nicest spots they'd found. A trickle of fresh water fed the tiny lake, and a small stream led away, diving north into the crevice between hills. At first, they'd been too afraid to use it in daylight. As the days passed with no sign of a Dragon, their visits became more frequent.

"I need a full bath. Turn around."

"We *are* married." He grinned from ear to ear.

"Don't start that again." She smiled back, and pulled off her shirt. Will closed his eyes quickly, waiting until she splashed into the water. "Well, what are you waiting for?"

"I'm coming." He opened his eyes and started pulling off his own clothes. He brought the blood-stained shirts and a bar of handmade soap to the water's edge before jumping in himself. He swam to the top of the icy water.

"Toss me the soap."

Will sank into the calm pool again, swimming beneath the surface to the spot where he'd left the soap. "Still can't believe we made this stuff from animal fat, ashes, salt and water."

"I've learned more in the wilderness than I did at school or the College."

"Me too." He watched her lather her hands and neck.

"Wash my back?"

Without a sound, Will treaded behind her. She stood on a smooth boulder in the center of the small pool. Stepping onto the stone, Will's chest, shoulders and head bobbed above the waterline. She passed the soap, keeping her bare back facing him. He'd seen her breasts before, yet found his heart racing nonetheless. Lathering his hands, he started to stroke soap through her matted hair, and then ran his palms over her shoulders.

The sensation of washing Susan was the most sensual moment he'd ever experienced. They'd bathed here before, yet never shared a touch. She usually didn't let him even look at her while undressed. Now they stood naked in the pool, his hands caressing her back.

Ripples spread across the pool as he swam back to shore, clutching the soap. He heard Susan emerge on the other side as he started to scrub the clothes. They remained on separate sides of the pool as the sun dried them. Will fought the urge to turn and look at her, focusing all his attention on washing their clothes.

An hour later, they walked back hand in hand.

*When I first woke after my captivity, I thought I was in Hell. Now, I'm in Heaven.*

\* \* \* \*

*I am the flame.*
*They want me to watch them.*

Plumes of smoke drifted like leaning pillars from the rubble around him.

A shape slithered out of the shadows. Scales glistened off starlight above. A pair of glowing red eyes glowered in the dim light.

Mors lay in ruins. Will recognized fragments of the blue tower. An enormous scar covered the ground where part of Silver Fair once stood.

"No sign of them?" whispered a voice beside him. Will tried to turn, but his eyes could only follow the flickers of the flame.

"None," said another voice. "Wherever they're hiding, they're biding their time."

"We should burn the forests, and smoke them out." A shape like a snake formed of shadow slithered just out of sight.

"We do as the King commands. Or do you doubt him?"

"Of course not." The sound of sliding scales hurried into the distance.

Above, something screamed in the air.

*I am the flame.*
*And Mors is burning.*

* * * *

He bit into the apple, allowing its tart juice to trickle down his chin. A brisk wind ruffled the crimson and orange leaves above, casting many to the leaf-strewn ground below. Will pulled the deerskin wrap around his shoulders, and continued picking. He placed six more apples in the sack.

Michi approached, carrying a pile of small dirt-covered mounds. "I've got seven sweet potatoes from the garden. Mind if I add them to your stash?"

"Go ahead." Will opened the bag.

"If we live here much longer, we'll have to start planting more fruit. This single wild apple tree and our tiny garden aren't going to cut it."

"I picked a good haul today, got twenty or so."

"It'll be winter soon. The leaves are almost done falling. I'm worried we won't have enough food long-term."

"More than food concerns me." Will frowned, reaching up for another apple.

"She's still hunting with Frank. I think it's time we asked the Swarm for help."

"Without her permission? I don't want to go behind her back."

"Something's happening to her. Strangely, it seems to be the *only* thing happening."

"What do you mean?"

"Will, this *stillness* isn't right. The Dragons conquered Mors by May, and now it's November. What's going on elsewhere? Frank and I talked when you two hunted yesterday. He wants to leave, to see if there's anything the Swarm isn't telling us."

"Don't you trust them?"

"Do you?"

Will sighed, turning his gaze toward the golden trees lining Reaper Ridge. "I don't know. They brought us to these hills, and we've been safe so far. I'm the only one who's truly content here. Why are you all so eager to plunge yourselves back into chaos? What are you afraid of?"

"This isn't where we belong, Will." She touched his hand. The Elemental's calm face betrayed no sign of emotion.

He closed the bag, slinging it over his shoulder. "You and Frank are welcome to leave. We're staying, maybe for the rest of our lives."

"Don't you care about Susan's friends or the rest of the world?"

He glanced at the open sky above. The distant College drifted around the recesses of his mind like a dream after waking. "I am worried about Susan. Let's talk to the Swarm."

Michi nodded. They left the apple tree and walked through a long open meadow. At the edge of the grass, they paused at five rough furrows. Will glanced through the garden, however he saw nothing ready to pick.

"Come on, before they return from hunting."

"Do you ever miss being around other 'Mentals? Other than Frank, I mean."

"Not really. Do you ever miss humans other than Susan?"

"Yes. I like living here, and it's safe." He frowned; a long sigh slipped past his lips. "I do miss my friends. I want things to go back to normal, just like you."

Continuing past Reaper Ridge, they pushed aside the cave's flap. Overlapped animal hides formed a rough carpet. The stone-ringed fire pit smoldered with dim embers. Michi took a log from the wood pile and tossed it onto the simmering ashes, stirring them with a long stick until a burst of sparks danced upward, and a small flame emerged.

"We've come to talk." Will stretched his palms toward the small flame, bracing himself. The fire rippled, bending in a strange convulsion. The tiny blaze brightened into a large bonfire, and a thin tendril of orange snaked to his forehead.

The world vanished, and his mother's face started to take shape.

*No. I don't have time for this now. Stop showing me.*

The image snuffed away, replaced by a dull ashy blur.

*Any news from Cronk and the College?*

The swirling smoke faded, replaced by a dim, familiar room. Cronk stood in the Library with Hann, Agmundria, and a group of younger Deaths. Frenchie paced in front of the group.

"We need to fortify the College," said Frenchie. "I've said it before. No one listens."

"The Dragons haven't made a move in months," protested a Death he didn't recognize. Will looked down at a column of dripping wax, his vision dancing along the top of a tiny candle flicker.

Hann sighed, lowering his head to his hands. "Preparation is difficult. Half the College believes the Dragons are done."

"Th-th-they might be r-r-right." Cronk picked at his cheek.

"We're unprepared," continued Hann. "There hasn't been a mortamant shipment since summer, and Reapings have all but halted. The souls are building up. Soon, we'll have to attack the Dragons, just to get fresh mortamant."

"*We're here to discuss Susan.*" Michi's voice cut through the image. At once, the Library vanished into a cloud of ashy haze.

"*THE SCYTHE WIELDER.*" A chorus of fiery voices screamed from every side.

"*She's in trouble.*" Will tried to ignore the strange sensation of speaking, or rather communicating, without a body. Clouds of swirling gray ash fringed with flickers of white flame filled his vision. It billowed and danced without pause. "*Susan has nightmares every night. She screams, watching Grym's life.*"

"*THEY'RE LEECHING.*"

"*What does that mean?*"

"*SHE IS GRYM, GRYM IS THE SCYTHE WIELDER, THEY ARE ONE.*"

Michi's voice cut through the void, her tone harsh. "*Stop speaking in riddles. Grym's sealed. Is Susan in danger? How can we help her?*"

"*NO HELP, NO DANGER, ONLY DEATH.*"

"*That's unacceptable.*" Will slammed his fist into the air, and the tongue of flame disengaged before grabbing his forehead again.

"*ONLY DEATH. ONLY DEATH.*"

"*What do we do to save her?*"

The Swarm receded into their ashy blur.

"*ONLY DEATH.*" Long after their voices faded into nothingness, the words continued echoing in his mind.

*ONLY DEATH.*

\* \* \* \*

Snow poured from the sky, falling in blankets of relentless white. Will drew his deerskin cloak tighter around his shoulders. Wiping snowflakes out of his eyes, he knocked on the cave's wooden door.

"It's me. Hurry up, it's freezing out here."

Sounds of moving timbers accompanied grunts from inside. The door, covered in furs, slid back. Susan and Michi sat huddled around the roaring fire. Smoke wafted up through the narrow crevice they'd cut, however much of it lingered in the air. Will coughed, bending to enter, while Frank slid the door and its braces back into place. He shook the snow off his boots and coat.

"We've got a clear path for now, but if it keeps snowing I'll have to go back out."

"We can't let it block the entrance," muttered Frank. "Snowed in this cave won't be good for any of us."

Will walked to the bonfire, flexing his fingers to ease their icy pain. "Any word from the Swarm?"

"Fire's blazing, but they aren't making a sound." Michi shook her head in disbelief. "Maybe the blizzard's making it hard to establish contact."

"They're watching." Frank stared at the flames, pulled up a log stump, and sat beside the others.

"How are *you* doing?" Will cuddled up to Susan, whispering.

She took his arm, yet her listless eyes glazed.

"I never thought I'd miss Susan's library." Michi ran a hand through her red hair. "I'd give anything for a book right now."

"You and Frank grew up together. What'd you do for fun?"

The two Elementals exchanged a look and started laughing.

"We threw things at each other." Michi grinned.

"You threw bugs at me. I just ran a lot."

"I liked you—how better to show it than to use my insects? Besides, you know I could barely control them back then."

"It feels like so long ago." Frank shook his head.

"You remember the time we hit the goat-faced guy's face with a mud ball?"

Frank's expression sobered. "Athanasius. I'd forgotten that time."

Will turned to Susan. "The 'Mental you watched Sindril kill?"

"Athanasius was the first person I met after Cronk, he gave me the contract and told me I was a Death. I thought he was crazy."

"I was there," said Frank. "It's when I decided to disguise myself as a Death. In some ways, that's when our entire adventure began."

"Although, in other ways, this conflict's been raging for a million years." Susan ran her fingers across her forearm. The dancing firelight cast an orange glow over the webbing encasing Grym. "At times, I feel like I'm a million years old; like I've been waiting for this moment in darkness." Her eyes widened, reflecting drifting sparks. "No, not this moment. A moment still to come, when the Eye ignites."

"Susan?" Will touched her shoulder, and she looked up, startled.

"Forgive me, I'm not sure what I was saying."

Michi met his eyes, shaking her head.

"Do you ever dream of Lovethar?" Frank rose, stoking the fire.

"Like the images you showed me?" Susan's eyebrows furrowed.

"Those were creations, my perception of what might have happened." Frank sat again, sinking into the dancing shadows and firelight. "You're dreaming through Grym's eyes. Have you learned anything new?"

"It's not easy to remember everything." She shifted her feet, casting her gaze to the floor. "Now that you mention it, I do recall one time Lovethar and Orryn became trapped for two weeks during the war. A Dragon general named Ryuuda conquered what's now the College, and Deaths had scattered throughout the Northern Forest. It's strange to think of her living in hiding with Grym, just like us now."

"I hope our battle goes better than hers did."

She glared at Will. "Lovethar lived a long life, and faded. She succeeded at much, even after the Elementals and Deaths both betrayed her. They tried to kill her child, and she fought them to the end."

"How did she help?" Will frowned. "It always comes to that question. If she lived, and the Dragons were defeated, what did she do? Did the Deaths overpower the Dragons in the end? If so, why vilify her?"

"It's so hazy." Susan waved her hand, pushing an invisible cloud away. "Lovethar and her husband Orryn loved each other, despite the protestations of both Deaths and 'Mentals. The Deaths tried to burn them, and Gesayn, their son was injured. Orryn despised Grym. He wanted

Lovethar to bury it, and she agreed. He blamed Grym for Gesayn's injury. She gave the bracelet to an Elemental who locked it in the library's vault. That's why my blood opened it. Only blood tinged with Lovethar's remnants, the blood of Elementals and humans bonded, could open the door. Yet, once Grym was sealed in the vault, his memories faded. He woke from a coma, trying to piece a million missing years together from fragments and whispers. I don't know what happened to Lovethar after the war, or if she made a difference in the end."

"She did make a difference." Michi rested her head on one hand. "The Elementals sing of her bravery to this day. Lovethar rallied the Elementals for a final stand against the Dragons. Without their help, the Deaths would have perished."

"And we repaid by enslaving you into years of servitude?" Will shook his head. "The Deaths owe their survival to you."

"Things didn't go bad overnight," said Frank. "For generations the two races knew peace, however over time, Deaths grew to fear us. Not until now has reconciliation started. Perhaps if we remember our common enemy, the Elementals and Deaths will unite again."

Will stood, his fingers touching the sore spots on his shoulder and arm. Even now, months after the vika's bites, he sometimes imagined the searing pain sinking into his skin. "That account doesn't match what White Claw told me. Gesayn was kidnapped, and his hand was severed to form a Dragon Key. The Deaths didn't injure him, the Dragons did."

"In the flames, the child was missing one hand." Susan's voice spoke with a hollow monotone. She waved her arm in front of her face again. "You're right. The Dragons made a Key, and the Key failed. Yet, the Deaths blamed Lovethar and her family. They burned them, or tried. Orryn saved them." Her expression hardened, and she jumped up. "He hated me. Orryn claimed Lovethar was obsessed. The Scythe drove her crazy. It's his fault I was imprisoned for a thousand millennia! It's his fault they failed to ignite the Eye!"

"Susan! Get a hold of yourself." Will rose, wrapping his arms around her trembling body. "You're not Grym, you're here with us. You're a Death, a human, a wonderful person, and we love you." He tightened his grip. "I love you."

Her trembling ebbed and she relaxed in his arms. He knew Frank and Michi watched, but he held her close, stroking her hair. For a moment they stood in silence.

"It's hard to control sometimes," she whispered.

"I know." He kissed her softly.

"I'd forgotten what you said before." Frank's eyes shifted in the dim, flickering light. "The Dragon King couldn't get what he wanted, so he used the Key to make himself immortal. He probably weakened himself with the Key's power, at least temporarily. That'd help explain why the Dragons lost the war."

"Setting the stage for a second attempt." Michi shuddered. "It took thousands of generations, yet now he's ready to try again. With no chance of a Dragon Key, the Dragons had no reason to attack the Deaths. They've been biding their time, allowing Deaths to reap souls."

"Which is why we've got to stay hidden." Will let go of Susan, facing the others. "We can't let them get to her. She's the first female Death, and she'll be the last. We'll live our lives in hiding, until we fade."

Susan looked at her feet. "There is one other way."

"What?"

"Kill me."

"Susan!" Michi and Frank both sprang up.

Her hands spread in a posture of surrender. "All the Dragons want is a Dragon Key, and their only means to one is through me. If I die, I'll cease, and there's no reason at all for the war."

"It's not an option." Will embraced her again. "We have a fine life, we just need to remain hidden."

Her body stiffened. "You couldn't kill me if you tried." She burst into deep maniacal laughter, and collapsed onto the cavern floor in tears. "Help me, Will."

"I'm trying."

Michi walked over, putting her hands on Susan's shoulders. "She's losing herself to Caladbolg."

Susan wept in his arms.

The fire behind them roared, and tongues of flame snaked outward, joining each of their foreheads.

Smoke and ash whirled around Will's vision as he drifted into the collective consciousness of the Swarm. An inferno engulfed him, casting him into a storm of fire.

An image appeared, fading into view.

Cronk's face looked down, as he bobbed atop a tiny flicker. Hot wax pooled beneath him on a slim taper.

"M-M-Mortamant all b-but g-g-gone. N-N-No n-n-new D-D-Deaths. N-N-no R-Reapings."

Will wanted to respond, however he was nothing: an ethereal filament of flame on a slender candle.

"D-D-Dragons have st-st-started m-m-moving again. They've b-b-been seen as f-f-far s-south as the r-r-river. C-C-College is n-n-not r-ready."

A voice sounded behind Cronk, and he hurried to blow out the candle, sending Will's mind drifting back through other fires old and new. Conflagrations blinked into life and snuffed out, smoke poured around him, and a dizzying panoply of fiery images blurred.

The orange tendril dislodged from his head, and Will blinked to acclimate to the dimmer cavern light.

"Susan?" She lay sprawled on the floor beside him, and he bent down to help her.

"I'm okay. The Swarm helped. He's gone, at least for now."

"I don't know how long they held us in their minds." Frank stood. "I'm going to check outside. We might have to clear the path again. Sounds like the snow's let up."

Michi caught his eye. "No new Deaths. They're out of mortamant. No Reapings. You know what that means?"

"The Dead don't go to the Hereafter?"

"It's more than that, Will. You saw what happens to un-Reaped souls. They're devoured by Dragons. The enemy has starved the College out of supplies, while fattening themselves with a glut of souls. While all this happens, thousands of innocents will never know peace."

"What do we do?"

"For now, we shovel." Frank shrugged. "All we can do is wait. It's horrible having to watch, yet the alternative's even worse."

"Let me shovel." Susan walked to the door.

"Susan, are you sure? A minute ago, you didn't even know yourself."

"I need to work through this. Whatever's happening with Grym will end, I'm sure." She grabbed one of the coats and pulled her arms through.

Will helped her slide the timbers from the door. With a grunt he pulled the door open. She lowered her head, ducking out of the cave. A gust of icy wind swept inside.

He turned to his friends. "We need to do more. Can't you use your powers to cure her? Can't we rip Grym out of her somehow?"

"When Lovethar used Grym, it was a tool, the bracelet you discovered." Frank frowned. "It's not the same now. He's part of her. There's nothing we can do."

"That's not good enough."

"We'll help you keep an eye on her." Michi's eyes widened. "We're just as worried as you are."

Will swore under his breath and hurried to put on a coat. The door was still open, and another gust of wind tore through the cave, sending the fire into convulsions. Frank stood. Ducking outside, Will heard the door slide closed behind him

Susan pushed the hollowed log section with a branch attached, shoveling a clear path before the door. The sun lay buried beneath the horizon, yet snow still fell. Behind the mountain range, the moon shone bright through a gap in the clouds. Drifting snowflakes caught the moonlight, forming a halo of white around Susan.

"Do you need help?"

"I'm fine." She continued shoveling, without turning around.

A frigid breeze started his teeth chattering. He hugged his arms around his chest for warmth. "Susan, talk to me. What's going on?"

Pushing another mound of snow aside, she sank to the ground. He hurried to sit beside her. For a long moment, they stared up at the falling flurries.

"Why me?" She wiped snow from her face. "I'm not Lovethar, and I'm as related to her as you are. It's been a *million* years, Will. Thousands of generations. The first war predates Ancient Egypt or the Bible, hell, it probably happened before human civilization. Why now? Of all the girls to force here, why me?"

"Your Elemental grandfather was a direct descendant of Lovethar. You know this. It doesn't matter anymore, you're here. I'm here."

"They'll come soon enough for me. They'll take the College, sweeping in on their terrible wings, and we'll have nowhere left to run."

"You're sounding like Grym again." He frowned.

"No, that was me." She sighed, staring up at the sky. "Do you ever miss life before the World of Deaths?"

"Sometimes."

"For a long time I didn't. Once we started living here, though, memories kept surfacing." She caught his eyes. "Not just Caladbolg's memories, but *my* memories from the Mortal World. My mom, dad, and brother. My friends, my school. I feel...stretched. Like my former life is pulling me one way, and Grym's past is pulling me the opposite direction. I hate him, Will. Ever since he killed those women in front of us, I've hated him, and now he's *within* me, tearing my soul apart."

"The curse can't last forever. If things with the Dragons die down, perhaps we can visit Frank's father. The 'Mentals might be able to help."

He pulled her close, wrapping his arms around her shoulders. The frigid, wet snow beneath them dampened their pants and shoes. The snowfall softened, until single snowflakes wafted down one at a time.

For a long while, they sat in the cold, wet snow. One by one, stars emerged above, and the night sky cleared.

"The Swarm kept showing me my mother." Will dropped his hands to Susan's waist. "I thought she'd have forgotten me by now, yet she still lights a candle every year on my birthday." He laughed, watching the steam escape as a dissipating cloud. "At first, the sight of her raised guilt and remorse. However, I wouldn't change anything, Susan."

Susan shuddered from the cold, and turned, kissing his cheek. "Let's go dry off."

"I mean it. Things have been difficult, yet everything will work out in the end."

She stood. "I appreciate your optimism, Will, but I'm not so sure."

Pulling the flap aside, she knocked. He heard timbers slide against stone, and the door opened. She ducked inside, and Will turned a final time, glancing at the glowing moon. A shadow swept past, and Will's breath caught in his throat.

For a horrifying instant he thought he saw bat-wings, and the glow of Dragon eyes.

The form turned. It was only a raven. The bird cawed loudly, circling back to the mountains.

*Only a raven. Only a bird.*

"You coming in?" called Frank.

Will shook the snow from his coat and leaned down, forcing his eyes back to the door.

\* \* \* \*

"Come on." Susan laughed as she rounded the bend in front of him.

"Look at the clouds." Will chased her, smiling. "It'll rain soon."

The fragrant air was thick with the scent of pollen, flowers, and blossoms. A pair of bright pink cherry trees swayed in the spring breeze; their weeping branches cast a shower of rose petals dancing into the air. Gentle birdsong wafted into Will's ears as his grin deepened.

"You heard the Swarm, it's my birthday again. We've been here over a year, Will. I'm sick of the same routine. We're going to go exploring farther than ever today."

"We've already done that. Reaper Ridge is at least four miles behind us. If we don't head back soon, we might have to camp overnight in the forest."

Susan spun, letting him catch up before she tossed her arms around him. "You make that sound like a bad thing."

"What's gotten into you today?"

"I'm sick of being cooped up. Nightmares every night, followed by monotony every day. Wake up, hunt, garden, talk, go back to the nightmares each night. Get angry at Grym, get over it the next day, and then repeat. It's only my birthday once a year. Let's be reckless for once. If we end up camping out, or getting caught in the rain, who cares? We've been through far worse."

"That's certainly true."

They stopped at a clearing in the forest. The outline of a jagged mountain cloaked in fog stood in the distance. A row of pink and white magnolia trees lined a small open field of thick, matted grass and clover. Small violet flowers and dandelions poked through the meadow's greens. The entire clearing smelled of sweet grass. The couple sat, watching a pair of hummingbirds hover and dart away. Behind them, the familiar peaks of Reaper Ridge seemed small, poking just above the blossoming trees. Will pulled out some venison jerky from his pack, and passed a piece to Susan. Above, bands of gray-bottomed clouds continued to roll in from the east, masking much of the sky.

"Can't believe it's been a whole year." Will broke off another piece of venison and chewed slowly.

"I still don't know how old I am." Susan frowned. "I've been alive sixteen years, my body's twenty years old from the curse, and memories spanning thousands of years flood my dreams each time I close my eyes."

"End of May means I'm nineteen now, however age isn't important. We are who we are. I doubt anyone in the Mortal World could imagine the things we've been through."

She laughed. "That's true."

They shared a long moment of silence. The trees bent and trembled in a gust of wind.

"You know, now that we're alone, do you ever consider becoming an *actual* married couple?"

"What do you mean?" She cocked her head coyly.

Warmth rushed to Will's cheeks. "I mean even if the Dragons didn't really marry us, we're a couple, and we've never… you know. I mean, we're alone now, Frank and Michi aren't around."

"I've thought about it." She pulled a strand of hair out of her eyes.

"I just mean if we're going to live the rest of our lives here in the wild, we could be, you know, I mean if you're ready and want to, then maybe we should—"

"You're not very eloquent today, Will." She leaned forward and gave him a deep, lingering kiss. Their tongues flitted over each other, probing and dancing. He held her soft hair in his fingers, relishing the sensation. Without a word, she broke the kiss, leaned back, and pulled her shirt over her head.

"Have you considered the repercussions?" His voice trembled. "If we have a child—"

"We'll protect them. We won't allow Sindril or the Dragons to dictate our life."

They kissed again. Will's fingers moved down Susan's bare back.

Thunder rumbled in the distance. Beads of rain started to fall, gently at first, yet with growing intensity.

Susan pulled away and slipped her shirt back on. "Let's find shelter."

They rose, looking around. "We didn't pass anywhere."

"There might be a cave or something by that mountain ahead."

He nodded and they started jogging through the forest. The rain hardened, coming down in sheets. The sky lit as a jagged bolt streaked down, accompanied by a booming roar. Sparks burst somewhere to their right. They kept moving, ducking against the plummeting water.

"We've got to find shelter soon, Susan. If lightning keeps hitting the trees, it could start a forest fire. It's been dry until now."

"I think the Swarm would protect us."

He tripped, sliding on a puddle. The world around them vanished beneath blankets of plunging water. Rain pounded the soft ground, turning dirt to mud and sending branches above careening against the downfall. He took Susan's proffered hand. "I don't think the Swarm has that sort of control."

"Come on, keep moving."

Half-jogging, half-slipping, they pushed forward. The trees grew denser and taller. Large cedars and pine spread twisted roots across the muddy forest floor. Their pace slowed, yet the rain continued, unrelenting. Will crouched beneath a tree, pulling Susan beside him.

"Maybe we should wait here. There's other taller trees around, this one's less likely to get hit."

Thunder groaned in the distance and the sky flashed, lighting the clouds and the sheets of falling silver.

She clung to him, their soaking clothes sticking together. The thunder receded to the west, or was it east? Will realized he'd lost track of their location. He tightened his grip on Susan, as the rain continued to plummet down. The trees around them buckled and swayed.

"This isn't how I expected the day to go." Susan buried her face into Will's chest.

"Me either." He patted her soaking back.

They endured the storm in silence. The torrent abruptly ended, leaving the forest in a misty silence.

"This might be the eye of the storm." Will helped Susan up, wiping the matted mud from her shirt. "Let's find better shelter quick."

She nodded and they hurried forward through the sodden woods. With no clear path, they worked their way past the trees. For a moment, the sky brightened enough to reveal the nearby silhouette of a large mountain. Will pointed and they hurried toward the cliff face.

Wind howled past their damp faces, and a second wave of rain plummeted down. Water pelted them in torrent after ceaseless torrent. Will tried to track their route, yet the rain blinded him. The trees above offered little protection, as unending water tumbled down.

"What's that?" Susan gestured to a shadow on their right. The rain spattered off a structure, lurking like a large shadow between a grove of trees.

"Looks like shelter."

They stumbled and slipped to the building's side. Nearing the edifice, Will saw eaves and shingles. "It's some kind of house."

"We're miles and miles away from any civilization. Who built it?"

Will pounded on the door, and it swung open. Thunder pounded behind him, and the sky flashed in warning. "We'll worry later. We need to get out of the storm."

Susan followed him inside. A potted jar of flowers started to glow, and their dim, dust-covered light illuminated a room strewn with waste. Will closed the door. Shards of shattered pottery littered the floor. A half-splintered chair, covered in cobwebs, sat in one corner.

"Look at this." Susan stood beside half a tapestry, hanging limply from the wall. A crude painted tiger stood in the upper part, leaning over something that was cut off in a large jagged tear.

"Whoever used to live here seems to be long gone. We'll wait here until the storm passes, and then head back."

"Do you smell that?"

He sniffed. "It smells like food."

"It's coming from there." She approached the wall behind the chair, and pressed on one of the beams. A hidden door swung open. Light poured out of the opening, emanating from a bright kitchen on the other side. Pots and pans hung from hooks above two long counters. A single potbellied stove stood between the counters.

"Doesn't look abandoned to me," muttered Susan.

"Hello? Is anyone there? We're trying to get out of the rain."

Susan ignored his calls, and hurried to a large pot of soup boiling atop the stove. Will placed a hand on her back in warning, however she dipped a finger in.

"Ah, hot."

"What are you doing?"

"I'm hungry."

"I don't think we should—"

He broke off as a shadowy figure dislodged from the wall. An ancient form with long, gray hair and loose, wrinkled, pocked skin emerged from the shadows. Tattered, dusty clothes, riddled in tears covered his, *or was it her*, thin frame. Skin hung from bones visible underneath. Sapphire eyes stared at them as if they'd never seen another soul.

"I'm sorry, we didn't know there was anyone home. We're just coming out of the rain." Will held his palms open in a gesture of supplication. "If you'll let us stay until the rain passes, we'll be on our way."

The man, yes, Will decided the figure was a wizened old man, stared at them. His withered lips parted, revealing dark yellowed teeth, which seemed to jut out at an assortment of wrong angles. The expression wasn't a smile, but more of a baring of teeth.

"The soup smells delicious. I'm very hungry." Susan edged forward. "Could I try a bite?"

The man's lips snapped shut, and then opened again. His sapphire eyes never blinked. He stared at them with icy coldness.

"What's your name? I'm Will and this is Susan. We didn't think anyone lived here."

The soup shifted, and a large bubble popped on the surface. A tiny white glow emerged above the liquid, and then vanished. For a moment, Will thought he heard a scream.

"I know what you are." Susan's voice lowered far below her range, and her posture shifted.

"Susan?"

"Back away, William. This is a *gheiraq*." She raised her right arm, and the thin webbing encasing Grym pulsed. Her arm gleamed blue beneath the webbing, with light that grew brighter every moment.

"Susan, what's going on? Talk to me."

The man's eyes bored into them with the same intense stare, yet he remained still. Susan backed away, keeping her hand raised.

"He was once an Elemental, however the power consumed him. Too much of his soul was lost. He lives in exile, anathema and accursed to all life. The gheiraq lose themselves, and consume other Elementals, seeking to gain the power they've lost. They forever strive to replenish their splintered soul, yet with every death shred it to smaller pieces."

"How do you know this?" Will backed to the doorway.

She shook her head, wincing. Her voice raised in pitch. "He's growing, Will. He's trying to help, but I can't shut him out."

"Stay strong." He reached toward her glowing arm, yet stopped as bright blue and white rays spread from the webbing. One touched his finger and he drew back in pain.

"Your finger." She stared.

"The light is sharp. It cut me. Is Grym waking up?"

Something growled behind him, and Will slammed to the floor.

"Will!"

A pair of daggers shot into his leg, sharper than the vika's fangs, pulling him backward. Light exploded above him, and timber fragments shot into the air. The pain released.

Will tried to rise, before crying out in agony. He pulled himself around. The old man had vanished. In his place crouched an enormous beast with staring sapphire eyes. It had the general look of a massive white tiger, yet its fur stood on end, forming jagged spikes like a porcupine. Beads of glowing white liquid dripped from every spike. The gheiraq bared its teeth, and the massive fangs dripped with blood from Will's leg.

"Run, Susan!"

The creature started forward, snarling. Its spikes bristled, and the creature turned so that a row of quills faced Will. With a high-pitched whistle, darts of brilliant white sped toward him, streaking trails of light. He braced himself. The glowing blue form around Susan's arm extended, and the glowing projectiles slammed into a translucent wall. Each one fell to the ground and dimmed.

The gheiraq spun again, baring its fangs.

Susan sprinted forward, toward the creature. Before he could protest, she leaped into the air and spun. The outline of an enormous blade shone around her arm in lambent turquoise.

The gheiraq jumped to meet her, yet the glowing blade grew. It knocked the creature's fangs out of its mouth, and tore the beast in half. Crimson blood splattered everywhere, accompanied by pools of luminous white.

Susan landed, the blade vanished, and her arm stopped shining. She stared at him, imploring, her hands covered in the creature's blood. With a thud, she collapsed to the floor.

"Susan!"He struggled to rise, fighting the pain. Pools of red stained his left leg. With a scream he pulled off his shirt, and pressed it against the fang marks.

"Susan! Wake up!"

The blood didn't stop, and she didn't move. She lay lifeless amid the creature's carcass. He grimaced and ripped the shirt apart, tying it around his leg. He grabbed a shard of timber and slipped it under the makeshift tourniquet, spinning and tightening until he couldn't pull any harder. He couldn't feel the bottom of his leg, yet somehow managed to stand.

"Aaarggh." Agony shot through his entire body. He ignored it, staggering to Susan.

"Talk to me!"

Susan lay lifeless in a pool of blood and gore. A pool of liquid glowed beside her, fading from brilliant white to dull gray. Will knelt, almost falling when the pain coursed back up. He touched her face.

"Oh God, Susan. Please, talk to me."

Her skin was cold and clammy. Placing his fingers on her throat, the tiniest tremble of pressure answered once, and then again.

*A pulse.*

She wasn't moving. Leaning in, he felt a slight hint of air escape her mouth.

*At least she's breathing. This is Grym's doing, I'm sure of it.*

Wedging his arms under her body, he tried to stand. He half rose, before toppling over. Cursing under his breath, he clamped his jaw shut, grimacing against the pain and weight. Lifting her, he staggered to the front door, leaving the gheiraq's body and strange dwelling behind.

He fell hard against the door, and it snapped open, breaking off its rusty hinges. Will regained his grip on Susan and hurried into the twilit forest. The rain had stopped. Stars twinkled between parting clouds, and the sun now slept beneath the dim horizon.

*Frank!*

He screamed the word in his mind, calling with what he imagined was the loudest voice possible.

*Frank! We're in trouble!*

No voice answered, yet Will sensed something at the edge of thought. A guiding image, faint and fading. He wasn't sure if it was real, however it came from the direction he guessed home must be.

Staggering through the forest at an excruciating pace, he carried Susan. He couldn't feel his legs or arms. He couldn't breathe for lack of water, and his throat constricted and protested every step. Still, he pressed on.

Tree after tree passed. Branches scratched his legs. He staggered on through sheer determination.

Hour after hour he did not rest. He walked, knowing at any moment he'd collapse, and both Susan and he would be lost.

*Will? What's happened?*

Frank's voice ebbed into his mind. He didn't have the strength to answer.

This is the woman I love. I will carry her to safety, even if it kills me.

This is my one final task.

Vision blurred as he sank to the ground.

Two forms appeared in the haze above. They spoke, yet their words faded to distant echoes in the wind. Will was back in Hell, ready to die. This time for real.

"Help me carry them."

"Are you all right?"

"We have to get them to my father, Giri."

Will sought the words, reaching into his final reserves of strength just to move his lips.

"No, bring Susan to the Mortal World. She needs a proper hospital."

"The Swarm can't transport between worlds. If we use the scythe, it could kill her."

"She needs…she needs…"

The world blurred into darkness.

CHAPTER TWENTY-FOUR—SUSAN

# Fear

**A** narrow band of orange sky stretched in a thin line from left to right, miles overhead. Behind her, a sheer cliff face formed a solid wall of granite. From horizon to horizon, the rocky wall rose to impossible heights, soaring thousands of feet skyward. The endless precipice soared behind a narrow pebble beach, running the immeasurable length of the rocky escarpment.

Susan stood upon the beach, staring ahead. A gauzy white robe covered her otherwise naked body.

Tiny ripples of water lapped against her bare toes. At the beach's edge, the water deepened into an enormous ocean. A few yards away, the sea surged upwards. Countless tons of water gushed higher and higher, forming a reverse waterfall. It flowed heavenward to a foaming crest, parallel to the distant cliff ledge behind her, extending beyond sight on either side.

A gentle, salty breeze blew across her face. Strands of loose hair fell across Susan's eyes; she brushed them aside.

In the center of the rising water, a thirty-foot tall iron door rested: the Door to the Hereafter. She'd been here before, leading souls to their final destinations. Glancing left and right, she half-expected to see a Reaper. However, she stood alone.

*Am I dead? Have I ceased?*

The narrow expanse of ocean between the Door and the beach frothed. Bubbles burst atop the waves, as a row of stones emerged, connecting to form a bridge.

*I'm not ready. No, I don't want to go.*

Strange runes and carvings bordered the iron Door. The more she stared, the more she realized she'd never looked at it closely. Its surface was rough, covered in dozens of etchings. The runes glowed with a faint, distant light, like reflected starlight rippling on the surface of a lake. Somehow, one foot took a step, and then another. She moved forward onto the bridge, mesmerized by the Door.

Another breeze blew, whispering outward from the Door itself. Familiar smells hung in the air, memories she couldn't quite reach.

She stared at the etchings on the Door. At the top, a woman lay in a hospital bed, a bearded man beside her.

*Mom and Dad.*

The engraved images quivered and bent, like sunlight dancing on a river. She watched the baby grow, arguing with an older boy.

*Joe.*

The girl aged, becoming a teenager. Susan watched her own life play out on the surface of the door. Every major event was encapsulated by a carved image that then swirled to a new picture. She strode forward, touching the cool metal.

At her finger's contact, the Door trembled. The etchings vanished.

The wind whipped against her face as the metal slid. The Door to the Hereafter opened, parting in its center, swinging inward. A soft, welcoming white light appeared on the other side.

"Susan Elizabeth Sarnio." The words sang from the luminous void, spoken by her own voice, although she hadn't said a word.

*I'm not dead. I can't be.*

The light pulsed: a double pulse, followed by a pause. Pulsing light pierced her skin. Light swam all around and through her body. White split apart, breaking into every color, a rainbow of sensations and memories, a river of emotion. The light ebbed and flowed with her own heartbeat. Susan stepped forward again, drawn by the swirling tide.

*No.*

The prismatic rays reached around her with gentle fingers, pulling her into the Door. She shook her head, unable to resist the light. She couldn't keep away from the voices calling. Calling her name, beckoning.

She belonged on the other side.

Susan stepped through the Door.

* * * *

A single bead of water hung by an invisible thread: a tear shed long ago in a fleeting world. Suspended over a boundless void, the crystalline droplet floated alone, its surface reflecting an inner light.

She flew closer and closer to the solitary tear.

Thin ribbons of rainbow stretched colored fingers around the tiny globule, massaging its elastic surface. Specks of silver and gold floated within the lonely water.

Susan tried to see her own reflection, but she was gone, a whisper of imagination in an unseen world. The tear grew in size at her approach, until it filled all of sight. Pressing her hands against its edges, she peered into the luminous liquid.

Tumbling inside, she splashed into light.

An infinite number of Susans appeared before and behind her.

Countless faces, all her face.

She touched her hair.

Every Susan touched her hair.

Eternity extended in every direction…

and she was everyone.

She tried to smile.

The strain shattered something within.

A wind howled out from her.

Wind blew through the crowd,

wiping the faces away.

As each face vanished, its body remained.

A perpetual sea of Susans surrounded her, each one faceless.

Faceless.

A dull blur sat in the center of every head,

Every faceless Susan.

Rainbow spiders crawled up bodies, settling where faces should be.

Every form dissolved,

Every form cried,

A well of tears,

morphing into someone she'd known.

Every face she'd ever seen:

Faces from the Mortal World,

Faces from the World of Deaths,
Faces from the dreams of Grym.
Everyone appeared around her.
Everyone.
She stood alone, a solitary tear,
Surrounded by a void.
Friends and strangers in a procession
Whirling around and through her.
Every face has a voice.
Every soul has a name.
One by one they spoke,
Each person spoke a single word.
The words flew by so fast,
Susan barely registered them.
One after another, a face appeared,
With each face, one word:
*Susan.*
*Elizabeth.*
*Sarnio.*
*Born.*
*Died.*
*Lived.*
*Loved.*
*Longed.*
*Cried.*

Susan gasped for air. She drowned in a sea of voices, a flurry of faces that swam around and through her. They said nothing and everything. She pushed outward, trying to stay afloat, yet a new wave pulled her down.

*Death.*
*Must.*
*Live.*
*Hold.*
*Hope.*
*Inside.*

She broke free again, treading hard. The ocean of bodies around her roiled and frothed, casting silver and gold light to the surface. Sparks fluttered out of the strange sea, catching on the edges of the watery tear around them. Its edges glistened with trapped sparks, shining like stars. Susan kicked her way out of the bodies, grasping for those infinitesimal stars.

Struggling up, she climbed.

Higher and higher, reaching.

Reaching.

Her fingers touched the light.

A river of tears showered down, raining shards of starlight.

Shattered stars dripped,

Pouring into a waterfall.

\* \* \* \*

Mom and Dad stood in a tight embrace. Dad's back was to Susan. He wore a dark suit, which was odd, because he rarely dressed up. Mom's hair was pulled back in a tight bun, another strange choice. She wore a long, black dress.

"They're waiting for us." Her brother entered the kitchen, also in a suit. Joe's expression was somber, and his shoulders hunched. He shoved his hands deep into his pockets, looking away from their parents.

*What's going on?* Susan thought the words, however no sound came out. Joe walked to the refrigerator, passing straight through her. She dissolved in a blur of smoke, and re-coalesced beside Mom.

Pulling herself out of Dad's embrace, Mom turned. Her mascara ran beneath her eyes, forming dark lines. Dad mumbled something, gesturing, and Mom walked to the bathroom. Dad looked right at Susan.

*Dad?*

"She's still alive, Joe."

Spinning around, Susan realized Dad's gaze was directed *through* her, at her brother.

"It's been three years."

"We'll never give up hope." Her father wiped the corner of his eye.

*I'm here, Dad. I'm here.*

Mom reappeared, adjusting her necklace and dress. She smiled weakly: her lips parted in an obvious effort to convey an emotion she didn't feel.

"Let's go." Dad spoke with a soft, determined voice.

Susan followed them out of the kitchen. Joe paused a moment and shut off the lights. As the house fell dark, something caught in her throat. Where were they going?

She walked behind her family as they got into the minivan. Susan tried to grasp the door handle; however, her fingers passed through, touching nothingness.

*Am I a ghost?*

She floated into the car, passing through the metal.

For a moment, she remembered a different door, a massive Door of etched iron standing in a reverse waterfall.

*I entered. This is what lies beyond.*

She drifted to the back seat. No one spoke as Dad started the engine. A light rain fell, drizzling onto the windows like angelic tears. The car backed up, and started down the street.

The lights of Damascus, Maryland glowed with a dull neon haze in the twilight rain. Mom's fingers played with her purse strap, tracing an invisible pattern. Joe stared out the window. They pulled into the parking lot of her old middle school.

*I only went to eighth grade for two days before Cronk arrived.*

A crowd waited in the parking lot. Mom, Dad, and Joe got out, and she drifted behind. She started to sigh, before she realized she wasn't breathing.

People walked over, greeting her family. Faces she didn't know. No, they were familiar, just older. A tall, lanky redhead walked over, carrying an unlit candle.

"Thanks for coming, Crystal." Joe kissed her on the cheek.

*Crystal? My best friend before I left the Mortal World? She must have gotten contacts. Why is Joe holding her hand?*

Dad gestured for them to join the others. A teenage girl with tiny eyes walked up, shaking Mom's hand.

*Monica?*

One by one, she recognized the others. Nurse Cherwell, who everyone called the Gingerbread Nurse on account of her sunny disposition, stood to the side frowning. Ms. Warwood, her teacher for all of two days, and even Dr. Fox was there. Others too, dozens of strangers Susan didn't recognize.

Dad walked to the top of the front steps, and raised his voice. "Thank you all for coming today. Tonight is Suzie's sixteenth birthday." He stopped, looking down. Mom hurried up, taking his hand.

"My daughter," he continued in a trembling voice. "My daughter vanished three years ago. There's been no note, and no word. The police call it a 'cold case,' however we will not rest. Suzie's out there, somewhere. Somewhere, Suzie knows it's her birthday, and we all just want to see her come home."

He broke down, and Mom helped him rejoin the silent crowd. One by one, people lit their candles, touching tapers to other wicks, spreading the light. Soon, everyone held a glowing candle. The gentle drizzle continued to fall, and people shielded their flames with cupped fingers or umbrellas.

"Come home, Suzie," said Joe beside her. He and Crystal held a single candle together.

Susan watched with a growing detachment. She wanted to cry out, but no one would hear her.

*I could've come home, but I chose to stay. I thought you'd forget me.*

She walked away from the crowd, not caring where she went. The wet pavement glistened with the reflection of streetlights. She continued away from the crowd, not daring to turn around.

*What do I do now?*

A wind blew, and every bead of water paused, freezing in mid-air.

The droplets hung, suspended by invisible cords.

The world stopped,

Time stopped.

She reached out, touching a single raindrop,

A tear.

The scene around her melted into a river of amber light.

A beagle appeared, its familiar face grinning.

*Bumper.*

*I really am dead, then?*

Colors swirled around and through her.

The dog disappeared,

The world disappeared,

Susan disappeared.

* * * *

Feng, Mel, Olu, and Gordon sat around a table.

*My teammates.*

"It's not like anyone else is playing boskery." Mel drummed his fingers.

Susan stood in the corner of a room similar to her home at Eagle Two. This must be another dorm in the College.

"That's not the point." Feng stood and walked to the window. Outside, the shadowy towers loomed large against a sunset sky streaked with orange and gold. "Three of our friends are *gone*, vanished to God-only-knows where."

"What do you want to do?" Olu raised his hands in question. "We talked to Erebus, and he told us to forget them."

"I've heard a rumor." Feng continued gazing at the earthy canyons and gnarled stone towers of the College. "Hann's up to something, possibly with Cronk. I think those two actually know what's going on."

"And what do *you* think is going on?" Olu pulled his hands behind his head, leaning back in the chair.

"I think the Dragons didn't just invade Mors. I think they're already here, hiding in the College."

"Dragons can't get beyond the Ring of Scythes." Gordon laughed. "Everyone knows that."

"I don't know who to believe anymore," continued Feng. "They've cancelled Reapings, and won't let us leave the campus. Yet, are we training to defend ourselves? No, we wait like rats for something to happen."

"You think practicing a couple boskery moves will help if a Dragon attacks?" Gordon stood. "This is ridiculous." He walked to the wall, passing right through Susan. She dissipated in a puff of smoke.

A river of light flowed through her.

She swam past a rainbow,

And the sunset collided with falling stars.

She doubled over when she coalesced.

Her belly ached, and she gasped for air. Her lungs cried out in pain.

A river of light formed a single globe:

A circle,

A window.

It took a moment to recognize the office.

The Headmaster's Office.

Hann sat behind a desk stacked with papers and books. An enormous circular window looked down from East Tower like an eye peering over the College. An array of telescopes stood beside the glass portal, pointed in various directions.

From this office, she'd proved Sindril's involvement with the Dragons.

From this office, she'd watched the 'Mentals start a revolution.

Hann rose, responding to a sound behind her.

Four tall men in hoods and masks strode into the room, brushing by Susan without noticing her.

"May I help you?" Hann's voice was calm and steady. He stretched his hands.

"We're placing you under arrest, Headmaster." One of the men held out a pair of handcuffs.

"May I ask the charge?"

"Conspiring with the Enemy, and failure to protect the interests of Deaths."

"You're making a mistake." Hann remained behind the desk, his tone held hints of warning.

"Come with us." Two of the men pulled short scythes from their robes. The snaths were blunt, like swords.

"Take me into custody, and the College will fall. I am the last hope against a Dragon incursion."

"Tell it to the panel."

"Who set you up for this? I am on the Council, and the Headmaster. You have no authority over me."

The two men stepped forward, lowering their blades. "This can go smoothly, or can be difficult. The choice is yours."

Light behind the window brightened, pouring in a steady stream.

The world vanished once more, and she again swam in a golden river of light.

Faces flowed past in a rushing procession. The train of images each shed a single tear, and one by one the drops of water coalesced.

Thousands of tears became one tear.

Susan floated around the prism-laced tear, watching the sea of bodies within.

The hellish forms writhed and groaned as a single mass: a trapped basin of limbs and faces.

Strangers and friends reached out to her,

Crying for her,

Crying for the world.

She turned away, gliding through an expanse of drifting stars.

She floated, until a single tear formed in her own eye.

Colors swirled around her, like paints mixing on one of Cronk's easels.

A cloud of thought coalesced, taking shape.

"What can we do?" Frank stood in a strange house, his hand resting on her arm.

She gazed down at her own body. Susan lay face up on a large bed, her eyes closed. Her thoughts watched, hovering above in some ethereal manner. Will sat beside her lifeless head.

Giri, Frank's father, stood behind her head, gazing down. His white hair framed a pale face lined with deep furrows. His blazing, fire-green eyes glanced up, and for a moment, looked straight into her ghostlike eyes: the eyes of her thoughts, her soul. He turned away.

"She straddles the worlds of life and death." Giri frowned. "I believe Grym and Susan are leeching off each other."

"What does that mean?" asked Will.

"You said Susan *aged* on the boat. Sindril stole four years from her."

"That's right." Will ran a hand through her lifeless hair. Susan tried to touch his hand, yet her fingers slipped through like vapor.

"Whatever Sindril did caused her *body* to age. Now, her soul catches up. She's aging rapidly, stealing years from Grym. The strain is far too much for any mortal. Grym's lived for generations. There is nothing we can do. She must fight this battle on her own."

"What will happen to her?" Frank's fists clenched.

Giri sighed. "She'll probably die."

*No.*

Will stood. "After all we've been through, I don't accept that. She's strong. She survived Sindril's curse already."

"She *prolonged* her exposure to the curse, however she hasn't survived. Not yet." Giri turned away. "Confronting the gheiraq brought things to a head. From what you've described, it was only a matter of time. The nightmares, the mood swings. Perhaps if you'd brought her sooner, but now..." His shoulders heaved, and he touched his forehead. Looking up, he stared right through Susan's watching eyes. "I've never seen a Death so close to their own demise. She has little hope."

Suddenly, Will and Frank both turned and stared at her.

"You must survive," they said in unison.

A million faceless forms emerged from every shadow.

"YOU MUST SURVIVE," screamed the choral voice of the Swarm.

Giri raised his glowing green eyes, the same fiery eyes that warned her countless times when she first arrived at the College.

Green fire spread through the room.

Smoke lingered, dissipating.

The room emptied, leaving only her own lifeless body.

Her spectral soul floated above her body.

She stared at her own corpse,

alone in the empty room.

Reaching down,

she touched her own face, her own fingers.

The body sat up.

Its eyes popped open.

"You must survive," whispered Susan.

Susan flew backward, the world rushing past at an impossible speed.

Blurred colors sped in a dizzying array, shooting around her with increasing velocity.

The world ripped apart,

Split by an infinite number of scythes.

Sunlight climbed through rips in the universe,

Oozing in like glowing blood.
All faded to black.
Lightning flashed in the distance.
Rain spattered her face,
Wet, heavy rain,
Passing through her skin,
Damp as fallen tears,
Dripping to the ground below,
Frigid,
Turning icy white.
Snow blew off the mountaintop.

Susan shuddered in the sudden cold. She stood knee-deep in snow, beneath the shadow of an enormous white-capped craggy peak. Gusts swept past, carrying thousands of tiny white crystals in their wake. Snow fell in constant sheets from the gray skies above.

Three hunched figures in layers of thick wool cloaks struggled against the glacial wind. One waved them to a stop, pulling out a rolled paper.

"It should be here." The man's voice caught in the breeze. The words weren't English, or any language Susan knew, however she somehow understood their meaning. He gestured to the paper, a map.

"I can't see anything in the blizzard."

"It's now or never, Masrun."

The man with the map nodded, shuddering against the icy wind. He tossed the paper into the snow, and gestured the others over. One by one the men stooped down, brushing aside the snowdrifts, digging.

*Masrun?*

Susan's mind raced. She knew the name, yet couldn't place it. The entire scene was somehow familiar, like déjà vu.

One of the cloaked men pulled a small wooden box from the snow. "It's here. The map was right."

Masrun took the box, opened it, and pulled out a golden bracelet with an emerald hourglass.

*Grym.*

The snow thickened, falling heavier and heavier,
The scene dissolved behind clouds of frigid white,
White faded to gray,

Clouds separated into tumbled masses.
Sunlight spilled down,
Obfuscated by pillars of smoke.

"Look out!" A group of Deaths crouched to the ground, hiding in a rocky crevice of the College. One of the towers stood nearby; dark copper veins webbed its surface. The entire area looked different, less weathered somehow. Plumes of thick, black smoke wafted up in gnarled columns beside the tower.

A bolt of flame shot downward. One of the Deaths vanished, and the others threw themselves out of the fire's path. Steam drifted off the scorch mark left on the canyon walls. A pair of shadows swept past, and Susan turned her gaze skyward.

Two Dragons roared. One, with glittering silver scales catapulted another bolt of flame into the College. The other, a crimson and violet Dragon, headed for the tower. With a shout, a volley of iron arrows flew into the sky. Most bounced off the Dragons, yet one sank between the silver Dragon's tail scales. The creature bellowed, turning mid-air, and sprayed a furious jet of flames in the direction the arrows launched from.

"General Masrun, are you all right?" One of the Deaths near Susan crouched beside a man lying on his side. Without the blowing snow, she was surprised at how young the general was. His face looked eighteen, with the hints of a beard only just starting to emerge on his teenage face. His arm jutted from his body at an unnatural angle. Around his wrist, the gold bracelet with emerald hourglass glinted in the sun.

"My arm's broken." He groaned, a trickle of blood appearing on his lips. "Lovethar, you have to take Grym. It might be our greatest hope in this war."

Lovethar nodded, her wild black hair blowing in the wind.

*Lovethar. The first female Death. She looks no older than him, maybe eighteen or nineteen.*

Susan tried to touch her ancient ancestor, however her fingers slipped through Lovethar's shoulder.

Pulling Grym off Masrun's wrist, the first female Death snapped the bracelet onto herself. She closed her eyes, breathing deep.

"We have to keep moving!" One of the Deaths in front of them gestured to the sky. Three more Dragons, each bone white, circled toward them.

"One of you stay with Masrun. Don't let him die." Lovethar stood, holding the braceleted wrist out. A sapphire glow emerged from her arm, taking the shape of an enormous translucent scythe blade. "We're going to finish this."

"The Eye of Donkar?" asked one of the Deaths. "Is it even ready?"

"We have to try." Lovethar smiled. "If I ignite the Eye, we might stand a chance."

"You can barely use that thing," yelled another Death. "Besides, we don't even know what the Eye will do."

Lovethar shook her head. "It's our only hope. Cover me."

Susan stood rooted to the ground. She watched her ancestor of thousands of generations past sprint away, leading other Deaths.

*I wondered if she was a proto-human, a Neanderthal or something. She wasn't very different from me.*

Shadows blotted the sun. The white Dragons growled, flying close enough to smell their sulfuric breath.

The ground beneath opened up.

Susan fell into a crevice,

The world vanished behind

A gash in the universe:

A rainbow-laced tear,

Shed by an uncaring world.

Prisms danced around its elastic surface.

An ocean of anguished faceless souls pressed against its edges,

Reaching outward,

Grasping,

Clawing.

Susan floated outside the salty tear,

Looking in,

Watching.

Slivers of white-hot light,

Searing the sky,

Burning.

Susan stood beside a roaring bonfire.

The nearby glimmering waters of Silver Lake and distant shadows of West and East Towers on the horizon revealed her location. She stood atop Widow's Peak.

Lovethar screamed.

A crowd of Deaths surrounded her, watching Lovethar burn. In her arms, she clutched a bundle: her son Gesayn. Flames licked the bottoms of Lovethar's legs, and she screamed again.

"You betrayed us." Masrun stood before her with a stony expression. "Hiding Grym is cause alone to execute you. Taking a 'Mental lover made the situation worse."

"Please, Masrun. I know how you feel about me, but be reasonable!" Lovethar struggled against the ropes. "The Eye of Donkar failed. I couldn't ignite it. The 'Mentals were under attack. What choice did I have? I used Grym's power to save them, not to betray anyone."

Susan watched, absorbed with the scene. The sense of déjà vu swept through her again. She *remembered* this.

A wild-eyed man ran into the crowd. His reptilian eyes glowed with fury.

"You have no business here, Orryn." Masrun gestured and two of the Deaths lowered scythes, holding the blades toward him.

Orryn didn't respond in words. He opened his mouth, and a piercing screech rang out. The Deaths covered their ears, one even dropped his scythe. Susan placed ethereal hands on her ears, yet it didn't stop the noise.

The water of Silver Lake frothed and foamed. Four massive forms emerged: waterspouts with the heads of serpents. The fluid snakes raced toward the tiny hill of Widow's Peak. The bodies of the creatures spun in twisters of whirling water. One serpent smashed into the bonfire, dousing it into steam. One by one, the other snakes attacked the Deaths. Each whirlwind of water opened its fangs, diving and plunging. Two of the Deaths vanished. Masrun ran down the opposite hillside, fleeing in terror. Gesayn, the infant, wailed and cried.

Orryn waved his arms and the tornados of serpentine water broke apart, splashing to the ground like rain. Lovethar clung to Gesayn, panting hard.

"Are you hurt?" Orryn pulled off the ropes around his wife.

Gesayn thrashed against his mother's arms. One of his hands was missing.

"We'll be fine."

"We lost, Lovethar." Tears welled in Orryn's eyes. "They stole Gesayn's hand, and created a Dragon Key. The Deaths turned their backs on you for saving me. Everybody won, except for us."

"You're wrong. We have each other, and that's all that matters."

A wind picked up, howling from the East. Lovethar and Orryn stared at each other.

The wind blew their faces away, leaving only faceless bodies.

The wind continued to strengthen, blowing colors like spray paint.

The world emptied, leaving Susan alone on Widow's Peak.

A man appeared before her, with short black hair, and a suit of rainbow scales. His green eyes burned like fierce emeralds. *Grym*.

"They should have died." Caladbolg shook his head, waving to the charred timbers. "If Lovethar perished that day, you and I would have never met; the Donkari and Deaths would never face extinction; the entire world would be safe and unchanged."

"I can't change the past." Susan put her hands on her hips. "I'm proud of my ancestors. I'm proud of what Orryn did to save his family."

Grym laughed. "That's the absurd thing. He *didn't* save anyone. He *prolonged* their suffering. Lovethar, Orryn, Gesayn, even the other Deaths you saw, they're all dead."

"They passed naturally."

"What difference does that make? The result is the same. Everything dies, Susan."

The world blurred, colors converged and parted.

Dust turned to stars,

Stars fell into dust again.

Faces spun past,

Forms pointing in anger,

Bodies wearing Grym's face.

Susan staggered as ground appeared. She stood beside Will in the Hollywood makeup room. Two women lay on the ground before her, each bearing a massive wound. Blood covered the eviscerated bodies. The scene was frozen in time, like a three-dimensional photograph.

*What were their names? God, why can't I remember?*

"You killed them." Grym strolled forward, staring with his fire-green eyes.

"You did this, not me."

"Me, you. It doesn't even matter. They're dead. If they hadn't died here they would've died a few years later. *Everything dies, Susan.* Your body itself is formed from the ashes of a dead star. The planet you walk on is littered with decaying and decomposed corpses. You eat dead beings every day to prolong your existence, until you die as well. You call yourselves Deaths because you've forgotten who you used to be. *Donkari* translates to *life.*" His lips parted into a wide grin. "Ironic, isn't it? Yet in the end, even they embraced what all things are: mortal."

"What's your point?"

"Susan, it's time for you to embrace the same fate. This is your death."

Grym vanished, and the two corpses sat up, still dripping blood and intestine. Their eyes popped open.

"Time to die," they said in unison.

Will unfroze, turning to her. "Don't listen, Susan. You have to fight it."

"What's happening to me?"

"You have to survive." Will's face melted away, yet his words remained. "Survive."

"Will! Help me!"

She screamed into nothingness.

The make-up studio spun into a whirlwind.

An explosion of color and sound,

From darkness to light,

Susan's life flashed before her eyes.

She was born,

She learned to talk,

to walk,

Making friends,

Mistakes,

Leaps,

Bounds,
Joys,
Sorrows,
One by one
every event spun by.
Cronk appeared,
She became a Death,
failing the Final Test,
and discovered Grym
in the Library.
Susan sat in Sindril's prison,
trapped in the Dragonspine Mountains,
a forced wedding,
surrounded by fangs,
She fell from her captor's claws,
She plummeted,
Diving deeper,
Through the fiery Swarm.
Living in isolation,
Alone.
The dim outlines of a cube-shaped room emerged.
She stood on a transparent piece of glass, one side of a glass cube.
Beyond each wall, a void stretched to infinite depths.
A mirror appeared.
Susan stared at herself.
*Who am I?*
She stepped forward, touching her fingers to the glass.
*Is this the end?*
A tear welled in her eye, threatening to fall,
Threatening to shatter the world.
*I am alive.*

"All things die, Susan." Grym stood behind her, his hand around her waist. Pulling aside Susan's hair, he kissed her neck. "Even if you ignite the Eye of Donkar, defeat the Dragons, and save your family, you would still die at some point. Why prolong your fate? Embrace your oblivion."

The tear fell.

Down and down it plunged,
Rainbows wrapped around the salty tear.
It grew, filled with faceless forms,
And she dove inside.
Splashing into the sea of bodies.
Faces whizzed by her,
Faces of friends and strangers,
Every soul had a name.
One by one they spoke,
Each person uttered a single word.
The words flew by so fast,
Susan barely registered them.
One after another, a face appeared,
With each face, one word:
*Susan.*
*Elizabeth.*
*Sarnio.*
*Born.*
*Died.*
She struggled to the top of the bodies, pushing them out of the way.
*This isn't the end for me.*
Grym stood atop the writhing sea of faceless corpses. "It's pointless."
He spread his hands and shrugged. "Just give in."
*No.*
Limbs clawed at her, tugging her down. Fingers and arms scratched
at her legs.
She kicked.
*No!*
"Why fight your fate, Susan?"
"This isn't my time."
"*Time?*" Grym laughed. "What do you know of time? I languished
in darkness for a thousand millennia. A million years trapped behind a
wall. I want nothing save oblivion, and you alone can grant that wish.
*Time* is my enemy. Time is something I want no more of."
The bodies pulled harder. Susan sank to her neckline.
*I have a choice.*

The images around her paused, sensing something within.

*I have a choice.*

With her mind alone, she pushed the bodies away, rising to the top.

*I have a choice!*

She stood atop the sea of forms.

"You think this is up to you?" Grym's eyes widened, and the countless bodies erupted into green flame. The inferno spread around her, until the enormous tear filled with ashes.

Susan smiled. "I'm sure you'll die someday, Grym, but not today."

She stood atop the expanse of barren ash and spread her arms wide. "This is not my time. I have a choice."

Caladbolg turned around, his eyes wide with confusion. "You shall die, Susan. Everything, every plant, animal, every soul ends. You will turn to dust, and your ashes will lie forgotten in the void."

She laughed.

"Have you gone mad, girl?"

"You're pathetic, Grym. You're so desperate to die that you've forgotten how to live. I know you're alone and are tired of darkness. I know this isn't the life you wanted. You think I expected to be a Death? Few get what they plan, yet that's no reason to give up. I may be a Death, yet I am *alive!* This is not my time."

While she spoke, the rainbows webbed around the tear started to glow. Grym's feet sank into the ash.

"You are a child. This will not stop me." Caladbolg leaped out of the ash, his arm morphing into an enormous sapphire scythe, formed from pure light. He slammed the blade into Susan. She didn't flinch. The blade shattered, and shards of luminous blue fell atop the sea of ash.

"You can't hurt me." Susan smiled again. "Don't you understand? I see life for what it is: a gift. It doesn't matter if it's finite, that just makes life more precious. I *cherish* every moment. Every sunrise, every breath, every heartbeat. I shall fight to live until my last dying breath." She stepped forward, and Grym fell into the ash. "I know this isn't my time because you've told me to lay down and do nothing, to accept my mortality and cease living. I won't do that. I will *never* do that. If you want to give up, fine. I am alive. I choose to *live!*"

The glowing sapphire shards melted with each of her words. They shifted and blurred, becoming tiny incandescent butterflies. Each sapphire butterfly swarmed around Caladbolg. He tried to bat them away, however they surrounded him, pulling him to his feet in a cloud of fluttering blue light.

Grym's tone changed, and his voice softened. "What do you have that's worth so much?"

"I have hope. I have faith that the world is a good place, and that life is filled with beauty. I have joy and love with my friends. What more do I need?"

He shook his head and the butterflies vanished. "I don't know anymore."

"You once showed me a vision of your creation through Dragonsong. You were the very essence of love and beauty. Bear with me a little while longer, Grym. Let's change the world together. Let's show everyone that life's worth living."

Grym smiled. Beneath their feet, grass started to climb up through the ashes. "Death isn't the end, anyway. Deaths leads to new life. I don't know if life's as precious as you claim, however you've impressed me. You've won, for now."

"All I've done is remember who I am. You helped remind me." She paused, staring at the strange sea of ashes. Weeds and wildflowers blanketed the gray dust, stretching to the droplet's edge. "These visions, these sights, was any of it real?"

"Yes. All of it was real, Susan. There are powers greater than you or I. Powers of life and death, powers of fate and choice. You've helped shape your fate today."

"What happens next?"

"That is up to you."

\* \* \* \*

Susan opened her eyes.

Timbers stretched beneath a thatched roof above. Will sat beside her, his head resting on his chest, asleep. Sunlight slipped between two emerald curtains. The smell of strawberries was thick in the air.

Will stirred, blinking and yawning. "Susan?"

She nodded.

"Are you? My God, you're…I didn't know if you'd—"

"I'm here." She smiled, and he threw his arms around her, knocking her back to the bed. The dampness of his falling tears wet her neck.

"Susan!" Frank entered the room, a huge toothy smile stretched across his face. "I knew you'd pull through. Father! Michi! She's awake."

Her friends surrounded her, grinning and speaking words of praise. Each spoke at once, and the jumble of well-wishes became a chorus of jubilation. Susan's eyes filled with tears. She tried to speak, yet the words jammed in her throat.

Everyone hugged and smiled, laughed and cried. The world made sense again, and her friends reveled around her. Susan just smiled, letting the flow of relief and joy wash over her.

Giri waved the others quiet. "How do you feel?"

"Alive. I feel alive."

"You've straddled life and death, trapped in a coma for two weeks."

"Two weeks? Was it really so long? I remember a strange creature like a tiger. After that, I walked through the Door to the Hereafter. The rest…the rest was like a dream. At one point I was here, watching you all."

"What do you mean, watching?" Frank frowned.

"I was like a ghost. I saw so many things. *If* they were real." She put her hand to her head.

"Take your time." Giri patted her shoulder. "Just relax."

She stared at her wrist. Thin gossamer webbing still covered Grym's mark. "It's still here." She closed her eyes, however couldn't sense Caladbolg's presence. "He's still buried within me. I thought it might be different."

"Wherever you went, you saw the First Scythe, didn't you?" Giri's fiery green eyes flashed.

"We fought. I can't put it in proper words. He wanted me to die, yet I refused. What happened?"

Frank stepped forward. "My father thinks that it's because of the curse, when Sindril attacked the boat. Your body aged, however your soul didn't. With Caladbolg's ancient soul buried within yours, you've started to leech from each other. You encountered a creature we thought was extinct—"

"The gheiraq." Susan nodded. "It's coming back to me now."

"Elementals lose a sliver of soul every time they use their power." Michi wrapped her arm around Frank's waist. "In the past, some 'Mentals went mad, losing too much soul. They started killing other 'Mentals, feeding off others' power, always craving more."

"We banished the gheiraqs generations ago," Giri's voice lowered, and he shook his head. "Many were hunted off and killed. I'm not proud of that fact. Still, it allowed our race to survive. You inadvertently discovered one of the sole gheiraqs left."

"It was alone, unique in the world, and I murdered it." Susan's eyes fell to her hands.

"It was trying to kill us," added Will. "Besides, you weren't yourself. Even your voice sounded different."

"Grym."

Giri nodded. "Yes. The attack occurred at an opportune moment. Grym leeched strength from you, while you leeched age from him. Together, your body acted in self-defense, yet the effort threw you into the void."

"I thought you might die." Will leaned back, sitting on the bed beside her. He took her hand in his.

"Will carried you through the woods." Michi caught her eyes. "He was injured, and yet managed to shoulder your unconscious body for miles."

"Thank you, Will."

He blushed. "You'd have done the same for me. You'd just saved us from the gheiraq after all."

"Frank and Michi used the Swarm to bring you here to Karis." Giri turned, looking out the window. "Few know you are here. I'd like to keep it that way. I've treated you with Frank and Michi's help. The three of us have channeled power to your stomach, since you couldn't eat. Will's given you water. He hasn't left your side since arriving."

"Again, thank you. Thank you all, for taking care of me."

Giri smiled. "Our job was easy. You, on the other hand, survived an impossible journey. You battled death and returned. Rest for the next few days. Michi, Frank, come with me. Let's get her some food."

The three 'Mentals left, and Susan sat up. Her legs and arms trembled.

"You heard him, just take it easy."

"Will, you didn't have to—"

"Of course I did."

They gazed into each others' eyes with no words. There was so much more she wanted to say. Words weren't enough. The flutter in her heart didn't do the emotion justice.

*I love him.*

"Will, I saw so much. Grym claimed it was all real. I don't know how it could be."

"We don't know what happens to souls when we Reap them. Maybe your soul was detached, at least for a time. I'm just glad it came back."

She turned away, and looked at the covers. "I saw my parents. That was the worst part. They haven't forgotten me. Mom, Dad, and Joe went to a candlelight vigil on my birthday. They think I'm just missing somewhere."

"The Swarm showed me my mother lighting a candle. I thought she didn't care about me, but I was wrong."

"I'd stopped missing them, Will. I didn't even remember Maryland anymore. Now, I'm ashamed that I forgot my family. They never gave up on me."

"There's nothing we can do. We're Deaths now."

"Death." Susan shook her head. "That's all Grym wants: his own oblivion. He lived in isolation for a million years. It drove him insane."

"I'm glad you didn't give in."

"Even when he was telling me to die, another voice kept calling for me to live. It was your voice."

They paused, staring deep into each others' eyes. Will leaned forward and kissed her. With parted lips, his soft tongue entered her mouth.

"Sorry to intrude," said Michi. "I have food."

Will broke away, blushing.

Michi laid a wooden platter on Susan's lap. An assortment of fruit and small cakes surrounded a cup of steaming tea.

"Thanks, Michi."

"You need to eat."

Susan took a bite of one of the cakes, letting the taste of lemon and sugar dissolve across her taste buds. Her stomach growled, calling for more. She started stuffing mouthfuls down, followed by fruit and tea. Michi smiled, rising to get more.

"Let me digest a little first. I haven't eaten in a long time, I need to make sure I keep it down."

Frank and Giri opened the bedroom door.

"Thank you for the food, and for taking care of me." She smiled.

"Take as long as you need to recover." Giri gestured to the window. "The town doesn't know you're here, yet even if they did, they'd do anything to protect you. We think of you as one of our own, Susan."

She nodded, leaning back onto the bed. "You've all been so kind." She paused, closing her eyes. An image crept into the back of her mind, and she bolted up again. "The Swarm. Can we contact them?"

"Of course." Frank frowned. "What is it?"

"One of the things I saw. Hann's been arrested. There's no one protecting the College."

"We'll ask them for you." Will patted her hands. "Rest, Susan. When you're strong enough, we need to decide what to do next."

"What do you mean?"

"Will wants to return to Reaper Ridge." Michi glanced at Frank before continuing. "Frank and I think it might be better to head to the College."

"We can't risk Susan's recapture."

"We can't sit idling as our world falls," snapped Frank in retort.

"Not now." Giri's flaming green eyes blazed. "Let Susan rest. There's plenty of time to discuss this. She just woke up, and has endured a trial greater than any mortal should ever have to face. Give her time." He waved the others out of the room.

Will lingered at the doorway. "Call out if you need anything."

She nodded, and he left. Giri remained behind, closing the door.

He turned, lowering his voice. "I don't think you should stay."

"You're worried about the village. My presence puts you at risk."

"Take the time you need to recuperate. However, plan your next move with care. Sindril and the Dragons waited a year. I hoped they were regrouping. When Will brought you, I started to reconsider."

"You think they knew this would happen?"

"I don't know, Susan. I can't answer for certain. However, what are they waiting for? Why haven't they stormed the College? Whatever seal they placed over Grym still seems intact, even after you two battled in the void. If this was part of their plan—"

"I've placed the village in grave danger."

Giri nodded. "Take your time, heal, and make a choice." He left Susan alone, closing the door behind.

She sighed, rolling onto one side.

\* \* \* \*

She awoke from a dreamless sleep, the most restful slumber she'd had in two years. As her eyes fluttered open, she relished the tranquility.

*I didn't dream of Grym, or Deaths. I didn't re-live terrors, or watch through other's eyes.*

Faint gossamer webbing still sheathed her right forearm, yet Susan felt alone.

*So glad to be alone.*

Pulling off the cover, she swung her legs over the bedside. At first, her muscles wavered, and she wasn't sure if she'd be able to stand. She took a deep breath, and forced herself up. She stood in the dark bedroom, breathing in the strawberry 'Mental scent.

She wore only a long, white nightgown of sheer silk, with embroidered lace sleeves. The garment was finer than anything she'd worn before. It hung loose around her slender frame, draping low from the neckline. *It must have been Kasumir's.*

Her bare toes wiggled on the cool slate floor. She walked to the lavender curtains, parting them and peeking outside. Starlight twinkled in the serene night sky above. A sickle-scythe moon gleamed dull silver. The shadow of a large willow tree bent and swayed in the breeze, its gentle branches dancing to and fro. A tiny light emerged and vanished, and then another. Dozens of fireflies flew across the willow's silhouette, appearing in bright flashes, streaking for a moment, before vanishing again. Behind the tree, flower lights dimmed in several windows. Karis slept.

She heard the door behind her creak, and Susan spun, startled.

"You're up," whispered Will. "I'm sorry, I was just coming to check on you before I went to bed."

"Stay. Close the door." She released the curtains. At her movement, a jar of flower lights on a table started to glow. She sat on the bed, motioning Will to sit beside her.

"Are you feeling better?"

"Yes. Thanks for checking."

She stared into his eyes. His pupils gleamed with dim flower light. "I was so scared, Susan. I'm glad you're—"

She cut off his final word by leaning in and kissing him deeply. Her hands wrapped around his shoulders. He sank into the kiss, pulling his fingers through her hair.

Her heart quickened with the taste of his tongue, the gentleness of his grasp. She broke the kiss.

"I love you."

"And I, you."

"Will, I've journeyed through life and death. It's you who brought me back."

"You brought yourself back, and I'm glad you did."

She smiled. "I can't imagine carrying anyone through mud, especially while hurt."

"There's nothing I wouldn't do for you, Susan."

They kissed again, even deeper than before.

Her whole body cried out, yearning for his touch. She needed this, needed *him*.

Her hands traced the outlines of his shoulders, his back. Her tongue traced the contours of his mouth. She broke the kiss, and stood. Pulling the nightgown over her head, she lay naked beside him in the bed.

\* \* \* \*

"We've tarried too long." Frank pounded his fist into the table. "We should leave. It's been a month since Susan revived."

"We've been through this." Will pushed his bowl away. Remnants of the delicious duck and rosemary stew Giri and Hinara had prepared littered its edges. "You and Michi refuse to return to Reaper Ridge, and Susan and I won't return to the College. Nothing's happened since Hann's arrest. The Dragons are still waiting."

"They won't wait for long."

"We can split up."

"No. The four of us should stick together. We've come this far."

"Return to the cave with us. We led a good life there."

"I'm not going back to the damn cave. The College—"

Michi rose. "Susan, why don't we let the boys argue this out again."

"Same discussion they have every night. We'll be outside when you're done."

Susan nodded to Hinara, Frank's aunt. The Elemental smiled back, and resumed cleaning the pots. She and Giri had been very kind, like parents, for the past month. However, Susan knew their patience grew thin. They couldn't stay much longer, and Will and Frank faced an impasse.

Bala sat in the front room, looking bored.

"We're taking a walk." Michi gestured.

The young boy with purple hair and bright violet eyes nodded. He rarely spoke to them. His sad eyes fell on Susan's, and a lump welled in her throat.

*Anil and Ilma.*

She'd scarcely known the two Elementals. Three years ago, they first guided her back to the College after her initial trip to Karis. The pair was instrumental in the 'Mental revolt from the College. The following year, they'd masked their ship on the journey to Donkar. Anil and Ilma always worked as a pair, manipulating light and wind to create invisibility. With all her discussions atop the crow's nests, spanning a full month, she'd learned so little about them. She didn't even know the twins had a younger brother.

The memories surfaced every time she saw Bala.

*Sarmarin flew toward the ship and released a blast of flame. Even from his talons, she felt a wave of heat. Fire rocketed toward their ship, engulfing it in an inferno.*

*Anil and Ilma. No!*

*The ship burned in the icy sea. Susan raised her head, and saw Will, unconscious in the white Dragon's claws.*

Giri and Hinara took Bala in after that, nurturing and caring for the ten-year-old. Frank claimed his presence helped ease all of their wounds. Bala had lost his parents. Giri and Hinara had lost Kasumir. Aside from Giri and Hinara, he was the only 'Mental in Karis who knew of Susan's arrival.

Forcing her mind back to the present, she gagged. The ever-present smell of strawberries disgusted her. The awful stench filled her nose, making her dizzy. She'd never disliked the smell before, yet something was off now. She coughed, waving her hand in front of her face.

"Susan, are you all right?"

"Just need some fresh air."

Michi nodded and Bala stood. Without a word, the young 'Mental moved his hands in a circular pattern. The air around the room shimmered, glistening like sunlight off a lake. Knowing the three of them would now be invisible, Michi led Susan and Bala outside.

They walked in silence, careful to use the balls of their feet, and avoided other 'Mentals. A path cut through the woods near Giri's house, leading straight to the open forest behind the village.

Susan gagged again. The awful stench of rotten strawberries.

Michi paused, touching her arm. Her eyes probed Susan's, and her lips mouthed the word: *what?* Susan waved her away, and they continued walking until the houses disappeared from sight.

Sitting on a mushroom-covered log, Susan vomited.

"Are you ill?" Michi sat beside her, placing a hand on Susan's back. "Should we go back?"

"You stink. You all do. The smell is sickening."

"What are you talking about?"

"It's never bothered me before, but now…" She held her head in her hands, trying to stop the world from spinning.

"We shouldn't have come out here if you're sick. Do you want to head back, or should I leave you here with Bala and get the others?"

"I'm sorry, Michi. I'm fine. Just a sudden wave of nausea."

They sat together in silence for a moment, and the queasiness subsided. Crickets chirped behind her, and a gentle breeze rustled the canopy above. Sun filtered through the leaves, dropping to pine needles and grass at the forest's feet. Bala leaned against a tree, looking bored again. He continued to move his arms, and the air still glittered.

Michi reached behind the log and picked up a small black and yellow beetle. The insect crawled up the 'Mentals' arm. "I'm worried about Frank." She took the beetle and moved it to her other hand, before letting it walk back to the log.

"Why?"

"I'm not a seer or anything, however I can sense something growing in him."

"You said after the soul snatcher, he grew a new power. It's probably his natural way of rebuilding himself."

"I hope that's all there is to it."

"You think the boys will come to an agreement?"

"I think we'll head back to Reaper Ridge. Will's right, we have to keep you safe."

Susan nodded. "I hate this. I want to be a part of the battle, not keep hiding from it."

"There's no battle yet, and if we're lucky we'll avoid one. You feeling better now?"

"Yeah."

"Frank and I used to play here as kids." She grinned, eyeing a mass of tangled roots beneath a series of twisted, overgrown trees. "Once I freaked him out by sending a full colony of ants up one of his legs."

"Is that how 'Mentals flirt?"

"Sometimes. It was also a goodbye. Plamen meant a lot to me." She turned back to Susan, running her fingers idly over the rough, mushroom-laden log. "Back before anyone called him Frank, he volunteered to work in the In-Between with Athanasius. I suspect he'd already planned to fight for 'Mental rights. He envied my power. His started late." She sighed. "I wish he'd tell me whatever's going on within him now."

"He'll be okay, Michi."

Bala yawned.

Michi glanced at the boy, and leaned back, raising her eyebrows. "Enough about me, how are you and Will?"

"Good. Really good."

"That's *all* you want to say? Come on, Susan, it's just us girls."

"And Bala."

"What?" The young 'Mental looked up, however Michi waved her hand and he leaned against the tree again, ignoring them.

"He's not listening. You and Will have been spending a number of nights together."

"And you haven't spent any with Frank?"

Michi's eyes glinted with amusement, and her lips parted, revealing a slight smile. "At least I'm not expecting."

"Expecting what?"

"Susan, sometimes you forget my insects. Your scent has changed *drastically* the last couple of weeks. At first I wasn't sure, so this morning I asked Giri to sense your soul. There's no question. I've been waiting to tell you."

"Tell me what?"

Michi shook her head. "You honestly don't know? What is it human girls have? A period? Isn't yours late?"

Susan felt the blood rush to her cheeks. "You're not saying—"

"You're pregnant."

Bala's hands stopped moving and he walked over. "Is it true?"

A large bush behind their log moved, its leaves pulling up and away from them.

"Hide us," demanded Michi. Bala circled his arms, and the air shimmered again.

The foliage receded further, drawing into a human shape. A familiar green face emerged from the leaves. "It's me," said Lucina, the foliate Elemental who'd first shown Susan the way to Karis. "I overhead everything." Leaves and branches withdrew inside her naked green body. "I'm so happy for you."

"No one can know we're here." Michi glared, her face stern. "It's imperative you don't tell anyone what you learned today, *especially* about her condition."

Susan's mind spun. *Pregnant?* She'd been feeling ill, and it wasn't entirely unexpected. Yet, the news still filled her with dread.

*My child is a potential Dragon Key.*

*The one thing they want.*

*What have we done?*

*Pregnant.*

"My lips are sealed." Tiny branches emerged from Lucina's face, forming an X across her mouth. "She has done so much for this village, and for Elementals as a race."

"You never saw us." Michi rose from the log, backing up. Bala's arms spun in wider circles. Susan stood.

"I never saw anyone." Lucina sank back into the ground, vanishing into shrubs and bushes.

"We should go." Michi glanced around.

"Are you sure?"

"I don't want to stay here a moment longer, we have to be even more careful—"

"That's not what I meant. Are you *sure*?"

Michi touched her arm, her face serene. "Yes. It's definitely true, and this is a *good* thing. You weren't forced into this, you *chose* to act."

"But it's what *they* wanted."

"Not quite. You were prophesized to give birth. They wanted to manipulate the circumstances. You've taken control away from Sindril. I repeat, *this is a good thing.*"

Susan frowned, a whirlwind of emotions playing through her mind. "Let's go back. I need to talk to Will."

\* \* \* \*

Will squeezed her hand. His excitement didn't surprise her, and continued to grow every day. She tried to share his exuberance, yet couldn't ignore the knot of fear resting at the base of her throat.

The stench of strawberries was unbearable, and never abated. She'd screamed at Frank yesterday morning for smelling up the room.

Giri sat at the foot of the bed, his fingers arrayed in a strange formation, and his eyes tightly closed. "I think it's growing faster than normal." He opened his eyes, breathing deep. "I've never seen a human pregnancy, so it's hard to be certain. The growing soul within you now draws energy both from your bond with Grym, and the traces of your 'Mental ancestry. You hold three separate souls in your body. This state affects all of you, I'm sure." He stood, his lip twitching. "I wish I could do more."

"Thank you, Giri." Will smiled as the Elemental left, closing the door.

"You heard him." Susan frowned. "The baby's not coming naturally, she's drawing power from Grym. What if she turns out to be some sort of twisted killer?"

"What makes you think we'll have a girl?"

"Are we doing the right thing, Will? We've created a Dragon Key."

"We don't know what the child will become. We're having a child of love, not of hate. Could our son become a Dragon Key? I don't know, but I don't regret our choice at all. We knew the risks when we slept together." He gazed into her eyes, placing one hand on her tummy. "I love you, Susan."

"I love you, too."

He winced, pulling away.

"What is it?" she asked.

"A sudden pain." He touched his shoulder. "It's gone now. For a moment, the old vika wound flared up."

"Don't talk to me about pain. My whole body hurts, and I'm exhausted. This isn't fun."

He grinned, pulling her into an embrace.

"Don't hug me. This is your fault."

"You didn't help at all?"

She laughed, hitting him with a pillow. "Nope, it was all your idea."

"That's not how I remember it."

He grabbed a pillow, tossing it at her.

"Hey, you're attacking a pregnant woman."

"Well you started it." They laughed until tears fell from their eyes.

The door flew open and Frank appeared, his eyes wide. "We're under attack. Grab what you need, we're leaving."

"What?"

"You heard me."

The house trembled and a thunder-like roar exploded outside. Susan and Will jumped out of the bed. She started packing clothes into a bag, until Frank grabbed her arm.

"We need to leave *now*. Take essentials only."

"You have the scythe?" asked Will.

"Michi does. I have the boskery blade."

The window shattered, and Susan dove onto the bed, covering her face. Shards of glass shot across the room. Billows of smoke poured in.

"Susan, Will," said a voice behind them. She turned and saw Samas perched on the windowsill, his tiny golden tail flicking back and forth. "White Claw's here. We'll hold them off, but you must flee."

"How did you find us?" demanded Will. "How did any of the Dragons find us?"

"I followed the attack. We have spies in high places. How they knew, I do not know. This place isn't safe."

"Come on." Frank waved, running out of the room.

Susan shoved some more clothes into the bag and ran into the kitchen behind the others. Michi stood with the scythe. Giri and Hinara watched the windows.

A winged shadow sped by. The kitchen window erupted into a cloud of glass and smoke. A Dragon screamed outside.

Samas flew into the room. "Use the Swarm!" He bat his small, gilded wings. "Flee!"

The house shook violently.

"The ceiling's coming down." Will grabbed Susan and pulled her, diving onto the cobbled stones outside. Giri's house collapsed into a cloud of swirling dust.

Susan spun, looking back. "No, we have to help them."

An enormous lavender colored Dragon with silver spikes bellowed atop the pile of debris. It screamed, piercing the air. Yellow-tinged smoke wafted from its nostrils. Rearing its monstrous head around, the beast bared rows of razor-sharp fangs, each over two feet long.

A whistling noise sounded behind them, and Susan turned again. Tiny blue stripes emerged in thin air. Ribbons of azure light coalesced, becoming solid. The light vanished, and Hinara stood with her arms outstretched. Giri, Frank, and Michi gasped for air beside her.

Hinara touched her heart. "Thank God, you're okay. I didn't know where you were."

The Dragon bellowed again.

"Move!" Will grabbed her hand, pulling her away. An enormous claw dove into the ground, sending a geyser of stone and dirt into the air. The Dragon scraped the spot they'd been sitting in only moments before. Glistening purple scales covered a leg fifteen feet wide, ending in foot-long silver talons.

Will and Susan ducked behind another house. She gagged in the thick stench of sulfur and blood. Frank and the others vanished from sight. A river of white flame jetted overhead. With a crash, walls around them dropped bricks and timber onto the road.

A glimmer of tiny gold wriggled out of the debris. "Hurry." Samas beckoned with his head.

Rounding a bend, they watched the lavender Dragon raze two more houses with its tail. Spewing a fountain of fire, the beast set four roofs aflame. The entire village swam in chaos. Plumes of smoke billowed from Dragon fire, and building after building collapsed.

An Elemental ran up behind them, waving his arms. A column of stone vaulted skywards, piercing the lavender Dragon's neck. A second 'Mental joined the fight, sending a geyser of water into its face. The beast spat, hissing, and reared back. It spread its enormous wings, and took off.

A green Dragon dropped from the sky, landing on the lavender Dragon's back.

"Brandr!" shouted Will.

The two Dragons wrestled, demolishing house after house. The purple beast was more than twice Brandr's size, yet the smaller Dragon continued to pin its rival down.

Four white Dragons sped into sight, chased by three crimson Dragons.

A bank of stones, each pointed like massive spears, rocketed out of Karis, changing direction mid-air, and plunging into the red Dragons. Two of the stones bounced off. Others sank beneath scales. One Dragon plummeted, throwing arcs of angry flame in all directions.

Dragons and 'Mentals battled. Boulders flew through the air, water and fire clashed, and Karis vanished into dust and smoke.

"Come on, stop gawking." Samas flew to her shoulder, digging his talons into her skin. He waved his head at a burning wall. "Go. The Swarm will do the rest."

Frank ran up, his face covered in soot and sweat. He grabbed the tiny Dragon by the neck. "You creatures destroyed my home."

"We're here to help."

"We don't want your help."

"Frank, what are you—" She broke off as he threw the golden Dragon at the burning building.

He nodded to Michi. They grabbed Will and Susan's hands.

"I'm sorry," muttered the Elemental. "I don't trust the Swarm." He took the scythe, and swung.

Colors blurred and smells catapulted by.

Susan's soul tore into three. She sensed Grym, ripping free from her arm, and the child screaming in her womb.

Light, sound, smell, taste, and the constant flow of her own tears all blurred into a single whirlpool.

The world tore open, and Susan followed the others through the gash in space.

Down, down they tumbled.

Light streamed by in rapid daze.

Frank's grip tightened around her wrist, however she still felt like she'd break away.

Falling.

She opened her eyes, blinking at the harsh sunlight.

There were two suns.

One star resembled the sun she'd grown up with, the sun of the mortal world and the World of Deaths. Behind it, a dimmer star, three times larger than the sun, glowered with a muted cherry light.

*The In-Between.*

An unbearable pain swelled from her belly.

She doubled over in agony.

Will knelt beside her, his fingers tense, yet tender. "Frank, what have you done?"

## CHAPTER TWENTY-FIVE—FRANK

# Shadows

**F**rank placed the boskery blade behind his back, tying it to his shoulders.

Susan gasped, clutching her belly.

Will leaped up, grabbing Frank by the shoulders. "You fool. She's pregnant. What are you trying to do?"

"I'm all right," said Susan, breathing hard.

"I'm sorry, Susan, but it was the only way." Frank gazed across the fields of withered brown grass. Pillars of crumbling stone poked up from the barren plain. The Gatehouse rose before them, a squat three-story mass of marble and iron.

*I never thought I'd return like this.*

"What do you mean? We could've used the Swarm again. White Claw was helping. Didn't you see them attack that Dragon?"

Frank pulled Will's hand away. "We've been in hiding for over a year. The moment we learn Susan's pregnant, Karis is attacked? This isn't coincidence. I don't trust White Claw." He glanced around the barren wasteland. Besides his three friends, Frank saw no signs of life or movement. "I don't trust any of the Dragons. I took us out of the World of Deaths. They shouldn't be able to track us here. When we're secure, we'll contact my father with the Swarm, maybe Cronk too. We should be careful not to reveal our location. I think the Swarm's intentions are good, yet all Dragons breathe fire. We don't know which Dragons might be watching."

"So, what now?" Will wiped soot from his face, helping Susan stand.

"How do you feel, Susan?"

"I'll be fine. Next time, warn me before pulling me into a scythe's tear."

"I'm sorry."

Michi joined them, her knuckles pressed tight around the boskery blade's handle.

"The Gatehouse." Frank pointed. "We'll be safe for a while at least."

He started across the stony wasteland. The air was still and silent. The suns hung low in the sky, yet he knew they wouldn't move. *The sun and its frozen reflection. Trapped in this sliver of a plane between two worlds. Most who come never realize both images are the same star reflected twice: once through life, once through death.* Time still flowed in the In-Between, however nothing else moved the way it did elsewhere. *A place of calm to ride out this storm.*

The others walked behind him, their feet shuffling across the desiccated grass. Frank didn't turn. Did they trust his decision? Not that it mattered, they'd already arrived. He regretted quarrelling so often with Will. However, the Death never listened. This was in *all* of their best interests.

He touched the cool iron of the rune-covered door. Two skull doorknobs stared back.

A flood of memories welled up at the back of his mind. His decision to leave Karis and work for Athanasius, and his subsequent change of plans upon Susan's arrival. For a moment, he hesitated.

"Come on." Michi touched his back. "We've come this far."

Opening the door, he entered the shadowy hall, stepping onto the white marble floor. Flower lights glowed with a faint, half-light. Dust covered much of the abandoned hallway, and scattered weeds poked through cracks in the stone.

"What happened to this place?" Susan's whisper echoed in the hushed passage.

Their footsteps reverberated, and Frank found himself stepping lighter. "There are no new Reapings. No need for a Gatehouse."

At the end of the corridor, they entered a small chamber strewn with papers. Contracts for Deaths lay heaped on the floor, piled in clumps on the desk, and littered about the room. Cobwebs covered the large mahogany desk that once belonged to Athanasius. A scant light glowed from a few flowers poking out of one mound of tattered contracts, yet shadows blanketed the room. Out of instinct, Frank walked behind the desk, tracing a finger through the dust.

"This is where I signed my contract." Susan picked up one of the papers.

"Me too," added Will.

Frank reached for the drawers. Pulling them open one by one, he searched.

"It's also where I first met you, Frank. Do you remember?" He ignored her, probing another drawer. A thin layer of dust covered cards and quills.

"After Athanasius's death, who ran this place?" Will tapped the top of the dusty desk.

"I don't know," murmured Frank. "Aha. Here it is." He pulled a small glass jar from the back of the drawer and unscrewed the cap. A small dollop of silver liquid beaded on the jar's bottom.

"What is that?" Will raised an eyebrow.

"Strength. Athanasius's abilities allowed him to manipulate it. Taking a portion of his own stamina every day, he bottled strength. I'd hoped there might be one phial left. This is the last of Athanasius's soul. Susan, take it. For you and the child."

Susan frowned, taking the jar. "I called him friend, but to be fair, I didn't know Athanasius. He signed my contract and gave me a piece of cake, saying to eat if I felt weak. He must have put his soul into the cake." She sighed. "I ate, not knowing what I consumed." She shook her head in disbelief. "That's why I felt so upset when Sindril murdered him."

"He was a good teacher." Frank closed the drawer. "I worked here for a year. It was a quiet time, but a good one nonetheless. Use it. You need extra strength more than any of us."

Susan opened the jar, smearing the silver liquid onto her belly. "If it makes my child stronger, it can't be bad."

Frank glanced around. "Nothing else to see in this office, unless you want to search for your contracts as mementos. Let's head upstairs."

He led them back into the corridor, turning the other way. At the hall's end, they pushed open a wooden doorway, climbing a steep bank of stairs. Each step they took creaked, disturbing the calm silence. The second story of the Gatehouse was arrayed in a number of small chambers. Nondescript doors lined either side of the empty hallway. Two large chandeliers, each filled with flower lights and covered by a thick layer of cobwebs, started to glow.

"It's too quiet." Will brushed some dust off the wall.

"The first four doors on the right are supply closets. We'll find provisions: food, water, blankets, and even clothes there. The first four on the left are offices. The last door on either side is a sleeping chamber, each with its own bathroom. We should be safe here for a while."

* * * *

Frank's eyes opened from strange dreams. *Visions of Dragons. An ancient song calling.* He remembered two Dragons, one black as shadow, the other plated in rainbows and light. The Dragons danced together, their bodies spinning in a circle. Singing as one, they faded into distant memory.

Michi turned over beside him, still asleep. Shadows covered the bed, hanging over much of the room. A shaft of crimson sunlight from the never-setting twin suns slipped past the curtains, painting the ceiling red. He eased aside the blanket and stood.

Sneaking into the empty hallway, he closed the door softly behind him. Time was difficult to notice in the In-Between, yet whatever the hour, the others all slept. Treading with gentle footsteps, he walked down the hall, not giving the flower chandeliers time to brighten.

He opened a door. Inside the office, a row of tall hourglasses lined a long shelf, leading to an open window. Each held a different amount of colored sand. A small table and two chairs stood against the opposite wall. He approached the window, peering out across the endless expanse of barren grass, dotted by scattered crumbing pillars of stone.

*This was my office.*

A cough to his right startled him. It'd come from the bedroom he'd just left. Was Michi awake?

He returned, passing through the open door. In the dim light, he saw a shadow hovering over the bed, its claws poised to strike.

"Stop!"

The shadow looked up, startled. Frank ran forward, yet the beast threw itself at him. The weight knocked him down. Legs and claws flew by in a blur.

"What's happening?" Michi bolted upright in the bed, drawing the sheets close.

"Someone was here." Frank struggled to his feet, hurrying into the hallway. A cloak disappeared down the staircase. He pursued. He heard footsteps below, but couldn't see anyone.

Reaching the bottom story, Frank's heart skipped a beat. He slowed, approaching the long marble corridor.

Something leaped from a corner, knocking him to the wall. The figure clawed at him, growling. Frank collapsed, out of breath. Wild sapphire eyes emerged in front of him, centered on a snarling lupine face.

The creature's wolf-like nose and yellowing fangs contrasted his robes and human legs. His shaggy hair hung at odd angles across his shoulders, falling down his back. His hands had human fingers, yet each ended in a long claw.

"Who are you?" snarled the lupine Elemental. A single claw pressed against his neck, piercing the skin. "You've stolen from the storehouse, and sleep in my chambers. Give me a reason not to kill you, thief."

"I used to work here, with Athanasius. I didn't think the Gatehouse was manned, since Reapings have stopped."

"*My* Gatehouse." The Elemental bared his fangs, pressing his claw deeper into Frank's throat. "I don't believe you."

"It's true, let me go. We'll talk this over."

"You're Dragon spies." His sapphire eyes widened. He leaned forward, breathing next to Frank's face. Frank sensed the creature's *hunger*. This Elemental was mad, ready to devolve into a gheiraq.

The creature spun back. Hundreds of insects crawled up its skin. Centipedes, beetles, and spiders swarmed over its cloak. The lupine Elemental screamed, trying to brush the insects away. Michi hurried downstairs, holding a nightgown closed with one hand, and holding her other hand outstretched, her fingers shaking with the effort.

Frank stood. The Elemental writhed on the ground, his eyes staring in fear and confusion.

"We don't want to hurt you." Frank opened his palms. "We just need a place to hide."

"I'll never tell you anything. I'll never sell myself to the Dragons." The mad Elemental laughed, its face contorting in hysterics. "You tried before, and it didn't work. It won't work now, not with your insects or your lies. I'll never tell." He clawed his own throat, opening a gash beneath his chin.

"What are you doing?" Michi screamed, and the mass of beetles, spiders, and other bugs fell off the Elemental's body, scurrying out of sight.

Frank ran to the creature, pressing his hand against the bleeding wound, however it was too late. The strange Elemental's head lolled back.

Michi fell to her knees, breathing hard. "I didn't mean for him to die."

"The poor man was insane. He said Dragons came before. We don't know what they did to him." He let the stranger fall. Turning to Michi, he shook his head. "You saved me, Michi. He tried to kill you in your sleep, and would've killed all of us if he got the chance. He was almost a gheiraq."

"You've saved me plenty of times."

"Thanks." The two held each other's gaze. Frank wanted to embrace his oldest and closest friend, but blood covered his hand.

"Have you checked on Susan or Will? What if he went to their room before ours?" Michi breathed hard.

"You spent too much of your power. Rest. I'll check on them."

Frank touched her shoulder with his clean hand, then leaned in and pecked her cheek. He walked up the stairs, pausing to glance back at Michi.

He pounded on Susan's door.

"I'm coming."

"Are you and Susan both all right?"

"Yes, we're fine." Will opened the door, blinking and yawning. "What's going on? Are we under attack?"

"It's over now. Go back to sleep."

*We almost lost everything. If the gheiraq attacked their room first... No, he couldn't bear to consider what almost happened.*

Will shook his head, closing the door.

Frank searched the other offices. He went to the tiny third level, a single large storeroom, yet it was empty. He returned to Michi. She sat on their bed, holding her head in one hand.

"Are you all right?"

"I've never called so many insects at once. I can't describe the feeling. I heard their souls, screaming as I pulled them out. It's more than pain. It was unbearable. I've never been so frightened. I didn't want to lose you, Frank."

"Thank you." He paused. "At first, all I could think about was protecting you. I forgot everything else. Nothing mattered except keeping you safe. I...I care about you."

"I care for you too."

Frank blushed. "I checked the rest of the Gatehouse. When you're up to it, I'd like to keep a few extra eyes around, just to make sure I didn't miss anything, or anyone."

"I'll use some insects. A couple of the beetles are still under my control. There were so many, I couldn't release them all at once. Who was he?"

"I think he was Athanasius's replacement. If Dragons came, it's possible they did something to him. We'll have to get rid of the body. For all their rules, Deaths never manned this position. If a Death had come, we wouldn't be burying them now. They'd have ceased." He frowned. "Let's hope this is the last challenge we have here."

She sank against his chest, and he wrapped his arm around her back. Stroking his fingers through her matted hair, Frank sighed.

\* \* \* \*

"Should we say a few words?" Will leaned on the shovel, gesturing to the mound of fresh dirt.

Frank frowned, yet nodded. He gazed across the barren plain. The Gatehouse stood silhouetted by the twin suns on the horizon. A crumbling stone pillar covered in moss stood beside the burial mound. Susan and Michi held hands, watching.

"I don't know this Elemental's name, however I can guess much of his story." Frank laid his shovel down. "He attacked us, not out of anger, but out of fear. The enemy twisted his mind, forcing him to become something he wasn't."

As Frank spoke, his attention drifted. Something deep behind his conscious thought stirred. With every word his mouth formed, a different sentence seemed to echo in his heart; different thoughts whispered by a different soul:

*They misunderstood.*

"This Elemental was a good man."

*Grym was a gift.*

"He worked at the Gatehouse."

*It wasn't his fault.*

"Just as I used to work here."

*I live still.*

"May he rest in peace."

*I will rise again.*

Frank pressed his fingers to his temple. The words made no sense. His power was gone, taken by the soul snatcher. Yet, something lurked there now, something far more powerful than he dared to imagine.

*I will rise again.*

\* \* \* \*

Frank pushed the pointy-hat figure forward. He sat back, surveying the pieces.

"We've been through this." Will returned the figure. "The bishop moves diagonally."

"This game is pointless."

"There's nothing else to do. Four person boskery won't work well, especially with one boskery blade and no ball. You're the one who discovered the chess set."

Frank rolled his eyes. "Sometimes trash from the Mortal World makes its way here. Items people cling to when they're brought to be Deaths, or things we've caught Deaths smuggling. If this was a normal time, you'd see Deaths passing through the In-Between at regular intervals. I'm not used to this quiet, this *stillness*."

"Well, *quiet* is perfect for a good round of chess. Try again."

The large iron door behind them opened a crack. Will looked up. Michi and Susan entered, shaking their heads.

"Nothing?" asked Frank.

"Other than the Gatehouse, there's nothing at all except grass and those old rocks." Michi rubbed her eyebrows. "No flies, no animals, nothing."

Will rose, walking to Susan. "How are you doing?" He embraced her, before stepping back and placing a hand on her belly.

"I'm fine."

"The child grows at an alarming rate." Michi shook her head. "We have provisions for another couple of weeks, however, we have no means to deliver a baby. Once the child's born, we'll be even worse off. This is our fourth unsuccessful scouting attempt this week. Frank, I think we need to consider leaving."

"I'd hoped to stay longer. We've only been in the In-Between for two weeks."

"We have some time." Will smiled. "She's barely showing. Giri thought the child was growing faster than normal, yet even if he's maturing three times a normal rate, we'd have another month."

"No, Michi's right." Frank peered out the open door, and swung the slab of rune-covered iron shut. "Once the supplies upstairs run out, we have no means to replenish. I have a suggestion, something that's been nagging at the back of my mind."

Susan and Michi sat on the extra cushions he and Will had carried downstairs. Will pushed the chessboard to the side, and the three looked at Frank expectantly.

"I think we should head to Vyr."

Will frowned. "The other 'Mental city? What makes you think it hasn't been attacked?"

"The Dragons attacked Karis because they knew we were there. Someone told them. We'll contact the Swarm, see if it's safe first. Maybe we could lie, saying we've decided to return to the College. Anyone watching the Swarm wouldn't know our true destination."

Michi shook her head. "The 'Mentals might have supplies, *if* they haven't been attacked. If we go, the Dragons will strike Vyr. How much of the Northern Forest will burn while we continue to run?"

"What other answer is there?" Frank held his hands up.

"We return to the cave at Reaper Ridge." Will took Susan's hand. "We have supplies, and know how to live off the land. We survive, and remain in hiding. If Frank's suspicions about the Swarm are true, and we use the scythe, no one will even know we're there."

"You want me to give birth in the wild? Is that how you plan to raise our child?"

"I want us to be safe."

"There's a third option." Susan turned to the iron door. "We can't stay here, and don't trust the World of Deaths, yet we have a scythe. We can go to the Mortal World."

"Michi and I might be able to survive there, I'm honestly not sure. However, you and Will are Deaths. Your souls will pull away. You'll lose weight until you die. I remember Athanasius explaining the situation to you just down this hall."

"I've been thinking. After fleeing the Dragons, the Swarm showed us images. We watched through the eyes of flame, not just flame in the World of Deaths, but scenes from the Mortal World as well."

"I saw my mother." Will nodded.

"And I saw mine. Which means the Swarm exists in more than one world. They moved our souls and bodies, carrying us first to Reaper Ridge, and later to Karis. If they can hold souls, and see more than one world, maybe they could support us."

"Support us how? What do you mean?" Frank's head spun.

"We return to the Mortal World, using the scythe. We ask the Swarm to strengthen our souls." She shook her head. "I don't know, maybe they can bridge the divide between worlds, and stop our souls from returning here, or at least slow it down. Somehow, they might be able to give us more time in the Mortal World."

Frank stood and paced the hallway. "We have no idea if the Swarm's even capable of what you're suggesting. The idea's based on a lot of assumptions. Besides, if the Dragons discovered us through the Swarm, we'd be revealing our location."

"We don't know how the Dragons discovered us." She stood, and Will quickly rose with her. Michi sat, scratching her chin.

"Our child could be born in a hospital." Will voice quivered with hope.

"It's worth asking the Swarm." Michi nodded. "The Mortal World is a logical choice. If Dragons can't cross realms, we might even be able to live there permanently. It's the safest place for all of us."

"So we just turn our backs on the World of Deaths?" Frank gestured. "We abandon all our friends? Our families?"

Michi stood, walking to him, and placed a hand on his arm. "Giri and Hinara survived the attack."

"We don't know that."

"No. I just have faith. We'll see them again. This decision, *if* it is possible, would allow Susan's child to be born in the Mortal World. Frank, the enemy wants a Dragon Key. If their child's born on the living Earth, maybe it won't even be a Dragon Key. It'd be a normal human baby. The Dragon's goal would be lost. You want to help our friends, this might be the way."

"We need to think this through." *Was it even possible? Could they trust the Swarm?* "You remember the last Reapings we tried? The scythe broke, shattering. We don't know how much mortamant is in this scythe. We might use it, and become trapped in the Mortal World. We already know the Swarm can't transport us between worlds. Deaths *cannot* live there for long. I remember telling countless new arrivals those exact words."

"This is different. No one knew the Swarm exists. You use flower lights so they can't see you, yet forgot the reason. Like Grym, the Swarm's an ancient secret we brought to light. Since they see into multiple worlds, we should ask if they can help us."

A thunderous explosion rocked the Gatehouse.

Will stumbled, clutching Susan. "What was that?"

Michi's eyes widened. "They're here. They've found us."

A screech pierced the air, so loud and shrill that they heard windows shattering upstairs. A roar answered it, and the Gatehouse trembled again.

"Grab the scythe and the boskery blade!" Susan ran upstairs. "I'll grab some food. We're going now."

Frank crept to the door, pressing his ear against the iron.

*Impossible. We never contacted the Swarm since arriving here. No one knows where we are. How did the Dragons find us? How did they cross into the In-Between?*

A sound like rushing wind crashed against the door, and the metal heated. He backed up.

"Frank! Snap out of it!" Michi grabbed his hand, pulling him to the steps.

Susan ran back downstairs, clutching a bag. "I saw at least five Dragons. One's clawing in the window. We leave now!"

Will snapped a tether to each of their waists, the type they used to wear on Reapings. Frank tried to focus, standing in an awkward daze. *Impossible. How did they do it?*

Michi slapped his face. "Frank, I don't know what's going on in your head, but this isn't the time." She shoved the boskery blade into his hands, double-checking the tether.

"Hold on." Will glanced at Susan, tightening his grip on the long snath.

A cloud of dust fell down the stairs, and parts of the ceiling crumbled.

Will sliced the air, opening a gash of light.

Colors blurred around them.

For a moment, Frank watched the Gatehouse crumble. A host of Dragons bellowed into the air.

A man with a scythe stood on the barren field, watching.

Sindril shouted something, and the Dragons bellowed again.

The scene dissolved into a dizzying maze of rainbows.

Two suns become a single sun, which collapsed behind a shroud of twinkling stars.

The tether jerked, the world took shape, and a gentle rain fell.

They stood in a dark alleyway. Cars honked in the distance.

"You brought us to the Mortal World?" Frank turned to Will. "We didn't ask the Swarm if Susan's plan was possible. This was foolish." Beads of glowing white light dripped on the scythe blade. The snath trembled, and the blade split into two shards, which clanged to the ground.

"No." Susan lifted the pieces, putting them in her bag.

"We'd better find the Swarm fast," said Frank. "We have no other option. Let's just hope your theory is true. Leave the snath here, it won't do us any good."

"Hide the boskery blade." Michi picked up a blanket laying in the alley, and tossed it over the double-bladed weapon in Frank's hands. The wet blanket smelled of urine. He grimaced, using the tether to strap it on his back.

"Come on," whispered Will. "Let's see where we are. Once we're alone, we'll start a fire. All I thought of was Earth. We could be anywhere."

The street outside the alley seemed deserted. A stray cat hissed, darting back into the shadows. Frank's back dampened from the wet, smelly blanket, and the soft drizzle which continued to fall. Darkened stone buildings rose on either side, each with some lit windows scattered in odd places. A pair of headlights appeared at the end of the street, and a car drove past. Frank pressed his body against the wall behind him, keeping his head low. They walked to a cross street. Four cars sped by, and a man in a yellow parka hurried past on a bicycle. No one paid any attention to them.

"There are lights over there." Susan pointed. "We'll at least get a sense of where we are."

"You want people to see us?" asked Frank.

"What does it matter? We're just strangers. No one knows us here. We've hidden the boskery blade, and the scythe's broken."

Frank nodded and they crossed the street. Stone houses, three stories high, stood arranged beside each other in long rows. Ornate cornices hung beneath many of the roofs, above bright windows. Strange stone faces poked out from some of the shadowed walls. A crowd of people walked in the well-lit street, huddled under umbrellas and bustling between shops and restaurants.

"Look at this." Will stopped by an iron sign with arrows. It was difficult to read in the dim light and drizzle. "I think we're in England. Bodleian Library and Radcliffe Camera are that way, along with a University Museum. What university?"

A red bus pulled up on the other side of the road. A group of people got off, hurrying away. Susan read a label on the back of the bus.

"This is Oxford."

"Now we know where we are." Frank shifted his weight, impatient to get out of sight. "Let's get out of the crowd."

Susan nodded.

They continued through the crowded street. On a corner, they saw a homeless man huddled under a tarp. *That'll be us soon. We've no money, no shelter, no plan. This was a bad idea.*

The smell of fried food drifted out from several restaurants. Old painted signs with pictures hung in front of some buildings, other shops looked more modern. He'd never been good with human customs or fashions, however the tantalizing smells made his stomach grumble. At the end of the street they turned right. The rain lessened.

Streetlights lined the broad street. Cars and busses passed on their left. A brightly lit stone structure with a small white cupola appeared ahead, surrounded by high iron fences.

"This must be the palace where their headmaster lives," muttered Frank.

"I don't think it works like that." Will pointed to the fence. Enormous shadowy heads with bizarre faces stood upon stone pillars, looking away from the building. "Odd statues though."

"It's a concert." Susan pointed to a sign. "Selections of chamber music from Mozart and Haydn, featuring 'The Hunt.' Performing at the Sheldonian Theatre, 20 August."

"Is that today?" Will glanced down the street. "I'd lost track of time."

They paused, staring at the glowing windows. The strange stone faces gawked down at them from their five-foot plinths. The muted sound of string music touched Frank's ears.

"Have you forgotten we're hiding?" Frank shook his head. "We need to find somewhere secluded before you two start to fade away."

Susan winced, clutching her belly. "Let's hurry."

They continued. An enormous darkened dome, covered in shadow loomed behind ornate stone buildings to their right.

Will pointed to another metal sign. "There's a park that way."

They turned left, and passed more large stone buildings. One three story structure with a high pointed roof in its center reminded Frank of the Gatehouse. He shivered, pressing on. They saw no people, and the cars grew less frequent. Occasional streetlights provided the only illumination around darkened buildings. At last they reached a low iron gate with trees and an open field on the other side.

"Oxford University Parks," read Susan, squinting in the dim light. "It's closed."

Frank took off the boskery blade and threw the sack over the fence. "I'll get the gate." He jumped, grasping the top rail, and clambered over. Michi followed, pulling herself over with ease.

Frank unlatched the gate, pushing it open. Susan glanced around, and then walked through the entrance holding Will's hand.

"Let's go further in."

The park was silent and desolate. With no light, trees loomed over them like monstrous shadows. A cloud moved, and the moon appeared. They walked in silence.

Frank grabbed Michi and pulled her off the path. A light bobbed ahead. Susan and Will met his eye in the darkness. They crouched in the shadows, hiding behind a hedge.

A small cart rolled by, with a tiny light waving over the empty fields. They waited until it was gone before continuing.

"It's ironic," whispered Susan. "We face Dragons, yet hide from a park guard on a golf cart."

"We don't want to be seen." Frank pointed to a long row of trees ahead, silhouetted against the night sky. "There'll be cover there."

The path led to a small river. Even at night, Frank heard the streaming water. For a moment he thought of a different river, and a grove of sad birches. *Birches singing*.

He couldn't place the memory. It irked him, like a half-remembered dream.

A narrow bridge crossed the slow-moving water. "We'll shelter under the bridge." He walked carefully to the water's edge. A thin ledge of mud and grass led to a small alcove of rock beneath the path. "It's a good spot to hide." Placing the boskery blade down, he climbed back to the others. "We need to start a fire. Will, help me gather some dry branches. Michi, Susan, keep an eye out for visitors."

Michi hid the scythe and Susan's bag beneath the bridge. She closed her eyes. "I can still feel the insects. It's different here, like using my power through a fog. I'll place extra eyes on us always."

"Good idea." Frank took some sticks, and walked to a spot away from their shelter. "I'll set the fire away from where we'll stay. We need to remain hidden. How did Dragons discover our location in the In-Between?"

"We hadn't contacted the Swarm." Will handed him more branches. "Whatever tipped them off, wasn't through the flames."

Frank nodded. He rubbed branches together, much as they'd done at Reaper Ridge. Blowing onto the pile of sticks, sparks blossomed into a thin tongue of fire. Glancing at each other in the dancing light, the two boys sat before the small cluster of sparks and flickers.

"Swarm?" Frank reached out with his voice, trying to push his thoughts through the flame as well. "Are you there?"

The fire blazed brighter, and an orange jet snaked to Frank's forehead.

*"YOU BROUGHT THE SCYTHE WIELDER TO THE MORTAL WORLD."*

Frank swam in a blur of fire and smoke. The sensation was different than the previous times he'd contacted them. He rode atop flame, watching through a clouded veil. The Swarm's chorus of screaming voices echoed in the distance, like thunder rolling off hills miles away.

*"We're in danger. We had to flee."*

Will's voice sounded closer than the distant Swarm. *"Susan and I are Deaths. Our souls will flow back to the World of Deaths without your help. Can you keep us alive in the Mortal World?"*

*"WE SHALL HELP YOU. HELP THE SCYTHE WIELDER. HELP HER LOVE."*

Frank struggled to breathe, fighting the swirl of smoke and flames. *"You can keep them alive?"*

*"NOT FOREVER. THEY CANNOT STAY.*
*WE SHALL HELP. WE SHALL DELAY."*

Will's voice called out again. *"What does that mean?"*

*"A YEAR AT MOST.*
*DELAY THE FLOW. WE HELP."*

*"What about money or supplies? Can you give us anything else?"*

*"WE EBB THE TIDE. IN THE END, YOU MUST RETURN.*
*WE HELP. WE HELP."*

Frank fell back to the grass. The tiny fire fizzled out, leaving a wisp of smoke. Grabbing the branches and dirt, he worked to hide any evidence of their activity.

"They'll slow our decay, up to a year. That's what they meant, isn't it?" asked Will.

"You're Deaths. You can't live here forever. However, it'll be long enough for Susan to give birth in this world. The child will be safe, and won't have the power to become a Dragon Key."

"Are you sure of that?"

Frank ignored his question. *No, of course I'm not sure*. "They've given us a chance. Besides, if the Deaths finish the war on their own, it won't be an issue. They won before."

"That was a long time ago." Will sighed. "The Swarm ignored my request for other supplies. Let's tell the others that Susan and I are safe, and maybe get some sleep. Nothing we can do until day."

"There isn't much room beneath that bridge. Might as well sleep on benches. It'll be more comfortable."

"That's fine. One person should stay awake at all times, in case anyone comes checking the park. Michi's insects will help too."

"Agreed."

They walked back to the bridge. Will embraced Susan and started to explain.

*We're safe.* Frank tried to take comfort in the thought, yet doubt nagged him.

*We're safe. For now.*

\* \* \* \*

*"Can you hear me, oh my love?*
*As ever sunsets drift away,*
*Where is the joy we sang to life?*
*Where are the broken souls*
*And the faded day?"*

*Birches shot into the sky: filled with golden light. Always singing.*

*A song he couldn't remember, yet dared not forget, lingering at the edge of thought.*

*Frank stood on the banks of a river.*

*Birches higher than mountains stretched into the sky, pillaring the heavens.*

*The song wound through him, ebbing and flowing with the water's waves.*

Frank opened his eyes, breathing hard.

The dream receded into obscurity, however the image of trees lingered.

Mist covered the river, wisping over the narrow bridge. Willows bent low over the gentle water. He sat on a stone bench. They'd moved twice during the night, avoiding occasional park workers. No one saw them. He'd scarcely found time to sleep, and the cold winds hadn't helped. Dawn now crept against the fading night. Amber shafts pierced the tree line on the opposite bank.

"You up?" Will stood.

Frank nodded.

"We should go into town. You and me. We'll need food and other supplies. We don't have money, so we'll have to improvise."

"The girls?" Frank glanced at another bench. Susan's head drooped in her hand, as she slumped on a bench. Michi stood above, watching the paths.

"Someone should stay here, and keep an eye on our belongings. The park will open soon. At that point, we'll just blend in." Will lowered his voice. "I want Susan to relax. After yesterday's strain, she needs to take it easy."

"All right." He walked to Michi and touched her arm. "Will and I are going into town to find food. Keep an eye on Susan and the blades."

She pecked his cheek, and then bent, picking something off the dirt. "Take this." Michi placed a tiny beetle on his shoulder. "If anything goes wrong, I'll be listening."

"Use your insects to tell us if you need help as well. Thank you, Michi. Once people come, just blend in."

"Good luck."

Will and Frank retraced their steps from last night to the now-open gate at the other end of the park. Two young women in bright outfits jogged past. Small wires hung from the joggers' ears, and their heads bobbed to some unheard communication. *Perhaps humans have their own forms of telepathy.*

"They're listening to music." Will caught him staring. "You really don't understand humans, do you?"

"I'm learning."

"Oxford's a famous university. A college, like the College of Deaths. I've never been here. Since it's an English-speaking place, we should have an easy time getting around."

"All right." Frank suspected his words would be understood by any mortal. 'Mentals and mortals never had issues communicating, yet perhaps this would make Will and Susan's stay easier.

A sign identified the street as Parks Road. A bus rolled past. The street was otherwise deserted. They passed the steep-sloped building again. In the light, the building looked less like the Gatehouse. The smell of food greeted them when they approached the center of town.

The stonework grew more elaborate with every step. Carved faces watched them from hidden places on walls, and ornate doors and roofs faced every marble building. Compared to the towers of the College of Deaths, this place was low, yet far more opulent.

"Entrance to the Radcliffe Camera," read Will, when they stopped at a large squat dome surrounded by grass. "Come on. This looks like it's all part of the school. We'll keep going around that church." He paused, scratching his chin. "Strange to see a church. My mom used to make me go. They're places obsessed with death and what happens next. Well, in a normal time, *I'd* be next."

"Look over there." Frank hurried to the iron fence surrounding Radcliffe Camera. A glowing form sat slouched against the rails. A teenage boy looked up at his approach. His features were dim and blurred. His skin shone, illuminated from within.

"A soul?" asked Will.

"You can see me?" The boy's voice echoed from a great distance.

"How long have you been here?" Frank reached down, surprised when his fingers slipped through the soul.

"Help me." The soul quivered in the wind, blurring further.

Will grabbed Frank's arm, pulling him away. "There's nothing we can do. Reapings stopped, remember? We can't return now, and he's already fading out of sight."

"Help me." The boy stared up, trying to stand. His form fell through the fence, floating above the ground. His edges blurred out of sight.

"Come on." Will pulled again, nodding to a man on a bicycle who'd started to watch them. "We don't want to attract attention."

Frank pitied the soul, yet turned away. He heard a low sound, like faint crying. They pushed ahead, passing the church, and reached a large street. Here, cars and busses drove by.

"Which way now?"

Will surveyed the scene. "I don't know. I'm not even sure what we're looking for. Let's head right."

They walked slow now. Frank spotted two more souls, yet said nothing. They sat side by side on the street corner, their edges fading in the wind. *Will's right, there's nothing we can do. I do care for those poor people. Strange, sometimes I think more like a Death than a 'Mental. Or perhaps it's my own loss.*

He pictured the soul snatcher, with its monstrous spider-legs and cloud-like mouth. The chimera, the power born from his soul, torn away. Left alone. His soul was no different than the souls they passed. It languished in isolation somewhere in the forest, facing oblivion. He turned to the two souls again.

"This should do." Will gestured. "A covered market with lots of shops. Come on."

Frank forced his eyes away from the souls, and followed Will into a building with tall red ceilings. Shops lined either side of the path. Many were just opening. A rumble in his stomach reminded him why they'd come. Here, people milled between the shops. Frank bumped into one old man, and offered a hasty apology.

Will and Frank walked the entire area twice before returning to the street. They sat beside a building, speaking in low voices.

"I'm starving." The Death scratched his chin. "Must be nearly lunch-time, and we haven't eaten breakfast."

"The fruit and vegetable stand at the end is our best bet."

"And the bakery." Will placed a hand on his stomach. "Did you smell those pies?"

"We still have no money."

"I hate to steal, but we need to survive. Do you have powers here?"

Frank closed his eyes. Michi kept insisting his power would grow back, that the soul snatcher only took a part of him. He tried to focus on one of the passers-by, a man with a black hat.

An image of glowing birches shot into his mind. Tall, sad trees singing.

"What did you do?"

Frank opened his eyes. The man stood staring at the road. Now he shook his head, breaking the trance. Adjusting his hat, he glanced around. Frank and Will looked at each other, avoiding the man. The stranger frowned and hurried away.

"I have something. Michi thinks my powers are growing back."

"It'll do. You distract the shopkeeper and any others who might be watching. I'll nab what I can."

They returned to the fruit stand. Row after row of fresh fruits and vegetable lined the corner of a large store, under green and white awnings. Separate stalls with more food stood in the center of the paths, all under the high red ceiling above. Frank walked a slight distance away, and found the four people, including the shopkeeper, most likely to spot Will. Concentrating on each, he reached to the spot behind his thoughts where his power used to lie.

*Glowing birches taller than sight.*

*"Can you hear me, oh my love?"*

*A pleading song.*

At the edge of thought, he saw four people staring away from Will. Frank struggled to concentrate, focusing on the empty spot within his soul. *Not empty, filled with something different.*

*The birches glowed brighter, swaying in the wind.*

*"Return to me," sang the trees.*

*The most beautiful song ever dreamed.*

Will gestured with his head, walking away. Frank released the power. It faded from memory like smoke from a candle. *Perhaps my power is growing back. Michi must have been right.*

Will clutched a large bag filled with food. "If I carried it in my pockets, that'd look a lot more suspicious. No one questions people with bags."

They leaned against the same spot on the stone wall outside.

"Thanks for your help, Frank."

"Of course. Let's get back to the girls."

\* \* \* \*

Susan and Will sat huddled beneath a large willow tree. Morning rain dripped off its long branches, splashing their large red umbrellas.

Frank and Michi watched.

"Should have swiped more than two umbrellas."

"It's just rain." Michi took his hand, smiling. "I like it."

Mist covered the River Cherwell, masking both the bridge and the spot where the blades remained hidden. Frank felt the map in his pocket. It'd been a strange two weeks, hiding in the Mortal World.

"We should head off." Michi glanced around. "Park's open by now. It's our turn to go scavenging."

"Stealing, you mean."

"Surviving. It's what we do."

Frank nodded. *This is no way to live.* The dropping rain darkened his mood even more.

"It's Thursday, and raining. That'll help. We'll hit the Farmer's Market in Gloucester Green before we visit the Covered Market."

"You've left some insects with Susan and Will?"

"Of course."

After saying goodbye to the two Deaths, they walked toward the town center. Frank kept his head low in the soft drizzle.

"How have you been doing?" Michi asked. They walked past the Natural History Museum, with its steep-sloping roof and petrified tree trunks. In the gloomy rain it again reminded Frank of the Gatehouse.

"What do you mean?"

"You're withdrawn. You don't talk unless Susan or Will are around, and always seem distant. I know you don't like our lives right now. However, we need to stay, at least until Susan delivers."

A poncho-wearing bicyclist sped by.

"I'm sorry. This place is alien to me. It's been difficult. That's all."

She stopped, taking his damp hands in hers. He looked up, meeting her eyes. "And your soul? Your power? It's growing back stronger than ever, helping us thrive. This is *good* news. I knew the creature hadn't devoured all of your soul, and now you're returning to normal."

He turned away, sighing.

"Frank, what is it? What aren't you telling me?"

"It doesn't feel right. My power, I mean." He shook his head, brushing rain from his forehead. "Yes, it's growing and it's helped us steal food and supplies, however it's different. The power's changed… something else now grows inside of me."

She placed a hand on his heart, leaning forward to kiss him. Her lips sank into his. They parted, and she looked at him, running her fingers through his wet hair. "I can't imagine how frightening it must be to lose something, and have it grow back as if you were an infant again. Of course it's disorienting. Besides, you're a different person now from when we were children. Your power *is* growing differently, because *you* are different."

"You're right. Of course that's it. Come on, let's get going."

They continued to Broad Street. On the Sheldonian Theatre's steps, a glowing figure sat beneath one of the strange heads. An old man sat hunched against the plinth. Each drop of rain sent his outline quivering.

"I see him too." Michi continued down the street. "We can't help."

"I notice a new one every day. What will happen to them?"

"Even if the war ends, I'm not sure they could all be Reaped. The souls we're seeing are already free from corpses, which means they're not recent. I've seen some so faded, they're almost gone."

"Will said un-Reaped souls become Dragon food. That must be where they're fading to. I don't know any of these people, and yet it saddens me. Do you think it's our fault that they won't pass on?"

"We didn't start this war, Frank. None of the 'Mentals started it. We're doing what we can." She reached an arm up, touching his. "Stop being so hard on yourself. You've done a wonderful job keeping us safe, helping to feed us, and helping look after us. You rescued Susan and Will, and discovered the Swarm. What more could we do?"

*She always knows what to say.* He grinned and they continued.

The rain lessened, stopping when they reached Gloucester Green. Rows of brick houses surrounded the open market. Stalls lined the square, under colored, dripping awnings. Walking the perimeter, they scouted the best stand to pilfer. Michi gave a slight nod at a corner with loaves of bread.

Frank leaned against a bicycle stand, eyeing customers and sellers. He counted six pairs of eyes most likely to spot Michi. Concentrating on those six people, he reached for the power.

*A grove of glowing birches pillared the sky.*

*With waves of golden light, they sang.*

Pushing the power toward the six strangers, Frank struggled to maintain his concentration.

*The eternal song spun around him.*

"Hey! That girl just nicked some bread. Stop her!"

Shaking his head, Frank looked up. A man he hadn't seen before pointed to Michi. "She's a thief!"

A policeman nearby hurried over and Michi sprinted away. Frank hurried into the street.

Michi darted into an alley, crossing onto a side street.

"You! Stop right there!"

Frank paused, and focused on the pursuing officer.

*A grove of glowing trees.*

*An ancient song.*

The man stopped, staring at the wall.

Someone bumped into Frank, and he lost his focus. The officer ran ahead again.

Frank hurried after the officer, who kept close behind Michi. She slammed into a man with a suitcase, knocking it over. Frank lost the officer twice, yet spotted him again each time.

A police car rolled up, and two more uniformed men stepped out. One swatted something from his face. She must be using her power.

Michi turned, ducking into a church with a huge tower.

*"Wait there,"* whispered a voice on his shoulder. A beetle shifted, clinging to his shirt.

The three policemen ran into the church. Frank leaned against a fence, pulling out the map, and pretending to be engrossed. He heard shouting inside. The three police emerged, holding a bag of bread.

"I don't understand. That's a bloody one-way staircase. The girl disappeared."

"Can't have, Clive. She's here somewhere. Head to the back."

"Well, we have the stolen goods. I'm not chasing some shoplifter all day."

"She pulled a Houdini right in front of us. Doesn't that make you angry?" With a start, Frank realized the map was upside-down. He adjusted it, listening to the bickering men walk off.

The beetle on his shoulder fell off, dead. A fly landed in its place.

*"What happened?"*

"I must've miscounted the people watching. I'm sorry."

Glancing at the map, this time for real, he started walking. At an alley, Frank paused. No one was around. The fly flew up, and with a shudder of light became a girl again.

"I didn't want you to carry me all the way back." She grinned.

"I'm just glad you're all right." He shook his head, and they walked to Cornmarket Street, the busiest pedestrian section of town. Shops and businesses lined either side of the road. The two Elementals leaned against a wall, breathing hard.

"It was bound to happen eventually." Michi started laughing.

"You think this is funny? You were almost caught."

"Yeah, but we weren't. I knew you'd save me."

Frank rolled his eyes. Three elderly women walked by, eyeing them. He lowered his voice as they passed. "Let's get back to the park. We can find other markets later."

"Agreed. You and Will should go. Keep an eye out for police on the way back. We don't want more trouble."

"Are you sure you don't want me to carry you?"

"You know how you try to forget the soul snatcher? Well, I don't like remembering the *months* I spent living as an insect before Susan's class took their field trip. No, thank you, I'll walk."

They took a long, meandering route back to the park, avoiding major roads. Michi kept her head down, and they changed direction several times when they saw police cars. The sky cleared, and shafts of sunlight slipped onto the streets.

Frank broke into a run when they reached the park.

Michi laughed, jogging behind him. They passed the cricket fields, continuing through the trees to the river. Frank halted. Susan and Will sat on a bench talking to a girl with long, wavy, copper-red hair, even brighter red than Michi's hair. She wore thick glasses, which she pushed further up her nose at Frank's approach.

"Back already?" Susan's belly poked out beneath her shirt, clearly showing the approaching child.

"We ran into…difficulties."

Michi stepped up behind him. "Who's you're friend, Susan?"

The redheaded girl popped up, adjusting her glasses. She extended a hand to Frank, shaking vigorously. "Hello, I'm Elizabetha. Elizabetha Parkinset."

"Frank."

"Michi."

She shook Michi's hand next. "Michi, that's an odd name. My name's odd too. It's like Elizabeth, but with an A at the end. I go by Betha, which is what you can call me." She grinned. "Yeah, my parents are kind of freaks. Mum used to study history, especially Elizabethan times. Like my name, but with an N at the end. You get the idea. Thought today would be a great day to visit the Uni Parks, after the rain I mean. The city's so empty during summer. Are you two freshers as well?"

"I'm sorry, I didn't catch all that." Frank's head spun. The girl peered at him through her glasses.

Susan stood. "Betha was telling us that her family's renting her a house. The college provides lodging for new students when the term starts, however that hasn't happened yet. Since her family's away, and she came early, they've rented her an *entire* house. That's so much nicer than what our parents did, isn't it?"

"What?" Frank was still having trouble grasping what Susan was trying to do.

Betha cocked her head to one side, brushing her coppery hair aside. "Don't get me wrong, Michaelmas term's three weeks away, but my parents were both leaving the country. It's my dad you see, he's a really important official at this oil company, and he's got tons of money. I'm not trying to say I'm rich, I mean I'm not. He is, but I'm not. My parents are pretty well-off, though. After all, they're paying for a whole flat, and it's not even a flat, more of an entire house, especially since mum doesn't want me rooming with others. It's the boys." She turned to Michi without pausing. "Your parents didn't keep you away from boys. I mean look at you two. It's so liberating to see girls who're having babies still going to Uni, and not just dumping themselves on welfare benefits. Not like that's an issue with me. No, my parents would rather throw me in a cell and hide me from the world until I'm married. How am I supposed to do that, if they won't even let me meet anyone, do you know what I mean?"

Frank put his hand up. "I'm sorry, I'm not following you. Susan, Michi and I wanted to talk to you and Will."

Susan smiled. "Betha's very nice. I explained how I met you three right here in the park, and how our parents dumped us here for school with no place to live."

Will stood, taking Susan's hand. "Susan and I told Betha how *mean* our parents have been. How my parents discovered our pregnancy and threw us out. How you two are in the same situation." He raised his eyebrow, nodding to Michi. "The four of us met just last week and have been living homeless, even though we're all going to be Oxford students."

"It's absolute rubbish, if you ask me." Betha pushed the glasses higher on her nose, sticking her chin out. "The whole British schooling system's rubbish. Here you sit at one of the supposed great schools, in the *world* mind you, and you four are homeless. How are you supposed to study if they won't even give you a place to live? I mean they will when school starts, but you're pregnant and can't go home. It's all rubbish."

"Yes. Michi and I are…studying here too." Frank nodded.

"And I'm pregnant, with Frank's baby." He heard the laughter edging into her voice. Susan glared at her, and Frank pressed his fingers around Michi's.

"Well that settles it." Betha tossed back her hair and straightened her glasses yet again. She tugged on the collar of her jean jacket. "You're all coming to live with me. There's room for everyone. We'll all be grand friends, I'm sure. Come on and get your stuff. Can't be living in the park. I'm over in Botley, it's a fair walk. Right by the train station, should you need to get anywhere. Not that there's anywhere you need to get. I'm really glad I ran into you four, this will be fun. When are you due, Michi? Sorry, don't mean to be rude, but I mean you're hardly showing."

"They only just found out," said Will. "Frank, why don't you collect our stuff?"

He nodded, walking to the bridge. *This is crazy. Why are we talking to this mortal?* The answer was obvious, Susan was tired of living outdoors. Still, what would they do if this loquacious girl discovered what they truly were? Her voice continued prattling in the distance. *She's going to be trouble.* He glanced around before climbing under the bridge to retrieve their bags. They had a little food, two broken scythe fragments and the large boskery blade. He tried covering the weapon in the now soaked dirty blanket, yet the double blades still poked out. He clamored back to the riverbank.

"Oh neat." Betha smiled. "Are you re-enactors or cosplayers? Looks like a fancy piece you've got there."

"Yes, that's right." Frank adjusted the blanket and strapped it to his already damp shirt. His filthy clothes itched. It'd been a week since they'd changed. Perhaps they could steal this girl's money and buy some decent supplies, food, and clothing. *Maybe it's not such a bad idea.*

He frowned. *What am I thinking? Stealing food's bad enough. What am I becoming?*

"Come on, let's head out. I know you're going to be very happy. I mean anything's better than staying here in the park. Still, I'm sure you'll be thrilled with the house. I'm actually really glad some people are moving in with me, it's just so damned quiet. Did you see the town yet? Looks like no one lives here but tourists and old folks. I mean I was at Blackwell's and the place was deserted. Just wait until Fresher's Week, everything will get crazy. That's what my friend Rhiannon told me. She's nice, still in Wales until term. You'll like her."

They followed Betha out of the park and toward the town. At one intersection, Michi threw herself against Frank, burying her face in his chest. A police car rolled by.

"Wow, you two are really in love." Betha grinned. "That's beautiful. I hope to meet a man who appreciates me that much. I went out for two months with this guy Steve, but he was so boring, and he never talked." She spun back to the road.

"Did you give him a chance to speak?" Frank whispered, without thinking. Betha didn't turn around, yet Michi snickered.

They passed the areas Frank knew, and continued moving. At the end of Cornmarket Street, they turned right, heading away from the center of activity. A large empty hill appeared on their left surrounded by a low stone wall. Two busses drove by. Few people walked this section of town.

Betha led them past the train station. They continued through a narrow tunnel beneath the tracks, approaching a row of houses.

"Here we are." Betha ran up the staircase of a large stone house.

*No one stopped us. We've made it this far.*

Frank took a deep breath, and followed the others inside.

* * * *

"Mmmmm."

Michi snuggled next to him, pressing against his arm.

Frank opened his eyes. The memory of glowing birches and a beautiful song ebbed into the recesses of his mind. The dream's joy lingered like a pleasant, cooling shadow on a sunny day.

He sank into the soft bed with each breath. Michi moved again, pressing even closer.

Behind the thick, gray curtain, bright sunlight slipped into the bedroom. Thin blue stripes covered the walls. The enormous bed was the most comfortable thing he'd ever felt. Thick down pillows rested under his head, and a warm white blanket covered them.

"Mmmm. We should get up soon. The others will think we're having too much fun."

He pulled her closer, relishing her warmth. "It's cozy, I admit, however we're here through deceit. I didn't like stealing, and I don't like lying to this poor girl."

"How well did you sleep last night? Our first night in a bed since Karis, and this was much nicer than that anyway. Why complain?"

*Why complain indeed. Once they finally slept, it'd been very comfortable. And before…*

"It was nice." He smiled. Leaning forward, they kissed. "All right, it was wonderful." His tongue lingered against hers, until he pulled away. "What if Betha discovers what we are?"

Michi shrugged. She rolled away, flopping against the pillow. "You worry too much. What's she going to do? Even if she told the Headmaster of this college, and whatever Council rules the Mortal World, I doubt they'd contact the Dragons and let them know we're here. Besides, who'd believe her? We have nothing to lose." She paused, sitting up, and faced him. "You spent a whole year at the College of Deaths lying to everyone, including Susan. Now, when we need to survive, you feel moral qualms?"

He nodded, pulling himself out of the bed. "I suppose you're right. We have nothing to lose."

She grinned. "So let's enjoy it. Come back to bed with your *pregnant* girlfriend."

He tossed a pillow at Michi and yawned. "Not now. And I know you're not pregnant."

She remained quiet, and Frank's stomach tightened. "I mean, you're not, are you?"

"No." She smiled. "But I had you worried for a minute there."

"You're incorrigible." Walking to the closet, he pulled on his jacket. "If she'll loan us some money, let's buy some new clothes." He ran his fingers across the handle of the boskery blade. It rested against the back of the closet.

"Did you see what was in the living room?" She raised an eyebrow.

"The fruit? It looked tasty."

"No, I meant the fireplace. If we can get Betha out of the house, we can use it."

He nodded, glancing at the blue-striped wallpaper. Striped like Aunt Hinara. "We still don't know if they survived."

"It's been far too long since we checked in with Cronk at our *actual* College. Susan thought Hann was arrested, remember?"

"A month on the run, and everything else fades into distant memory. Come on, Michi, let's see if the others are awake."

They dressed, and left the bedroom, walking down the flight of creaky wooden stairs. The hallway was plastered with gaudy red wallpaper, several pieces of which curled away from the walls. Susan and Will sat in the kitchen. A flat screen on the wall seemed to be relaying a stream of images and sounds. It reminded Frank a little of the Swarm, yet this form of telepathy seemed removed and distant. The creatures controlling it could only show images in the thin frame.

Betha greeted them with an enormous smile, handing each of them a mug. "Just brewed some fresh tea. I've got toast and eggs ready too. Did you sleep well? Sorry, forgot to even start with good morning. Good morning. Glad you're liking the place, roomies. Frank and Michelle, wait, was it Michelle?"

"Michi. We slept wonderfully, thank you, Betha. It's very cozy here."

"Michi, that's right. I should remember odd names, having such an odd name myself, and all." She laughed. "I talk a lot, I know. But I want to know more about all of you. How did you two couples meet? What are you studying when term starts? Do you have plans after school? Go on, oh, here's the jam for your toast."

"What is that?" Frank pointed to the frame. A man inside was talking, gesturing to a glass building behind him.

"Oh, it's just the news. I'll turn it off." Betha waved a small box at the frame and the image vanished.

"How are you able to see images? I don't understand."

"Well, my folks foot the cable bill. I mean, it's not like I sit around all day, but I put it on sometimes. Don't forget, I didn't have any flat mates until you lot moved in last night."

Susan shot him a look. Frank sat, nibbling on the breakfast. He'd have to ask Susan to explain later.

Will put his mug on the table. "Susan and I went to school together. She was new, so I showed her around, and fell head over heels. We're studying...transportation."

"Transportation?" Betha leaned back in her chair. "I didn't know you could study that. So you research new modes of travel? Going green, and all of that?"

"That's right."

Frank felt a new sense of appreciation. Will hadn't told a lie, however, still kept Betha in the dark. Impressive.

"What about you two?"

"Frank and I grew up in the same village. We're also studying transportation."

"Four transit majors staying with me. What are the odds? Well, you four finish eating. I just got a check yesterday. Mum sure splurged this time. You want to go shopping with me? We'll get some food for the house, and I don't know, maybe the girls want to pick some new clothes up? Of course, I'll take you both to the doctor first. If you've been in the park, I'm sure you're anxious to get the babies looked at."

"Michi, do you think you should be going outside? After yesterday, I mean." *We don't want more trouble with the police. Besides, what happens when they discover you're not pregnant?* He raised his eyebrows.

"I had a doctor's appointment yesterday," lied Michi. "No home but they still saw me. Doctor said I'm getting too much sun. Susan, why don't you go without me? It's been a while since your last appointment."

*You've never had one, not by a human doctor.* Frank hoped for Susan's sake, the child was all right. *Would they notice how fast it was growing?*

"I'll come too, of course." Will placed a hand on her arm.

"Thanks, Will." Her shirt stretched tight across her swollen belly.

"Well, I'll just freshen up and we'll leave in a few minutes." Betha pushed her glasses up, running a hand through her auburn hair. She turned to Frank and Michi. "Is there anything you two want while we're out shopping? Any food you need?"

"Susan and Will know us well. Whatever they're in the mood for would be great." Frank paused. "Some extra clothes for us would be great too, if you can spare some."

"You can come shopping with me tomorrow. Today we'll focus on food, and getting these two sorted out." She paused, adjusting her glasses. "You'll have to help out, of course. I like being charitable, but we'll discuss chores, cooking, straightening up, you know. I don't want you to think I'm just give, give all the time. I mean, I'm really glad you're here, and don't want you to go—"

"We don't want to outlast your generosity." Will stood, clearing the table. "We'll be happy to cook and help around the house. You've been more than kind, Betha."

"He's a charmer, Susan. All right, give me a few minutes, I'll be right back." She walked upstairs.

"Transportation?" whispered Frank.

"It's what we do." Will grinned. "Why are you two staying?"

"Michi got caught yesterday. We didn't even have a chance to tell you."

"Well, it looks like we won't have to steal for a while."

Michi pointed to the fireplace. "Keep her with you, and take your time. We're going to contact the Swarm."

"That's a good idea." Susan glanced upstairs. "I want to know what's going on with Hann and the College."

"We'll check." Frank heard water running above, and motioned to Will. "Before you head back into town. What is that thing?" He waved at the blank frame. "It showed images. Mortals don't have powers."

"It's a TV, a television. Wow, sometimes I forget you two aren't from the Mortal World. It's a machine, an instrument that lets people see through other machines. Yeah, that's a terrible explanation. Susan?"

"It's a tool. Like a scythe, or a boskery blade. Television is a form of communication."

They heard the door open, and the sound of steps on the staircase.

"Stay safe." Frank placed his hand on Will's arm. "Be careful."

"We'll be fine."

"You two ready to go? Looks like it's going to be great weather. Of course the forecast's rain by three, but you know how often they make up stuff. I honestly don't know how anyone gets paid to sit in an office pretending to know the future. I suppose that's what governments do too, isn't it?" She laughed, until she noticed that no one else was joining in. Frank looked at Susan, who shrugged. "Well, um, at any rate, we'll be off. There's food in the fridge, feel free to help yourselves, just clean up after. If you need to head out, here's a spare key. Make sure the deadbolt's turned. Do you have mobiles?"

This time Susan looked at him. He turned to Will, yet the Death shook his head, shrugging.

"Mobiles?" Frank scratched his head.

Betha pulled a small box from her purse. "You know, *phones*, some way to call you?"

"No, we don't have phones," said Will.

"Stuck in the park with nowhere to live and no phone. I'm sorry if this sounds rude, but you four all have the worst parents imaginable. Your family's aught to be ashamed."

Frank tensed. The image of Kasumir's body sinking into a pool of white light flashed into his mind. "My mother—"

"Frank's mother was murdered." Michi took his hand. "It's a touchy subject."

Betha's eyes widened. "I'm sorry, I didn't know. We'll look at picking up some mobiles in town." She opened a drawer and pulled out a sheet of paper, scribbling something. "I've written my number here. You can use the landline if you need anything. Let's see, what else. Fresh towels in the closet if you haven't showered. Internet doesn't start until tomorrow, so there's not much to do on the computer. I'd rather you don't use mine, and well, I guess you don't have your own. Well there are some books to read if you get bored. I always carry a few novels with me. Haven't gotten into the whole e-reader craze yet, still prefer the touch of pages. I've got a few in the family room, just don't move the bookmarks. Guess that's it. Enjoy your day."

Betha spun, her copper-red hair waving down her back. She wore a white and lilac dress and had bare feet with sandals. She gestured for Will and Susan to follow, and the three headed to the front door.

"We'll see you later." Will waved, closing the door behind them.

For a moment there was silence. Michi started clearing the remainder of the table. "Let's give them a few minutes before we start a fire. Wouldn't want them to come back forgetting something."

Frank helped her clean up.

"That shower you showed me last night was wonderful." She took a cloth, wet it, and started wiping the table. "Water falling from above. Humans are clever with their fancy tools."

"We showered at the College of Deaths, however I've never seen anything like that tell-ye-vision before." He strode over to the thin frame. "It's like they harnessed Elemental abilities and put them into this slim box."

"Again. They're clever."

"Leave some insects outside the door, we'll need to know when they're on their way back."

"There are two butterflies watching the house. I've got an emerald dragonfly near Susan and Will, keeping an eye on them directly. I'm nervous about them examining Susan, but it's a good idea nonetheless. The dragonfly will warn me if anything's amiss."

"What's a dragonfly?"

"He told me that's what humans call their species. It's a magnificent animal. Strong fliers, and predatory. Smaller versions of Dragons, perhaps."

"Leftover from when this world was created, even if only as an echo." Frank walked to the family room, sitting on the couch.

"You think the Swarm's safe to contact?"

"We hadn't used it when the Dragons found us at the Gatehouse. However they're tracking us, it's not through the Swarm."

He nodded. "It troubles me. Keep an eye out for Betha. Let's start a fire. See any fresh wood?"

"We don't need it. A spider on the wall over there's watched people light it." Michi strode to the large brick fireplace and turned a dial. There was a hiss, followed by a click. A small blaze started.

"Another of their fancy tools?" He walked up, and knelt before the flames. He called out with both his words and his mind. *"Swarm. Can you hear me?"*

Michi knelt beside him, watching the flickers.

"We want your help. *We need your help.*"

Two thin tongues of flame snaked out of the fireplace, bending to their foreheads.

Fire and smoke whirred around him, blurring into a clouded haze. Again, he watched the images through a veil, and heard the chorus of screams echoing from a great distance. Riding atop the crests of flame, visions poured through and past him.

A man lit a candle, walking away.

Dead grass crumpled under fading wildfire in the In-Between.

The visions jumped from scene to scene in rapid succession.

*"SCYTHE WIELDER IS SAFE."*

Michi's voice rang out from far away. "A month ago, we fled Karis. Our families were under attack. Please, can you show us what happened to them?"

The world vanished into a haze of smoke and dust. Frank rode atop a downward falling blaze, spewed from a Dragon's mouth. Karis burned, hissing plumes of white smoke into the sky. He landed on a house, crawling over its shingled roof. A 'Mental raised her hand, sending a stream of water to the roof. The scene blurred and changed.

He watched from the end of a burning stick, poking out of the ground. Around him, most of the town lay in ruins. His father and Hinara walked into sight. Hinara limped, leaning hard on Giri's arm.

"They've gone." Hinara's voice was even more removed than the Swarm's. It sounded muffled, as if Frank was deep underwater, and his aunt stood on land above.

Giri answered, yet Frank couldn't decipher the words.

"Kevara?" His aunt paused, grimacing. *Michi's mother. Her only family after her father's death.*

"Fled to Vyr." Giri pointed. "Many have—" His words faded again when he pointed.

They walked to a body on the ground. Hinara's face contorted with rage, and she screamed. Giri knelt, pulling up Bala. The young boy's purple hair hung from his head, which flopped against his neck. Giri clutched the body, looking heavenward. *They took him in, cared for the orphan. They loved him, and needed Bala after Kasumir's death.* When Giri placed the child down, a bloodstain covered his shirt.

Giri took Hinara's arm again, limping to a razed building. Aunt Hinara leaned against the ruins of a wall. *Their house is gone as well.*

Giri walked right to the smoldering fire, seeming to approach Frank. He lifted the stick. Frank's vision followed the torch, spinning and riding the tiny flames as his father waved the stick at the ground.

A thirty-foot silver Dragon lay face up in the dirt. Blood oozed from between many of its scales, pooling in the dirt below. Long shafts of stone, like enormous spearheads, protruded from the Dragon's belly in four places. Giri circled the beast, approaching its open eye. He waved the torch at the creature, yet it didn't move. He stabbed it, sending Frank straight into the monster's pupil. The image dissipated.

*"Our parents are alive."* Michi's voice called through the distant haze. Smoke and ash danced around him. *"I'm sorry about Bala, and wager we lost many friends. The village was destroyed."*

*"What of the College? How have they fared?"* Frank called with his mind, not aware of any body. Only ash and flames surrounded him.

The world blurred and flickered, flaring into a shower of sparks that clung to the night sky.

Stars twinkled overhead. His vision rode the crest of a slow-burning campfire. Large shadowy trees stretched finger-like branches high into the twilit sky on either side. Cronk sat in front of the fire. Glowing red and orange light danced across his face.

Agmundria approached, pushing the overgrowth aside.

"Were you seen?" Olu walked into Frank's field of vision, approaching from the opposite direction. His voice echoed from far away, muffled by an unseen void.

Agmundria's hands moved. The young Fearmonger spoke telepathically, so Frank couldn't make out her response. Cronk stood.

"T-t-they have H-H-Hann. W-w-we c-can't trust anyone."

Agmundria waved, probably saying something else.

"F-F-Forty? C-C-Camped t-t-two miles away?"

"What are they waiting for?" Olu stamped his foot.

Frenchie walked into sight, placing his hand on Olu's shoulder. "Does it matter? They're here. We should strike now, before they attack us."

"N-N-No. They'll s-s-slaughter y-you all."

Agmundria pointed to the trees.

"Impossible." Olu's eyes widened with terror. "They wouldn't dare."

"Both Erebus and Eshue." Frenchie shook his head. "The Ring of Scythes might already be deactivated. If those two are under a spell, Rayn's been working his evil for months, and now Hann's been taken."

Gordon walked into Frank's sight, running a hand through his curly red hair. He scowled and moved out of view.

"W-W-we r-r-return to the L-L-library. N-n-no one is s-s-safe at the C-C-College."

Frenchie nodded. Cronk's eyes drifted to the fire, and for a moment he seemed to look right at Frank. He kicked sand into the flames, and the vision evaporated into swirls of ash.

*"They need our help."* Michi's voice sang from somewhere in the swirl of dust and smoke.

*"What can we do?"*

*"What happens if we don't return? What hope is there for the College?"* The haze of smoke, flame, and soot whirled into a new pattern. Somehow, Frank sensed this vision was different, perhaps something that occurred long ago, or that hadn't happened yet.

The College of Deaths burned.

Flames danced along the tops of the earthen mounds. The two enormous towers seemed connected by lines of fire. A bridge of solid flames linked the towers. Smoke clouded the air, making it hard to see.

One of the towers toppled to the ground, and there was a peal of booming thunder.

The sky flashed, not with lightning, but with millions of glowing, angry souls.

*"SCYTHE WIELDER MUST HELP. SCYTHE WIELDER IS OUR ONLY HELP. SHE MUST IGNITE THE EYE OF DONKAR. IGNITE THE EYE."*

The chaotic scene vanished into the familiar haze of smoke. Sparks lingered, dancing around the edges of sight.

*"What is the Eye? What do you expect Susan to do?"* Frank's mind ached from the constantly-shifting visions. He felt the fury of the fire, the heat of the conflagration around him.

*"HAVE HOPE."*

Frank tumbled backward into the family room. The tongue of flame snaked back into the fireplace, and the fire snuffed out.

He turned to Michi, who was breathing hard beside him.

"Our families are alive, but the College is in trouble."

Frank nodded. "The Swarm's convinced that Susan's the only one who can help them, however they don't know how." He stared at the empty fireplace. "Do you think that was the future?"

"I think it was fear. They think if we don't help, the College will fall. Don't forget, if the Shadow King has his way, the last million years will be re-written. Everything will cease, including the Swarm."

They sat on the floor in stunned silence, waiting for the others to return. Doubt gnawed Frank's heart with every passing moment, and each thought led to graver fears.

Michi stood, walking to the window. She peered out.

"We need to go home. Just you and me, Frank. They're safe. Susan and Will are with other humans. There's nothing more we can do here." She gazed up at the sky. "The others should return soon. There's a storm on the horizon."

Frank sighed. "The Ring of Scythes has failed. The College is ready to fall. No, Michi, the storm is already here."

## CHAPTER TWENTY-SIX—SUSAN

# Hope

*D*ad broke down, and Mom helped him rejoin the silent crowd. One by one, people lit their candles, touching tapers to other wicks, spreading the light. Soon, everyone held a glowing candle. The gentle drizzle continued to fall, and people shielded their flames with cupped fingers or umbrellas.

"Come home, Suzie," said Joe beside her.

Susan opened her eyes. Will slept beside her on the soft, large bed.

She rose, easing the door open, before closing it softly behind. Shadows filled the hallway. The faint gleam of pre-dawn light ebbed at the edges of Botley Road outside the window. She entered the bathroom, splashing cold water onto her face.

*It wasn't a dream. Grym claimed the visions were real. The Deaths said our ties were severed. They lied. My family never gave up on me; they think I was kidnapped or ran away.*

Of all the terrifying sights she'd encountered while close to death, the scene of the candlelight vigil in her honor haunted her most of all.

*I abandoned them. I abandoned my parents and my life.*

She blinked, staring at the woman in the mirror.

*They wouldn't even recognize me. I'm twenty-one years old, and pregnant.*

The baby stirred in her womb. She placed her hands against her belly, thinking about the awkward visit to the OB.

*I've been pregnant for less than three months, yet I'm huge. Giri said it grew faster than normal, because of Grym. The doctor said the baby's healthy.* She sighed. *This child won't wait long.*

She sat on the toilet seat, placing her head in her hands.

*Why is this happening to me? I'm not some Helen of Troy worth warring over. The Dragons and Deaths think I'm some second Lovethar. I'm just a normal girl who got caught up in a ridiculous set of events. And now I'm... Now I'm...*

Her eyes welled with tears. They slipped down her cheeks, falling to the tiled floor below. The baby kicked.

*How am I supposed to raise a child? I have no support, I'm the only damned woman in the entire World of Deaths. If I stay here, I'm living on borrowed time, until my soul drifts away. How many more months will we have, and will the child be born as a mortal or a Death?*

She remembered the doctor's office. Will wanted to know the sex, but she convinced the doctor to keep it secret from both of them. The sonogram was a blur she barely understood.

*What if it's a girl? There are no other female Deaths.*

A new wave of fears rushed over her.

*If the child's mortal, I'd have to leave it here. I'd have to abandon it. I wouldn't even have a choice. If it's a Death, we'd have to return and brave the Dragons. Either way, I lose!*

She sank into herself, letting the tears continue to flow out. For the first time, she wished Grym was present. Even his voice would remind her that she wasn't alone. She considered waking Will, but for what purpose?

Someone knocked on the bathroom door.

"J-just a minute." She wiped tears away, and pressed the toilet's flush lever, although she hadn't used it.

"Susan?" Michi's soft voice called through the closed door. "Can I come in?"

"I'm fine."

"I can see you crying. There's a spider in the corner. I just want to talk."

Susan wiped her face again, opening the door. Michi slipped inside, closing the door. She sat on the edge of the bathtub, pushing aside the purple shower curtain, and reached a hand out to Susan.

For a time, they sat in silence.

"I'm scared, Michi."

"The Dragons can't reach you here. This is the safest you've been in a long time."

"It's not Dragons that frighten me. I'm having a *baby*. I don't know anything about kids. What if it's a girl? You know how difficult it is being female in our world. We don't even know *what* the child will be. The doctor claimed it's healthy, but what do they know? They thought I'd been pregnant almost nine months, when it hasn't even been three! If they're born here, will their soul be a part of the Mortal World? Will the child become a Dragon Key? I spent time in a Dragon prison, threatened with rape and worse. I walked through the Door to the Hereafter, battling Grym and facing my own mortality. Why should having a child fill me with so much dread?"

"Susan, calm down. You're bringing a new life into existence. It's normal to be afraid."

"Normal? What in *our* lives is normal? What does normal even mean?"

Michi patted her hand. "Frank and I looked into the Swarm while you shopped yesterday. They believe in you, Susan. So do I."

"What did you see?"

The Elemental sighed. "The College is in trouble. Dragons wait outside the Ring of Scythes, which was de-activated. Erebus and Eshue are under Rayn's control, and no one's seen Hann since his capture. Cronk, Agmundria, and your boskery friends are hiding in the library outside campus."

"It's my fault. This whole war wouldn't have started if I hadn't come to the College. Sometimes I wish Cronk never appeared at my door."

"You can't blame yourself, Susan. You've done all you can. Frank and I want to return to the College, and see if we can help during the approaching battle. However, if you want us to stay, we'll wait here with you."

"I don't think it'll be long before this child comes. My life's going to change so much, no matter what happens." She sighed. "Do you remember the night at Reaper Ridge when the boys went hunting, and you and I sat gazing at the stars?"

"Of course."

"You're a good friend, Michi. You and Frank came for us when we stood on the brink of despair. I can't ask any more of you. If you want to head back, go. The scythe's in two pieces. That leaves one for us to use."

"You said yourself, the child won't be long now. We'll wait until after the delivery. We're not abandoning you now, Susan."

They stood, embracing.

"I'm going to see if Frank's still asleep. Let me know if you ever need anything, even just to talk." The Elemental opened the door and exited.

Susan turned to the mirror. Streaks of moisture lined her cheeks, trailing from her eyes. Her hair was matted and disheveled, and her new nightgown left half of her swollen belly exposed.

*There's one other thing, something Elementals wouldn't understand.*

She eased down the staircase, careful not to creak the steps. Outside the window, the first rays of sunlight poked through clouds on the horizon. Susan walked into the family room, picking up the mobile phone Betha purchased for her.

*I shouldn't do this. Even if they answer, and it must be the middle of night in America, what would I say?*

Her fingers moved across the screen, pressing number after number.

She clicked the phone off before finishing, laying it back on the table.

*You chose this life. You chose to stay.*

Joe's voice echoed in her mind.

*"Come home, Suzie."*

She walked into the kitchen, and poured water into the kettle.

Glancing at her wrist, the webbing was there still. It seemed fainter in the Mortal World, like strands of transparent gossamer. Betha hadn't noticed it, and Susan guessed most people wouldn't see it without staring. She moved her arm back and forth, watching light gleam off the latticework encasing her wrist.

*If he could, Grym would tell me to ignore my parents, to never see them again. I can't tell them why I left, or what I've become. And yet...*

Her mind drifted back to the candlelight vigil, and Dad's tears as he thanked the crowd.

*"Come home, Suzie."*

* * * *

Reaching into the bag of chips, she took the last two out.

"They're like shrimp potato chips." Will studied his before taking a bite.

"Prawn cocktail crisps." Betha smiled. "How long have you been in England? Everyone loves crisps. Never tried prawn cocktail? I love 'em. There's a Thai chili flavor that's my favorite. You two are American, right?"

"We've only been here for a month." Will grinned. His ease lying bothered Susan. Yet, they seemed to do it constantly now. How much longer would they take advantage of Betha? "Our parents were both on a trip over here, dropping us off. Then they split, heading back to America. Leaving us with just our student visas. No money, no place to live, nothing. We'd probably be in a homeless shelter if you hadn't taken us in last week. You can't imagine how thankful we are."

"No worries. It's so nice to have friends to talk to. I've got no use for all the extra room, and you four have got the house spotless. I mean, seriously, really clean. I walked down to the counter, and I swear my reflection was better than in the mirror. And the cooking's been terrific. That meal Frank made last night. Never knew you could do that with chicken, it was amazing. I'm not much of a cook, as you've noticed."

"Tuesday's stew was…good."

"Don't lie, Will. You're such a flatterer. Susan, you really did find a keeper in him, you know?"

"I know." She glanced at the obelisk memorial standing in the center of the open courtyard. They sat in Bonn Square, on a cool marble bench. The late summer sun beat down on them from a cloudless sky. Students now appeared in greater numbers, with term only two weeks away, although Betha claimed the city still felt empty.

On the memorial's stone steps, two figures hunched over. Their forms glowed with faint shifting, blurring light. Susan couldn't shake the sensation that the souls watched her, waiting for her to do something.

A third soul walked aimlessly through the center of the road, heading toward Queen Street. A bus drove through its blurred form, scattering light, which coalesced after its departure. The indistinct form was faceless, yet Susan swore its eyes stared at her, filled with accusation.

"All right." Betha's voice dropped to a whisper, and she looked around, as if ready to impart something dire. "We've known each other a week, and I think of you two as friends now. It's secrets time."

"What?" Susan turned to the smiling redhead.

"You know, we tell each other one thing we wouldn't tell other folks. We're housemates, we might as well get on well, right? So we should tell each other things, get to trust each other. All right, I'll go first. I'll tell you a secret, but you can't freak out, and you can't tell anyone. And, you have to tell something that's *really* secret and special." She gave a big wink, and grinned.

"See the memorial over there?" Betha pointed.

"Yeah." Susan nodded, glancing again at the two vague blurs.

"Sometimes, I see *ghosts*. Right now, there's a ghost sitting on those steps."

"What?" Susan tried to mask her surprise. Mortals couldn't see souls, could they? Of course, it'd explain the obsession some people had with ghosts.

"What exactly do you see?" Will raised an eyebrow.

"It's not specific, more like a shift in the air, a faint kind of shadow. There's definitely one there. I've seen them all over town. Seems like there's more recently." She lowered her voice. "Remember, you're not allowed to think I'm daft or anything. Now, I told you a secret, it's your turn."

Susan's gaze turned back to the souls. Could Betha really see them? "I died once."

Will jumped up. "Muscle cramp." He stared at Susan.

"I mean, I almost did. I was injured, and Will brought me to help. While unconscious, I saw things."

"Oooh, you mean you saw a light? Or did you see the Grim Reaper?"

"Both." Susan smiled. "I can't describe it any better than that. Well, that's my secret."

"I can't believe Will saved your life. He really is amazing. Will, do you have a secret?"

"Um, not really."

"Come on, Will, we both shared something."

"Yeah, come on, it won't hurt you."

"Well, if you insist…the very first time I met Susan, I thought she was kind of annoying."

"Really?" Betha smiled. "Not love at first sight?"

"I never told her that. Never told her my initial reaction. She was the first girl at an all-male school. She was so *different*. I mean, I love her now. I didn't know any better, yet my first reaction was to wonder what she was doing there."

"Susan, you're so brave. You helped make a school co-ed, and were the *first* girl there? I'll bet the boys all went pretty crazy for you."

"Something like that."

"You guys hungry?" Betha stood. "How about some Cornish pasties? My treat. Well, more like my mum's, but same thing."

Betha's exuberance and unending charity were godsends, however, Susan followed the eager, bouncing redhead with trepidation. She pulled on Will's arm, whispering.

"She saw those souls."

"It's odd, I agree. Still, that doesn't mean she's connected to our world at all."

"Will, we're completely reliant on her. If she's not who she says—"

"Then we'll leave. I think you're overreacting."

Betha spun around. "You two lovebirds chatting again? Don't look now, but I see another one on the side of the road." She gestured, again pointing to a glowing soul.

Susan shuddered, yet said nothing.

\* \* \* \*

"I'm not ready for this." Will shook his head.

They sat on a bench, watching shoppers pass by. A single green-domed tower stood where the road met the horizon. Oxford's towers seemed like tiny bumps compared to East and West Towers at the College of Deaths. With a sigh, Susan realized she missed the gargantuan columns of gnarled stone. The child stirred within her womb.

"I'm not either, Will." Clouds banded the sky above, fringed with echoes of crimson and copper. Sunset approached fast, and the Cornmarket Street shops already blazed with light.

"We're having a *baby*. Any day now, at the rate it's growing." He put his head in his hands. "What were we thinking? We're not cut out to be parents. We can barely fend for ourselves."

"We didn't have a choice. Either spend our whole lives running, or bring a child of love instead of hate into the world. Will, they brought me there to *breed* me like some animal. They're disgusting. I hope our child *is* a Dragon Key, and uses her power to tear those monsters apart. I'll ignite that *Eye of Donkar* thing Grym kept whispering about. I don't even know what it really is, but if it helps kill Sindril—"

"What then?" He raised his eyebrows, glancing around. No one paid any attention to them. "We'll still have a baby to raise. Where will he live? How will we feed him? There are no babies in the World of Deaths, and the Swarm can't keep us here forever."

"I think we should move to Vyr. If the war ends, we raise our child with Frank's parents and the other 'Mentals."

"Why not move back to Reaper Ridge?" He paused, as a gray-haired woman hobbled by with a cane. Once she passed, he took Susan's hand. "Forget fighting back. Forget revenge. We live in hiding, until we're old and gray. Our son won't even have to face the Dragons, and the war will play out on its own, far away."

"They'll find us. I know it." She grinned. "Besides, what makes you think we're having a boy?"

"I just guessed, I mean Deaths are male."

"Before me. Those rules don't apply now."

"You think we'll have a girl?"

She put her hand on her belly, and Will's fingers rested next to hers. The child kicked, and Will smiled. "We'll find out soon."

They lapsed into silence. The street grew quiet as evening approached. Two glowing souls sat on the curb across from them, their edges blurring and refocusing with each gust of breeze.

Susan's eye popped open. "Something's happened."

"What?"

"The team. The boskery team back home."

"What about it?" Will squeezed her hand. "Susan, what's wrong?"

"Someone died. Time's been re-written."

"How on earth would you know?"

"A boskery team has seven players. I remember that."

"So?"

"We competed in the finals with only *six* players? We never took a seventh?"

"It does seem strange, now that you mention it."

"Mel, Frank, Gordon, Feng, you and me." She counted the players one by one on her fingers. "I think someone else was killed. Whoever the seventh player used to be. They've *ceased*."

Will shook his head in uneasy silence.

She frowned. "We don't know for sure, but it makes sense."

"I hate the idea that we had a teammate, and now we can't even remember their name. You're right, Susan, it is possible. Likely, even."

"We forget, staying here, that the Deaths are at war."

"I haven't forgotten. Come on. We should start heading to the house, it's getting dark."

She nodded, and they stood.

They walked west, toward the setting sun. The streets grew empty. Will and Susan walked hand in hand. Her new violet dress hung over her pregnant belly, its soft cotton swaying against her legs. Will wore a new outfit as well, a brand new pair of jeans and a plaid shirt, more of Betha's ceaseless hospitality.

"Do you think Betha really sees souls?"

"She sure seemed to." Will paused. "Don't let it bother you. We don't know how these things work. Maybe dozens of living humans are able to see them. If I remember from years ago, people claim to see ghosts all the time. Maybe they weren't lying."

"Perhaps."

Passing the quiet mound by Oxford Castle, a large hill with paths, they paused. Streaks of orange tinged the clouds ahead, while the road behind darkened.

"I'm scared, Will. I don't want to give the child up, but I'm terrified to be a parent."

He took her in his arms. "I'm worried too. It's normal, but we're here for each other."

"This *isn't* normal. We don't even know if the baby's human! If the pregnancy's going this fast, what if they mature faster than normal their whole lives? What if they turn eighty before we turn thirty, or have some sort of terrible curse? What if they have to stay behind in this world, while we return to the College? This isn't fair." She broke down, letting the tears slip out.

Church bells chimed in the distance. Will held her close, and she buried her face into his shirt. She heard cars and busses pass. Tears poured out until their wells ran dry.

Wiping a hand on her sleeve, she looked into his gentle blue eyes. "How do you stay so strong?"

"I'm not half as strong as you, Susan. Everyone needs a hand sometimes." He wrapped his fingers around hers, leading her down the road. "I'm just as scared as you are. Even if everything goes well, and that's a big *if*, we don't know anything about parenting. However, I do know that I love you, and we're there for each other."

"I love you too."

They stood on the street corner, and his lips sank into hers. With the slightest pressure, her lips parted, and their tongues caressed.

*Even when my world is upside-down, Will loves and supports me. He's my family now.*

The nagging image of a candlelight vigil tugged at her thoughts.

*"Come home, Suzie."*

She pushed the memory aside.

They continued past shops, restaurants, and stone townhomes until the train station emerged on their right. Susan paused, leaning against a railing. Cars drove by beneath them.

"What's wrong?"

"I just got a terrible sensation in my stomach." She glanced at the pedestrian tunnel beneath the train tracks. They'd walked through the narrow, graffiti-filled fifty-foot long tunnel dozens of times. It connected Botley, where Betha's house stood, to Oxford. She'd never paid a second thought to the tunnel, yet now her legs froze. Staring at the opening, something filled her with dread. "I can't go in the tunnel."

"There's nothing there."

The world stilled. For a moment, Susan hovered over the Dragonspine Mountains again, hurtling downward, out of the monster's claws. Every fiber in her body screamed to run away.

"Susan, this is the only way to Betha's house. We can go back and cross the street for the sidewalk, however it's already late. Can't we just use the tunnel?"

The road was five feet beneath them, separated by a steel railway. A sidewalk on the opposite side of the street offered a path beneath the tracks, yet they'd need to backtrack for several minutes to cross the street. She stared at the tunnel again.

*I'm being paranoid. It's the hormones.*

She took a deep breath, and nodded, letting Will lead her into the tunnel.

Overhead, the florescent lights flickered. Something caught the corner of her eye.

"Just some spiders, relax." Will took her arm.

"Look at their centers. Those aren't spiders." A line of arachnids crawled along the wall. Each had eight legs, however where the bodies should be, she saw only blurs.

"It's what Frank described, only smaller." She broke into a run, and Will hurried to keep up. "Bodies of a spider with a cloud in the center. They're soul snatchers."

One of the creatures jumped off the wall, flying toward her. She yelled, and Will knocked it aside, but it clung to his hand. His face paled, and he fell to his knees.

She grabbed a rock, and slammed it into his hand. He yelled in pain, and the tiny soul snatcher scurried away.

Sprinting out of the tunnel, they stumbled into a sudden halt.

Lying on the sidewalk, a soul glowed faintly.

Two shadowy forms leaned over the soul. Men, dressed in black leather, bent over the glowing form, their faces buried in its light. Susan heard a sound like sipping water.

At the soul's feet, a cluster of small soul snatchers clung on. The soul's light poured into the clouds where their bodies should've been.

Susan and Will stared. He grasped her hand so tight it hurt.

The two men looked up.

Their eyes caught the light: bright yellow reptilian eyes, the eyes of snakes, shone bright against shadowed faces. Their skin seemed loose and ill-fitted to their forms. Around their serpentine eyes, she caught the faint ridges of scales.

*Dragons.*

"Run." Will whispered the word, however it might as well have been a scream.

They turned and sprinted back through the tunnel.

Two soul snatchers leaped off the wall, flying toward her belly.

She tried to tear them off, yet they dug into her right hand like thorns.

She felt a surge from within her wrist.

With a flash of blue light, both tiny arachnids flew off her hand, trailing smoke.

"Come on!"

They exited the tunnel, and she risked a glance behind. The two Dragons stared at her. They walked with a slow confidence. The lights above them went out at their approach, so only their glowing serpentine eyes lit the dark tunnel.

"*Ssssssussssan.*" She wasn't sure which one hissed her name, yet they recognized her.

*How? How did they find us? How are they here at all?*

No time to think.

She turned and sprinted back toward Oxford, with Will trailing.

"We've got to get to Betha's house. We need help." He panted, trying to keep up.

She reached the cross street, and ran across. A car whizzed by, blaring its horn.

"Do you have any soul snatchers?" She grabbed his shirt, staring at his wrists.

"No, I made it through this time."

The two Dragons stood on the opposite side of the road, glaring with their golden snake eyes. She heard a hiss, and their leather coats flapped in the breeze.

She sprinted up the footpath, through a row of parked bicycles. Will trailed her.

*"Grym. Help us."*

There was no answer. He might have freed her from the spiders, yet the webbing still covered her arm.

She ran to the train station, darting inside.

"Where are we going?" Will ran after.

"Hey you two! Slow down!" A policeman stood, rising from his chair.

"Officer, there are two men chasing us." Susan pointed to the door. "Two men in all black, wearing leather."

"Well, you two stay here, no one'll be chasing anyone." He walked to the door.

Susan backed away, walking fast. She grabbed Will's hand, pulling him past the counter and crowd.

The entrance doors slid open, and the Dragons strolled through, hissing.

The policeman started to say something until one of the shadowy leather-clad men dug his hand straight into the man's chest. The policeman fell over, blood pouring from his stomach. People in the station screamed, running.

Susan wasted no time. With no one paying any attention to them, she ran through the wheelchair door for ticket holders and sprinted toward the tracks. She pushed past a small number of people waiting to board a train.

"Wait—there's a bridge." Will pointed to a pedestrian bridge.

They ran up the stairs two at a time.

Sweat poured down Susan's face. At the top of the bridge she paused. The baby kicked, screaming at her mother's exertion. "I can't keep running."

The two Dragons appeared at the bottom of the stairs. A steady commotion of yells poured from the station itself.

"If we cross to the other side, and make it to the road, we'll get to Betha's. Frank and Michi can help."

She took a deep breath, wiping the sweat from her forehead. They crossed the pedestrian bridge, running down the stairs.

More shouting. Gunshots rang out from the other side of the bridge.

Reaching the opposite platform, Susan and Will ran toward a door marked emergency only. A loud alarm blared. They shoved the door, sprinting out of the station.

Susan paused again, breathing hard. They stood on a side street. She saw the cars on Botley Road just down the hill.

"Almost there, honey, you're doing great. I think we might have lost them."

The baby kicked and kicked. Susan let out a moan of pain.

They jogged now, hurrying to the road. Crossing the street, they saw no sign of pursuit. Will helped support her as they darted past houses. Another two bridges to cross, over the Thames, and they'd be safe.

At the second bridge, Susan saw them. Four men, all in black leather with glowing serpent eyes. They stood on the opposite side of the street staring. A loud hiss filled the air, and the faint scent of sulfur wafted on the evening breeze. The last vestige of dusk vanished behind the clouds, and dark, threatening woods loomed on either side of the river.

"Can you run again?"

"We have no choice."

They sprinted across the final paces of the bridge.

The Dragons crossed the street. Their slow confidence and steady stares terrified Susan to the core.

Running at full speed, Will and Susan dashed the final few paces to Betha's house, turned the key, and flung open the door. Will slammed the door behind them, bolting it.

"What's wrong?" Frank rushed to her side, but she collapsed on the floor, groaning.

A sudden soaking sensation flooded her panties, as liquid spilled out. She moaned in pain.

Betha hurried into the room. "Your water's broken, hasn't it? We've got to get you to a hospital."

"Frank, they followed us. They're here."

"What?"

"Outside. They chased us."

Frank went to the window, drawing aside the curtain. He jumped back, breathing hard.

"How many?" Will panted, holding Susan's hand.

"At least six. Maybe more."

A clawing sound scratched at the door, followed by a loud hiss.

"What in hell's name is going on?" Betha walked to the window, pushing Frank out of the way. "Oh my God, what are those things? Their *eyes*."

"They chased Susan and me. I don't know what to do. More will come."

Michi walked downstairs. "You have to leave. Frank and I will fight them."

"I'm calling the police." Betha pulled out her mobile and started dialing.

"Don't." Will put a hand on her shoulder. "Look, we have to get Susan to a hospital first. As soon as we're away from the house, you can call them, but get us away from here first."

"No cops." Susan forced the words out. She pictured blood oozing from the policeman's stomach at the train station. "No one else needs to get hurt. We run."

"We'll protect you, Susan." Frank turned to Michi, nodding. The two walked upstairs.

"Betha, do you have a car?" Will helped Susan away from the door, leading her to the living room. "Any way out of here?"

"I have a friend." She paused, typing into her phone. "She's not answering. Dammit, let me call again."

"We need to get her out of here, to a hospital."

Susan caught his eyes. "They're still out there." The words escaped as a whisper, but she cried out when a wave of pain shot through her.

"We can't stay. Frank and Michi will protect us." He raised his voice. "Call the police."

"No." Susan waved Betha to stop. "They'll be too many questions. Not after the station."

"Call a taxi, then." Will's fingers squeezed around hers. He looked up. "Hurry."

"All right, all right." Betha dialed, walking to the other room. A moment later, she hurried back. "There's a taxi coming." Betha paced, her face a mixture of shock and worry. "I told him to honk when he arrives. He'll take us to a delivery center. Some of the best hospitals in the area, I'm told. Those things, those weird things. Are they even human? I mean, of course they are, just kids with contact lenses, right? Why are they here? What's happening?"

Susan walked to the bathroom, and used a towel to help dry off. Fluid covered her legs. *The baby's coming.*

She screamed. A sudden wave of intense pain shot down her womb, ending at her legs.

Will pounded on the door. "Are you okay?"

"Arrrrgh." She gripped the sides of the toilet. "It's the baby, it's coming."

"Those things are still outside."

Washing her hands, she walked to the window, pulling aside the curtain. Three pairs of yellow reptilian eyes stared back from the shadows.

"Sssssuussssssan."

A loud crash sounded above. Broken glass flew down.

Frank and Michi jumped from the second story window. Their bodies seemed suspended in mid-air, falling to the ground in slow-motion. Hundreds of tiny insects disengaged from their clothes as they approached the street.

Two of the Dragons looked up. Their hands sloughed off, revealing razor-sharp talons.

Frank brandished the double-bladed boskery blade, and Michi waved her bare hands.

Susan stared from the window, as Frank whirled the blade, slicing into Dragon after Dragon. A beast jumped up. Frank spun, twirling the blade into a ring of silver. The creature flew back, slamming into the sidewalk. A second one roared, diving at Frank. He sliced its throat. Four leather-jacketed men soon lay sprawled on the ground.

Swarms of insects flew toward the other two, and they hissed, clawing at their eyes. Frank stabbed each of them with the boskery blade, and they crumpled.

"You four aren't students, are you?" Betha stared at the carnage from the window by the door.

A pair of headlights approached, and a loud car horn honked.

"Come on." Will grabbed her arm. "Before any more come." He unbolted the door and they pushed it open, shoving hard to move against the collapsed bodies.

"Are they—?" Betha stared, unable to complete the sentence.

"Just get in the car." Will ran to the taxi, opening the door.

"What the bloody 'ell is going on?" A man with a thick, bristled moustache stared at them.

"We were attacked, and we're running. Here's forty quid extra." Betha slammed two bills into his hand. "Please, help us get away, my friend's pregnant. We're calling the police at the hospital." She glanced at Will, then turned back to the driver. "Please, just get us out of here."

"I don't—"

"Sixty quid." She slapped another note into his palm.

"All right, all right. Get in. If they ask me, I'm giving a full report, mind you. Never been a liar."

Will helped Susan into the back seat. Sitting beside her, he never released her hand. Betha sat beside them.

Frank left the boskery blade on the porch, nodded to Michi, and walked to the taxi's front door.

"I don't want any trouble." The driver shook his head. "No funny business."

"We just want a ride."

Frank got into the front passenger seat, and Michi squeezed in beside Betha. The cramped riders slammed the doors closed, and they sped away from the house.

"I'm sorry about your window." Frank leaned back, turning his head.

"Yeah." Betha stared ahead. The poor girl who'd been so kind to them looked ready to faint.

A second wave of pain swept through Susan and she cried out.

"Hurry." Will banged on the driver's chair. "She's in labor. We have to hurry."

Oxford blurred by in a whirl of shadowed stone and glowing lamplight. Twice, Susan swore she saw luminous snake eyes staring from the roadside, only to have the glows become streetlights when they drove closer.

They reached the hospital, and Susan was ushered into a wheelchair.

"Aaaarrgh." She yelled as another contraction wracked her body.

She closed her eyes, dimly aware of people talking.

"Doctor will be right with you."

They wheeled her into a white room. Curtains partitioned other sections from view. Machines beeped and hummed on the side wall. They helped her to a bed.

Near the head of the mattress, seated on the tile floor, a glowing soul turned and stared.

* * * *

Will walked into the room with a bottle of water and some crackers. She sat up smiling, as he bent and kissed her cheek.

"We're alone in the room. You're the sole patient in this bay tonight."

"The labor's moving fast. Doctor expects I'll deliver in an hour. Thanks for the crackers, I'm hungry."

"Betha's the one to thank. She's saved us many times over, Susan. Now, she's filled out all the paperwork, forging our names and addresses, so we qualify for British healthcare."

"Why's she still helping us? After what happened—"

"She's Gordon's sister."

"What?"

"Gordon, from the Gray Knights. We played boskery for so long, I'd forgotten his last name. Gordon Parkinset. Frank made the connection this afternoon. He hasn't told her who, or *what* we are, however he's hinted that we know Gordon. She's lonely. Her parents dump money on her as compensation for her brother's disappearance, and she has nowhere to put it. Now she encounters us, and Frank tells her we know where Gordon is. She's confused, yet still helpful."

"We need to tell her the truth. All of it."

"I agree. Maybe this is connected to why she sees souls. It's fate. There are forces at play working to help us, Susan."

A contraction wracked her body. She grimaced.

"At any rate, they're in the lobby. Betha's shaken up, to say the least."

Susan leaned back on the pillow. "They did an ultrasound, and the baby's going to be okay. We're having a girl."

"A girl." Will's eyes welled with moisture, and he bent down, kissing her forehead. "Susan, I love you."

"We have to pick a name. With all the worrying and running, we never discussed what we'd name her."

"How about Susan, after you?"

"Absolutely not. I don't even like my name."

"Elizabeth? It's your middle name, and it'd thank Betha as well."

"It's a possibility."

Beside the bed, the soul stood. Its features were clearer than many she'd seen, which meant it hadn't been dead for long. A silver-haired woman looked at them, with soft amber light pouring from her skin. The soul shook its head, pointing to Susan's heart.

"You don't like Elizabeth?" Will's eyebrows raised.

The soul pointed again, placing a hand on its own heart.

Susan nodded. "It has to be more heartfelt. This is an important decision. Will, what's the one thing you and I have held on to since meeting? The one thing we held even in the Dragon's prison, or at the threshold of death?

"Hope." The word came from the soul, Will's lips, and from Susan's mouth all at once.

Smiling, the glowing figure walked away.

"Our child is Hope." Will placed his hand on her belly.

"Hope for peace, and a better life." She smiled. "It's the perfect name."

\* \* \* \*

With the gas mask over her mouth, she took a deep breath. The pain lessened at once. She nodded, handing the mask to the nurse. Will clutched her hand.

"You're doing great, Susan. Just keep breathing." The doctor stood between her outstretched legs. "I can see the head. When I say to, I want you push as hard as you can. Ready, and PUSH."

Susan groaned, pushing with all her might.

"Again. PUSH."

Her fingers tightened around Will's.

*Hope. Our child. Hope is what we need more than anything.*

"PUSH."

*I have Hope. I have faith in you, Hope.*

"PUSH."

With a surge, she felt Hope emerge. She heard a cry.

In a flash, the hospital room vanished.

She stood on an endless sea, stretching beyond every horizon. Purple clouds hung against an empty gray sky.

Caladbolg stood before her.

*"You were foolish."* The ancient king stared at her, his feet lingering on the surface of the still waters.

*"What are you doing? Why am I here? Bring me back. Bring me back to Hope."*

*"You thought creating a child in this world would spare you pain. You were wrong. Your soul was tethered to the Swarm, and was filled with fear. Hope is a powerful Dragon Key, more powerful than even Sindril realizes."*

*"Bring me back now, Grym. I don't have time for this."*

*"Calm yourself, girl. You haven't gone anywhere. I wanted you to know what your child will become."*

*"I'll keep it in mind."* She breathed hard, her body aching.

*"We are one now, you and I. The chains restraining me shattered with this birth. I am free."*

She raised her hand in warning. A surge of strength coursed from head to toe. Concentrating on the water, two streams snaked around Grym's legs, holding him like ropes. *"I defeated you once, passing through the doors of death itself. You don't frighten me."*

Her anger grew, raging through her veins with heat. How dare this scythe continue to threaten her? How dare he taunt her?

The blood pumped faster through her arms. She smelled smoke, letting the rage boil.

With a gust of wind, the sea vanished, replaced by an ocean of fire. Grym smiled.

They stood atop an endless flaming sea, a conflagration even mightier than the Swarm.

*"Your ancestors controlled fire as well. Finally, you start to come into your own. Do not worry, Susan. I respect our battle, and I will bring no harm to you, your friends, or your child. I am your tool, as you are mine."*

The ocean of fire flared up, and dissipated.

Clouds of gray, vanishing, fading…

*I am your tool, as you are mine.*

The machine beside her bed beeped.

"Susan! Susan!" Will's fingers squeezed like a vice.

She opened her eyes.

"She's stabilizing. Get that IV going. Susan, can you hear me?"

She nodded. Hope wailed in the distance.

The doctor stepped to the head of the bed, shining a light in her eyes. "You passed out for a second. Probably just a reaction to the pain. Colby keep a close eye on her vitals."

"I will."

"How do you feel?"

"I'm all right. I'm very tired, but I'm all right. I want to see her."

"Of course. Susan, this is Hope. At five pounds, seven ounces, she's a little underweight, yet nothing to be concerned over."

Wrapped in a blanket, the tiny creature was the most beautiful thing Susan had ever seen.

"She has your eyes, Will."

"For a moment, I thought I'd lost you."

Susan stared at their child.

*A powerful Dragon Key.*

This sweet innocent creature.

Hope squirmed, staring with unseeing eyes. Her tiny fingers clenched in a tiny fist, and her small mouth opened, pushed by a miniscule tongue.

"One of the calmest babies I've seen." The Doctor jotted some notes on a pad.

Susan looked down at Hope, at her pure innocence.

The child's lips widened, almost in a miniature grin. Her tongue slipped out again.

Will rubbed her shoulder.

Susan's head flopped back against the pillow. A sense of relief blanketed her.

*I will protect you from them. I will protect you from all harm, no matter what it takes.*

*"And I will help."*

The ancient voice echoed in the back of her mind. He was there now, waiting for her.

"You seem to be doing fine, but we'll keep an eye on you for the next few hours." The doctor stood. "Congratulations on a healthy baby girl."

*"Yes, congratulations, Susan. She'll make a fine Dragon Key."*

* * * *

"She's beautiful." Michi rocked Hope in her arms.

"How do you feel, Susan?" Frank placed a teddy bear beside her table. "Betha picked this from the shop by the lobby."

"It was nothing." Betha stood beside Michi, her attention on the newborn baby.

"I feel fine." Susan sat higher against the soft pillow. "Just tired."

This new room was smaller than the delivery bay, and again free of other patients. The smell of bleach and disinfectant hung over everything. In the distance, the constant sound of fans, beeping machines, and walking nurses echoed down the hallway.

Will drew the window blinds aside. "There's a storm rolling in. Lightning on the horizon."

"What time is it?" Susan yawned, stretching her arms.

"Five in the morning. Nearly dawn." Betha sat at the foot of Susan's hospital bed. Her face masked her emotions, and she stared at the wall. "Listen. I don't want to get mixed up in any trouble. Frank…Frank said he knew where Gordon was. My brother went missing three years ago. He'd be seventeen now." She paused, gripping the white sheets. "Whatever Gordon's involved with, maybe it's better not to tell me. What happened at the house was crazy. I think maybe I'll head back, and just let you—"

"You can't go back." Frank looked up, his eyes narrowing. "It's not safe."

Michi handed Hope to Susan. "He's right. They might come back."

"I'll call the police. Or is it something bad? Will Gordon get in trouble if I call the authorities? Oh, this is ridiculous. What is going on? Where is my brother? Do you really know him?"

"We do." Susan smiled at her daughter. Hope murmured, wriggling against her blanket. The baby's miniature fingers clenched into a fist against her cheek. "Gordon's safe, and he's not in trouble with the law. It's far more complex than that."

"Let me guess, you can't tell me. I open my home to you, go out of my way to help you, and you won't even tell me what connection you have to him?"

Susan continued gazing at Hope. "You helped us before any of us realized you were Gordon's brother." She looked up, smiling at Betha. "We're grateful. You've been wonderful, and we owe you more than you know. I promise we will explain everything. You just might find it hard to believe."

"You think we should tell her?" Frank started to pace.

"Michi. Keep an eye out, and let us know if anyone's coming."

"Already on it." The Elemental grinned. The thought of insects in a hospital bothered Susan. She shoved the thought aside.

"Are you religious, Betha? The souls you see, what do you think happens to them?" As she spoke, Susan thought out her words, keeping her attention on the baby. She'd never seen a more precious sight. Her body ached with exhaustion, however, she wanted this issue out in the open, before Betha abandoned them. If Elizabetha did chose to leave, it would be with all the knowledge she deserved. Besides, connecting with a family of a Death was strangely personal. What would her own family think, if they knew where she was right now?

"I go to church on Christmas, sometimes on Easter. Why? Don't tell me Gordon's joined a cult or something."

"The Gray Knights are no cult." Frank continued to pace.

Susan ignored him. "Have you ever wondered what happens after death?"

"You mean like Heaven and Hell? I see ghosts. Of course I think about it." Betha sighed. "I mean now that you mention it, it'd be impossible to prove one way or the other. There could be an afterlife, but are we just supposed to take everyone's word for it? I never accepted anyone's opinion on blind faith. I know what I see. Funny thing is I never saw *any* until Gordon went missing, and now it's like there's so many of them." Betha seemed to relax, falling into her loquacious patterns again.

"When a person dies, normally their soul is reaped by a Death, someone with a scythe."

"Death? Like on the old medieval churches, or in the comic books? The skeleton guy?"

"Before he went missing, did Gordon lose a lot of weight?"

"Yeah. He was real skinny, especially at the end. I kept telling him to eat more—"

"Gordon is a Death. It's a job. Will and I are Deaths too. Like Gordon, we were kidnapped from our homes and forced to reap souls." Susan looked up from Hope's wriggling face. Betha stared back.

"You're Deaths?"

"You've seen a lot of souls lately because the Deaths are at war. Reapings have paused."

"Deaths? You reap souls? Gordon too?"

"You saw my boskery blade earlier." Frank smiled. "It's just a type of double-scythe. Gordon's great with boskery blades."

"Boskery?"

"That's how we know Gordon. Boskery is a sport. We play it with him, in the World of Deaths."

"World of Deaths? Like the Underworld? That's where Gordon is? Guys, I think I need to wake up now, this is all more ridiculous than anything I could have imagined." Betha stood. "I should get going. Look, I won't tell the police. I won't tell anyone. When they ask about the window, I'll say—"

"They're here." Will's voice cut into the room, soft yet worried. "Susan, you'd better see this."

Susan handed Hope to Frank and climbed out of bed. She walked to the window, with Betha close behind.

Dark clouds covered the night sky. Beneath the window, a well-lit parking lot filled with cars stretched to the road. Around the lot, shadows deepened.

A fork of lightning bolted down, throwing light onto the surrounding fields.

Rows of leather-coated men stood just outside the fence, staring up at the hospital.

They faded into the shadows again.

The lights on the parking lot flickered and went out.

A second bolt of lightning shattered the darkness.

Four of the men scaled the fence. They stared up, with glowing reptile eyes.

"Those are the creatures the Deaths are fighting." Will pointed. "Everything Susan told you is true."

"Michi, did you bring the scythe blades?" Susan dropped the blinds, hurrying back to Frank. She clutched Hope in her arms.

"Yes."

"We're using one now. Will, you brought us to Oxford, leading us to Betha and help. I trust you to save us again. Bring us back to Karis."

*"Wait!"* Grym's voice thundered in her ears. *"The child's less than a day old, she's too fragile to travel by scythe. You will injure her if you do."*

Michi handed Will a metal shard, one of the two scythe blade fragments, and he turned it over in his fingers. Betha stared at the broken fragment.

"No." Susan's eyes widened. "Put it away. Grym's told me that Hope can't travel by scythe yet, she's too weak. We have to find another way."

"We need to get out of the city *now*." Frank peered out the window.

Betha pulled out her mobile. "I don't know what's true anymore, but those things out there terrify me. If you *are* Deaths, and Gordon's one too, well at least that slacker finally found a job. I'm calling my friend Genevieve. Girl's a tart, but she owes me a *major* favor after the stunt she pulled, and this certainly qualifies. Besides, she drives a bloody boat on wheels, and she lives up here by Headington."

Will handed the scythe blade back to Michi, and stepped close to Susan. He rested a hand on her shoulder. "We'll be okay."

"Looks like it's time to check out." Betha snapped the phone closed, and walked to the door. "She's on her way. Probably drunk off her arse. Still, she'll get us back to the train station. From there you can go wherever."

"I'm sorry we couldn't be more helpful." Susan cradled Hope. "Thank you again for everything, Betha."

"Susan, Betha, take at look at this." Frank pulled aside the window blind again. They hurried over.

"The ghosts!"

Hundreds of glowing souls launched themselves out of the hospital, flying through walls and floating over the parking lot. The stream of souls hurled itself at the approaching horde of Dragons.

"Why would ghosts help, if we weren't Deaths? What I told you is true."

Hope gurgled in her arms.

*The ghosts rushed to protect us? Or was it to protect Hope? Grym claims she's a powerful Dragon Key.*

"*They do not protect* her." Grym's voice boomed in her mind. "*The child protects herself, and* you."

Soul after soul hurtled down through the hospital walls. Many toppled at strange angles, as if thrown by an unseen force.

"I believe you." Betha stared down with them, watching the onslaught.

Flying luminous forms wrapped around the serpent-eyed men. The Dragons waved their arms trying to repel the souls. Some tried to eat the oncoming dead, however there were too many. Dozens of Dragons collapsed.

"I believe every word." She glanced down at the vibrating phone. "Come on, Genevieve's at the lobby."

They walked out of the room.

"You haven't been discharged yet," protested a nurse. "I don't think the patient should be up and around."

Ignoring the nurses, they passed through the corridor, dashing to an elevator. Susan clutched Hope against her chest. The baby started to cry.

"Just going for a walk," Betha shouted in the direction of the nurses' station, without pausing. At the lobby, a disheveled blonde girl in sweats accosted them.

"It's five-o-clock in the bloody morning. This better be good, Betha."

"After what you did with Brandon, I don't want to hear it."

"Don't you start. I do you this favor, and we're even, do you understand?" Genevieve's breath reeked of alcohol even from where Susan stood.

"You're drunk, Gen. You're giving me the keys, and we're all going to the train station. Once we get there, we're even and I'll never mention him again."

"You better not. I mean it was just one damned party. Who are your bloody friends? Not like I care. More losers, no doubt."

"The keys, Gen. Now."

"Here. Here. I'm not going anywhere. I'm going to sit right in this lobby and wait until you bring my car back."

"Fine with me. Come on." Betha grabbed the keys and ran out the front door.

"I'll kill you if you scratch it. I swear you better not do anything to that car!"

Susan ran after Betha, with the others close behind. Rain fell in sheets, pounding the ground. She slipped, falling to one knee. Will ran to her side, helping her up.

Betha unlocked a large silver car, ushering them inside. Susan, with Hope on her lap, sat between Will and Frank. Michi took the front passenger seat. Betha revved the motor, slammed it into reverse and pulled out.

Lightning flashed, followed by an enormous rumble of thunder. Two Dragons approached, walking between the cars. One stared with yellow eyes, the other crimson.

"Let's move." Will leaned over and buckled her seatbelt over her. The car raced away from the hospital.

They sped through the darkened city streets. The stone buildings of the colleges loomed like enormous threatening shadows in the rain. Thunder echoed in the distance.

"Can barely see in the bloody rain." Betha turned the car's wipers higher. Ahead of them, their headlights reflected off the falling sheets of silver.

"We have to leave Oxford, yet where can we go?" Will stared out the window, as another bolt of lightning cleaved the sky.

"I want to go to America. I'm going to Maryland, with Hope. Her grandparents need to know."

She expected an argument, however, Will nodded.

Susan glanced at Frank, but the Elemental shrugged. "At this point, there are no rules. If you want to go to your family, so be it. Just remember, you can't stay in this world for long."

*"Hope's soul is tethered to the World of Deaths."* Without prompting, Grym quelled one of her deepest fears. *"You'll have to take her with you when you return."*

"Hope's a Death."

"Grym told you?" Will kept staring out the window.

"He's free now. There's nothing burying him anymore." She glanced at her wrist. There were no gossamer threads, and the hourglass tattoo-like mark was visible once again.

"Be careful, Susan. He's a murderer."

Hope gurgled, nestling against her breast.

"Train station's just ahead." Betha pulled off the road, into a parking lot. In the rain, Susan just made out the building where they'd fled from Dragons only hours ago.

They parked and got out. Ducking in the rain they hurried toward the station.

"Look behind you," Frank called out, turning.

A Dragon stood on the roof of the car they'd just left. His serpent eyes gleamed with ferocious emerald light. Lightning flashed, and in its brief glow, she saw the bulge of wings beneath the Dragon's leather jacket. The creature turned its face skyward, lapping the rain with a forked tongue.

It bellowed, roaring into the night, louder than thunder.

Another streak of lightning struck a car in the corner of the lot, casting sparks and smoke in a plume. The noise deafened. The Dragon's mouth distended, and two rows of fangs emerged.

"Take Hope." Susan pushed the baby into Will's arms. "Get into the station now."

"What are you doing? We need to run."

"I'm through running."

The words felt strange on her tongue, however a new sensation rolled through her tired body. Anger, rage, and confidence stronger than she'd ever known welled up from the depths of her soul.

"Your arm." Betha pointed. "What's going on?"

"In the station. All of you. *Now!*" Susan glanced at her right arm, which was wreathed in glowing blue flame. Steam sizzled where the rain struck the brilliant incandescence of her fire-wrapped arm.

*I am your tool, as you are mine.*

The others ran into the station behind her. The storm raged above, as the green-eyed Dragon stared at her from the top of Genevieve's car.

One of its shoes split open, and a gash emerged in the creature's leather pants, revealing a taloned leg, covered in violet scales.

"The child." The creature hissed, digging its claw into the car's roof.

"Leave my family alone." Susan raised her glowing arm.

The Dragon opened its mouth, and a jet of hot flame shot across the parked cars.

Susan lowered her right arm, on instinct, and raised her left. The blaze struck her palm, and ricocheted away, careening into an empty area of the parking lot.

*"SCYTHE WIELDER!"*

A flood of images rushed through her mind at the flame's touch. She saw the Swarm, and an infinite number of fires throughout two worlds. She watched Cronk's face appear and vanish into smoke.

The blast of fire flickered out on the pavement, and the Dragon cocked his head. Susan's breath came fast and hard.

*"Thank you, Grym."*

*"That wasn't me. You stopped the blast yourself. Your grandfather was a fire Elemental. You've held traces of that power within, your whole life. Now you wield the First Scythe. You are the mother of the Dragon Key. You are strong, Susan."*

"Susan!" Will shouted from behind. "Train's leaving in a minute. Come on."

The Dragon bellowed, yet made no move.

Susan spun, following Will into the station. He pressed a ticket into her hand and they raced through the turnstile, and onto a waiting train.

"We're going to London." Will sat beside her, with Hope squirming on his lap. Frank and Michi sat across from them.

"I'm coming too." Betha hopped on the train, just as its doors closed.

"What about the car, and the house?"

"I'll take care of those later. I want you four out of sight, before I head back. Those things are after you, and they've certainly seen me. I might stay away from Oxford for a while. Gen won't mind too much, I'm sure."

The train shuddered, pulling away from the station. A piercing screech sounded outside the car.

"The Dragon's calling for help. We're not free yet." Susan leaned against the seat, glancing down at her arm. There was no glow.

*"The College of Deaths has fallen."* Sadness echoed in Grym's deep voice. *"It took me a moment to decipher what we saw when you touched the flames. Dragons have taken over both Towers. Cronk and a few of your friends hide in the Library, begging for aid."*

She relayed the message, and Frank stood. "There's nothing else Michi and I can do to help you here."

"Are you crazy? They're still chasing us!" Will adjusted his grip on Hope, and she started to cry. "We need you two now more than ever."

"Frank's right." The calm in Susan's voice surprised her. "If they don't help, we won't have a home to return to. Leave one scythe piece, and return to the World of Deaths." She glanced around the train. An old man near the front of the car slept, and a teenager with ear buds stared at his phone. "No one's looking. Go. Find White Claw and the 'Mentals. Do whatever it takes to survive. We'll be in touch through the Swarm."

Michi's face wrinkled in concern. "Are you sure you'll be all right?"

Susan nodded. "At the next station, we'll switch trains. We can do that a few times, and the Dragons will never know where we went or are headed. They're all in Oxford. As long as we stay away, we'll be fine. You, on the other hand, will walk into a war zone. Be safe."

Betha stood. "My brother. You're going to him, aren't you?"

"Yes." Frank placed a hand on her shoulder. "Gordon's a good friend, and I'm sure he's fine."

"Tell him, I love him. We never forgot him." She wiped her face.

"I will."

Michi handed a scythe piece to Susan. Glancing around again, she handed the fragment to Frank. He took Michi's hand, and swung. A gash of white-hot light brighter than lightning appeared, swallowing the two Elementals. They vanished.

The teenager looked up for a moment, before turning back to his phone.

The train sped on through the night.

"When is the next stop? I want to throw them off our trail." Unsure of where to put the scythe blade, Susan laid it on the seat.

"Didcot Parkway. Just a few minutes from here."

"In case anyone's watching, I want to switch railcars."

"We'll get off, and wait at Didcot for the next train."

"Betha, I can't tell you how much you've helped us. The words thank you aren't strong enough."

"Look after Gordon, and we'll call it even."

Hope started to cry. Susan pulled the child to her breast allowing her to nurse.

"You're a natural mother." Will smiled.

Susan watched the countryside whizz by in a gray blur. They pulled into Didcot, and stepped off the train. The rain lessened, and the sky above grew brighter. The area around was dismal, an empty industrial wasteland with trains and some cement smokestacks.

She kept an eye out for Dragons. None had followed them.

Betha sat on a bench, staring at the rails.

Behind them, a single glowing soul floated by.

"My whole life's gone topsy-turvy in a day." The young woman ran a hand through her thick auburn hair. "I thought there was something different about you two when I first met you at the Parks, yet I never dreamed it'd be like this. Those ghosts pouring out of the hospital like a waterfall. Gordon's a Death? A Grim Reaper?"

"Yes. At heart, he's just a normal kid, trying to survive." Susan bounced Hope on her lap, and the baby's eyes closed.

"I've seen so many adverts for missing children. Are they all Deaths? Is that what happens?"

"I don't think so." Susan did another survey of the empty tracks, keeping a wary eye out. "All Deaths were kidnapped, but most missing children don't become Deaths. Before me, there were no female Deaths."

"Now there are two." Will smiled down at his daughter. "The rules of our world will change."

She sighed. "Let's just hope there's a world left when we return. If the Dragons win, souls will continue to pile in this world until their king erases history."

"They were the original reapers, according to legend." Will stared at Hope. "If we keep our daughter safe, the Shadow King can't make a key. Maybe they'll start reaping souls, and there'll be no more Deaths, no more kidnapped children."

"You sound like you want them to win." Susan frowned.

"Who are they?" The redhead's foot twitched. "Who are these creatures you're at war with."

"Dragons," said Will.

"You're kidding." Betha shook her head.

"I wish we were."

"Go to Maryland." The redhead looked up.

"What?" Susan raised an eyebrow.

"It's where you're from before you were kidnapped, isn't it? I heard you say you want Hope to meet her grandparents. Tell them the truth. They deserve to know."

Hope wailed, squirming in Susan's arms.

"What is it?" Will frowned. "Is she hungry?"

"She just ate." Susan stared at the crying child. *I don't know anything about babies.*

Betha grinned. "She might have, you know, left you her first present."

"Present?"

"She needs to be changed."

"I only have what we took from the hospital. We don't have any diapers or anything. Hell, I don't even know *how* to change a diaper."

"Stay calm, Susan, you just faced a Dragon. I think we can handle a baby."

Hope's cries grew into a full wail.

"I'll get the station manager." Betha hurried off.

Will touched her arm. "You're doing great, honey."

Betha ran back several minutes later with a large bag. "It's amazing what money, a proper question, and a smile will do. Turns out the station manager's wife just had a baby last week. I've got all kinds of stuff in here."

"He won't need this?" Will looked through the bag.

"The money and the smile, as I said. Here, I'll show you how to change a nappie. I'm guessing neither of you ever babysat?"

They shook their heads. Betha took Hope and rocked her. She laid her on the bench and demonstrated. Susan looked skyward, silently thanking the heavens for Betha's unending support.

The next London-bound train pulled up, and its doors slid opened. The rain was little more than a soft drizzle. Hints of crimson tinged the gray pre-dawn clouds.

"Come on." Susan stood, adjusting her hold on Hope, and the others followed her onboard. They passed two men in business suits, and a blind woman beside a guide dog. An Asian woman in a gray dress typed into a laptop.

She led Will and Betha to the next car, which was empty.

The train started, and a conductor walked up, asking for their tickets.

"These have already been punched. Got on at Oxford?"

Betha smiled. "My niece here is just a day old, we had to get off at Didcot for her."

"Ah, lovely child. Hey there. Hey. Hi." He made a series of strange faces and Hope wriggled. "No worries, you lot just hang tight til Paddington. Got an hour." He smiled, tipping his hat and walked away.

"Thank you, Aunt Betha." Susan laughed.

The train sped east, rushing to meet the dawn. Grassy fields and clumped towns passed, blurring after each other. Leaning her head against Will's shoulder, Susan's eyes grew heavy. She started to relax, when the entire train shuddered.

"What was that?" Will's face pressed against the window.

"Probably some debris in the track." A hint of doubt quivered in Betha's voice.

The train shook again, and its interior lights flickered out.

*"They're here. On the roof of the train."*

"I have to go." Susan wrapped her fingers around Hope's tiny hand, handing her to Will. She kissed him fiercely. "I can stop them."

"What can you—"

"I can do this. You believed in me, Will, when we first met, and no one wanted to trust a girl. Believe in me now."

The train jumped, and something pounded on the roof of the train car. A geyser of sparks shot past the window as the train skidded on the track.

"Go." Will clutched Hope. "Be careful."

Susan stood, and the blue flame engulfed her right arm.

*I am your tool, as you are mine.*

She felt the air around her, and waved the First Scythe. Grym's edge gnawed at open space, sensing her desires. Moving her arm from side to side, the blue flame became a blade, feeding on the empty air.

Grym reached into the air, opening space, chewing through the void.

With of flash of blazing sapphire, Susan stood atop the train's roof. At once, she dropped to her hands and knees as forceful wind pounded her. The blue flames on her arm rippled in the gale.

A monstrous roar bellowed from behind.

Susan spun around, struggling to balance. With growing confidence, she stood.

A leather-clad man stood facing her, with emerald reptile eyes. Both legs of his pants were torn beneath the knee, revealing enormous muscular legs covered in violet scales. Talons dug into the trembling steel car beneath them. The beast hissed.

She held her right arm like if it was a sword, extending from her shoulder to fingertips. Fingers of dancing blue flame coalesced into a solid saber, an enormous scythe blade of solid light.

"Ssssssuusssssssan." The Dragon's face quivered, shaking in the wind like an ill-fitting mask. The human skin fell to the train, and the leather jacket tore open. Two enormous bat-like purple wings flapped in the roaring wind. He folded the wings, leaning against the railcar's momentum.

Wind whipped her hair. Susan took a step forward, still brandishing the First Scythe.

The Dragon's mouth opened, revealing sharp fangs. It threw a bolt of fire toward her. Susan deflected it with her left hand.

*"SAVE US!"*

The Swarm bounced away, and Susan felt rage and anger boiling in her blood. She curled her fingers, and the stream of fire circled back in mid-air, attacking the Dragon from the side.

*I understand. I see the fire.*

Fire was an extension of her thought, a current of wind, no different from fighting Grym at the threshold of death.

Flames accosted the Dragon, rushing over it. Surprised, the creature lost its balance, falling.

The train sped on.

With three flaps of its large wings, the creature landed back onto the railcar. It ran at Susan, clawing its way forward by piercing the train with its talons. The monster's fangs bared, and it screamed into the air.

Susan ran, diving beneath him. She landed on her back, clutching its legs. Holding her arm above her, she moved the First Scythe.

A ray of sapphire light erupted from her arm, slicing the Dragon. Scales and blood fell and the stench of sulfur made Susan dizzy. It roared, taking to the sky.

Susan stood again.

This time, the creature landed at the front of the train, spinning around. Green blood trailed down its chest, spilling onto the steel car. Dozens of scales hung off his body at strange angles, and gaps in the scales oozed with blood and pus. The Dragon staggered, staring at her.

"Leave my family alone." She raised her arm again, letting sapphire flames coalesce once again into an enormous translucent blade.

A wall slammed into the Dragon's head as the train dove into a tunnel. Susan dropped to all fours. The Dragon bellowed so loud Susan's ears rang.

They emerged from the tunnel, and Susan stood. Holding her arm, a second ray of sapphire sped toward the beast, striking its neck. The Dragon rolled from side to side, clinging to the train, and to life.

Susan checked her balance and walked to its gasping head.

The beast turned an emerald eye to her, staring. "You and the child will die. Others will come."

Susan raised Grym and sliced off the creature's head. With another wave of her arm, she re-emerged in the train's cabin in a flash of sapphire.

She sat, exhausted.

*"Don't relax yet."* She sensed Grym looking through her, staring around. *"I know how they've tracked you. It's Will. His shoulder. I should've seen it earlier."*

She stared at Will's shoulder, and through Grym's eyes she saw a tiny glowing dot.

*Another vika egg. Too small for the Swarm to detect, yet large enough for the Dragons to track.*

"Will. Give Hope to Betha."

"What's happening? We heard so much noise."

"Hand Hope to Betha now. I know how they've been tracking us."

Will nodded, and passed the sleeping baby to their friend.

"I defeated the Dragon that was here. More will come if I don't do this. I'm sorry."

She raised her arm, letting blue flames emerge.

*"We have to be careful, Grym. Don't hurt him."*

One of the fingers of sapphire fire snaked up, creeping to Will's shoulder.

"There's a vika egg. I'm going to remove it."

The finger of flame sharpened, becoming a single spike. It pierced Will and he cried out.

*"I have the egg."*

Grym and Susan pulled the miniscule egg from Will, and the flames tossed it into an adjoining seat. The sapphire light sharpened, focusing on the tiny dot. Wisps of smoke wafted up from the seat, as the egg disintegrated.

"It's gone now." She smiled. "The Dragons can't follow us anymore."

There was an enormous thud as something slid off the roof of the train.

Susan sank into the seat. "I'm really tired." She closed her eyes.

\* \* \* \*

She stood on an endless sea beneath a flaming sky. Where fire and water met, two figures faced each other: Susan and Grym.

"What am I?" Susan stared at the ancient king's face.

"You are a hero, a survivor, a mother, and a child."

"No riddles. I moved that fire in mid-air. I fought, using *you*, with a courage I've never felt before."

"You're being hard on yourself, Susan. I've seen that courage before. You fought me and won, and you gave birth to a Dragon Key. Your full potential has awoken. When you return to the World of Deaths you shall be a weapon to be feared."

"I just want to protect my family. That's all."

She took a step back, gazing at the endless expanse of flame and water.

"Your other family thinks you're dead."

"What?" She turned back.

Caladbolg stroked his white beard. "You're tethered to the Swarm. I see through the tether like watching sunlight reflect off the ocean. Sindril's realized you're in the Mortal World. He's probably known for some time. He's created a ruse, a lie for your parents."

"What? Show me!"

The water and fire met in a clash of steam, which swirled around her. The image faded, and Susan's eyes watched from the top of a lit candle taper.

Mom, Dad, and Joe were dressed in black. They stood around a casket with drawn, miserable faces.

"I'm alive. This is a lie!"

The image faded, and Susan again faced Caladbolg. "Why would he do this?"

"I suspect he's prepared a trap."

"I have to tell them. I can't let them think I've been killed, and I don't want them in danger."

"You should warn them, yes." He nodded, stroking his beard.

"It's not enough. What else can I do? You used to talk about some sort of eye. The Eye of Donkar."

"It's at the College. I wish it were here. The body of Karos, my Dragon long ago, was fashioned into a weapon to focus my powers. This happened after he died and I was sealed in the bracelet. However, I was buried behind the library wall before it was ever used."

"So we can't use the Eye, and Sindril knows I'm in this world. I'll call Mom and Dad. I'll tell them I'm alive."

The two stared at each other. The sky above rolled in constant flame, and the sea below quivered.

"I think you could go, if you wish." Caladbolg studied her with a cold expression.

"You're trying to kill me again? You just said it was a trap."

"It's a trap worth springing. It will take some training, but you need time for Hope's sake. Work with me, and you might be ready to fight.

If you can't tackle a few Dragons here in the Mortal World, what chance will you have against the Shadow King?"

The world faded from sight.

Susan opened her eyes.

"Paddington Station next stop," blared the intercom.

Betha yawned in the seat across from her. Will held Hope, rocking the sleeping baby. His eyes met Susan's, and they smiled.

The four departed the train. Susan glanced at the rows of tall steel and glass arches, stifling a yawn.

"What next?" Betha pushed a strand of copper hair away from her eyes. "I'd buy you guys plane tickets, but those are going to be a *lot* of money, and without ID, you won't even get on board."

"They can't track us now." Susan took a deep breath. "We've bought some time. We need a place to stay. If we can survive in the shadows for a few days, we'll be fine."

"You have a plan?" asked Will.

Betha ran a hand through her red hair. "Plenty of hotels around. Some time in a hotel's going to be a lot less than a plane ticket. I'll set you two up, maybe spend one day more here in town, and then I'm going to head back. No more Dragons?"

"I don't know, Betha. I don't know what they'll do now."

The redhead frowned, leading them outside. They avoided the hotels closest to the station, choosing a small, unremarkable one near an alley. Betha booked four nights in a single room.

The elevator creaked as it climbed wearily to the fourth floor. When they reached the small room, Susan flopped on the bed, close to sleep.

Her last thoughts lingered around an endless sea beneath a flaming sky.

*"What chance will you have?"*

# PART THREE

## BEYOND THE THRESHOLD

CHAPTER TWENTY-SEVEN—FRANK

# Serpent's Web

Colors, sounds, and smells blurred around him, streaming into a torrent of sensation.

The In-Between passed, a mirror between worlds. While it rushed by, he swore he saw cracks creeping through its sky.

The scythe blade fragment struggled, tearing its way through space. Sparks of every shade shot around his hand as he forced it through the void. Frank clung to Michi, straining to keep his fingers clamped around hers.

Frank hit the ground hard, rolling on dirt. He blinked, adjusting to the dim light.

They sat in a wasteland. Scorched trees yards away ringed acres of ruin. Stone rubble littered splinters of wood and brick, heaped into random piles. Mounds of muddy earth stood between gouge marks ten feet wide. The desolation stank of rotten eggs and decaying flesh.

"Where are we?" Frank's eyed widened, knowing, yet dreading, the answer.

"Karis. This was our home. They've destroyed it."

"I tried to bring us to Vyr. Your mother was headed there." He opened his palm, revealing a pile of silver dust.

"The scythe blade?"

"At least we made it to this world in one piece." He tossed the dust aside. "It feels good to be back. Even if the village is ruined, the Mortal World was odd. Running around in the shadows, surrounded by strangers."

Michi stood, shaking her head. "I hope Susan's okay. She seemed awful sure of herself. I'll reach out to insects. We need to be careful."

"Where are the survivors? We saw my parents here through the Swarm." Frank frowned. "Something's wrong."

"They might have gone to Vyr. It doesn't seem like anyone's around."

"Come on."

They walked through the desolation. A stillness lingered in the air. The two Elementals fell silent, walking hand in hand. Dawn crept into the sky above, breaking through scattered clouds.

*Jera's house used to stand over there, next to Forgyni's. Central Hall is nothing more than a large pile of rubble.*

Much of the village was unrecognizable. A leaning spire of stone shot out of the earth before them, a spear of granite fifty feet long used during the battle. Its broken tip lay on the ground a few yards away, covered in dried blood.

"Someone's coming." Michi grabbed his arm, spinning toward the forest. They ducked behind the leaning rock column, where it met a mound of mud and crumbling brick.

A solitary figure emerged from the woods, staring around her. Her hair was disheveled and dirt smeared her face. At first, Frank didn't recognize the woman.

With a start, he stood, smiling and waving.

Hinara stared up, shaking her head. Her lips mouthed a single word. "Run."

Michi pulled Frank back behind the stone. She shook her head, with a finger on her lips. Creeping to a crevice in the protruding slab, Frank watched from their concealed shadow.

Trees crashed behind Hinara, and two silver-scaled Dragons emerged from the forest. Hinara staggered. One of the Dragons reared its head back, tugging on a cord wrapped around his aunt's hands.

Another Elemental walked behind the beasts, pulled by a similar cord. A bleeding gash cleaved Giri's face across one side. One of his eyes was missing, replaced by a blood-stained hole. An open wound ran straight to his father's chin. Blood dripped to the ground.

Giri paused a moment before staggering forward, pulled by the rope.

A familiar voice sounded in his head, with an image of a single green eye, flaming. *"Run, my son. Karis is finished. Hundreds made it safely to Vyr. Hinara and I have spent months imprisoned here in these*

*ruins. They've tortured us, trying to find Vyr's location. Save yourself.
Run, before they see you."*

Frank stood rooted to the spot. The Dragons dragged Giri and Hinara to a mound of mud only a few yards away. The silver Dragons looked identical, each twelve feet long with glowering crimson eyes. Their scales shimmered in the blood-red dawn light.

Giri and Hinara hit the ground, thrown in the mud. One of the Dragons raised a claw, and opened its mouth. An awful sound, like a dark, evil song, rang out. Notes echoed off the ruins of Karis, shuddering against the scorched earth.

Streaks of black crept from the mud at the notes of the Dragon's dirge, forming narrow cords. Rising into shafts, the shadows bent around Giri and Hinara, wrapping around their bodies. Thick shadow webbings soon encased both Elementals. The dark webs formed a tight cage around each.

One of the Dragons snorted, casting smoke into the air. Settling down on its haunches, it folded its thin wings behind its back. It faced Giri, so that its head pointed away from Michi and Frank. The other Dragon growled and turned away, walking to the forest.

After a few minutes, a loud rumble sounded. The Dragon's belly raised and lowered in a slow rhythm.

"It's sleeping," whispered Michi. "We need to get away now."

"We have to free them."

"With what? Insects alone? We're unarmed, and the other Dragon will return at any moment."

A tiny voice below them spoke. "You need help."

Michi pulled a stone aside, and they heard a gasp. A thin golden head emerged from the rubble, glaring at Frank. Samas, the tiny Dragon he'd attacked before leaving, looked up.

"What's happening here?" Frank resisted the urge to wring the small creature's neck. He braced against the stones.

Samas crawled out, limping. One of his gilded wings was torn off, and gaps showed where golden scales once lay. Green skin pulsed beneath the wounds, riddled with dark bruises. His wrinkled face grew tight, wincing. "I am *not* your enemy, Frank. It's why I've stayed here, watching your family. For two months, I've been their only link to hope.

Now that you're here, we have a chance." The golden Dragon peered through the crevice, and fell against the stones, breathing hard.

"Prove your loyalty." Frank pointed. "Help us free them."

"We need others. Take me to Vyr. I cannot move well. Find the other 'Mentals, and I'll find the remainder of White Claw."

"I'm not leading a Dragon to Vyr."

"Frank." Michi placed her hand on his wrist. "We need help."

"Carry me to the trees." Samas nodded. "Blindfold me if necessary. You attacked me, and now I'm asking for your help. Neither of us trusts the other, and yet we need each other. The Dragons are my enemies too." He winced again. "Please. Elementals and Dragons worked together once, long ago. If we hope to defeat the Shadow King, it is our one option."

Frank rose, peering through the crevice again. Giri and Hinara lay helpless, trapped in the dark webbing.

Michi shook her head. "We can't win by ourselves, Frank." She picked up Samas, and sprinted away, toward the far side of the forest.

Frowning, Frank ran after them.

CHAPTER TWENTY-EIGHT—WILL

# Cries and Confusion

"**N**o, Gen, I'm in London."

Will heard shouting from the other end of the phone.

"I'll get the car to you when I can, don't worry."

More shouting. He glanced at Susan. Her arms moved in wild motions while she slept on the bed. Hope gurgled, and Will bounced the baby on his lap.

"That's the best you're going to get." Betha hung up, throwing the phone onto the table.

"Genevieve didn't take the news well?"

"I shouldn't stay with you lot for too long. For now, she's fine." Betha sighed. "Susan's out cold, and I don't blame her. I'm exhausted too."

Will stared at Hope.

*Our daughter.*

Her tiny eyes opened, squinted, and snapped back shut. Her fingers clenched and unclenched, and her whole body squirmed.

"Careful." Betha stepped over, adjusting the baby's position. "You have to always hold her head. I'm guessing they don't have parenting classes in the underworld?"

"It's not the underworld exactly, at least I don't think it is, but no, we don't."

"Use your elbow. There, that's it."

Hope nestled against his arm, breathing gentle, warm breaths, and drooling from her small lips.

"She looks like you Will, but with Susan's nose."

"Thank you, I think." His daughter looked like a doll, a small moving doll. Her presence changed everything, and yet it seemed unreal.

Susan murmured in her sleep, tossing to one side.

"I'm not an expert, but I've watched babies a lot. I nannied for a time, before Uni. Mum thought having a job would help me be responsible. Didn't really need the money. Still, felt awful good to make some of my own. Before I head back to Oxford, I want to make sure you and Susan are comfortable with Hope."

"You've already helped us far more than you should. If you want to head back now—"

Betha tossed her copper hair back. "It's for *her* more than you. A baby needs all the help it can get."

"Of course. Thank you."

Hope opened her mouth, letting out a loud wail. Her legs and arms moved back and forth, clawing at the air. The infant's head rocked against his elbow, her face scrunched up like a prune.

"What is it? What's wrong?"

"She's probably hungry." Betha glanced at Susan. "Time to wake mum up, or give her a bottle." The redhead reached into the bag from Didcot Station. "No formula in here. We need to pick up some supplies, clothes and the like. Nappies and dummies, a few towels and some lotion. It's a start, but not enough."

"Nappies? Those are diapers, right? What's a dummy?"

Betha pulled a pacifier from the bag. "A dummy," she said, slipping it into Hope's mouth. The infant turned, spitting it out.

Susan sat up, yawning. "I'm up. I'll feed the baby."

Will passed the wriggling infant to her.

Hope calmed at Susan's touch.

*Our child.*

*I feel so useless. I want to support her. Susan's a new mother who fought a Dragon atop a train. What am I? How can I even help?*

After Hope ate, Susan straightened her shirt. "You're still here, Betha? I expected you'd have left by now."

"I want to make sure the child's provided for. You and Will need help, supplies, and any support possible. It's bad enough there are

Dragons chasing you and all the ghost stuff, but you're new parents. That's a stressful situation in the best of circumstances. I'd be pulling my hair out if I was you, begging for all the help I could get."

"We do appreciate it."

Elizabetha sat down on the edge of the bed, launching into a long explanation of childcare, trying to cover every detail she knew. Her thoughts rushed out, each idea coming faster than the previous one, and often with no order. Will walked to the desk on one side of the hotel room, and using a pen and paper, started jotting down notes.

"Don't forget to sleep. Trade off, give Will turns watching her with the bottle, whatever you need to do. All the parents I talked to said they don't sleep at all for months. I'm exhausted now, after a day of insanity, don't think I could handle a month of this."

*I don't think most parents have quite the same situation.* Will jotted down the word sleep.

"Well, that's all I can think of now."

Susan rocked the baby on her lap. Clutching Hope close, tears streamed down Susan's face. Will hurried to her side, placing an arm around her.

"What are we doing, Will? I can't do this." She continued to cry, clutching Hope closer. The baby wriggled and started wailing herself.

"We're here together. We'll face this new challenge just like we've faced previous ones. Let me take her."

Will eased Hope away from Susan. Both mother and child continued sobbing.

Two glowing souls stepped through the hotel walls. They approached Hope, stretching luminous arms toward the crying baby.

At once, Hope calmed. Susan continued to cry.

"You see them too?" whispered Betha.

Will nodded.

The souls glided back through the wall, and Hope nestled back into the crook of Will's elbow, smiling.

*What strange power does our child possess?*

For a long moment, Susan sat on the bed, letting tears fall. Betha patted her shoulder, while Will rocked Hope. Noise from cars grew louder as the day deepened.

Betha stood, walking to the drawn curtain shade, and pulled it aside. "I'm getting hungry, myself. Let's head to breakfast. I'll let you treat."

Will looked up.

"I'm joking. Don't worry. Come on, both of you. We'll grab some food, and get some supplies. Once we have some bottles, you two can start trading off nap times. If I wasn't so hungry, I'd take one now myself. Are you all right, Susan?"

"No. But I will be." She wiped her eyes.

"That's good enough for now."

## CHAPTER TWENTY-NINE—SUSAN

# Training

"Thank you, Will. You sure you're able to watch her for a while?"

"Get some sleep, Susan." He kissed her on the forehead.

She sat on the bed, watching Will and Betha. Two purple straps along Will's shoulders connected to the new baby carrier. Hope faced him, hanging from his chest. Will raised the baby's tiny hand in a wave, and they exited.

Susan closed the blinds, masking the early afternoon sun. She glanced at the large shopping bags. They'd been to four stores after a filling breakfast.

She winced. The so-called full English breakfast included a bland fried egg, a mound of runny baked beans, something called black pudding that hadn't been pudding at all, bacon, two slices of fried toast dripping with butter, and a grilled tomato. The strangest *breakfast* she'd ever eaten, although after last night's exertions, it was very welcome. The amount of food reminded her of the last time she'd seen her mother. Mom overfed her, often making three meals' worth at once, and insisted she finish everything, since she was losing so much weight.

*My soul was fading into the World of Deaths.*

Susan shook her head. She *had* to see her parents, yet the thought terrified her. Whether Sindril planned some sort of trap didn't matter. *They think I'm dead. They've spent years hoping for my return, only to be told a lie. It's not right.*

Still, how would they react? She was four years older than if she'd aged naturally, not to mention that she now had a baby. *Their grandchild.*

She walked to the phone, and started to dial. Pausing before the final number, her mind filled with apprehension.

She clicked the final digit, listening to the phone ring.

"Hello?"

The voice on the other end was so familiar and yet so strange. For a year, Susan had yearned to hear that voice, to connect once again. Now, she sounded like a distant memory.

"Hello? Is anyone there?"

Susan ignored the lump rising in her throat. She forced her voice out. "Mom?"

"Who…who is this?"

"Mom, it's me. Susan. Su*zie*. I'm sorry I was never able to talk before."

There was a loud intake of breath from the other end. The voice quivered when she responded. "I think you must have the wrong number, my daughter passed away."

"I've been gone for three years, I know. Ever since Cronk showed up at our door and said I was a Death. You won't believe where I've been, or what I've seen, but I'm alive, I assure you. You remember the man with the scythe and the stutter? Joe thought he was wearing a Halloween costume. It was right after I'd lost all that weight."

After a pause, Mom's shaky voice responded. "I remember. I don't understand—"

*No time for doubts. I have to prove myself to her fast.*

"Mom, it *is* me. In your dresser, in the top left drawer all the way in the back, you've got a little box you think Joe and I don't know about. We found it one day and were freaked out. It's got all of our baby teeth."

"Suzie? My God, Suzie, it *is* you." Susan heard her shout something to someone else and the sound of footsteps and voices. "Suzie, where are you? We'll get you help. If you've been taken, we'll pay whatever they want."

"I wasn't kidnapped." *Not exactly, anyway.* "I'm alive, and I'm fine. I'm coming to see you soon. Just listen, if anyone tells you I'm dead, don't believe them."

"Susan?" Dad's voice joined the conversation. "They showed us a charred body, although we weren't sure. We were hopeful, but how—"

The pain was too great now. "I'll see you both soon." She choked up, suddenly full of guilt. "I have to go now. I love you."

"We love you too."

Click.

*I abandoned them. It wasn't just that I failed my test, it's that I forgot. They remembered me, and I forgot all about them.*

Susan shook her head again, focusing on the day so far, and ignoring the impending reunion. *The shopping helped.* She'd never imagined so many products existed just for babies and new mothers.

*A new mother. That's what I am.*

Susan lay on the bed, grateful for the reprieve.

Closing her eyes, she let the waves of exhaustion wash from head to toe. Her body ached, from pains where she'd delivered, to her sore breasts, not to mention bruises from slamming into the train's roof. Taking a deep breath, she ignored the pain, focusing on her weariness.

She slipped into darkness.

*Waves of nothing surrounded the world, washing away all thought.*

Opening her eyes, Susan stood on the endless sea.

Her bare feet rested on the surface of infinite still waters. The ocean stretched beyond sight in every direction, with only an occasional small ripple troubling the sea's crest. A white dress billowed in unseen winds, waving around her legs.

The sky above was a hemisphere of solid flame. Fire arced over and around her, bending from horizon to horizon.

Grym stood facing her, his wrinkled fingers stroking his wizened silver beard. He wore a black robe emblazoned with a green emerald hourglass.

"Susan Sarnio, the supposed Scythe Wielder." His deep, booming voice broke into laughter, sending ripples across the calm waters. "You don't know anything. You don't deserve to wield me."

"I defeated a Dragon while fighting on top of a moving train."

"Luck." The ancient king smiled. "Hormones surged through your body. You'd just given birth, after all, and to a Dragon Key. Adrenaline, fear, and good fortune combined to give you that victory. You won't succeed again, and you're not as strong as you think. You want to defeat the Shadow King? You plan to ignite the Eye of Donkar? If you want to spring Sindril's trap, you need training."

Susan raised her arms. "Where am I supposed to get training? This is the first Dragon Key in a thousand millennia. There hasn't been any sign of you in just as long. I doubt anyone's alive who remembers how to use your power."

"Don't be a fool. *I* shall train you."

Susan regarded Caladbolg. He'd murdered two innocent women during a Reaping, and battled her at the brink of death. She didn't trust him.

"You know our thoughts are one. I can hear your doubt, and while it's true that we've been at odds, you saw our potential when we work together. Don't rely on blind luck next time. Train with me here, within your mind. Sindril has no idea how powerful we are. His trap is meaningless."

"Very well." Susan's toes dug into the water, and she braced herself.

"I won't go easy on you. Damage in this place is just as real as damage suffered when awake. Don't hold anything back."

"Get on with it, Grym."

The ancient king spread his arms wide, and soared backward, coasting across the water. The calm sea frothed, churning into enormous, swelling waves. Susan struggled to maintain her balance. Two cyclones of flame twisted down around Caladbolg, folding beneath him. Hot mist steamed where the flames touched the water.

Flame, mist, and sea joined into a solid mass. Grym rode the back of an enormous Dragon, five times larger than the one she'd battled on the train. Its scales shimmered in a blend of sea-blue and flaming red, with silver sheen. The beast opened its mouth, and a stream of flame shot at Susan.

She threw herself to the left, avoiding it.

"No!" Grym waved his arm. "You control fire. Blasts like that mean nothing. Sense the power of the flame, the elements within the blaze dancing and moving. *See them*, and tell them where to go."

The Dragon reared its head again, and a second fire blast soared across the surging waves.

Susan took a deep breath, reaching out her left hand. She imagined the fire deflecting away. The waves swelled again, and her attention shifted to her feet.

The flames shot around her hand, scorching her. She screamed, diving into the water to quell the conflagration.

Sputtering to the top, she found she could no longer stand atop the waves. She treaded water with desperate kicks.

"You can't become distracted. It takes all your concentration to move fire, just as it takes all your effort to wield the First Scythe."

She nodded, gasping for breath.

"Take control, Susan. If that's not where you want to be, go somewhere else. What is the primary function of any scythe?"

*Transportation. Of course.*

With an enormous effort, she calmed her mind. Sinking into the surging sea, she ignored the water around her body, focusing on her wrist. A tingle shot from her right elbow to her fingertips, and without looking she knew sapphire flames encased the arm. She envisioned her destination, and swung.

*I am the scythe. The weapon and I are one and the same.*

The fingers of flame clawed into space, pulling her through a tear in dimensions. Light exploded and dissipated.

She stood on the Dragon's back, behind Grym. She raised her arm again, pausing.

"Never hesitate!" Caladbolg lifted his arms, without even turning to face her. Three streams of fire snaked down from the sky. They moved like serpents, coiling and preparing to strike.

Susan took a deep breath. *Concentrate. I control the fire.*

She lowered her right hand, lifting her left.

A fiery column sped down, baring serpentine teeth.

*I am in control.*

Within its form, millions upon millions of particles moved in a pattern, swirling in a strange dance. Elements combined and combusted, wreathed in a cloak of solid flame. The pattern filled her heart. The dance echoed around her soul. *I understand.* The ever-watchful eyes of the Swarm coasted on the fire's tips.

Clenching her fingers into a fist, the snakelike pillar of flame evaporated into a cloud of smoke. Two more jets of fire shot down. She waved a hand, and they lowered, striking the Dragon instead.

"Better." Grym turned, holding his arm. Sapphire flame, identical to the blaze encasing Susan's arm, wrapped around his entire body. "You're gaining some skill with fire, but can you wield me?"

Caladbolg's body burst into three rays of blue light. The rays grew brighter and larger, each forming an enormous curved blade. The blades ran at Susan, slicing the air with wild motions.

*Concentrate. I am the weapon.*

Susan let the sapphire flames on her arm coalesce. She deflected one attack. A second sliced into her leg.

A sudden memory flashed, of days spent training for boskery with Will and Frank, as well as the other Gray Knights.

Grym attacked again. Each of his arms was a solid glowing blade, and a third sapphire scythe hung from his chest. His eyes glowered with fierce determination. The scythe on his chest burst into a trail of light. She raised her arm to block. He jumped to strike.

*Just like boskery. Remember the basics: turn, rotate, pivot, attack.*

She jumped into the air, letting her arm's weight pull her. Clearing the blast from Grym's chest, she sliced at his shoulders. All three of his blades vanished.

Landing hard, she rolled, aiming her arm, and released a blast of light from her wrist. She flexed her left hand, and a coil of flames extended from the sky, wrapping around Caladbolg. The flames slithered around his neck, arms, and waist.

"Good."

The Dragon, flaming ropes, and glowing blade on her wrist all dissipated like mist.

She stood atop a calm sea once more, facing Grym beneath a flaming sky.

"Is that all?" Confidence and adrenaline coursed through every fiber of her body.

"That was just the first round. You're learning."

"What are you waiting for, old man? I'm ready."

CHAPTER THIRTY—FRANK

# Forgotten Fears

**F**rank walked with gentle steps, keeping a wary eye on the forest around them. Michi stretched her arms wide, the ends of her fingers had vanished. Frank knew she was in contact with hundreds, if not thousands of insects. Just like when she'd discovered the message in the library years ago, leading to Susan's discovery of Grym, Michi could even transform parts of her fingers into additional insects.

A cicada chirped loudly ahead, and Michi paused, waving them to the right.

They'd avoided Dragons since leaving the ruins of Karis yesterday. Progress was unbearably slow. Every time a beast flew overhead, they halted. The knot in his stomach never lessened.

*They have my father and Aunt Hinara.*

They passed through the woods in a silent, sluggish procession. Samas lay across Michi's shoulders. The golden Dragon gave Frank a look he couldn't decipher before turning back to face the trees. They moved forward, one agonizing inch at a time, careful not to make a sound.

Michi stopped again, holding up her hand.

Silence filled the forest. Frank heard no birds or insects at all. He started moving his mouth until she waved him silent.

From the base of the nearby trees, long shadows bled into their path, streaming toward them like rushing water.

*Darkness enveloped everything. In the distance, he heard Samas scream.*

*Fear pierced his heart.*

*This* can't *be real.*

*Kasumir appeared, staring at him with dead, empty pools in her eye sockets.*

*Giri and Hinara stood on either side of her, their faces contorted in anguish.*

*The three Elementals fell face forward, collapsing into the glowing pool of Elemental magic. Gordon pushed his way out of the water, staring. Betha emerged beside him, and both vanished into the pool.*

*One by one all the Deaths he knew clawed their way out of the pool, laughing, only to sink back beneath its luminous surface.*

*Susan and Will emerged last, holding something between them: a child.*

*Frank stared at the tiny bundle, seeing his own face.*

"Agmundria?" He heard Michi speaking nearby. "Is that you?"

The darkness and strange images faded.

Samas trembled, writhing on the ground. *I wonder what frightens a Dragon.* He helped the small creature back onto Michi's shoulders.

In front of them, Agmundria smiled. The sallow-faced young girl stood several inches taller; however, she still appeared disheveled and emaciated. Behind her stood eight other fearmongers, each with plaster-white skin and deep red eyes. Seven of them were creatures he'd encountered before Susan's abduction. The memories were dim and faint. His powers after Kasumir's murder had been erratic. He held vague recollections of training, intending to attack Dragons. The final fearmonger was different, an older man with soft features, although still an albino. *Gesrir Nallas.* He'd never told Susan the name. Gesrir helped save Susan from Sindril's attack during her first year at the College. Frank nodded to each of them in turn, smiling.

*"It's been a long time. What are you doing here?"*

The words of Agmundria's speech terrified him even more acutely than when they'd last seen her. *Her power's grown*, he mused.

"My father and aunt are being held by Dragons in the ruins of Karis. We need help freeing them. Will you aid us?"

*"Of course."* Agmundria smiled, filling Frank with dread.

"How are you here?" Michi waved at the forest. "I thought you were at the College, with Cronk."

Gesrir stepped forward, grinning. *"Cronk came to me in the hidden library, with Agmundria. With Cronk's permission, I led her away from the area, bringing her to meet others like us."*

With every word, shivers crept down Frank's spine. For a moment, the seven seemed to morph into seven albino wolves with crimson eyes, before melting back into their natural forms.

"You're fearmongers," whispered Samas. "I've heard rumors, yet never dreamed the power would be so terrifying."

Gesrir motioned one albino forward. The slender fearmonger cowered in front of Frank.

*"His name is Thyral."* Gesrir patted Thyral's shoulder. *"Years ago, you dove into his mind, Frank. He's never been the same."*

*When I lost control, after mother's death.*

"I'm sorry."

*"He's forgiven you, in his way. They're frightened of you, and will follow your lead, even to death."*

He nodded, thinking, and glanced at Samas, who still shuddered. "Dragons feel fear?"

"Are you kidding?" Samas twitched.

"Michi, call off your bugs, and prepare for the next strike. We're going back."

## CHAPTER THIRTY-ONE—SUSAN

# Homecoming

"**B**etha, I've said this before. We can't thank you enough." Susan threw her arms around the redheaded woman who'd taught them so much.

"I suppose I'll never see you two again."

"If you see either of us, it means you're dead." Will shook his head. "No, don't plan on it."

Susan picked up Hope, strapping her into the snug baby carrier on her chest. She sighed. "I mean it, Betha. I wish there was something we could do. You were a true friend." She squeezed Betha's hand, and an idea sprang to mind.

"I know that look." Will frowned. "Susan, what are you planning?"

"Get the scythe blade. We're leaving it with Betha."

"We need it to return to the World of Deaths."

Susan laughed. "I wield the First Scythe, the most powerful scythe ever imagined. No, we don't need that broken piece of metal at all. Get it, please."

Will nodded, fishing the silver fragment from their bag.

"Why would you leave this with me?" Betha took the scythe piece from Will, holding it at a distance.

"This is a piece of our world. Once we've gone, you won't be able to tell anyone what you've learned about the World of Deaths. This is a token, a reminder that your brother's alive and well. Think about him whenever you see it, and remember us as well. You saw the birth of a Death. The first Death *born* in millennia. You're a witness to history, and you've helped shape it as well. Even if it's a secret you have to carry to the grave, you're the only human with any sense of what might happen next."

"What happens if I use this? Could I visit Gordon, or you two? Can I see the World of Deaths."

She reached for Grym's presence, glancing at the hourglass mark on her wrist. He remained silent.

"I don't know, Betha. I doubt it." Susan took the woman's hands again. "You don't need to see us to remember our gratitude. We will never forget you." Hope gurgled against her stomach, wriggling her fingers.

"If I told anyone what I've been through, I'd be locked up in a funny farm. No, I'll keep your secret. Still, do me a favor."

"Anything."

"Tell Gordon I love him, and he's chosen good friends."

"We'll tell him." Susan smiled.

Betha sniffed, wiping a tear away. "You three had best be off already. I'm no good with goodbyes. Don't need to drag it out or anything."

"We're still going through with the plan?" Will raised an eyebrow. She knew he wanted to return to the College.

"I need to. After all those hours spent in the library, I have an actual way to see them. This might be my last opportunity."

Will nodded.

"Goodbye, Will and Susan. You too, Hope."

"Goodbye, Betha."

Susan's body ached from the hours of training. Somehow, the pain experienced within her mind manifested on her body. However, she now knew how to control Grym, as well as her own abilities.

*I'm ready. Sindril has no idea who I've become.*

She gave a last glance to the hotel room. Will shouldered a backpack laden with supplies, and lifted a separate duffle-bag, equally packed. He took her left hand, squeezing tight. Hope gave an awkward smile.

*"You're certain she's able to travel?"*

*"Travelling will not harm her."* Grym's voice echoed with warning. *"I can't say the same for Sindril. You could leave her here, with Will."*

*"Something tells me this is the last time I'll ever see my parents. No, I want them to meet their granddaughter, and Will, even if it's only this once."*

*"You remember the leeching? My confidence and power seeped into you, but your logic and caution seeped into me. Listen to reason, Susan. She's a Dragon Key. Leave Will and the child here. Come back for them afterward."*

*"You want me to take on a trap? What better motivation than to protect my family. No, Hope is going to meet her grandparents, and her father's coming. I've made up my mind."*

*"You've taken on my stubbornness as well. So be it."*

She lifted her right arm, allowing the blue flame to emerge and coalesce into a solid blade of light. Adjusting her stance, she tightened her grip on Will and waved her arm, tearing into space.

Light shattered into sound, dissolving into smell.

A blur of colors sped by, whirling into a cavalcade of rapid images.

She sensed Hope on her chest, scrunching her face and trying to scream.

Will clung on, his fingers locked in hers.

A blaze of sapphire erupted and Susan staggered.

Streetlights lined the road, casting their glows onto puddles. A gentle drizzle fell from gray clouds above. A single car rolled by.

"This is where you used to live?" Will released his grip on her hand, adjusting his hold on the duffle.

"Damascus, Maryland. Yes."

She took an awkward step down the street. The houses stood close together. Each house looked similar to the others, each a one-story building with beige vinyl siding and a dark shingled roof. Hope started to cry, and Susan pulled the baby's hood tighter trying to keep her from the sprinkles above. Will followed behind in silence. The smell of wet grass lingered in the distance.

Every step she took was harder than the last. Glancing to her left she saw Crystal's house. *My best friend, in a different life. Now, she's Joe's girlfriend.* A light was on in the upstairs window. Susan glanced up, still walking.

She kept an eye out for Dragons, not seeing anyone at all on the deserted road. At the end of the cul-de-sac, a large willow dripped with water from the soft rain. Susan walked to the narrow paved driveway beside the weeping willow, and took a deep breath.

"This is it."

"We're here with you."

"I don't know what to say. I'm not sure if I can even do this."

*I don't look anything like the girl they lost.*

Hope shifted, her face scrunched into a tight mass of wrinkles. Susan looked down at her daughter, and glanced up again. Lights shone from the living room and kitchen. Both cars sat in the driveway. Will touched her hand, his fingers moist from the soft rain.

She started up the driveway, forcing each foot to move forward.

Susan pressed the doorbell.

The door opened, and her brother Joe stood in the frame. He'd grown a slight beard. Although his hair was longer and pulled back, he was still the Joe she remembered. For a moment she just stared, all speech caught in her throat.

"Can I help you?"

*He doesn't recognize me.*

"Joe." She managed to choke the word out. Hope started to fuss again.

"Do I know you?"

"It's me. It's Susan."

"Susan? Is it really you?"

The door swung open. Joe stared deep into her eyes, and then gave her an awkward hug. He shook Will's hand, and ushered them into the living room, before shouting to Mom and Dad.

Mom barreled down the steps so fast, she tripped, slamming her elbow into the banister. She rose, with tears in her eyes.

"Suzie? It is you. Oh my God, you look so much older. Suzie, oh God, Suzie." Susan passed Hope to Will and then sank into the sea of embraces and tears.

For a long time all anyone could do was hug and smile and cry. Minute after minute passed with no words, no stories, no questions, and yet a flood of emotions.

She wanted to say more, she yearned to tell them everything, but Susan held back.

Dad broke the silence. "You haven't introduced us, yet. Who's your friend?" Dad studied Will, seeming unsure of what to make of him.

"This is Will, and this is our daughter, Hope."

"Daughter?" Mom walked straight to Hope, who gurgled.

"Your granddaughter," added Susan.

"In all this time, where have you been?" Dad sat in the recliner, his fingers working a steady nervous pattern through his moustache. "On the phone—"

"It doesn't matter," said Mom suddenly. "She'll tell us when she's ready. It's all right, honey, we don't want you to feel any pressure. You're home, where you belong."

"*Whatever you plan to tell them, make it fast.*" Grym's voice thundered in the back of her mind. "*Four Dragons just appeared outside the house.*"

She glanced at Will, who sat with Hope on his lap, looking like he wanted to run away.

"Can I get you something to drink?" Mom stood.

"We can't stay much longer," said Susan.

"Can't stay?" Dad frowned. "You just got here."

Inside her mind, Susan searched for Grym's presence. "*I control you. I can come visit them any time I want.*"

"*We both see it, Susan. I can't explain why or how, perhaps it's the Swarm showing us, through your tether. Yet, I know it's true. This is the last you'll ever see them.*"

Susan took a deep breath. "I don't have time to explain, and there's no words to describe what I'm feeling. For a time, I ran, and was bullied for it. Now, I've been selected for a job, a very important job. It just might change the entire world. Will works with me, and our daughter lives with us. It's a secret job, one I can't tell you any details about, but you must believe that I'm alive and well, and that I'm happy."

"You're some kind of secret agent?" asked Joe. "Like CIA? You're just a kid."

Will grinned. "Where we work, she's more than a kid. She's a hero. A leader."

The baby cried.

"You held a candlelight vigil on my birthday. I got the message. It took me a long time to hear, but I want you both to stop looking for me, and stop grieving. Our work is top secret." She glanced at Will. *It's not the whole truth, but it's not a lie, either. Betha saw Dragons and souls, she understood. Mom and Dad on the other hand...* Hope thrashed, wailing.

Something slammed into the roof with a thud.

"What was that?" Dad got up.

"That was our cue. We have to go." Tears welled in her eyes again. There was so much more to say, but at least she'd seen them. "Goodbye, Mom, Dad, Joe." One by one she embraced them. Two more thuds sounded above.

"They're here," said Will, pulling on her arm.

"What's happening?" asked Dad. He pulled out his cell phone. "I'm calling the cops, we'll protect you."

"No cops." Susan held up a hand in warning. She nodded to Will. She wasn't going to explain fully. She'd said goodbye, but she wasn't going to let Dragons attack the house either.

"Your arm!" shouted Mom.

Blue fire rippled down her arm, and Susan vanished into sapphire light.

She appeared on the roof, and plunged a ray of light straight through a Dragon's chest. Spinning, she lopped off the head of a second beast.

The front door open and Will ran out, followed by her awestruck parents.

Mom's mouth looked ready to fall off.

"Military weaponry's come a long way," muttered Dad.

"How did she do that?" asked Joe.

Susan waved her arm, appeared beside Will, and then slashed the air again.

With an explosion of sapphire, they stood in a cemetery.

"Where are we?" Will staggered.

Susan walked through the rows of headstones. A large patch of fresh muddy dirt lay beside a blank marker.

"This is where the police claimed I'm buried. I've got them away from the house, this is where they'll come next."

"Are you all right?"

She smiled. "Yes. I got to say goodbye, something Deaths never get to do. Besides, even if I couldn't tell them everything, they saw enough."

"You've still got Grym. After the War, you can come back and explain things to them, if you like."

*No, the Swarm's right. That was the final time I'll see them.*

CHAPTER THIRTY-TWO—FRANK

# Terror and Flight

Frank peered out from the line of trees, gripping the bark. His fingers dug into a scorched section, wrapping around a torn branch.

In the center of the ruins, his father and aunt Hinara sat back to back. Rope-like threads of solid shadow snaked around their bodies, even covering their mouths. Bristles of spiked shadow pointed at each of Hinara's stripes, and a spike stood poised before Giri's single remaining eye.

"They're toying with them." Frank turned, whispering to Samas, "The Dragons kept them alive for all this time, hoping to break them."

"It's also a trap." The golden dragon nestled atop Michi's shoulder. "They hope to lure the Elementals out."

"How many Dragons?" Frank ignored Samas, moving his gaze to Michi.

"I count three total in the area. If they call for others—"

"Let's hurry, before that's an issue. Samas, if we get to Giri and Hinara, can you undo those cords?"

"Yes. It's a form of shadow power. It won't be hard to break."

"Good. Get ready."

He motioned to Gesrir, who waited by a tree several yards to the right. At once, all nine fearmongers approached the wasteland, stepping from nine different points in the forest. Their hands waved.

Something bellowed in the distant canopy. A Dragon leaped into the air, writhing and contorting in violent spasms. It flew to the west. Agmundria pointed to the woods, clenching her fingers into a fist.

A second Dragon emerged, stumbling. It jerked around, and collapsed on the ground, shuddering.

Gesrir waved to Frank.

Frank and Michi darted out of the forest, jumping over rubble and heaps of mud. They reached Giri and Hinara.

"Quick." Frank grabbed Samas, placing him at his father's feet. The Dragon shot him a look, before turning to Giri, singing.

One by one, the shadow cords unwound from Giri and Hinara.

"Hurry." Frank glanced around.

Agmundria stood before a trembling Dragon, her arms outstretched. The other fearmongers faced away from the center, each holding their hands skyward. One of the albinos motioned.

Three Dragons sped above the tree line, their fangs bared.

The albinos clustered at the Dragons' approach, arraying their hands in a strange pattern. Two of the beasts broke off, falling into the trees. The other opened its mouth, sending a jet of flame rocketing toward them.

The cords untangled, and Hinara jumped up. "Take my hand!" she shouted.

Frank and Michi took hold, just as the fire drew close. At the last second, he grabbed Giri's hand. The flame's warmth singed Frank's skin.

The ribbons on Hinara's skin flared out, and with a flash of light they stood on the opposite side of the clearing.

"The others?" Frank stared at the area they'd been standing in before. Smoke rose from scattered flames. The albinos rushed together again, this time sending the Dragon roaring away.

Agmundria lay on her side. Frank ran back into the desolation. Flickering fire riddled the area. Hurrying to her side, he picked up the girl.

The Dragon she'd been facing rose, baring sets of razor-sharp fangs. Its silver scales glinted in the sunlight, and its red tongue swept out of its mouth. The monster bellowed, sending plumes of sulfur and smoke into Frank's face.

*I'm not afraid. I fought a Dragon once before.*

He reached for his power.

*White light.*

*An ancient song singing in a grove of glowing birches.*

The Dragon paused. Something moved at Frank's foot, and Samas emerged from a mound of ash. The tiny creature climbed onto his boot.

Frank focused again.

*A grove of glowing birches pillared the sky.*
*With waves of golden light, they sang.*
*An eternal song.*

The silver-scaled Dragon closed its mouth, turning away. Unsure of what he'd done, Frank turned and sprinted as fast as possible, while still carrying Agmundria.

A moment later, the beast roared again, running through the desolation.

"They're here. They've come." Samas panted, clinging to the worn leather of Frank's boot, and the bottom of his pants.

A large green Dragon soared over the horizon in front of them, landing behind Giri and Hinara.

Hinara grabbed Michi and Giri, pulling them together. The blue ribbons on her skin expanded, wrapping around the other two Elementals.

"Wait!" He ran faster.

All three vanished in a flash of blue.

Frank stopped.

The two massive Dragons faced each other, with him in the middle.

Both monsters screamed.

# Breach

**W**ill knelt beside Susan, putting the duffle on the ground beside the fresh grave. Hope cried, her tiny voice shrill against the quiet evening.

Susan's fingers clenched and released. She touched Hope's face, and turned to him. "I shouldn't have brought you here. I put you in danger, but I'm glad you got to meet my family."

*Don't you understand, I won't leave you. I want to be here with you.*

"You killed those Dragons in minutes. Was that all Sindril had planned?"

Hope quieted, waving her arms. One by one, a handful of glowing souls emerged from the ground, including the fresh grave.

*Is our daughter doing this?*

"These are all souls who must've died recently, after the Reapings ceased." Susan stood.

The glowing forms ringed them, forming an outward-facing wall. Will counted thirteen souls surrounding them. Their bodies shone with faint golden light, and their edges blurred into the night air around them.

"Susan, what's happening? Why are they circling us?"

"Hope has strange abilities. I think she called them."

"But why?"

One of the luminous forms shifted, and Will saw what was beyond.

A dozen leather-clad men stood in the drizzle, each with gleaming reptilian eyes. Serpent tongues darted out of some of their mouths. Twelve Dragons waited outside the circle of glowing souls.

A low hiss emanated from the shadowy Dragons.

"Ssssuusssssan. Give usssss the child."

Two of the men took a step forward, their shoulders bulging in unnatural ways. Even in the dim light, Will saw a hand slough off, replaced by steely talons.

"Susan. Use Grym. Bring us to Frank. Get us out of here."

From the corner of his eye, he watched sapphire flames pour out of her shoulder, encasing her right arm.

"No." She took a step forward. "I'm through running. Why run from one battle to another? Grym's right. I can handle this."

He grabbed her left arm. "I know you're upset, but we have to get out of here!"

She glanced at Hope. "This shouldn't take long."

"Don't do this, Susan. I need you."

She stared into his eyes. "I need you too." She kissed his cheek. "However, I also need you to stop doubting me. I repeat, I can handle this."

He clung to Hope, dumbstruck. *I don't doubt you, I just want to protect you.*

Susan walked through the glowing ring of souls. The ethereal light wafted apart like smoke, coalescing into a single form after she passed. The blue flames on her arm blazed with a ferocity that matched her determined steps.

"Be careful!"

He shouted the warning to empty air.

In a blur, far faster than his eyes could see, Susan vanished and reappeared behind one of the Dragons. She slashed her glowing arm. A bolt of sapphire lightning shot through two Dragons at once, and they each crumpled to the ground.

Hope gurgled, smiling. The souls around him remained still.

Susan vanished again.

Two men shed their human skin, and enormous wings appeared.

Appearing in a sapphire burst, Susan emerged, flashed the blue scythe, and vanished again.

Will stared.

One by one, Dragons collapsed in blurs of whirling blue light. Screams pierced the air, and the stench of sulfur grew acrid.

Hope gurgled again.

The glowing souls shifted, and Will spun.

Behind him, a human face fell to the ground. A leathery Dragon bared its fangs, sending a rocket of flame toward the ghostly ring.

"Susan! Help!"

Sapphire exploded in front of him, and Susan faced the fiery stream with her left hand. It ricocheted to the side, barreling into another Dragon.

Another scream pierced the air, and Susan vanished again.

Only three Dragons remained. All three stood in their natural forms, beating bat-like wings against the sky.

A black Dragon dove, its fangs open. Susan rolled to one side, and slashed its neck. The beast's head rolled off, and its body fell back in a geyser of dark blood.

A red Dragon clawed at Susan. She vanished, and his talons dug into the yellow Dragon instead. The monster screamed. Susan emerged in a burst of blue a moment later on the red Dragon's back, slashing down. The beast collapsed. Raising her arm, a bolt of sapphire lightning struck the yellow Dragon, splitting its hide in two.

She turned to Will, walking with a smile.

"I told you I could handle it." She limped forward. The blue fire encasing her arm vanished.

The glowing souls sank into the ground, and Will ran forward.

Susan collapsed on the ground, breathing hard.

"You're amazing! Susan, I can't believe I ever doubted you. We'll win the war for sure. You're terrifying, but amazing."

She nodded, still struggling for breath.

A deafening sound like shattering glass crashed above them.

Will and Susan stared at the sky.

A crevice of white light split the heavens, cleaving the hemisphere in two.

"My God." Susan gaped.

"What's happening?" He clutched Hope's fingers.

A fissure of light, filled with tiny moving forms ran from hemisphere to hemisphere.

Thousands of Dragons soared into the Mortal World.

CHAPTER THIRTY-FOUR—FRANK

# Crossfire

The green Dragon arched its forty-foot back, snarling. Its yellow eyes narrowed, and white smoke drifted from the beast's nostrils.

Sunlight glinted off the silver-scaled Dragon. Its wings flapped in the wind. Clawing the mud, it thrust its talons into the rough ground.

Frank froze, caught between the two monsters. Agmundria lay still in his arms.

The silver Dragon moved to one side, and the two creatures began circling each other.

"He's here to help," shouted Samas, still clawing to Frank's leg. "Brandr! I'm here."

The green Dragon snorted, opening his mouth. "Move, 'Mental. Let me deal with this one."

Frank spun around, eyeing the two great winged worms. The silver Dragon's mouth widened, and a stream of flame raced out. Frank jumped to one side, yet he couldn't move well with the unconscious fearmonger.

Brandr leaped forward, blocking the flames with his scales.

At once, the Silver Dragon pounced, sinking his fangs into Brandr's side. The Dragons grappled, rolling through the mud.

Frank tried to run. A tail or leg flashed in a moment of silver, sending him flying through the air. Agmundria slipped out of his grip, hitting the ground a few feet away. Samas tumbled off, vanishing into a cloud of dust kicked up from the melee.

Another Dragon appeared above, with scales blacker than night and eyes crimson red. The Dragon flapped down, landing with its mouth open. A wave of white-hot flame sped out, torching both of the two wrestling Dragons.

Brandr and Silver-scales disentangled, shaking the flames off with rough undulations of their hides.

Agmundria moaned, her legs twitching. Frank hurried over.

"Are you hurt?"

*"I cannot move my leg."*

He lifted her again, this time holding the girl on his back. He scanned the area without seeing Giri, Hinara, or Michi.

With a roar, a fourth Dragon with white scales like clouds appeared. The black Dragon jumped into the air, colliding with the white one. The two tumbled through the sky in a spinning blur of white and black, until the black one bit the white Dragon's tail.

Meanwhile, Brandr pinned the silver Dragon to the ground, slashing its throat. An enormous fountain of blood erupted.

When the green Dragon started toward Frank, the Elemental backed away.

"It's all right!" Samas waved a talon from Brandr's shoulder. "I told you he was an ally. White Claw is here to help."

The golden Dragon scrambled to the ground, half climbing, and half falling. He hit the dirt hard, and wriggled there, pulling his face out of the mud to grin. Brandr spread his wings, soaring into the sky.

The white Dragon struggled, trying to shake the black Dragon from its tail. Brandr flew straight to the black Dragon, sinking his talons into the beast's back. With a screech, he released White-scales.

White-scales spun in mid air, tearing into the chest of Black-scales. Between Brandr and the ivory Dragon, Black-scales bellowed, collapsing back to the ground.

Dust hung in the air, mixed with the stench of smoke.

"Plamen! Look out, I'm coming."

Spinning, he saw a cloud of buzzing locust scurrying across the ruins.

"Wait." Frank shook his head.

The grasshoppers paused, hovering in mid-air. Michi, Giri, and Hinara emerged from the haze behind them.

He turned to Samas, who'd clambered onto his boot again. "You swear White Claw wants to help?"

Brandr snorted behind him, stomping his foot. "The Shadow King would kill us all if he succeeds. We want to survive. I don't care for 'Mentals or Deaths, however I won't condemn my race to extinction fighting them. In this case, we *are* allies."

A deafening screech split the air, ending in a shattering sound. A gash of blue light cleaved the hemisphere above, splitting it like shards of broken glass.

All eyes turned skyward.

"What is *that*?" Frank stared, adjusting his hold on Agmundria's legs. The girl trembled on his back.

The locust dispersed, flying to the forest. Michi stumbled forward. "Frank. The sky! The barriers between worlds."

"Hurry." Giri ran forward. "We're no longer safe here. You Dragons helped us at the last battle. I remember you in particular." He pointed to Brandr. "We have no choice but to work together. Come with us, we've got to get help."

"You're leading Dragons to Vyr?" Hinara scowled. "Is that wise?"

"The worlds are breaking. Wisdom is no longer an option."

CHAPTER THIRTY-FIVE—SUSAN

# Lake of Blood

The crack in the sky opened wider. Countless Dragons sped out, hurtling toward the ground below.

"We're leaving." Susan took Will's hand. "Hold on tight. If the barriers between worlds are breaking, this is going to be a rough ride."

He nodded, slinging the duffle over his shoulder, and clutching Hope. He still carried the backpack as well. Her fingers tightened around his, and Susan's right arm vanished behind flowing sapphire flame.

*"Hurry."* She heard the concern in Grym's words. *"They're coming"*

The first Dragons opened their mouths, casting a storm of fiery columns to the ground.

Susan waved her arm, tearing into space.

For a fleeting instant, she saw Earth reflected like a plate of glass. Fractures of white light cracked the glass, forming an intricate web. Through every crack, the universe drained like water through a sieve.

Susan slipped through, pulled past the splintering fragments of the Mortal World.

She clung to Will's arm, pulling him and their daughter through the void.

Color became light, burning into smell, which roared into sound.

The In-Between, a reflection of the shattering worlds, raced by.

The taste of rancid strawberries and rotting eggs tore across her tongue.

An explosion of cobalt-blue, tinged with sapphire sparks and azure lightning erupted.

Susan staggered, falling to the ground.

The air stank of sulfur, smoke, and blood.

Her right arm tingled, cooling from Grym's use. She flexed her left fingers, which closed on empty air. Will and Hope weren't there.

*My family. No!*

She darted up, searching the area.

Debris and scorched, barren wasteland extended for acres behind her, with a line of dense forest ahead. Above, the same crack stretched across the open sky, although she saw no Dragons.

"Will?" She whispered the question, and then screamed, "Will!"

"Here." He emerged from the trees, carrying Hope and the bags. "I lost my grip at the final moment, but I'm okay. We both are." He gave her a quick kiss.

Susan smiled. "I feel the difference already. My soul feels strange. I'm not sure how to describe it."

"Stronger." Will touched his stomach. "I feel it too. We've been away from the World of Deaths a long time. Even with the Swarm's help when we were in the Mortal World, it's better to be back."

"You see the sky?"

"It's here too." She stared up.

Hope started to whine. Despite her complete exhaustion, Susan allowed the baby to nurse. They stayed on the edge of the forest, keeping a careful watch on the fractured sky above.

"Where are we?" Will gazed around. "Are the worlds breaking? Are normal people back there overrun by Dragons, or were they just after us?"

"I don't know the answer to either question." Susan reached for Grym's wisdom, yet the ancient king remained silent.

"We need to find Frank and Michi." Will dug into the backpack. Drinking from a water bottle, he passed it to Susan afterward.

"Agreed."

She dove into her soul, standing on the boundless sea under a burning sky. Grym's back was turned, so she spoke with her mind.

*"Are they at the College? What does the Swarm show you?"*

*"Your soul's not tethered by the Swarm anymore. I can't reach their eyes, as once I could."*

*"How will we find Frank and Michi?"*

*"Even as we dove through the splintering void, I saw a battle. Two Dragons facing each other with Frank in between. It couldn't have been more than an hour ago. He's close."*

Grym turned, and she saw the wasteland change, coalescing into a village she knew well.

*"This is Karis?"*

*"It was."*

She withdrew from the infinite expanse, turning to Will again. "Grym thinks they're nearby. We have to try and find them." She paused, surveying the destruction again. "This was Karis, Will."

"Are you sure? There's nothing left. It could just be—"

"This is where the village stood before the battle. The one we fled. The area's been razed."

He nodded. "If this is Karis, we should head north, deeper into the forest. If Frank's close, he's probably trying to find other 'Mentals."

"Good idea." She took the baby harness from Will, strapping their daughter to her chest. She flexed her fingers, rubbing the dark hourglass mark on her right wrist. "Any idea which way north is?"

"No. Doesn't Grym know?"

"It's not a compass. The First Scythe doesn't work like that."

Hope gurgled, wriggling her arms and feet. The wind shifted, blowing toward one end of the forest. She yelped, and the wind strengthened. The baby stopped moving, and the wind ceased. Susan and Will looked at each other.

"That was a coincidence." Will glanced down. "Just wind."

"Let's try that direction."

They crossed part of the ruined landscape, before walking back into the trees. Susan kept a wary eye on the heavens. Light slipped through the crack, which stretched from horizon to horizon. The disconcerting sight vanished above the dense forest canopy when they entered the woods, and Susan felt a sense of relief.

After an initial line of scorched trunks, the forest thickened, seeming untouched by battle. Birches, pine, and oak soared into the air, masking the heavens. Dense bushes and overgrowth made walking slow.

For thirty minutes they wandered along the same route, until they reached a slight path. Susan stumbled out of a bush onto a patch of low grass, snaking between the trees. They turned, following the path deeper into the woods.

Shadows deepened, darkening into a web around them. Susan halted, staring around.

"What's wrong?" Will put the duffle down.

"There's something here."

Sindril stepped out of the woods, a broad smile stretching across his face.

Without pause, she held out her arm, reaching for the sapphire fire. None came.

"Grym!"

She couldn't sense him at all.

Sindril strode closer. He carried an enormous scythe.

Hope started crying.

Sindril held out his hand, and the baby harness vanished. Hope soared through the air, pulled away from her by invisible threads. Sindril swung the scythe, and the child vanished in white light and crimson blood...

She screamed with every fiber of her soul.

"Susan!"

Will stood beside her, shaking her arm. The shadows receded.

The moment of panic swept away, when she saw Hope sleeping in the baby harness.

"What happened?"

Three albinos stepped from the tree line.

"Fearmongers." Will stepped in front of her, shielding her and Hope from the Elementals.

"Susan?" Two bushes pushed aside, and Michi ran out, smiling. "They're friends. Don't hurt them."

Susan's breaths came in deep gasps. She'd watched Sindril murder her baby. It hadn't been real, however she couldn't escape the terrible image, or the visceral fears it'd raised.

Frank emerged from the woods next, carrying something on his back.

"Susan! Will!" His face lit up. Rushing forward, he embraced Susan. Will wrapped his arms around Michi.

With a crash, two Dragons emerged from the forest. One had white, cloudy scales, and the other was green. Samas, the golden Dragon she'd met long ago clung to Frank's boot.

"A happy reunion, indeed." Samas smiled up at her. "I see you've had a child, as was foretold."

"Keep away from her. She won't be turned into some Dragon Key."

"We're on your side, Susan. This is Brandr, whom Will has already encountered, and this is Jurna, another member of White Claw. Jurna is Elkanah's sister. Elkanah died, helping to protect you."

The memory stirred in her gut, and on instinct she raised her arm. "I remember Elkanah. He was on the boat, and captured Will."

"If he hadn't brought me to the Dragons, they'd have killed me." Will's face creased with concern. "I trust them."

"They are allies." Giri emerged from the woods, with a drawn expression. A bloody cloth covered one eye, and a scar ran down his cheek. Hinara and five more fearmongers followed him. "We were on our way to Vyr to recruit as much help as possible."

Grym stirred within her subconscious. *"Not Vyr. There's a job that must be done first. Susan, ask if the 'Mentals have anything hidden. The worlds shatter. I can mend the tear, but need power."*

She paused, unsure of how to relay the strange message.

"What is it?" Frank lowered Agmundria to the ground.

"Grym thinks it's more important to fix the break in the worlds, the crack in the sky. He thinks he can do it himself, although he doesn't have enough raw power. He's asking for help."

Frank and Michi exchanged a look.

"No." Giri stepped forward. "I don't know what the Scythe suspects, or how he's looked into my thoughts, yet I will not bring outsiders there."

"The barriers are cracked." Frank stared at the canopy overhead, shaking his head. "The Shadow Dragons will tear everything apart until they reach Hope and use her to destroy time. The King's convinced them that this will bring a golden age to the Dragons. They're misguided, but follow his will." He sighed. "If the barriers break completely, we won't have a world left to save."

"He's right." Hinara put a hand on Giri's shoulder.

"Mother said it was a last resort." Frank turned back to his father. "I used it when I shouldn't have. Now the time has come."

"What are you talking about?" Susan sat on a tree stump.

"I won't bring the Dragons there." Giri's expression hardened. "Samas, we might be allies for a time, but there are limits."

"I don't know what you're planning, however, I shall wait here with Brandr and Jurna." He flexed his one unbroken wing. "We'll send word to the remaining members of White Claw. We've suffered setbacks, yet the true battle is soon to begin. This is the final chance for our race, and for all races. When you return, White Claw shall be ready."

"The fearmongers will remain here." Giri nodded. "Will and Susan, take Hinara's hands. She'll come back for Frank, Michi and myself."

Michi stepped forward. "You're going to the lake? Take Agmundria. Heal her."

"No fearmonger has seen the lake. No Death has either." Giri sighed. "Very well. All things are changing."

Susan stood, holding Hope tight to her chest. She took one of Hinara's hands, and Will took the other.

The blue stripes on Hinara's skin glowed and ballooned outward, wrapping around Susan, Will, and Hope. With an azure flash, the world vanished, and they re-emerged at the side of a large lake with calm water.

The gash of light arced above the clouded sky like a tear in the heavens. The strange glowing breech mirrored on the placid waves, spanning the lake.

"Wait here, and do *not* touch the water." Hinara's stripes glowed again and she vanished.

A moment later, she reappeared, a few feet away, alongside Giri, Michi, and Frank. Agmundria clung to Frank's back, and he helped her to the ground.

"The Lake of Sorrows." Frank's eyes glistened with a far off look.

Giri strode forward, walking straight to Susan, staring with his one eye. "You guessed this place existed, didn't you? The First Scythe told you."

"I had no idea. Where are we?"

Grym watched from behind her eyes. *"Elemental power never truly dies, even when one of their kind passes on. I remember when the first*

*Twelve formed from Dragonsong. I suspected they buried their dead somewhere special, where the powers would remain untouched."*

"Grym only knew that Elemental power doesn't die. He didn't know this place existed." As she turned to the lake, Susan saw hundreds of ghostly forms emerge, hovering over its surface. Elementals from thousands of generations, whose power rested in the calm waters.

"The Lake of Sorrows is our greatest secret." Giri shook his head. "The Scythe is correct, our power changes, yet never vanishes. For a time, Deaths trained using the bones of our ancestors. Elementals took back the bodies of the Twelve, and founded the lake. For millennia, we've come here to bury our dead in peace. What we are preparing to do is sacrilege, and disturbs my mind and soul. However, *that* is worse." He pointed to the cloven sky.

*"The Twelve are here?"* Through Grym's eyes, she watched the ethereal bodies floating above the surface. They vanished one by one, sinking into the waves, until six men and six women remained. Their eyes glowed with pure white light.

"Frank, bring Agmundria to the lake. We'll heal her first."

He nodded, carrying the young fearmonger to the surface. He stepped in, wading until her back touched the water.

Hinara and Giri followed. Susan stepped forward, halting at a gesture from Michi.

Around the four Elementals, water glowed. A soft light enveloped Agmundria, and Giri touched the girl's forehead, muttering.

After a minute, they returned, and Agmundria stood.

Terror raced through Susan's mind, sending shivers along her spine.

*"I feel stronger than ever before."* The girl grinned, and Susan forced herself to smile back.

Hope chuckled, her tiny face scrunching and relaxing. The baby seemed unaffected by the young fearmonger.

Giri turned to Susan. His clothes appeared dry, despite his trip into the water. He frowned. "It's your turn. I don't know how you intend to do this."

Susan unfastened the baby harness, handing Hope to Will. Taking a deep breath, she reached within her soul, sensing Grym.

*"What do I do?"*

The ancient voice echoed. *"Step onto the water, I shall take care of the rest."*

She approached the Lake of Sorrows. Turning, she saw the others staring at her. Even Hope's tiny head flopped to the side, and she watched her mother with a smiling face.

Susan took a step.

Two inches beneath the surface, her foot stopped, pushed by something.

Unlike the inner world of the endless sea and burning sky, where she could walk atop an ocean with her mind, here she felt something push back against her weight. Thousands of invisible fingers pressed upward from the depths of the lake, keeping her from entering deeper into the water. She struggled over the hands, trying to push past them.

"What's happening?" she heard Will mutter.

"The Elementals don't want her to touch their power," responded Giri. "I suspect they're trying to keep her out."

She walked forward with slow deliberate steps. Kasumir appeared, with her alabaster skin and deep eye pools of solid black. Behind her, other Elementals stood, with outstretched arms, barring her way.

*"They're not there,"* Grym assured. *"Continue."*

Susan took a deep breath, walking into Kasumir. Her body became a red blur, melting into a pool of blood. One by one, the other Elementals each turned to blood, collapsing into the lake. Around her, bubbles frothed to the surface. The clear water reddened, turning to a lake of crimson blood. With every swell of the blood-waves, the pungent stench of rancid strawberries wafted up.

On instinct, Susan raised her right arm, staring at the cracked sky. Tingles crept from shoulder to fingertips, and sapphire flames burst from her skin.

At once, she sensed a pull, like a tether pulling her toward the sky and down to the water at the same time. Ripples of blood appeared, creeping toward her. One by one, each raised circle pulled inward, stopping beneath her feet.

With a blast of power more furious than anything she'd experienced before, a surge of heat flew from the lake, rushing skyward. A man appeared beside her, with glowing eyes. Another Elemental in ancient clothing materialized next, appearing from nowhere. Soon, the dozen Elementals she'd seen before circled her, staring with eyes of solid light.

The heat coursing over her body and up past her arm burned, searing her skin. Her arm shook, trying to stay still. A column of red light erupted, flying into the sky. A nauseating stench of rotten strawberries clawed into her nose.

Pulled from her body with a sudden jerk, Susan watched herself. She stood between two of the twelve First Elementals.

Her own body stood before them, standing in the center of the circle. The face aged, growing a beard, and she saw Caladbolg's face, concentrating. Ripples of glowing blood continued to flow inward, gaining speed. The column of intense crimson now reached the tear in the sky, pulsing with powers from generations upon generations of Elementals.

The twelve Elementals each raised their palms, moving in perfect unison. With a deafening roar, twenty-four bolts of white-hot incandescent lightning shot into the clouds, forming a glowing cage around the pillar of glowing blood. The cage pulsed and sizzled with energy, streaming in an endless surge of power.

"Susan! What's happening!" Will's voice sounded miles away. Struggling to turn, her soul remained fixed in place, watching Grym channel power upward.

Sensing something behind the sky fissure, she imagined great wings, far larger than any other she'd seen. A shape that filled her with dread.

A form uncoiling from a spire of rock, where she'd been forced to marry.

*The Shadow King.*

Somehow she knew the Shadow Dragon tore the gash between worlds, and now fought Grym, who tried to seal it.

Sparks shot off the lightning web surrounding Grym's pillar, and one of the Elementals vanished. A second one sank to her knees. The streams of refulgent white ceased.

The twelve Elementals sank back into the lake, and she stood alone, facing Grym.

*"I can't do this."*

She closed her eyes, and sank into her own body again.

Despite unbearable pain, she pushed with all her might, channeling and molding the ancient energy.

The red column dissipated, and the First Scythe receded into the depths of her soul. Her arm throbbed.

"Susan?" Will stood on the side of the lake, his eyes wide with worry. Hope wriggled in her carrier.

She staggered to her family. Collapsing on the bank, she stared at the clouds.

The fissure shrank until only a small crack of light remained. Frank hurried over with a bottle of water, holding it to her lips.

"We can do no more. The crack's sealed, however it's temporary, like a bandage over a deeper wound." She took another drink of water, letting the cool liquid slide down her parched throat. "The Shadow King tore that gash, he alone can mend it."

"How do you know?" Frank knelt beside her.

"I'm not sure, exactly. Grym recognized the First Elementals. I think he remembers their birth, or creation. He understood more of what happened than I did."

"You saw the Twelve?" Giri walked over, his voice reverent.

"Didn't you?"

Will shook his head. "We saw you walk to the middle of the lake, standing on the surface. There was a flash of red light and you returned. We never saw anyone else."

Michi turned to the sky. "If what you said is true, even if we didn't seal the breach completely, we'll prevent Dragons from moving between the worlds. I'm sure that will get their attention. Nowhere is safe anymore."

"We'll return to the College soon." Frank stood. "We've something to do first. Agmundria, Michi, Father, Hinara. There's power remaining in the lake. If we fail in the upcoming battle, there'll be no Elementals to even remember this place. Mother told me this place was a last resort. Well now is the time." He gestured, walking into the water.

Giri turned, just before stepping in. "Susan, you should come as well. Grym's spent much of his power sealing the world. We need you both more than ever."

She nodded, and Will helped her rise.

Following the Elementals, she stepped into the water again. This time, her feet sank into the water without resistance. There was no trace of blood.

Around each of the six figures, golden light shimmered. The Lake of Sorrows rippled, with circles flowing around every wading person.

The sensation was alien, and at first she bristled. Energy crawled up her legs like thousands of tiny insects, burrowing beneath her skin. Each droplet of energy held a unique feel, a unique past, and yet all blended into a single stream, nourishing, *strengthening*.

Her power grew, her soul grew stronger, fed by the power of hundreds of previous Elementals.

Lives flashed before her eyes, countless stories glimpsed for a fraction of a second.

One Elemental stood before her, a man with long silver hair and eyes of red flame.

*Orryn.*

His power seeped into her last, and she smiled at the sudden swell of ability.

She turned, and following Frank's lead, started to climb.

The Lake of Sorrows was gone. A large empty crater stood in the center of the forest.

Reaching the shore, she flexed her fingers.

*I was strong before. Now, I'm invincible.*

"*You* are *strong,*" replied Grym. "*Yet, the Dragons remain stronger. This will not be easy.*"

CHAPTER THIRTY-SIX—FRANK

# A Memory of Song

The image now lingered behind every thought. He couldn't escape it.

*A glowing grove of trees, singing an ancient song.*

Frank tried to ignore the strange vision, yet it consumed him. The added power from the lake coursed through him in violent waves, crashing against his soul. Every pulse of energy added to the melee within, always resulting in a stronger sense that he was *missing* something, something very important.

*Journey to the heart of pain;*
*Sing the ancient promise new;*
*Find love again.*
*Find love again.*

The words echoed in his ears. They made no sense. Who'd sung them? Why couldn't he escape the image of glowing birches?

"Frank?" Michi touched his arm.

"I'm fine. Just feels strange, with all the added power."

She nodded.

Hinara appeared in a flash of azure ribbons. She'd already brought Susan, Hope, and Will back to White Claw and the fearmongers. Now she gathered Giri, Frank, and Agmundria into a huddle. The stripes on her skin ballooned, wrapping around their bodies, and they vanished into blue. A moment later, they stood in a wide clearing surrounded by forest.

"How?" Frank started, staring at the huge crowd surrounding them.

A hundred Elementals circled the area, plus an additional twenty Dragons.

"White Claw is ready." Samas limped forward, grinning. "These Dragons remain loyal to our cause. They shall make a difference."

"Vyr is here as well." A woman with short, matted hair like cobwebs stepped forward. *Michi's mother.* Frank smiled.

"It still isn't enough." Giri shook his head. "They've fortified the College. I cannot see the Shadow King with my visions; however, I sense he's near."

"Use the Swarm." Michi gestured to the Dragons. "We need information. One of you, start a small, controlled fire."

Brandr clawed the ground, opening his mouth. A small jet of flame engulfed a nearby holly bush. Brandr closed his jaws. Flames licked the leaves and branches.

Frank approached, his palms open. "Swarm. Show us the College. Show us everything that might assist us now."

A tiny snake of fire jetted out of the blaze, arcing to Frank's forehead.

He rode atop the flickers of a billion fires.

His body burned, turning wood to smoke.

A cloud of gray ash whirled around him, and the world vanished.

Frank's vision watched from the top of a small fire in a fireplace. He saw Betha, turning away from the blaze, sitting on a couch in the living room. Her hands clutched a broken fragment of scythe blade, and her eyes glistened with tears.

Betha lifted a small box, and the black panel Will called a television sprang to life, showing strange images. A woman spoke directly into the room, pointing behind her.

"The light in the sky seems to have lessened, but remains visible across the entire world. Scientists remain baffled over the spectacle's composition or why it's appeared now."

Betha pressed the small box, and the image changed. A man at a desk, reading from a stack of papers now faced the living room.

"Thousands across the globe gather in groups, claiming the light marks the End of Days. The so called Skymark continues to terrify and inspire people in every nation."

Betha looked at the fire again, still holding the scythe fragment.

The image faded into gray cloud.

Whirling through ash and spark, flames and flickers, Frank rode atop the dancing fires.

A new image emerged.

Watching from the embers of a dying torch, he saw two familiar men walk forward. Senchion and Vestru, the strange priests who'd captured them before reaching the Dragons, walked to a pile of wood. Three other robed priests appeared, dragging a screaming Death.

The Deaths screamed again. The priests brought him to the wood, binding his wrists and ankles. Moving away, they started to chant and sing.

An enormous silver Dragon sped from the sky and devoured the Death in a single bite.

For a moment, a memory tugged at his mind, fading to the dimmest corners of thought.

"Prepare for the next sacrifices." Senchion spun, walking away.

The image dissolved into a cloud of dust and ash.

Frank stepped back, as the Swarm disengaged from his forehead.

"What did you see?" Michi held his hand.

"The humans in the Mortal World panic over the breach. Something's happening at the temple where we were captured. I can't recall all of it, yet they mentioned new sacrifices. I think they're bringing Deaths to the temple, where Dragons devour them."

"We must hurry." Giri kicked dirt over the fire, extinguishing the flames. "If they've started emptying the College, we have no more time."

"The hidden library." Susan rubbed her right wrist. "If there are any Deaths left to help us fight, that's where they'll be waiting."

"Sindril knows the library." Will shook his head. "It isn't safe."

"Nowhere is safe. If they've taken the College and Mors, where can we go?" She sighed. "Besides, if there's any secret left that might help us in the final confrontation, we'd discover it at the library."

*"Let us go first."* The voice sent shivers through Frank's spine. Gesrir gestured to the other fearmongers. *"We shall clear a path. With our skill, they won't even know why they flee. We'll secure the library, and from there we'll plan our offensive."*

Glowing birches stood behind his eyes, singing a strange song.

Frank nodded. "We have one chance. This battle will determine the fate of our world, the In-Between, and the Mortal World. All hope rests on success."

Gesrir nodded, and the fearmongers departed.

CHAPTER THIRTY-SEVEN—WILL

# The Eye of Donkar

The bookcase swung open, revealing the words Librvm Exelcior on a wall. Will adjusted Hope and walked through the wall, passing onto the dim staircase. Flowers glowed, casting a faint yellowed light. He reached the bottom, joining Susan in the library.

Elementals crowded between the stacks of ancient books, scrolls, and rock carvings. One of the albino fearmongers gave Will a slight nod, making the hairs on his neck stand on end. The stuffy air smelled of mold, books, and strawberries.

"White Claw remains in the forest outside." Samas sat on Hinara's shoulder, watching Will and his daughter. "Now we plan."

"W-W-Will." Cronk stepped forward, his familiar pockmarked face stretched into a wide grin. Will nodded to the teacher.

Three other Deaths hurried from the shadows. Mel, Feng, and Gordon, his three teammates from the Gray Knights smiled, patting his back.

"Will, you had a baby?"

"We missed you."

"So glad you're all right."

Will grinned back. "Gordon, you'll never guess who we met. Susan and I fled to the Mortal World, and it was your sister Betha who saved us. We wouldn't be here, with our daughter, if she hadn't helped."

A shadow crossed Gordon's face, and he looked at the floor. "Betha?"

"She loves you." Susan put a hand on his shoulder. "In the end we told her the truth. She knows you're here, and that you can't go back."

Gordon nodded, pulling his lips tight before turning away. "She knows I'm here?"

"She does." Will took Susan's hand. "We left her part of a scythe as well. Who knows? After the war, maybe rules will change."

"Rules are already changing." Gordon turned back to them. "Deaths having kids, and Dragons everywhere. You've given me another reason to fight." He grinned. "I want to see Betha."

Frank stood on a large stone. "We'll have a proper reunion later, when the College is secured and the Dragons are defeated. Now, we must prepare."

One of the Elementals from Vyr raised his fist. "We've marched here with Dragons. Now they wait outside. I don't trust them. Why are they involved? Why are we risking our lives for Deaths? After the generations of abuse they've inflicted, let them suffer. This battle doesn't concern us."

"Have you forgotten the past? Have you lost sight of who and *what* we are?" Frank stared down at the crowd. His voice grew distant, almost wistful. "Dragons emerged as the first life on Earth. Beautiful, *godly* creatures who shaped the world, raising mountains and carving rivers through their voices. Dragonsong created what is now the Mortal World."

"We know the stories, Plamen." A different Elemental with yellow hair like autumn leaves shook his head. "You speak like a Dragon. First you lose yourself in the Deaths, now you've grown to love the Dragons?"

"I only mention what you've forgotten. It is more important now than it's ever been. The Earth Dragons created the Mortal World, shaping and guiding it. However, their shadows, the Shadow Dragons created this world, the World of Deaths, or what was once called the Shadow World. The conflict between Dragons never ceased. The Earth Dragons fought the Shadow Dragons before the first Donkari or Deaths held a scythe. Now, yet again, Dragons fight one another for the fate of the worlds."

"Are you saying White Claw is made of Earth Dragons?" The yellow-haired 'Mental spat. "It's a lie, we know the Earth Dragons are gone."

Samas shifted on Hinara's shoulder. "We are Shadow Dragons, just like every Dragon. However, the issue goes far beyond Dragons fighting Dragons. If the Shadow King is victorious he will unmake the worlds, turning back time. He will erase all Elementals, Deaths, and Dragons from existence until there is nothing left, except himself. Few Dragons realize why they're fighting, they follow orders and instinct. They don't realize the price of victory is extinction."

Frank gestured. "The same price would be paid by our race, should the Shadow King triumph. If you want to ignore your role in the world, turn back to Vyr now. If, like me, you cannot ignore the call of fate, then *fight*."

With every word, Frank's voice grew louder, more self-assured. "It's true Deaths mistreated us, and it's true that Dragons have long been our enemies. However, a threat far greater than either of them has taken hold of the College. The Shadow King wants Susan, a woman descended from both Elementals and Deaths, and he wants her daughter Hope, an innocent child. He wants to destroy the world we call home, and to *end* all of us in the process. Will you let that happen?"

The Elementals muttered, and some shook their heads.

"Will you let them kill your families, erasing your ancestors and descendants from existence?"

"No!" The 'Mentals pumped their fists into the air, growing angrier.

"It is time to put aside old hatreds. It's time to *fight*!"

"Fight! Fight!" The library echoed with a flood of angry voices.

"A rousing speech." Samas twitched, his golden tail flicking back and forth. "I'm grateful for the sentiment, Frank, but *how* do we plan to attack? The College is overrun by Dragons, the Ring of Scythes is inactive, and they outnumber us ten to one. The Shadow King, a Dragon far larger and older than any other Dragon, could defeat everyone in this room himself if he desired. Some of the strongest Deaths, including

Sindril and Erebus, have joined the Shadow Dragons for reasons of their own. I repeat, *how* do we proceed?"

For a long moment, no one spoke. Silence filled the ancient library, and Frank stepped down from the stone. Feng coughed and shuffled his feet.

Susan took a step, and everyone turned to her. "The Eye of Donkar. Grym asked if it was ever completed."

"Grym?" asked Gordon.

"The First Scythe." She met everyone's eyes, one by one. "The King of Donkar. Caladbolg. He's real, and he lives within me now. He's how we returned to the Mortal World. And now, Grym tells me we need the Eye of Donkar."

The crowd around them shuffled. Some seem surprised, others hopeful, while others appeared doubtful.

"What is the Eye of Donkar?" Samas scowled.

A Death walked out of the shadows. Professor Domen adjusted his robe. Will hadn't noticed the chubby teacher in the crowd. "Legends spring to life before our eyes. Grym, the power I've so long studied. Is it true?"

"We tried to tell you last year."

Domen shook his head. "I've also heard of the Eye of Donkar. A weapon created during the Great War, designed to unleash immense amounts of power."

"The Ring of Scythes is the Outer Eye." Susan rubbed the mark on her wrist. "There was supposed to be another part, something to focus Grym's power. He doesn't know if it was completed. The Deaths won the war without the weapon, and he was sealed away."

"No." Samas shook his head. "The Deaths didn't win. The Shadow King abandoned his plans in despair. He sank into a million-year hibernation when the Dragon Key failed. Without the King's guidance, the Dragons collapsed. The seeds of White Claw were born on that day."

"I s-s-saw it in a b-b-book." Cronk walked to one of the shelves, and pulled down a dusty tome. "I've s-s-spent s-s-so m-much t-t-time here. The Eye of D-D-Donkar." He handed the volume to Domen, who flipped through its worn pages.

"This says the Eye of Donkar was installed at the pinnacles of East and West Towers. It's never been used." Domen looked at Susan. Will wondered what the Death must think now. He recalled sitting in Domen's office, handing the doubtful teacher Grym, in its bracelet form.

"That's what we have to try." Susan glanced at him and Hope. "Grym says the Eye of Donkar was forged from the body of Karos, his personal Dragon. The Eye, when ignited, will focus his power, creating a weapon strong enough to attack the Shadow King." She paused. "I have to go, Will. I'll leave you and Hope somewhere safe. Only Grym can use the Eye of Donkar."

He wanted to argue, wanted to keep her safe with his family. A feeling of helplessness washed over him. In the end, Will just nodded. "If you must, I know you'll succeed."

"The Ring of Scythes needs to be reactivated." Susan walked to Samas. "How do we turn the power of the Ring back on? When I was locked out during my first year at the College, Sindril changed the barrier using a golden scythe."

"The Headmaster's Blade." Domen closed the ancient book. "It should restore power to the Ring of Scythes, however no one's seen Hann for months."

Samas twitched his broken wing. "My spies tell me he's being held in the Armory beneath the College. Perhaps his golden blade is there as well."

"This will be difficult." Domen looked at the outside of the ancient volume. "Both pieces of the Inner Eye must be fired at once for the weapon to work. The Donkari divided what remained of Karos and tied each half to an enormous rope. There are crossbows imbued with

'Mental power atop each tower, attached to each of the two halves. If I read correctly, we'll have to scale both of the towers, while a separate group attacks the Armory and reactivates the Ring of Scythes."

"I'll take the Armory." Giri's single eye raged with green flame. "My power's never been stronger."

"You should have the largest contingent." Samas twitched again. "Lead a group of White Claw and Elementals, and attack from the Lethe. You'll have to fight every inch of the way to the Armory."

"I'm going in through the tunnel." Susan spoke with a calm confidence. "Rayn was there, so they know of its existence. Still, it's narrow enough to prevent many Dragons from using it at once. With luck, it might even be empty. I'll need help, but the passage leads straight to East Tower."

"I'll lead the group to West Tower." Frank climbed the stone again. "My division will enter the College near the road to Weston. I want as many fearmongers as possible leading the charges with my group and my father's. Timing is essential."

Domen shook his head. "I'll accompany Susan. My knowledge of the Eye, combined with Grym's presence, should allow us to ignite this weapon."

Susan climbed beside Frank, looking over the throng of expectant faces. "The three attacks must happen simultaneously. For the Eye of Donkar to activate, the Ring of Scythes must be active, and both halves of the Inner Eye must connect from the tower peaks. When they connect, the latent power from Karos will ignite the Eye, and I can attack the Shadow Dragons, using Grym. We have our three groups. One group from the Lethe, one group attacking West Tower from the road, and my group traveling underground to East Tower. We'll only have one opportunity to try. If any one group gets ahead, they should wait somewhere safe, allowing the other groups to reach their goals, before the final strike."

The yellow-haired Elemental from Vyr scowled. "If this Eye doesn't work, what then?"

"We fight the Dragons, and take back the College through sheer determination." Susan grinned. "The Shadow King gave up once before. We can defeat him again. History is on our side."

"We can do this." Frank gestured to the group again, waving his arm the way he used to rally the Gray Knights before a difficult match. "We know the odds. If we each do our best, we can win. The fate of three worlds rides on our shoulders."

The Deaths and Elementals shouted.

Susan climbed down, walking to Will.

"I'm sorry, Will. You'll need to stay here. I can't risk you or Hope getting hurt. I'd stay if I could."

"I know."

Hope smiled, flopping her tiny head against his chest. Susan took his hand, and leaned in for a deep, passionate kiss. He tightened his fingers around hers.

"Susan, be safe. I'm—"

"I'll be back. I won't die, I promise."

"You think it's wise to stay in the library? Sindril's been here. He knows where it is."

"This was where I first defeated him. I think his pride's too great to return. Cronk's been here and hasn't seen him or Dragons. There's nowhere safe, but this place is close." She waved to Hinara. "Hinara, I know you want to help in the battle, but I want you here with Will and Hope. If anything happens, whisk them away at the first sign of danger."

Hinara shook her head. "You wield the First Scythe. Can't you use it to reach the top of one tower? With my power, I'd appear at the other pinnacle. Why risk a direct attack?"

"The Ring of Scythes has to be active. Someone would still need to attack the Armory. Besides, we can't let the Dragons gain any advantage. If you and I appeared atop the Towers, they'd attack and overwhelm us.

If three separate large attacks occur at once, they won't know where to fight. If we battle our way in, with three groups, it might divide their attention long enough for all three attacks to succeed."

She paused. "There's another, more personal, yet equally important reason." She glanced at Will. "The Dragons want Hope more than anything. I need you here, Hinara. Your ability is the best protection for my daughter, and for Will. I can't stay, however they *have* to remain safe. I wouldn't feel comfortable with an entire army around them. As long as you're here, you can pull them away, keeping them free from harm."

"I'll protect them, Susan."

"I'm remaining as well," said the golden Dragon on her shoulder. "With my injury, I doubt I'd be much help at the College. I'll place Dragons on guard outside. This place shall be as secure as possible."

Susan put her fingers on their daughter's head. Her eyes glistened with tears. "I'll use Grym to seal the door upstairs. No one will get in." She turned to face him again. "I'd be lying if I said I wasn't scared."

"I'm scared too." He kissed her.

The yellow haired 'Mental approached, bowing. "My name is Lumyr. It's a risky plan, but we'll help. My two sisters and I will divide among the groups. Our ability is communication. Susan, I'll go with you."

"Can someone stay here, so I know what's happening?" Will adjusted his hold on Hope.

"There are only three of us, and we alone hold this power." Lumyr frowned. "I'm sorry."

Will took Susan's hand again, and led her through the stacks of books to a quieter spot. "I won't even know if you succeed."

"I'll return. I have a family to protect, and I won't let anything stop me."

Will nodded, fighting tears. "We'll be here, waiting."

They kissed again. With every touch of her tongue, Will's heart threatened to explode.

CHAPTER THIRTY-EIGHT—SUSAN

# The College of Dragons

$A$ steady stream of confidence flowed from Grym. Grateful for the encouragement, she took a deep breath. Sapphire flames engulfed her right arm.

They waited beneath a cluster of tall pines. A pile of rubble stood nearby, masking a stairway that led to the passage. It seemed a lifetime since Hann sent her and Will through the tunnel, on a secret mission to discover a supply of mortamant. She reflected on their trip along the banks of the Acheron, and the happiness they'd known, if only for a brief period. That mission ended with their kidnap. Sarmarin and Elkanah, the first Dragons she'd encountered, had carried them into the mountains. Now, the distant College was overrun by the beasts.

Susan looked at her group, a contingent of soldiers following *her* lead. Times had certainly changed. Theirs was the smallest company, and the only one without Dragons. Samas divided White Claw between Frank's and Giri's squads, leaving the remainder to protect the library.

Agmundria stood beside Lumyr. Gesrir stood to the side. She'd learned his name for the first time today. The same albino helped her against Sindril at the end of her first year, and helped find Grym during their second year. Professors Domen and Cronk, two of her favorite teachers, each held a scythe. Gordon and Feng, from the Gray Knights, stood behind her as well. Feng held a dagger he'd made himself, with a broken scythe forming its tip. Gordon's hands gripped a boskery blade, hidden by Domen when the other blades were melted down. An

Elemental from Vyr named Mokosh, who controlled water, watched Susan with sea-gray eyes under long strands of coral pink hair.

Eight fighters helping Susan.

*"Not one of them is a true soldier."* Caladbolg remained present behind her eyes, watching with determined assurance. *"You are the strongest one in this group, Susan."*

Lumyr's eyes glazed, staring into space. "The other companies are ready. Giri's on the banks of the Lethe, and Frank's just outside the Ring of Scythes. They await your signal."

"Let's go." Susan motioned, and they sprinted toward the rubble.

A Dragon roared, spying the movement. It sped from the sky, and Susan pointed. "Agmundria, Gesrir. Get rid of it."

The two fearmongers raised their hands, and the Dragon screamed in mid-air, spinning wildly. Lumyr and Mokosh scrambled down the stairs. The others followed, with Susan joining last. Spinning, she waved her arm with a flash of sapphire, and the entrance collapsed into boulders.

Darkness filled the tunnel.

Susan walked forward, raising her glowing arm. "Follow me."

The smell of mold lingered in the dark, cool air. Patches of water covered the rough stone. At the back of her mind, she kept picturing Hope. This was the longest she'd been apart from her baby. She'd left bottles and diapers with Will in the library. Strange that even while approaching the battle she'd long feared, her thoughts continued to turn back to family.

Something caught her eye, and Susan whirled around. A glowing orb hung behind them. She raised her arm, letting the brilliant sapphire flames grow.

Mokosh held a sphere of whirling water, filled with light. "Added illumination." The 'Mental smiled. "I didn't mean to startle you."

Susan nodded, facing the long darkness again. Using Grym as a torch, the company walked in slow silence, with Mokosh and her water-light in rear. The noiseless march sent Susan's mind racing in a thousand directions at once. So many questions, fears, and possibilities.

After two hours they stopped. A boulder blocked the path, with a narrow opening at its base. One at a time, they climbed through. On the other side, they rested.

"We'll take a short break." Susan leaned against the boulder. She increased the light, yet saw nothing in the distance. The flames lowered again. "Lumyr, how are the other groups doing?"

"Giri's party just entered the boathouse. Dragons are swarming, and the fighting's heavy." His eyes glazed, and he paused. "Plamen's group has arrived at the Ring of Scythes. Dragons and fire everywhere." He shook his head. "It's chaos. I'm afraid that's all I see."

Susan glanced at the others' faces, and rose. "Let's keep moving."

The shadowy tunnel widened, and the stones grew smoother. Catching her breath, Susan halted, extinguishing the flames on her arm.

She pressed against a wall, motioning the others to follow. Mokosh's light went out.

A faint glow bobbed in the distance, and a trace of sulfur crept to her nose. The company remained pinned to the side of the tunnel, waiting.

"Third time this month, I've had tunnel duty." A voice echoed from the distance. "You've heard the rumors, I'm sure. They say Susan's back in our world, with her *kid*. Now the fun really begins."

"It's about time," answered a gravelly voice. "I'm sick of all this waiting."

The light crept closer. Two shadowy figures held glowing flowers.

"Do you smell something?"

The light paused, less than two yards away, and the figures started to sniff.

Susan yelled, blue flames enveloping her arm.

She froze as the sapphire light illuminated the figures. The men wore black robes with yellow skull patches. *Training robes.* For a moment she stood staring at them, unsure if they were Deaths or Dragons.

"It's her," snarled one of the men. His skin hung off his neck at an awkward angle, and his reptilian eyes glinted.

One of the Dragons released a bolt of flame. She caught the fire with her left hand, sending it to the other creature.

Agmundria raised her hand, and the Dragon collapsed to the ground, burning and screaming. Susan spun, her arm becoming a blade of light. She sliced the first Dragon, but he jumped back.

His mouth opened, exposing rows of razor-sharp fangs.

*"Concentrate! Remember your training, Susan."* Grym watched from behind her eyes, his tone filled with admonishment.

She waved her hand, appearing behind the open-mouthed figure in a flash of sapphire. He turned, punching her chest, and she flew back to the wall. Stones slammed into her back, knocking the air out of her. He opened his mouth again, sending a second fire blast.

A wave of water poured through the tunnel, sweeping past the Dragons. The creature's mouth oozed hissing steam. He put his hand to his face, ripping human skin away. He noticed the writhing Dragon on the ground. "Get up and fly! Warn the others now. Susan's here." Sharp talons emerged from his hand and he sprang at Susan. She raised her arm in defense, and a bolt of blue lightning sliced through his body. The Dragon crumpled in a pool of blood.

The other Dragon sloughed its skin, revealing a small beast, not much larger than Samas. It spread its crimson wings and soared away.

"Don't let it escape. Come on!" Susan leaped over the dead Dragon, swung her arm, and vanished in sapphire.

She appeared in front of the tiny Dragon, and sliced the air. He dodged, flapping his wings, racing past. Mokosh ran to Susan's side, and a jet of water sprang after the creature, smashing it against the tunnel wall. Susan ran forward and severed its head.

The others hurried to catch up.

"Are there any more?" Domen panted, leaning on the scythe.

Susan illuminated the dark, spying only stone ahead of them.

*"That was sloppy."* Grym echoed behind her thoughts. *"You're thinking about Will and Hope, not where you are and who you're fighting. If you want to save them, you'll need all of your concentration. Two Dragons shouldn't be an issue at all."*

*"I'll do better next time."*

Gordon touched her shoulder. "Susan, wow, that was impressive."

"Keep moving. We're almost at the end."

They continued through the dark until they saw the dim glow of flower lights and a door. A sleeping Dragon lay in front of the door, his scaled back rising and falling in slow rhythm. Susan vanished, appeared at his head, and severed it.

*I've become a ruthless killer. I'm no better than Grym.*

*"This is war, Susan. Kill, or be killed."*

She motioned the others to climb over the serpent's corpse.

"An elevator?" Gordon raised his eyebrow.

"It leads all the way to the Council Offices at the top of East Tower." She pressed the button, and they waited. The door opened, and she held her arm ready. The carriage was empty. She put a finger to her lips.

The car was just large enough for all nine of them. She pushed the button marked 101, the highest number. With a creak, the elevator lurched up, gaining speed.

Susan held her breath. *Don't stop. Don't stop.*

The machine reached the hundredth floor and paused, one story below the top floor. She shook her head, gesturing for the others to prepare. Gesrir and Agmundria opened their palms, and closed their eyes.

A muffled sound cried from the other side, as the door slid open.

For a moment, Susan stared.

She'd been in this hall before; it led to the Headmaster's office overlooking the College. Golden chandeliers filled with glowing white flowers hung overhead. Deep gashes and claw marks stretched down each wall. Fragments of charred red and gold wood separated the office from the hall, where doors once stood.

A figure hunched in front of them, waving an unseen foe away. Professor Rayn coughed. He wore a purple Headmaster's robe.

Susan ran forward, her arm transforming into the glowing blade. She held the energy at his neck. "Rayn. Are you working for the Dragons? What have you done with Hann?" Nodding to Agmundria, the fearmongers lowered their hands.

His eyes focused. "Susan Sarnio." He spat, grinning with a mouth full of sharp fangs. "You're too late. The child will be ours, and you as well."

She wanted to kill him. This was another Dragon. At the same time, he'd been her teacher. This was the first person she knew, whose life rested in her hands.

"Mokosh. Bind him."

The Elemental stepped forward, and thin ropes of glowing water snaked around Rayn's body. He struggled, unable to escape.

A massive sound crashed behind them, and the elevator carriage shook. She heard a Dragon screaming.

"Get out of there!" She waved her hand, and the others jumped into the hall, just before the elevator collapsed to the bottom of the shaft. A silver-scaled Dragon clawed down through the opening, roaring.

Susan ran into the Headmaster's office, followed by the rest of the company. A pair of wings flapped outside the large circular window, and a second Dragon, this one covered in shimmering purple, bust through the glass, sending shattered fragments across the office.

Susan and her eight friends stood in a circle, their backs against each other. The silver Dragon strode forward from the hall, and the purple Dragon bellowed from the broken window, with Susan's group caught in the middle.

Rayn walked up beside the silver Dragon, smiling. Wet streaks crossed his purple robe, however the liquid ropes had vanished. "Welcome to the College of Dragons. This is my assistant, Yurne. My friend in the window is Kindra. I'd love to meet your new friends, Susan, but the truth is, I don't care. Now that you've given birth, you're no use to us. This is the end for all of you." The skin on his face loosened and fell to the floor. With a roar, Rayn tore through his robe, revealing scales of bright orange.

Susan took a deep breath, quieting her mind. For a moment, she saw the endless sea beneath a burning sky. The world seemed to slow.

All three Dragons blew streams of white-hot flame toward the group at once. Susan leaped into the air, channeling the fire with her left palm. She allowed wave after wave of heat to course around her, and she spun in a whirlwind of flame, casting the fireballs back at the Dragons.

Cronk and Domen ran toward Rayn with raised scythes. The orange Dragon knocked Cronk to the ground. Domen slashed one of Rayn's legs, knocking scales to the floor. Lumyr dove, covering his head with his hands when Yurne slashed the group with his tail.

Agmundria and Gesrir raced to Kindra, waving their arms at the purple-scaled monster. The Dragon screamed, reeling in the window. Susan shot two bolts of sapphire at Kindra, slicing off her wings. The fearmongers waved their hands in circles, and she howled, falling out the window. The Dragon screamed, plummeting to the distant ground below.

Gordon slashed Yurne with the boskery blade, and the creature shuddered, fighting the waves of paralysis. Susan vanished, appearing on Yurne's back, and sliced off the Dragon's silver-scaled head.

Rayn roared, blasting Domen with fire. A wall of water splashed from the high ceiling, crushing Rayn beneath gushing waves. He struggled, splashing against the force. Susan killed him, slicing into his back, and the water receded, pouring into Mokosh's fingers.

Lumyr trembled in the center of the floor.

"It's over." Gordon helped the yellow-haired 'Mental stand.

Feng peered out the window. "Susan, you'd better take a look."

She walked to the shattered edge, and peered down at the College. Wind whipped past her face. In every direction, Dragons flew. At the base of West Tower, Dragons battled Dragons, sending streams of flame in every direction. Stone and water shot into the sky, guided by 'Mental hands. She couldn't see Frank's group, yet knew they were encountering trouble.

Turning to the Armory, she saw more fighting. Crowds moved beneath hundreds of serpent tails. A bolt of lightning shot from the ground to the sky, followed by a barrage of flame from Dragons above. Giri's company was caught in the melee.

Smoke wafted from every part of the College. Around the black cube of the Examination Room, enormous black scars covered the earthen mounds. Blood flowed through much of the labyrinth of stone beneath the two enormous towers. Grey clouds hung in the sky above, punctured by the glaring white scar that still ripped across the heavens.

A Dragon soared by, and Susan jumped back, hiding behind the wall.

"We can't stay here. They'll see us." She ran back into the office, turning to Mokosh. "Can you get us one floor higher?"

The Elemental nodded. Susan and the others stood on the edge of the empty elevator shaft. A wave of water emerged, pushing them into the opening, carrying them up. It curved, sloshing toward a closed door one level above. Susan slashed, and the door burst open.

Cronk squeezed the edge of his wet robe. Gordon ran a hand through his wet hair.

They stood in an empty, darkened room. Painted stars and constellations covered the vaulted ceiling. A single table surrounded by thirteen chairs stood in the center of the windowless chamber.

"Looks like the Dragons haven't been using this one." Feng walked to a chair and sat.

"The Council used to meet here." Susan gestured to the table.

"The others aren't ready." Lumyr trembled, shaken. "My sister's been hurt, but she can still communicate."

"Tell the other groups we're waiting. Once they're closer, we'll go to the peak and find that crossbow." Susan waved her arm, and the doors rose from the floor, sliding back into place. Threads of white light beaded across their surface, sealing the entrance. "It'll be safer here, where the Dragons can't see us. Hopefully, they're too occupied with Giri and Frank to notice what happened in Hann's office."

She looked around the empty room, and spotted a tall painting of a robed Death. The painting looked out of place. "Gordon, Feng, help me." The boys walked over, and they felt along the sides of the frame, until she found a tiny latch. The painting swung out, revealing a door.

"That's the way to the pinnacle of this tower. I'm sure of it."

She opened the door, revealing a steep, narrow staircase. Closing it again, she allowed the flames on her arm to recede. The magnitude of her actions crept into her mind. *I'm a killer. And I've only begun.* She buried the thoughts away.

Walking back to the table, she sat. "Now, we wait."

CHAPTER THIRTY-NINE—FRANK

# Ascent

Lyrna grabbed Frank's arm. "A message from my brother. Susan's group is near the top, waiting for us to be closer to our target."

A boulder flew through the dusty air, smashing into the earthen wall before them. Fragments of stone shattered all around. Frank wiped sweat from his forehead, turning his attention back to the fight. They'd lost ten fighters at last count, including a Dragon. That left thirty Elementals including himself, five Dragons, and five Deaths. He didn't even know most of the battalion's names. The company now cowered in four groups, hiding behind stony mounds near the entrance to West Tower.

"Any sign of Brandr, Jurna, or the other Dragons?" He shouted to the huddled figures behind him.

"They're out there somewhere." Michi's was the one face not covered in panic. "In this madness, we can't rely on their direct support."

Frank peered over the mound. West Tower stood a few yards away. A black Dragon flew to its gnarled side. After clinging on with a taloned arm, it screamed. The beast bared its fangs, and a fire blast scorched the mound hiding Frank. Intense heat seared around the stone, so hot he crawled back. He heard a second Dragon roar, and the sound of clashing wings and tearing fangs.

"Everyn, Koros, and any others who manipulate stone. Take the lead, followed by water 'Mentals and fearmongers. On my signal, we make for the door." He took a deep breath, trying to calm his racing nerves.

*A grove of glowing birches, and a lonely song.*

Instead of fighting the strange image, he reached for it, letting the calm music soothe him.

Digging his fingernails into his palm, he tightened his hands into tight fists. "Now!"

Everyn, a spry Elemental with a short purple beard and canine ears, jumped up. Koros, whose bulbous fish eyes stared in opposing directions, stood behind him. Each 'Mental waved their hands with fluid motions. The ground thundered, and a wall of stone emerged from the ground, opening into a tunnel.

Frank leaped over the mound, running into the new passage. He gestured the others to follow. The stone shook with violent convulsions, and dirt fell from above.

"Run!" He sprinted toward the base of West Tower.

Turning, he watched the newly-formed stone cave collapse beneath a Dragon's claws. Two of his Elementals vanished into the rubble. Three albinos pointed to the beast, who scowled and took off again. Koros stepped to Frank's side, and forty-foot spears of granite broke from West Tower's sides, flying into the Dragon-filled air. Winged serpents of every shape and color fought above the College mounds. White Claw was outnumbered tenfold, yet seemed better-trained. Two of the rocky projectiles rammed straight through Dragon necks, and the flying snakes plummeted to the bloody stones below.

"Come on." Michi pulled his arm. Everyn's fingers shook, and the ground beneath the door swelled like an ocean wave. The doors to West Tower flew open.

Frank and the others raced inside.

"What happened to the elevator?" Michi pointed. The three elevator carriages stood encased in glittering, transparent crystal. The edges of the crystal flared where frozen flames of solid diamond shone.

"This goes all the way to the top." Koros touched the jeweled sheath. "We can't use the elevator shafts at all."

"The stairs." Frank walked to a narrow door at the side of the entrance chamber.

"It's a hundred stories." Michi hurried behind him.

"A hundred and one. Come on." He opened the door. Flowers started to glow. Steep stone stairs spiraled up into the darkness. The narrow stairway forced them to walk single-file. Frank led, followed by Michi and Everyn. They passed a door and kept climbing.

*Second story. Third. Fourth.*

"If I use my power, I can push the entire company—"

Everyn's words vanished behind a roaring sound. Looking up, Frank's eyes widened at a growing light cascading down the spiraled stairs.

"Water, now!"

One of the 'Mentals beneath them must have heard, because a flooding wave surged around his feet, growing stronger as it sped up the steps.

With an enormous crash, flame and water slammed into each other. Frank flew backward, falling into Michi and slamming against the rocky steps. Water surged past his feet, and hot steam choked the air out of the narrow staircase.

Michi grabbed his arm, pulling him through a door. They stood in a narrow hall, surrounded by classrooms. Everyn stumbled out of the door a moment later, his face scarred by a dark red burn.

"The others." Frank spun.

"They'll be fine. The water 'Mentals are clearing a path. Most got out a level below." Everyn touched his burn, wincing. "We need to move faster. I'll lift us with stone."

Frank nodded, putting his hand on the door. It was cool to the touch, so he opened it, peering into the dim, winding staircase. Scorch marks streaked the walls. Two blue-haired 'Mental girls stood ankle-deep in swirling water. "It's clear for now," said one of the children. *Marella and Assana.* They were no older than eleven, and their eyes bulged with fear.

"You two did very well." Frank grasped their shoulders. "Stay close to me. We might need more help soon."

Michi and Everyn walked down several of the steps, vanishing behind the bend. Michi hurried back two minutes later. "We're ready to try Everyn's plan. I've let the others know."

Frank nodded. Water continued to fall down the steps, and he grasped the scorched walls for support. With a rumble, the steps moved. The damp ground swelled upward beneath his feet. He stumbled, falling into Michi. The ground continued to rise, circling around the narrow staircase. Doors flew past in a blur.

*Fifteenth story, sixteenth, seventeenth...*

With a loud screech, the moving stone underfoot halted.

"What's wrong?" He turned around, shouting.

"Something's blocking the power. The stone won't budge." Koros pushed his way past others on the narrow staircase. "Frank, there's something here."

Michi's eyes widened, and she spread her arms. Insects buzzed in every direction. "Brace yourselves!"

A two-foot long, slender, black, leathery serpent with golden eyes slithered from the shadows. A second Dragon, equally narrow and small emerged on the other side. One by one, the space around them lit with golden eyes. Tiny shadow-colored Dragons clawed on the sides of the narrow corridor.

"Attack!" Frank pointed, and Assana waved her arms. Nothing happened.

"These aren't normal Dragons." Michi clenched her hand. Her insects hovered in mid-air, directionless. "They're sapping our abilities somehow."

One of the Dragons jumped off the wall, wrapping around Marella's neck. The creature tightened. Frank ran to the girl, clawing at the beast. It turned its head, hissing.

*A grove of glowing birches. A song of longing.*

The Dragon relaxed, and Frank ripped it off, slamming it against the wall repeatedly. "Run! Continue up the Tower!"

He turned and sprinted. "Michi. Reach for your augmented powers. Use the ability we took from the lake. It will help. See if you can hold them off while we push on."

She nodded, and vanished, becoming a beetle. Hundreds of other insects passed, rushing down the stairs. Frank started climbing, taking the narrow, winding steps two at a time.

"Hurry." Frank climbed without pause. "Follow me."

He passed three more doors before he paused. He motioned the company to pass. Resting in the door's alcove he heard screams and hisses echoing from levels below. The last of their group ran past.

Michi, back in human form, appeared, running hard. Blood streaked her face. A Dragon clung to her arm, its fangs nestled in her skin. Frank grabbed the tiny serpent. Ripping a dagger from his belt, he slashed the creature in half, prying its fangs out of Michi's arm. She screamed.

The stairs below erupted in a chorus of hisses. Hundreds of tiny black Dragons scrambled from the shadows like a horde of golden-eyed snakes.

Frank pulled Michi up the stairs and they ran.

The staircase wound and wound without end. Frank's legs throbbed in agony, and his muscles felt ready to fall off. He saw the feet of his company rounding the stairs above with every turn, and heard the constant hisses of Dragons approaching from below.

A shudder shook the twisting passage. Dust fell from the walls.

Michi met his eyes, her hand clamped over the spot on her arm where she'd been bitten. "That came from outside."

Frank paused in a doorway, screaming between panted breaths. "Koros! Everyn!" Their names relayed up the steps. The hisses approached, and Frank climbed again, forcing his legs to move. Michi held his hand. The two earth 'Mentals appeared at the bend above.

"What can we do?"

"Can you use your powers outside West Tower? I know the Dragons here sap your strength, but reach beyond these walls." Frank risked a look below. The stories beneath them writhed with a mass of converging serpents.

Koros and Everyn extended their arms, closing their eyes. Frank stopped on the step below them, alongside Michi. The hisses approached, deafening and terrifying.

"I feel the stones of the tower wall." Koros nodded, his eyes still shut. "I can't use the power here on the stairs, but outside the passage, I feel it again. We're near enough to the outer edges. Yes, it'll work."

"Rip off parts of the outer stone and smash it back. We need to collapse this passage beneath us, or we'll be fighting these things forever."

Michi extended a hand, and thousands of insects sped in front, forming a solid wall of bugs. A pair of Dragon fangs snapped through the insects.

"Hurry." Michi trembled beside him. "I can't hold them for long." A second fanged mouth poked its way through the insect barrier.

Koros and Everyn scrunched their faces. Sweat beaded on their brows. Something thudded against the wall. A moment later, another crash thundered. With the third bombardment, the entire stairway heaved and shuddered. Stones collapsed onto the insects, which scurried away as the twisted passage fell. A mound of rubble blocked the way down, and the hisses erupted into distant screams.

"Let's go." Frank turned and ran back up the stairs. "That'll hold them for a little while."

They jogged up another five flights of stairs before Everyn called out. "My power's not blocked at all anymore. Brace yourselves, all of you. We're getting out of here."

A slab of earth emerged underfoot, carrying them up and around.

Door after door slid by.

They gained speed.

At last, the rock halted.

Frank followed the company through the final door, walking into an enormous domed room. A charred hole lined with crystallized flames stood in the center of the room, in place of the elevator. A vivid fresco on the ceiling depicted large green and black Dragons with glowing red eyes facing a crowd of Deaths with scythes. A burning figure stood in the center of the image.

Winds howled through the room. Shattered windows, supported by pillars of stone, ringed every wall. Frank took everything in at a glance, searching for access to the roof. He spotted the yellow-haired Lyrna. She'd collapsed on the ground, next to a group of breathless Elementals.

His own legs threatened to stop moving, but he forced himself over. "We'll rest for a moment. Tell Susan we're ready."

She nodded, closing her eyes.

"Any word from my father?"

"They've broken into the Armory. That was the last message I received. I don't think they've activated the Ring."

Frank stumbled to one of the shattered windows, kneeling and clutching a pillar for support. Wind howled past, whistling into the room.

Gray clouds mixed with plumes of smoke. The fracture of light hung in the center of the sky like a beacon. East Tower rose a mile away, its stone walls chipped and smoking. Beneath the two towers, a sea of chaos engulfed the College. Thousands of Dragons flew, fighting. Frank couldn't tell which side was winning, and his gut warned that he'd not like the answer if he knew. Much of the earthen labyrinth lay stained in patches of blood. To his left, bolts of fire clashed with streams of jetting water and stone. Giri's company was on the move.

He scrambled back to the center of the room, turning to Michi.

"Any idea on how to get to the roof?"

"Don't use Koros or Everyn, or any of the others for that matter. They're all exhausted, and we don't know what we'll find at the peak. Besides, if there's a weapon up there, they might damage it by mistake."

Frank nodded, surveying the room again. Between the windows, thin columns of stone arced to the vaulted ceiling. One pillar stood five times thicker than any of the others. He walked to it, motioning Michi to join him. She extended her fingers, and two beetles fluttered across the stone.

"Here." She pressed an indentation, and the pillar swung open, revealing a hidden door. A ladder extended on the other side. Frank climbed up, feeling the wind strengthen. He saw open sky at the top.

He climbed to the peak of West Tower and froze. Sulfur-laden wind slammed into his face. Michi's steps echoed on the ladder rungs behind him.

"I don't believe it." She stared, joining him.

Hundreds of Deaths sat huddled on the center of the roof, their hands bound. Spires of worn stone, thousands of large and small stalagmites, poked from the roof like weathered teeth. Frank ducked behind one, pulling Michi down.

They watched a crimson Dragon land in the group of captured Deaths. It lifted one of the screaming boys, grasping him in silver talons. Snarling, the beast flew away.

"I don't see a weapon." Michi whispered, pushing her mouth next to his ear in the bitter winds.

He motioned for her to follow back down the ladder. The Deaths hadn't spotted them. "We have bigger problems." He walked through the door, facing the company. "It's not just an attack. This is a rescue mission."

With a terrifying screech, an enormous silver Dragon flapped outside one of the shattered windows. Swirls of gray smoke enveloped the scaled beast, pulsing into undulations of dancing fog. The blanket of smoke vanished, and a leather-clad man with golden eyes stood in the window.

"Been a while." The figure smiled, baring sharp fangs. "I was at the house that day you jumped out a window." The Dragon ran a finger down a scar along his right cheek. "You paralyzed me. Probably thought I was dead."

Three other Dragons appeared around the room, each taking the human appearance Frank witnessed in the Mortal World.

The fearmongers spread their arms, and two of the creatures paused. Marella and Assana waved their hands in a fluid motion, and water gushed from their fingers, spraying one of the Dragons out the window.

"Up the ladder!" Frank gestured wildly. "Free the Deaths on the roof, see if they can help."

Michi ran behind him, scaling the rungs. Everyn made a gesture and a section of floor slammed into the Dragon who'd spoken. The creature spun, diving to the ground. An Elemental jumped into the air, her white hair blowing like smoke. The air pulled around her, twisting into a gale that accosted the Dragon. He struggled to stand, talons tore out of his boots, gripping the floor.

Everyn punched the air and the ground flew apart beneath the creature's feet. He vanished behind a cloud of swirling smoke, emerging as the silver-scaled Dragon again. His head whipped back into the room, and a jet of flame blasted across the floor. Marella countered with a wall of water, which collided with the fire in a blast of hot steam.

"Go!" Frank shouted again, waving everyone up the ladder.

The two remaining Dragons in human form jumped to the ceiling, clawing their way across the painting by digging sharp claws onto the mosaic. Tiles fell to the floor. An Elemental pointed a finger, and a bolt of lightning erupted, slamming the ceiling. One of the Dragons collapsed.

The silver-scaled Dragon wrestled against the ferocious onslaught of wind and stone bombarding it. Frank pushed his way around the concentrated gale. Even at its edge, his feet struggled to find balance. He grabbed a scythe from one of the Deaths. The winds eased, and he ran forward, slashing the creature's neck. It tumbled out the window to the ground.

The human-form Dragon jumped from the ceiling in the middle of their group. Assana spun in mid air, and a rope of water shot toward the creature. The beast sloughed his skin. Chomping down, his fangs impaled the young girl, with a rush of crimson blood.

"No!" Marella screamed, watching her sister's body crumple to the floor. A tidal waved emerged, gushing around all of the fighting. Frank lost his footing, carried with the surging water.

"Marella. You have to—"

He sputtered, trying to stay afloat. The surge pushed him toward a window. He grabbed for one of the pillars, but missed.

The wall of water pushed Frank out of West Tower.

He tumbled in mid-air, plummeting.

Water rushed down, surrounded by wind.

He fell.

Something slammed into his chest, knocking his breath away. He saw Brandr's leathery green wings flapping. The Dragon clutched him in tight talons, carrying him to the peak of West Tower. He tossed Frank onto the roof. A group of sharp spires caught his fall, breaking beneath him. His entire left side throbbed in sharp pain.

"Are you all right?" Michi ran up, making her way across the peak. "We're nearly all at the top, and the Deaths are free. Three Deaths were under some sort of spell, keeping guard. I bound those ones over there."

He rolled to one side, spitting up blood.

"Frank."

"I'll be fine."

Brandr flapped his wings overhead, landing on the roof. "I can't stay long. If there's a weapon here, you'd better find it soon."

"Thank you for saving me."

The Dragon snorted.

"Find the girl Marella. Or any of the others caught in that wave. See if…see if they survived."

Brandr nodded and took off again, flying into the battle below.

Michi helped Frank walk to the center of the tower. Deaths milled, rubbing their hands where they'd been tied. Some called out to him, yet he ignored their calls.

"Contact Susan." He grabbed Lyrna's shoulder. "See what we're supposed to do."

"I see it." Michi pointed to the perimeter of the roof. At first glance he hadn't noticed the ropes. Coiled around the entire circumference of West Tower thick ropes stood in tight bunches. "The ropes."

"There's a lever." Lyrna pointed. "They have the same thing on East Tower. Each rope's a half-mile long. They have to connect in the middle, fired simultaneously, to activate the Eye of Donkar." The Elemental paused. "There was trouble over there. There are Deaths on the top of their tower too. Someone named Eshue tried to fight them, under some kind of hypnosis. Susan cut his arm, but he'll be okay. She's ready now, if we are."

"The Ring's active?"

Lyrna nodded. "Giri's group faced heavy fighting, but they've activated the Ring of Scythes."

Frank ignored the pain coursing through his body. He limped, with Michi's aid, to the edge of West Tower. Wind pummeled his face. He struggled for balance. Dropping to his knees, he saw a machine jutting from the side of the stone, just beyond the rim.

A three-foot wide slab of stone jutted out from the wall below, extending from the tower like an outstretched finger. At its center, a crossbow arced in either direction, ending in a drawn piece of cord. The cord supported a dark sphere, which was attached to the end of the massive coils of rope winding around the tower.

"We have to fire that thing at the same moment Susan fires a similar one on East Tower?" Michi eyed the strange weapon. "What happens if the two halves miss each other? The towers stand a mile apart, the odds of this working are slim."

"We have to try. The sphere must be what remains of Karos, Grym's Dragon. This weapon's still our greatest hope of victory." Frank climbed over the rim, standing on the narrow causeway of stone. The thin bridge shuddered in the wind, and he fell back, slamming onto the rock. Something itched, and looking down, he saw a coil of insects wrapped around his waist like a belt.

"Tell me when." Frank reached for the lever beneath the cord. If he pulled it, the bow would spring, and the rope should fire.

"Susan's there. I'll count down. Five, four, three, two, NOW."

Frank pulled back and the stone beneath him shuddered. The bow sprang, shooting the black sphere at an unbelievable speed toward the opposing tower. A faint dot flew away from the other tower.

Rope uncoiled, flowing away from West Tower. A piece of rope hit his legs, and he stumbled, falling. The insect belt tightened, pulling him to the rim, and he scrambled back to the peak.

Coil by coil, a seeming impossible amount of rope sprang away from West Tower. He watched the two rope lines approach the center of the College, above the black cube of the Examination Hall.

"They're going to make it." Michi shielded her eyes from the wind. "I don't believe it."

A Dragon flew up, knocking into one of the ropes. The other one struck the center, its cord growing taut. It fell.

"It didn't work. The ropes didn't connect." Frank stared as their greatest hope plummeted out of the sky.

CHAPTER FORTY—WILL

# Snare

Will held the bottle to Hope's lips, watching her suck. He wiped a line of spit off her mouth when she finished.

Hinara paced through the stacks of the library, her fingers flexing under her chin. Samas stretched his broken wing, watching from a table.

"They'll be fine." Samas nuzzled against Will's duffle. "Susan is stronger than you realize. This weapon of Grym's might work."

Hinara ignored the Dragon, pacing again.

"At the very least, could you stop worrying? It's upsetting the baby."

"Hope's fine," countered Will. "Don't bring her into this."

Samas sighed.

Will laid Hope on the table and changed her diaper. The baby's piercing blue eyes watched above a smiling mouth. Faint wisps of brown hair crowned her forehead. He finished, rocking her in his arms.

The sound of sliding stone surprised him. He turned to watch part of the wall move, where they'd discovered Grym's hiding place years ago. A man emerged from the nook, wearing a long white robe.

*Sindril.*

"Will!" Hinara darted forward. Sindril rolled a small ball on the floor, which spewed gas into the air. The Elemental grabbed Sindril's arm, coughing.

"The smoke. It's doing something to my power."

Sindril strode forward, a large grin plastered across his face.

"Hello, William. I've grown tired of waiting."

Will took a step backward. Samas hobbled toward the stair.

Grabbing a dagger, Hinara sliced in wild, desperate motions. Sindril ducked, laughing. He slammed her arm into a wall, knocking the dagger out. With a laugh, he kicked her in the chest. She collapsed onto a stack of books.

Without waiting for her to rise, Sindril held the dagger to her throat, and slit. A trail of blood flowed down her clothes.

Samas screamed, yelling for help, but no one answered.

Samas leaped at Sindril, clawing in desperate motions. Sindril rammed the dagger into the golden Dragon's mouth, and then again into his chest. He tossed the bloody corpse to the floor.

"Now, where were we, William? Last time I saw you, you'd just been married. I see you've decided to start a family."

"Stay away from us. You're a monster."

Will clutched Hope to his chest, coughing. Smoke filled the library. His daughter's head lolled against his chest as he staggered backward. Sindril stood between him and the stairs. There was no way out.

The former headmaster smiled. "I have to thank you. Not only have you provided us with a Dragon Key, but by discussing your plans here, in the predictable spot Susan never fully abandoned, we know exactly what you intend to do. Rest assured, the so-called Eye of Donkar shall fail." He gestured toward the hidden alcove. "A wonderfully hidden area. I'm guessing you found Grym there? Installing a small portal behind that wall wasn't easy, but we've been here for some time." Sindril shook his head. "You really are pathetic."

Will took another step backward. There was nowhere to go.

Claws grabbed his back, and he saw a flurry of leathery wings.

Sindril reached for Hope.

He fought, screaming. Talons dug into his arms, pinning them to his side. Something slammed into his head from above.

The world turned to fog.

Fighting to stay conscious, he squinted.
Hope slept in Sindril's arms.
The world went dark.

## CHAPTER FORTY-ONE—SUSAN

# Firefall

Susan stood on the ancient crossbow, staring at the dangling rope beneath her. The plan had seemed so close to success. Each stretch of cord now hung limply from the tower peaks.

She glanced over her shoulder. Finding Eshue and other Deaths under some sort of hypnotic spell was disturbing. Eshue sat on the far edge, under Agmundria's watchful eyes. The group of newly-freed Deaths milled around the center of East Tower's apex.

"What happened?" Gordon leaned over the edge.

"It didn't work. The ropes didn't connect." She paused, thinking. "Get Lumyr. I have an idea."

Gordon nodded, scrambling back to the pinnacle. The wind slammed into Susan. She smiled. It should be terrifying to stand on the narrow ledge of stone jutting away from East Tower. The Eye of Donkar stood over a thousand feet above the rocky labyrinth of the College. *A hundred and one stories, as high as the Empire State Building.* The thought trickled into her mind from some distant memory. *I'm alone on a three-foot wide stone plank, completely unafraid.*

Above, the breach in the heavens glowed brighter than the sun. Dark clouds and plumes of billowing smoke surrounded it. Below, Dragons continued to fly in every direction. The busiest part of the battle now concentrated near the boathouse. *Giri activated the Ring, but the Dragons will change that if we don't hurry.* She scanned the horizon, searching for a leathery green figure.

*"Brandr!"*

Unsure if she'd yelled or called with her mind, she felt relief when the enormous Dragon flapped in her direction. He approached, hovering before her. Grasping the side of East Tower with silver talons, he turned his head. His snarling fangs dripped crimson blood.

"The plan failed." He beat his wings in constant rippled movements, fighting the ferocious winds. Every gust that thundered around the Tower, however, dissipated into a harmless breeze before it touched her. The sapphire flames barely quivered.

"The orbs need to touch. That's all. Fly down and grab one. Have one of your Dragon friends do the same, and meet in the center."

He snorted, growling at the order.

Susan pointed. "Go now."

Brandr spread his wings, diving like a rocket into the tumult below.

"I'm here." Lumyr peered from the summit's edge, his yellow hair blowing across his face.

Susan climbed up from the ledge, joining him on the other side of the rocky rim. "We'll see if the Dragons manage to connect the ropes. If not, you're our failsafe."

*"They respect and fear you."* Grym echoed behind her eyes. *"You've become a leader."*

She turned back, peering down at the distant College.

Brandr and Jurna circled each other; the green Dragon seemed to be speaking to the cloudy white one. The two separated, racing toward the towers. Brandr grabbed the black dot beneath her, grasping it with an outstretched talon. He circled, flying back to the middle.

*Karos.* The thought welled from Grym. Seeing the orbs, and knowing they'd been formed from his flesh brought a mix of emotions to Susan's mind. She'd seen the Dragon many times through Grym's eyes. She pushed the memories aside, focusing on the present.

A host of black Dragons with burning red eyes shot from the other side of the campus, spewing a solid line of flame. They roared over the rest of the battle, rampaging with unbelievable speed.

Brandr flapped harder and harder, hurrying to meet Jurna. The white Dragon hovered near the center, far above the Examination Hall. Surging behind a tidal wave of sheer fire, the stampede of black Dragons slammed into Brandr. They clawed at him, grabbing his wings and legs. He wrestled free, yet the rope slipped through his claws. The attackers now threw flame at Jurna, who twisted and fled.

Susan motioned for Lumyr. "I suspected they might be too large. Dragons will attack any members of White Claw who try to assist. Tell your sister, we need Michi's help. She can do this. I saw her use insects to lower Frank from a window. Insects can join the ropes, and they'll be small enough to pass through the crossfire."

Glancing down, she watched the black Dragons retreat to the battle near the boathouse.

*They knew to stop us. Someone knows what we're trying to do.*

*"You can't worry about that now, Susan. The Eye of Donkar is still our best hope."*

Brandr shook off the last attacker, soaring up to the summit. Streaks of blood lined his leathery face. "I can try again, however, they attacked the moment we approached the center, and left once we'd dropped the ropes."

"Michi will help instead. Protect the ropes at all costs."

The Dragon snarled, his eyes fierce with inner rage. With a monstrous snort, he leaped off the writhing tower.

Lumyr tugged on her arm. "Michi is ready. She's never tried something so massive. Still, she's confident she'll manage."

Susan nodded.

Screeches and clashes of wings continued to sound from below. The sound of cries, and stone smashing, blended with echoes of roars and rushing feet. Yet, a new noise now began, one unlike anything she'd heard.

It started as a gentle clicking, almost imperceptible against the tumultuous battle. Growing louder every second, buzzing and clicking thundered across the campus. Dragons paused, searching for the source of the strange sounds.

A mile away, West Tower shot into the sky, a gnarled mass of twisted stone standing like a stalagmite over a thousand feet high. The twin of East Tower loomed with sides of earthen brown, granite gray, and streaks of red and white minerals stretching across its stony sides. Yet, even from her perch atop the rim, she saw lines of black. A sea emerged from countless unseen corners, a sea of tiny black specks, surging in a mass. Wave after wave of insects climbed up West Tower, as if a great black cloud slowly grew from the base. Soon, all of West Tower vanished beneath the mass of tiny specks.

The noise now deafened. Scrapes and wings and constant buzzing. Susan leaned over the edge.

East Tower was blanketed beneath a thick layer of insects. Billions of beetles, flies, winged ants, moths, wasps, bees, cicadas, locusts, fireflies and cockroaches scrambled over each other, racing in a mad dash up the rocky side. The insects clambered across the narrow stone crossbow, speeding down the limp rope.

With a roar, the stampeding black Dragons sped back. Ten other Dragons from White Claw joined Brandr and Jurna. One by one, each Dragon grappled, fighting. Jets of flame broke through, attacking clumps of insects. Each time a section fell to the ground, another swarm of insects rushed to take its place.

West and East Tower writhed beneath the living shrouds. Each flying insect grasped a part of the limp rope. Soon, the stone sides of the towers again became visible. The ropes twisted, flying into the air. A Dragon knocked one rope to the side, and insects fell off, but others scampered to fill the void. The ropes continued to climb.

"It's working." Lumyr watched beside her. Although she heard Deaths shouting in amazement behind them, she didn't turn.

*"Giri's in trouble."* Grym's fires brightened on her arm, growing with eager excitement. *"We have to ignite the Eye soon, while the Ring's still active."*

She watched the ropes again. Every inch brought a fresh battle. White Claw and the Dragons struggled, blasting flames and clawing with fierce talons. Fangs sank into tails, and insects fell. More bugs continued to surge forward.

The ropes snaked across the College, stretching in a perpendicular line to the towers. They bent and swayed, moving with the insects, avoiding the Dragons. Half a mile from Susan, two tiny black dots came closer and closer.

Susan held her breath.

*BOOM!*

Light exploded.

A glaring burst seared the sky, brighter than a thousand suns. A deafening crash louder than thunder accompanied the flare.

Susan flew back, pushed by a blast of power.

The orb glowed white-hot, like a tiny star, held in place by a mile-long span of rope connecting East and West Tower. Sparks flew from the central light, pulsing and dancing. The insects clung on, riding the trembling rope bridge.

With a roar, flames raced outward from the center light. Fire engulfed every insect, and the bugs fell to the distant ground, charred and dead.

A bridge of fire, with a star in its center, connected the two towers.

*"The Eye of Donkar."*

Susan waved her arm, vanishing in a flash of sapphire.

The world parted around her, and blue light dissipated.

She stood atop East Tower. The burning rope stretched to her side.

Frank stared up, his eyes wet. Michi lay in his arms.

"Is she all right?"

He shook his head. "The insects died all at once. I've never seen an Elemental use so much power, only to have it snatched at the end. She's alive, but barely."

"She did it, Frank. She connected the ropes. The weapon's active."

"Don't use it." He stared at her, and a hint of green fire filled his pupils.

"What are you talking about? We've worked too hard for this."

"I can't explain. Something's not right." His eyes widened. "I don't think the Dragons are our enemies. It was a misunderstanding."

*"He's gone mad. Come, Susan. We need to stand at the center of the Eye."*

"I'm sorry, Frank. Just wait here. Michi will be okay."

"Please don't go. He's coming." Frank turned back to Michi, shaking his head.

"Who's coming? Frank, what's going on?"

The Elemental didn't answer.

*"Enough. End this now, Susan. The center of the Eye."*

She stared at her two friends, unsure of what to do.

*"Go now."*

Susan waved her arm, vanishing into sapphire light again.

The world coalesced.

Tingles stretched across her body.

*Power.*

*Power greater than any she'd ever imagined.*

*Power beyond power.*

Susan stood atop a tiny star, at the center of a mile of burning filament.

A row of flames spanned the gap between the peaks of East and West Towers, a thousand feet above the College of Deaths, forming a perfect bridge.

*The Eye of Donkar.*

*Power beyond power.*

Sapphire flames spread from her arm, crossing over her chest and legs, engulfing her entire body. Where the blue flames met the dancing orange of the fire bridge, sparks of white and green shot into the air. At her feet, the white orb radiated sheer brilliance, feeding off the conflagration around it, and sending pulsing waves of power up through her limbs. Her fingertips trailed starlight and energy. Every breath escaping her lips glowed.

*"YOU STAND ON THE EYE OF DONKAR. USE US, SCYTHE WIELDER!"*

The Swarm connected the towers, wrapping around her ankles, and extending from her arms. She watched the battle far below with thousands of eyes. This wasn't just the eyes of the Swarm, this was *all* fire.

*Every flame that ever burned.*
*Every blaze yet to kindle.*
*All fires stand at my feet.*
*I control the Eye.*

Before her gaze, the battle slowed. She sensed every movement, and saw every detail. Her eyes darted to a solitary cicada corpse on one of the earthen mounds two thousand feet away. The tiny creature's legs had seared away, and its shell was charred. Her eyes shifted and she watched Giri face a Dragon. His hands raised in defense, as the creature's talon reached for Giri's throat. The scene seemed oddly frozen in time. Her eyes darted again, to Brandr wrestling three black Dragons, all paused in mid-air. Another shift of the eyes showed her Frank, still clutching Michi's gasping body, fighting for life. With another glance, she saw Jurna and a brown Dragon locked in a struggle, their bodies suspended out of time. One by one, she took stock of every creature fighting, and it all happened in a fraction of a second.

*Is this the power of the Eye?*

*"You've scarcely touched the power yet,"* Grym answered. *"Don't be afraid. It's what we've waited for."*

Susan reached forward. The clouds above condensed, thickening into a spinning wheel around the gash of light which still glared in the center of the heavens. Thunder rumbled. Within the cloud, she sensed fire darting between drops of water. She *felt* the lightning, eager to burst forth.

She opened her palm.

An enormous bolt of lightning forked from the firmament. Charging in a wild stampede from the heavens, it coursed to her fingertips, spiraling around her body.

*"USE US, SCYTHE WIELDER! USE US!"* The Swarm screamed with a chorus of voices louder than her ears could bear. Lightning danced around her, wrapping jagged streaks into a solid blur of incandescent white. Fire blazed: a strange blend of orange flames and sapphire flickers.

She looked back at the frozen battle: at time stilled by the sheer power radiating through Grym, channeled through her body.

Susan pointed, her finger trembling.

Flames coursed around her, and lightning waited, eager to surge.

She stared at the Dragon in front of Giri.

Lightning danced with flames.

*All fire: every flame that ever burned, every flicker yet to spark.*

Power erupted from her finger, racing down to the frozen battle below. Light poured through the Dragon, and the creature shattered into a billion pieces. Its talon fell to the ground at Giri's feet, and the 'Mental stared at the sky.

Spinning, Susan punched the air, rolling her arms in a smooth motion, letting the power flow where it needed to.

A surge of fire coasted from the clouds, and each of the black Dragons around Brandr collapsed, dead.

The scene still moved in slow-motion. Dragons turned, flying toward the bridge of flames. With slow, predictable movements, they flapped their oversized wings.

Spreading her arms wide, Susan reached into the cloud above. A thousand bolts of fire-wrapped lightning scorched down, striking only where she aimed. One by one, every enemy fell. Dragons lay sprawled across the mounds, covered in blood.

Something flashed in the corner of one of the Swarm's infinite eyes.

Erebus stood next to the Ring of Scythes, holding a golden scythe.

Susan turned, raising her hands. A surge of the all-fire danced at her palms and spun around her wrists, ready to erupt.

She hesitated.

Unlike Rayn, Erebus was a Death, and her teacher. He might be under some sort of spell, like Eshue.

Erebus slammed the golden scythe into the Ring of Scythes.

With a jolt of energy, the Ring de-activated.

In a flash, the battle unfroze. Her vision of the College blurred, and she could no longer make out individuals or details.

*"What's happening?"*

*"Without the Ring of Scythes, you can't focus your attention,"* warned Grym. *"Yet, you've already unlocked the power of the Eye. You still wield it through me. Just be cautious."*

She aimed a bolt at Erebus's feet. The ground beneath him erupted, tossing him into the air. He landed hard, with blood on his forehead.

Susan faltered. She hadn't meant to kill him. Would he survive?

*"Focus! Worry about him later."*

She turned back to the College around her. White Claw now outnumbered the remaining Dragons. Several creatures sped away, racing over the Ring.

*"We've done it."* She smiled, lowering her hands.

Something rumbled to the west. Turning, she saw an enormous black shape lift from the earth. A shadow larger than a mountain uncoiled from the forest, a black shape she'd faced before.

*The Shadow King.*

Four red Dragons flanked the gargantuan beast. His body was even bigger than Susan remembered. His wings stretched from horizon to horizon. With a monstrous roar, the Shadow King bellowed. Even miles away, Susan felt the wind from his breath, and smelled the stench of hot sulfur. The five Dragons flew toward the Ring of Scythes.

Snapping her attention back to the power around her, Susan reached into the sky. The spinning wheel of clouds and lightning lowered, belting her waist. She placed both of her hands together, facing her open palms to the west.

*All fire: every flame that ever burned, every flicker yet to spark.*

She channeled the surge of lightning, flame, and pure energy.

The Swarm flowed through her, swimming along the bolt of power.

Pouring everything into the blast, she fired at the Shadow King.

Fire twisted around lightning, blazing with white-hot intensity.

The blast of energy rammed into the Shadow King.

For a moment, the enormous Dragon paused. He screamed, opening his mouth wide.

A wave of darkness spewed from between the King's fangs, engulfing the all-fire.

Inch by inch, the blast of energy vanished behind a shadowed veil.

Susan fought back, urging the power to continue. She dipped into the Swarm, grasping with her mind, reaching for every possible trace of energy.

The Shadow King swept over the Ring of Scythes and slammed into West Tower, throwing his massive weight against the pillar of gnarled stone.

He burst through the other side.

Susan stared.

Frank, Michi, and hundreds of Deaths stood on the pinnacle.

West Tower collapsed.

Boulders toppled to the ground amid a rising cloud of dirt and debris.

Screams sounded from the peak.

With a horrible snap, the rope bridge ripped apart, and the flames vanished.

The orb beneath her feet shattered.

Susan fell, hurtling to the ground.

Power sapped out of her, sucked away with the vanished Eye.

She reached for Grym, yet a sense of exhaustion overwhelmed her.

The sapphire flames flared out.

Susan plummeted.

CHAPTER FORTY-TWO—FRANK

# Reunion

**F**rank's ears ached from the sound of the explosion.

He clung to Michi.

An enormous mass of stone beneath his feet fell through the open air.

Deaths and Elementals in every direction screamed.

Boulders crumbled atop loose stone.

Thick smoke clouded the air.

Down he fell, with the collapsing tower.

Down, down, down.

Everyn yelled something. Stones moved, water spouted.

The chaos was too great.

He watched through a blurred haze, turning his eyes skyward.

*The Shadow King.*

The enormous Dragon's body was magnificent. Stretching for thousands of feet, rows of beautiful black scales caught the light, sucking it away like shadows. His wings spanned as far as Frank could see, great powerful wings, gliding along the air with ease.

A terrible longing gripped his soul.

Even as he fell, he watched a grove of glowing birches.

The song sang through his mind and heart:

*Can you hear me, oh my love?*
*As ever sunsets drift away,*
*Where is the joy we sang to life?*

*Where are the broken souls*
*And the faded day?*

*Spin the broken wheel of fate,*
*Fold your wings and war no more.*
*Return to me, your once-bound wife.*
*Steer anger beyond death;*
*As once we swore.*

*Can you hear me, broken king?*
*Do you recall our dying plea,*
*Made on embers of a faded song?*
*Fold your wings and war no more.*
*Return to me.*

The Shadow King paused, hovering in mid-air. His wings flapped in a slow motion, stirring the cloudy wind.

*Can you hear me?*

In a flash of light, Frank stood on an open field, surrounded by sunlight.

Two enormous creatures filled the sky. One, a Dragon with rainbow scales, and the other a Dragon formed from black shadow.

"The Earth Dragons wouldn't approve." The enormous Shadow Dragon circled the Earth Dragon. He nipped her tail, but not in attack.

"I am the Queen, just as you lead the Shadow Dragons." The rainbow-scaled Dragon spun in mid air, butting heads with the other.

The two creatures landed, laughing. Fanged smiles stretched across each face.

The Shadow King stood on his hind legs, shouting at the sky. He sat, and the Earth Queen nuzzled against his chest.

"It's natural that you and I should come to this. You are my shadow, after all."

"Is that all I am to you?" The Shadow King playfully nudged her neck.

"I fear for the gift I tried to give. The figure I created, in the image of the Donkari, has become twisted."

"Caladbolg." The Shadow King spit. "My Dragons convinced him to attack a group of Earth Dragons. I am sorry, my love."

"My subjects are no better. This war must end."

The image grew brighter, until the vision faded.

*Return to me.*

Once again, boulders tumbled through smoke.

Frank's fall halted.

His shirt tore open.

Glancing to either side, he saw wings of gossamer emerging from his back. Each thin wing shimmered with a dizzying display of rainbow colors. He flapped them, still holding Michi.

"Frank?" She opened her eyes, staring at his face.

"I love you, Michi."

"What's happening?"

Answers flowed around his thoughts, just out of reach. The rainbow wings continued to flap. He stared at the Shadow King.

"The soul snatcher took most of my soul. A different soul found me, and buried itself in my body. It was the Earth Queen, the Earth Dragon who loved the Shadow King."

Michi's eyes widened. "The one he's trying to resurrect? Frank, how is that possible?"

"Her soul lived on, trapped in a forest. Michi, I can hear her thoughts, see with her eyes. She's becoming me."

"Fight it. You have to resist."

"That's not the answer. Don't you see? This is the solution we've been looking for. Do you love me, Michi?"

"You're scaring me, Frank."

"Do you love me?"

"Yes."

He embraced her. "I love you, too."

A soft white light enveloped them both. Distant screams faded into the background.

The Shadow King spun, facing them.

The light grew brighter, extending beyond his hands and wings. Michi became a part of him, a part of *her*.

*We are the Earth Queen, reborn.*

A million years of memories coincided with two tiny glowing souls. Two Elementals who loved each other.

For a moment, the smaller souls stood before the enormous, powerful song.

An ancient voice called out.

*"All love is precious."*

Three souls became one.

*We are the Earth Queen, reborn.*

The Earth Queen spread her wings, soaring toward the Shadow King.

CHAPTER FORTY-THREE—SUSAN

# The Shattered Door

Susan fell.

Debris and smoke shot past. Before the Death's eyes closed in exhaustion, the terrible sight of West Tower crumbling into a mountain of rubble filled her sight.

With a sharp jolt, claws wrapped around her stomach.

Brandr flapped his wings, pulling Susan from her freefall, and coasted to the ground.

The green Dragon set her down beside the Examination Hall. A Dragon's bloody corpse hung over the edge of the black cube.

Brandr wrapped his leathery wings around her, blocking the onslaught of dust and debris rushing from West Tower.

"Frank and Michi! We have to find my friends!"

Sapphire flames emerged on her arm, dim and weak compared to what they'd been mere moments before.

She stared at Frank, hovering above the ruins. Two enormous rainbow wings extended from his back. He clutched Michi to his chest. As she watched, a blinding light swept over them, and the Elementals vanished.

A Dragon with shimmering rainbow scales flapped its wings.

*"The Earth Queen."* Grym stared in disbelief. *"Somehow, she's been reborn."*

Frank and Michi were nowhere to be seen.

Susan stared and waved her arm, appearing with a blue flash on Brandr's back.

"Something's happened to them. Take me over there."

Brandr snorted. Flapping with slow, measured strokes, he approached the rainbow Dragon.

The creature flew higher, soaring toward the Shadow King. She noticed Brandr and Susan. Turning her head, the Earth Queen opened her fanged mouth.

Two eyes of swirling green flame appeared, hovering behind Susan's thoughts.

*With a flash of green fire, she stood on the endless sea.*

*A flaming sky filled the hemisphere above.*

*Her feet rested on the crests of gentle waves.*

*Caladbolg stood beside her, robed in sapphire.*

*In front of her, Frank and Michi stood hand in hand.*

*"This is goodbye." Frank took a step forward. "Susan, you're one of the best friends we've ever known."*

*"We'll miss you." A tear ran down Michi's cheek.*

*"There's no time to linger." Frank shook his head, his eyes blazing with green flame. "Sindril has Will and Hope. Stop him."*

*"I don't understand." Susan started forward, but Caladbolg grabbed her arm.*

*"They're already gone."*

Susan blinked, back on Brandr's back. She clung to a narrow spike protruding from his spine.

The Earth Queen and the Shadow King circled each other above, filling the sky with their slow, strange dance.

"Take me to the library."

"What?" Brandr snarled. "The Dragons. What should we—"

"They won't hurt us anymore. We need to get to the library, Sindril has my family."

Brandr banked to the right, and veered south, away from the smoky campus. Blood, corpses, and boulders covered everything. The College lay in ruins. A dark cloud hung where West Tower once stood.

They passed over the Ring of Scythes, landing near the Southern Forest. Susan ran forward. A Dragon's body lay face up outside the small ivy-covered cottage. She waved her arm, vanishing in sapphire light.

She emerged in the underground library.

"Will? Hope?"

Searching from side to side with dread she saw the duffle lying on the table. She ran to Samas. The tiny Dragon's body lay at an odd angle. She touched its wing. Her eyes darted to Hinara. Sprawled against the stairs, the Elemental sat in a pool of blood.

Susan waved her arm, vanishing into sapphire again.

She re-emerged on Brandr's back. "Samas and Hinara are dead. There's no sign of Will or Hope. I don't know where he'd take them."

The ground shuddered. Above the trees, something moved in the sky.

Brandr jumped, flapping his leathery wings.

They hovered above the trees. To her left, Susan saw the two enormous Dragons, still circling each other again and again. Overhead, the gash of light shone between clouds. To her right, a column of white streaked into the sky.

*"Those are souls, Susan. Escaping into this world, released from the Hereafter."* Grym's words echoed with urgency. *"Sindril must be at the Door."*

"I'm going ahead. Gather White Claw and join us at the Door to the Hereafter when you're able."

Brandr nodded.

Susan waved her arm, letting the flames claw through space.

In a flash, she stood on a narrow strip of land.

Behind her, a cliff stretched from horizon to horizon. A few yards away from the beach, water thundered skyward for hundreds of feet.

Up and up the water surged, into a reverse waterfall. Between the massive walls of water and stone, a narrow stretch of sky arced.

In the middle of the upward-flowing wall of water, a metal door stood.

*The Door to the Hereafter.*

*Where souls go to move on.*

The Door stood ajar, and searing white light poured through the crack.

Souls rushed from the open door, racing into the torn sky above, and vanishing into the glowing gash in the heavens.

"Susan. Right on time." Sindril smiled. He held something in his hand, something red. Two Dragons, each crimson, flanked his left and right.

Will lay a few yards away. Susan sliced the air, rushing to his side. She untied his bound hands, pulling a gag from his mouth.

"I tried to stop him, Susan. I'm so sorry."

"Where's Hope?"

Will's eyes darted.

She used Grym to appear beside her daughter. A gag stretched across Hope's mouth, and when Susan pulled it free, the baby screamed. Her tiny legs flailed in wild, jerking motions. Hope's left leg ended in a blood-covered stump. Three glowing souls stood at the baby's feet, pressing against the spot where her foot should be. A faint blue glow appeared on the wound.

"Save her," whispered Susan. "Save my daughter."

*"The souls stopped the blood loss. I shall help as well."* Sapphire light slipped from Susan's arm, wrapping around Hopes kicking leg. Susan pressed her hand to the baby's forehead, and she quieted. Power from the ancient scythe coalesced into a bandage, wrapped tightly around the limb. The three souls nodded, drifting away.

Susan brought Hope to Will's arms, and she turned to face Sindril. He stood on the narrow rocks in front of the Door.

Rage coursed through every fiber of her body.

"You sick bastard. You brought me to this world, tore four years from my soul, threatened me with rape, and now cut off my baby's foot? *You're insane.*"

Sindril laughed, turning to the Door. He held the severed foot like a trophy.

The crimson Dragons lunged forward, spewing fire.

Susan caught the flames, spun, and severed one of the creature's heads. The other Dragon charged. The sapphire of Grym shot forth in a bolt of lightning, and the Dragon collapsed into the water.

Sindril pressed Hope's foot into the Door.

"Behold, the Dragon Key." He laughed with maniacal frenzy.

The Door exploded. Fragments of iron shot in every direction. The reverse waterfall collapsed, surging down. A tidal wave rushed at the beach.

Susan stared. The sea roared, surging from the collapsing wall of water. Tumbling forward, water slammed into both beach and cliff.

With a quick breath, Susan grabbed Will and Hope. In a flash of blue, they appeared at the top of the cliff.

Wave after wave pounded into the rocks below them. The ocean churned, rolling in massive heaving swells.

Water surged and frothed beneath them.

The waterfall was nowhere to be seen. Only a seething ocean stood beneath the sheer cliff face. Behind her, a narrow plateau of open stone formed a long strip, stretching north and south to the horizons. The causeway was fifteen feet wide, a line of rock running twenty feet above the water like a bridge. Waves frothed on either side.

Will clutched Hope, sobbing. Susan turned back to the new-formed sea.

A pool of water glowed white, erupting into a column of energy.

Billions upon billions of souls surged toward the gash in the sky. Countless individuals, souls once at peace, screamed, pulled out of the Hereafter.

Sindril appeared in a flash of silver. He held a double-bladed scythe, yet Susan sensed this was no boskery blade.

"It didn't work." He frowned. "I should be back at home, in the Mortal World. Time should have been undone. Not just the waterfall and the Door, but *all time*. Perhaps a foot wasn't enough. I need *more* for a proper Dragon Key."

Susan ran forward, holding her right arm across her chest.

Sindril spun the blades.

Mortamant clashed against her wrist.

He jumped back, and she swung again. Sindril whirled the double-scythe into a wheel of silver, slicing the air.

"I only want to go home." He ran at her again.

Grym erupted with a blast of sapphire energy. Sindril dodged, jumping to the left.

"You brought me here. You destroyed my life, and threaten my family." Susan's jaw set. "I'll kill you."

Sindril jumped into the air, twirling the double-scythe.

Susan straightened, bracing herself, but held her arm still. He slammed the blade against her arm. With a clang, one of the blades broke, and shards flew in every direction. She spun around, blocking the other blade just before it nicked her leg.

With a roar, the Earth Queen and Shadow King emerged in the sky above. Their bodies moved in a constant circle, one half scaled in shimmering rainbow, the other half in black shadow. Their wings nestled behind their backs, while their enormous bodies swam on, moving as one. They danced, Dragon and Dragon, as they spun.

*"They are one."* Grym's voice dropped to a whisper. *"The two great powers. Earth and her Shadow."*

Susan looked up. Sindril smashed the scythe into her left arm. She collapsed to the ground, clutching a gash. Hot blood ran across her fingers.

The Dragons above sang a deep, powerful song. Their bodies blurred into solid light.

She saw a flash of flaming green eyes.

*"My final gift."*

A wall of sapphire flames engulfed Susan, dissipating in blue sparks. Caladbolg stood before her, facing Sindril.

Susan waved her arm, but nothing happened. Grym was no longer tied to her.

The ancient king's beard waved in the wind. He wore a long, black robe, with a bright emerald hourglass seal on the back.

Above, the sky flared and then dimmed.

Both Dragons vanished, and the gash in the sky disappeared.

A deep rolling sound, accompanied by the pungent smell of sulfur, echoed from the sky.

Souls turned in mid-air, streaming back to the ocean.

One by one, the glowing souls hit the water like falling stars. Splatters of water turned to heaving waves, as the ocean surged and frothed. The water moved in greater swells. Waves rolled and burst. The entire sea boiled, bubbling beneath the onslaught of rushing souls.

Caladbolg, Sindril, and Susan stared at the changing landscape.

The boiling sea sank away from the stony causeway. Water shrank back from the narrow strip of land, and a gap opened. A deep fissure widened, pushing the swirling expanse of ocean farther from them.

With a roar, foaming waves leaped upward. The reverse waterfall reformed. Where the Door once stood, a rectangular gap of searing white light now blazed.

"You've ruined everything." Sindril ran forward, but Caladbolg grabbed his arms.

Blue flames surrounded Sindril and Grym. The First Scythe turned his head. His eyes glistened with tears. "Goodbye, Susan."

He jumped, diving off the cliff. Sindril struggled while Caladbolg pulled him into the pool of glowing white at the center of the waterfall. Grym and Sindril vanished into the Hereafter.

Wind whipped past Susan. The wall of water transformed into a mountain of surging flame, and then blazed into a mass of solid sapphire light. With a deafening blast, the wall of water re-appeared.

Hope gurgled behind her. The baby cried out, uttering a strange word that sounded almost like "door."

The shards of iron flew into the air, reforming the shattered Door. Piece by piece, the iron solidified.

The Door slammed shut, vanishing.

Water flowed upward, toward the unbroken cloudy sky.

Susan turned to Will, throwing her arms around him.

"It's over."

The Deaths embraced, holding their daughter and letting the tears flow.

## CHAPTER FORTY-FOUR—WILL

# Aftermath

**B**randr folded his wings, landing atop the long cliff face.

To their left, twenty feet below, the sea stretched westward, ending at the just-visible shores of the mainland and the Acheron Delta. Will remembered the long explanation Elkanah gave him aboard the ship.

*That seems a lifetime ago.*

To their right, a chasm a thousand feet deep ended in a narrow strip of land. A few yards away, the upward-flowing waterfall brought wave after wave back to sea level. The sky beyond the waterfall cleared. Clouds parted, and the first evening stars twinkled near the dimming eastern horizon. The smell of salt filled the air.

Will gazed at Susan.

The woman he loved sat with Hope on her lap. Lines of dried blood covered her face and neck. Her black shirt clung to her sweaty chest. Her jeans wore torn in dozens of places, many stained red. Will's shirt wrapped around her left arm, bandaging a deep gash.

Hope squirmed. Her left leg was covered by the strange bandage Susan had created. The baby cried, kicking her legs and arms.

Brandr snorted, tapping his foreleg like an impatient horse.

Will stood, the cool sea air blowing across his bare chest. "What now?"

He took Hope from her mother, cradling the child. Susan rose, wincing when her left arm brushed against stone.

"Decisions have to be made." She stared at the spot where the hourglass mark once appeared. A faint reddish scar was all that remained of the First Scythe. "Brandr, we'll need you to fly us."

Jurna spiraled out of the sky, landing a few feet away. Other Dragons flew close behind.

"Where are we going?" asked the green Dragon.

"Let's return to the College. What's left of it."

"Climb on."

Brandr lowered his body to the rocks, flattening his chest against the causeway. Will put Hope on the ground, kissing his daughter on the forehead. After helping Susan climb up, he lifted the baby.

"You take her, Will. My arm hurts too much. Ride on Jurna."

He nodded. With no clear way of carrying Hope, he put her against his chest, and she rested her tiny arms on his neck. He supported her body with one hand, while struggling onto the back of the white Dragon with the other. Gripping a small black spike with his left hand, he clutched Hope with the right. Jurna looked so much like her brother. It seemed an age since Elkanah grabbed Will, carrying him across the sea.

"Let's go."

The two Dragons jumped into the air, and he felt the scales beneath him tense. The cloudy-white scales radiated a soft heat, pulsing with every breath. Jurna spread her long wings, catching the sea breeze. Wind whipped against his naked skin, and the scales chafed where his jeans clung to the Dragon's body.

The Dragons circled, gaining altitude. The strip of land at the Door appeared like a dark fissure beside a long, narrow stone road. They banked, heading west. Soaring past the forest, they soon saw the College.

The Ring of Scythes gleamed with a dull silvery light, around an enormous cloud of swirling smoke. East Tower stood before them, a gnarled mass of stone rising above the debris, the solitary tower of the campus.

Will's breath caught. "What happened to West Tower?"

"Destroyed in the battle." Jurna flew on, her wings gliding in gentle strides.

They circled lower, and the stench of blood and smoke choked his lungs. Corpses of Dragons and Elementals covered the College of Deaths. The once graceful maze of earthen mounds was a nightmarish disarray of smashed boulders and shattered stone.

An Elemental with a short purple beard and dog ears ran forward. One by one, the Dragons of White Claw landed in the debris.

"What happened?" shouted the Elemental. "Is it over? We saw the two Dragons vanish."

"The battle's done." Will slid off Jurna.

Susan nodded. "Gather everyone you can find. Elementals, Deaths, and Dragons. We'll meet on the boskery field outside the Ring of Scythes." She turned back to Brandr. "There are people on East Tower, at the summit. Have White Claw bring everyone there to the boskery field."

The Dragon snorted, jumping into the air. White Claw followed.

"I need to do the same." Susan winced again. "We have to figure who's alive, and how to proceed."

"You need to rest. You're hurt."

"They'll be time to rest soon. If we don't sort things now, the situation will deteriorate into another fight. We need things to change. Elementals, Dragons, and Deaths *have* to work together." She glanced at the ruins around them. "Remember the souls we saw in the Mortal World? Someone has to start reaping again. The College is a shambles, and for the first time in this world, all three races *must* work in harmony. It's the only way forward."

Will nodded. The love and admiration flowing through his chest could not be stronger.

"Take Hope to the field now. I don't want her breathing in this smoke."

"No." Will shook his head. "You might be the strongest woman in the three worlds, but you're hurt and you're tired. Besides, if Hope gets hungry, I can't help. *You* take her to the boskery field. Wait for me and rest. I'll gather everyone. We'll be there by sundown."

She nodded, a resigned, happy grin creeping onto her face. He handed Hope to her, and watched them walk through the Ring of Scythes.

Turning back to the chaos of the College, he started forward.

For over an hour, he worked his way over rubble, around bleeding corpses and cowering survivors. Progress was slow, yet continuous. Around one bend, a familiar figure brushed dirt from his purple robe.

"Headmaster Hann!"

"William Black. Never expected to see you again." The older Death clasped his arm around Will's back. Behind them, Professor Domen and Gordon staggered arm in arm through a cloud of debris.

"We're gathering everyone we can, all the survivors able to walk. Those who are too injured to move are remaining here. Everyone else is meeting at the boskery field."

Hann nodded. "The world's going to change."

"If you see anyone else, spread the word. I'm heading to the field now."

"It's good to see you, Will. I'll join you soon."

Will nodded, skirting the base of East Tower. A 'Mental with pink hair and sea-gray eyes stood near the doors.

"Is Susan all right?" The 'Mental leaped up, running to Will.

"Yes. I'm going to her now. Everyone is. You fought with her?"

"My name's Mokosh. I was in her company. When White Claw started evacuating East Tower, I used my power to climb down the elevator shaft and see if any others survived. I haven't found anyone."

"Thank you for looking. Let's go. Everyone's gathering at the boskery field."

They walked through the clearing smoke. Some sections of campus had fared better than others. Will paused, before moving past one of the bloodied mounds.

"What is it?" Mokosh hurried after him.

"I just want to check something."

He lingered at a low-lying wall. A layer of dark soot covered the side, and part of a charred desk sat on its top. Wiping the soot away, he revealed a painted eagle clutching two scythes in its hand. The door to Eagle Two stood ajar.

Mokosh followed him as he walked into the vacant building. He hadn't been here for years. Shafts of dim light streamed through shattered windows. At last, he reached the familiar door. Eagle Two, Room Five.

"I can't believe it's unharmed."

"What is this place?"

"This was our home." Will turned. "It *is* our home. Forgive the detour. Come on, the sun's almost down."

They left, passing through more of the ruined campus as they headed south. Beyond the Ring of Scythes, they encountered a growing crowd. Elementals, Deaths, and Dragons trudged toward the boskery field.

Will searched the throng for Susan, and found her on the bleachers, rocking Hope. He ran to his family.

"Eagle Two's one of the places that survived intact. We have a home to return to."

She smiled. "How long is it since we've been able to say those words?"

"Too long." Will kissed her forehead.

She nodded. "Let's get started."

Handing Hope to Will, Susan stood on the bleachers, climbing until she faced everyone.

"You all know me. I came to this world years ago when I was taken from my home. I wasn't given much of a choice. I never wanted to become a Death, or to wield the First Scythe. Many of you are here today because circumstances forced your hand. Elementals, Dragons, and Deaths fought for millennia. Three races forced to share one world, now brought together in a battle none of us asked to fight."

Wind blew Susan's hair as she waved her good arm. The sun sank behind her, outlining her clothes in golden-orange. "The time for fighting is past. The time to rebuild our world has arrived. I saw into Caladbolg's heart, and I do not believe he was created as a weapon. We all saw the union of Earth Dragon and Shadow Dragon. The power that shaped this world long ago was love. Love gave me a family, a man I adore, and a daughter I cherish. Through love, all three races must come together."

The crowd watched in silence. A breeze rippled overhead. Hope gurgled in Will's arms.

"The College needs to be rebuilt, but not as before. Let us welcome other girls from the Mortal World. We'll give them a choice, to stay if they *want* to. In time, generations will grow, and no one will need to be brought from elsewhere."

Some of the Deaths watching started to murmur.

"There's more." Susan stared at them. "We lost one of the towers. Many Deaths huddled on East Tower. I think it likely many were on West Tower as well. We might have lost hundreds, if not thousands of Deaths, and we don't even know they're gone. There are countless un-reaped souls, and a severe lack of mortamant. The solution is obvious. Dragons and Deaths must work together. Both races shall be reapers."

More of the crowd muttered. Some started to shift uneasily.

"I'm not finished." Susan held up her hand, quieting them. "Elementals once built and shaped this world. They created the College. It's natural that they lead the efforts to rebuild the World of Deaths. Yet, they are never again to be treated as servants or lesser citizens. Deaths, Dragons, and Elementals must work in harmony. All three are equal."

"What gives you the right to decide all of this?" Erebus struggled forward. His hands were bound with rope behind his back. Will felt it necessary to bind all of the Deaths who'd worked with the Shadow

Dragons. "I've been a Death far longer than you, Susan. Dragons reaping with Deaths? The idea's ludicrous."

"You helped the Dragons during the battle." She took a step down from the bleachers. "Eshue was under hypnosis. I sensed it with Grym. Were you? Or was it by choice?" Erebus bristled, scowling.

"Enough." Giri walked to the front of the crowd. "Susan's right. There's no other way. Souls need to be Reaped, and our homes need to be rebuilt. Our lives have been thrown into chaos. I lost my sister and my son today."

*What? Frank? He's gone? And where's Michi?* Will stared at Susan, and she gave a slight shake of the head.

"I've suffered just as everyone has. It's our choice. This battle was not in vain. Their sacrifices will not be forgotten." Giri paused, and his voice softened. "When the two Dragons joined in the sky, I received a message. A last communication from my son, Plamen. He told me that love was the foundation of the three worlds. The walls have risen again, however the Mortal World, the In-Between, and the World of Deaths are all bound by the love used to create them. When the Shadow King and Earth Queen sealed the gap, they ensured that new Dragon Keys could never be formed again." Giri glanced at Hope. "Deaths can have children. Susan's right. If we start families here, in time we won't need to harm families in the Mortal World. Dragons can once again live in peace, without the obsessed longings of an ancient king. Their race shall thrive again. Elementals will earn the respect they deserve. We have suffered in the shadows for too long."

Brandr turned his head to the twinkling stars emerging overhead. "I speak for White Claw. We support this change. Let this night mark the birth of our new world. It is no longer the World of *Deaths*. This is the World of *Shadows*. That is how it began, and how it shall be known moving forward."

"The World of Shadows." Susan nodded. "It's a world I'm proud to call home."

"The World of Shadows." Giri stared up at the dusking sky. "Plamen would be proud."

The crowd nodded. Will walked to Susan and took her hand.

"There's so much to be done." Hann walked to the front of the group. "Susan, you have shown yourself to be a great leader. I am grateful."

She nodded.

Will squeezed her hand as she turned away. "Frank and Michi? What happened to them?"

"Their sacrifice saved us all."

## CHAPTER FORTY-FIVE—SUSAN

# Funeral of the Nameless

Susan opened her eyes. Sunlight slipped past the curtains of the small bedroom in Eagle Two. Will lay to her left. She slipped out of bed, careful not to wake him.

She tiptoed to the stone bassinet Everyn built. Hope slept soundly, her small face stretched into a smile. One of the baby's arms pawed at the air. Moving the blanket aside, Susan surveyed her daughter's legs. Her right toes squirmed, clenching and releasing. She pushed aside Grym's bandage. Her left leg ended in a stump, now scabbed over. Susan slipped the bandage back, kissing her daughter's forehead.

Opening the bedroom door, she glanced at the bed. Will snored. Sneaking out, she closed the door gently behind and walked to the kitchen.

Narrow banded clouds streaked the sky. East Tower loomed in the distance, its gnarled walls reaching skyward like an enormous stalagmite. Beneath East Tower, the rest of the College lay in ruins. A dusty haze still lingered over much of the campus, even now, a week after the battle.

Susan sighed. She glanced at her forearm, and the tiny red mark almost invisible above her wrist. She couldn't shake the feeling of emptiness.

*I don't miss Grym. I hated him. Didn't I?*

Flexing her fingers, she glanced at the distant tower peak.

*I stood above the College, more powerful than a god.*

*I won the battle. I defeated Sindril.*

*Why do I feel so hollow?*

For a week, they'd searched for other survivors. Hann insisted on making her a leader, at least in name. She was the "Ambassador of Deaths," whatever *that* meant.

In the back of her mind, screams echoed. This was unlike Grym's visions, or even Frank's messages. She tried to ignore the memories, yet they persisted like a nightmare lingering in the recesses of thought long after waking.

*How many did I kill?*

"You're up before Hope?" Will stood in the doorway.

"This time. She's up every couple of hours."

He embraced her, and she sank into his comfortable arms.

"Susan, what's wrong? You were staring out the window again. The same far-off look."

"The funeral's today. It's been a week since the battle. I just can't stop wondering how many *I* killed myself. If I'd waited, and the Shadow King vanished, would the Dragons have stopped fighting?"

"You know that wouldn't have happened. They'd have killed you. Hope would have no mother, and I'd be lost. What's worse is that neither of us would even know why. Susan, you did what was necessary. Stop beating yourself up."

He stroked her hair, rubbing his tender hands down her back.

Will glanced outside. "We should get ready. They'll begin soon."

Susan followed him back into the bedroom. Will changed into his training robe, the black hooded cloak with a yellow skull embroidered on the front. Even four years later, it fit. Susan's clothes didn't fit at all. Mokosh had loaned her a long black dress with satin sleeves. Will helped her tie the back after Hope ate.

Carrying the baby into the kitchen, she sat at the table. He made some toast and poured two glasses of water.

"If all continues on schedule, Reapings should resume next week." Will sat beside her. "Hann's been working hard coordinating with Brandr. I don't know how the Dragons will Reap, they *eat* souls."

"Dragons formed the Door to the Hereafter. They opened that gateway in the first place. Maybe every Dragon has their own pathway within."

Will raised an eyebrow. "The Dragons take souls to the Hereafter through their stomachs?"

"It wouldn't be the strangest thing we've seen. Besides, we know so little about them."

"That's true." He shook his head. "At any rate, yesterday Brandr said he was sending two members of White Claw to investigate the temple Frank mentioned. The one where Deaths worshipped the Shadow King. I suspect they'll be the last ones to welcome this new world."

"Not the last. I visited Erebus in the Armory. He still refuses to join the new College or even to acknowledge that he was a part of the enemy's plan. I don't know what will happen to him."

They lapsed into silence, staring at their food. Hope gurgled, pressing against her dress.

*We're not running for our lives, or fighting for survival. I should feel happy.*

Will touched her hand.

"I miss them too, Susan. Frank and Michi were our closest friends."

She nodded, rising. "Let's get going."

She placed Hope in the carrier, strapping it around her chest.

They left Eagle Two.

Hand in hand, they walked through the campus. Others joined them, walking in silent procession. Will nodded to the other Deaths, and smiled at the 'Mentals. Susan stared straight ahead, forcing one foot after the other.

They joined a growing crowd at the rubble on the western edge of the College. Deaths, 'Mentals, and Dragons stood in a clearing surrounded by shattered boulder fragments. No one spoke.

At one end of the clearing, a large timber pyre stood, where the doors to West Tower once opened. On the pyre, the tiny golden Dragon Samas lay between two Elementals. On one side, Lyrna lay face up, her yellow hair tied back behind her head, and her hands clasped at her chest. Her brother Lumyr gave Susan a curt nod. Hinara's body rested on the opposite side of Samas, in a similar position. Behind the pyre, three empty chairs sat, each piled high with flowers.

Brandr, Giri, and Hann walked to the pyre.

Hann wore his purple Headmaster robe. "This week has been arduous. I thank you all. Together we've recovered the injured and removed the corpses." He held the golden scythe used to seal the Ring of Scythes. Tapping it on the pyre, he straightened. "Now, we lay the final three bodies to rest."

Giri's fingers clenched and unclenched. "Today, we celebrate the lives of my sister and my son, as well as my dear friend Michi. We also honor the Elemental Lyrna, and the Dragon Samas." He paused, turning his single eye to Michi's mother, who stood listless in the front row. "We remember the hundreds of others lost: comrades and former enemies alike. For on this day, there are no more enemies. This is a new world, the *World of Shadows*, a place where Dragons, Elementals, and Deaths share a single heart and single purpose. On this day, let no one shed tears. Let us rejoice in the knowledge that their sacrifices have brought the greatest change the three worlds have ever seen."

Brandr nodded. "Samas was my mentor and my friend. He taught me a great deal. Many good Dragons perished. Others who died were misguided, following a mad king to their own destruction. I've never considered Elementals or Deaths friends before." He turned, looking at Susan. "Yet, I'm ready to try."

Hann lifted the golden scythe. Everyn and Koros stepped out of the crowd, walking to him. A deep gash ran along Koros's face, and one of his ears had torn completely off, yet he smiled now.

"This scythe was used to seal the Ring around the College." Hann handed it to the two 'Mentals. "As our first gesture of peace, I have decided to never again seal the College from anyone. This scythe shall become part of our monument, a testament to peace."

Giri smiled. Susan saw the pain behind his one good eye. "The Elementals dedicate some of our powers to this monument. Using... using power once in Hinara and Lyrna, this monument will serve as a testament to peace."

Brandr grinned, baring white fangs. "The Dragons give flame to the monument. We also want peace."

Giri and Hann stepped down, joining the crowd that faced the pyre. Brandr opened his mouth, and a blast of flames engulfed the three corpses.

For ten minutes, the bodies burned before the silent crowd. Crackles rippled over sparking flames, and a stream of smoke wafted up. Everyn, and Koros walked forward, with palms raised.

The flames solidified, becoming black marble. An enormous block of stone emerged, and the pyre and corpses vanished. At the edge of the marble slab, the golden scythe lay, embedded into the monument. A thin column of gnarled white stone, a six-foot image of West Tower, climbed from the rear of the block.

Mokosh walked forward next. Waving her arms, a tiny moat appeared around the stone monument, and on each corner, a fountain leaped into the air. After a moment, the fountains began to glow. Four tiny flames emerged, one atop each fountain.

Susan smiled. The monument honored Elementals, Deaths, and Dragons equally. A wave of pride ran through her.

Hann stepped up to the memorial. "The water and fire in this monument will never go out. They shall serve as a living testament to our commitment toward peace between the races. Before we depart, I ask each of you to remember the Deaths especially. We will never know how many Deaths perished. Unlike Dragons and Elementals, the fallen Deaths have been wiped from history. We shall not rebuild West Tower. Instead, we shall remember. The Deaths who fought here are nameless, but like the Dragons and Elementals, they've forged a new world."

As one, the crowd chanted "A new world."

For a moment, no one knew what to do. Slowly, Deaths, 'Mentals and Dragons began walking up to the new memorial.

Susan and Will joined the crowd, admiring the strange, moving sculpture. The tiny flames dancing atop the fountain water intrigued her. She wanted to reach out and question the Swarm, however she refrained out of respect.

At last the crowds thinned.

Giri walked up to her, his face heavy with grief.

"I miss them."

She embraced him. "I do too."

CHAPTER FORTY-SIX—WILL

# The Second Wedding

$A$t the base of the hill, Silver Lake glistened in the afternoon sun. The calm waters reflected a blue sky with scattered white clouds. On the opposite bank, the small deserted village of Weston sat. The homes lay empty, like shells of a ghost town. Beyond Weston, at the edge of sight, the solitary spire of East Tower climbed over the horizon.

*This was once Widow's Peak.*

*I took Susan here, during her first day in this world.*

*There couldn't be a more perfect spot.*

He turned. Lovethar's Peak, as Susan renamed it, now stood cleared of weeds and overgrowth. The sides of the lone hill remained steep. A long row of new terraced steps extended from the lakefront to the top. He glanced at the far side of Lovethar's Peak.

*She's waiting. The woman I love, and the mother of our child.*

Despite the flurry of emotions he'd experienced since being brought to the Shadow World years ago, he'd never felt anything like this. His heart beat so fast it threatened to pop from his chest. His mouth ached because he couldn't stop smiling. Beads of sweat trickled over each palm.

"You nervous?" Gordon gave his shoulder a playful slap.

"G-G-glad my s-s-suit fit." Cronk grinned.

Will wiped his sweaty hands on his pants, and adjusted the jacket. Starting up the steps, he took a deep breath. Each long tier ended on either side with a bush of glowing flowers. Will walked with a steady stride, higher and higher, until he approached the top of the low hill.

Four massive rose bushes bloomed. Lucina, the foliate Elemental they'd met when they first journeyed to Karis years ago, grinned next to her handiwork.

Hann walked to Will, shaking his hand. Will's friends stood near the steps, facing them. Glancing behind the roses, he saw the ruins of an ancient staircase and a crumbled tower. On her first day in the Shadow World, Susan insisted on climbing this peak alone, and she'd fallen into those ruins.

Two girls in bright dresses started up the hill. Agmundria walked first, followed by Mokosh, who carried Hope in her arms. His daughter wore a pretty yellow dress that one of the Elementals sewed just for today.

Susan stepped into the sunlight. With every step up the stairs, Will's breath grew quicker. Mokosh and Agmundria joined the audience. Susan walked up to the pedestal.

She wore a long, flowing cream-colored dress studded with pearls. The bodice was tight, ending just above her breasts, and leaving her shoulders and arms bare. Beneath her waist, long waves of creamy satin stretched in a train. A circlet of silver and pearl crowned her sleek black hair, and she held a small bouquet of glowing flower lights.

*They stole that outfit from the Mortal World, just for us, and I'm not complaining.*

Hann gestured for the couple to hold hands. Susan passed the flowers to Agmundria, and took his fingers in hers. She smiled. For the first time since the battle, Susan seemed genuinely happy.

CHAPTER FORTY-SEVEN—SUSAN

# Eve of Tomorrow

**S**usan knocked on the door.

Hope burped, wriggling in the carrier.

Glancing around, the progress impressed her. Houses lined the street, masking the decimation that covered the village.

She knocked again, clutching the book in her left hand.

The door opened a crack. A single green flaming eye greeted her from the shadows.

"Come in, Susan."

Giri ushered her inside, closing the door behind them. Despite the new walls, most of the house was empty. Two wooden chairs sat in the corner of the otherwise vacant room. Giri sat, motioning for Susan to do the same.

"We missed you at the wedding."

"My apologies. Congratulations to you both. The grief is too fresh for me."

They lapsed into silence. Neither looked at the other. Susan ran her fingers along the book in her lap.

Giri rose. "Would you like anything? I can make tea."

"No, thank you."

"How are things at the College?" He adjusted his eye patch.

"Life's moving on, albeit slowly. Will's led a lot of the cleanup and rebuilding crews. He plans to coach boskery once they re-start the games."

"Sounds like he's doing well. What about you?"

"Hann asked me to lead one of the first joint Reapings. I refused. I don't want to Reap anymore."

He nodded, seeming unsurprised. "What will you do?"

"I'm going to teach. Someone at the College needs to teach the incoming girls about Lovethar, and about Women's Studies in general. It feels fitting."

Giri nodded again. "You think many will stay?"

"I don't know. Hann re-wrote the College's rules. They won't force people to become Deaths anymore. Brandr and White Claw helped, reshaping the way contracts are drafted. Souls won't be pulled here. Deaths will have to recruit, at least until families start developing. Still, with the Dragons helping Reap, we should be fine."

Another silence lapsed, broken by a low gurgle from Hope.

"You know why I've come, don't you?"

"I can guess. Before you ask about her, I repeat the question. What will *you* do?"

"I don't understand."

"You have a husband, a new position in the College, and an entire world that looks up to you. My entire family gave their lives to protect you, Susan. Yet, the one thing we each search for still eludes you."

"What is that?"

He turned, watching with his single eye of green flame. "Happiness, Susan. I see the same sadness consuming you that fills my heart."

"I'm happy. Things turned out the way we'd hoped."

Giri rose, and paced the vacant room. "Going through Plamen's things I found a parchment Hann gave him. It promised him any one request, if they came back from a rescue mission with information. I can see my son's face, convincing the Deaths to mount an expedition into the Dragonspine mountains." He sighed, turning away. "We both know what I've lost. As a seer, I also sense your loss. You held a power greater than any of us dream of, and it was snatched away. You murdered dozens of souls, and their faces haunt your dreams."

"It was war—"

"You killed them, didn't you? Susan, the same doubts tear at my heart. Like you, I suffered personal loss. Frank, Michi, Hinara, and even Kasumir before them. War isn't pretty and it isn't kind. War tears our hearts through the mud, and even if you win, you've lost a part of your soul forever. War is the greatest soul snatcher the three worlds shall ever see."

Susan stared at the book. *Lovethar's Diary.* She'd found it tucked in the back of her closet, forgotten for so long, a birthday gift from Frank. The distant ancestor who'd suffered persecution and witnessed a war.

"Things have to change." She spoke through clenched teeth. "For Hope's sake. How can I protect her from so much pain?"

"You can't."

She looked up.

"You expected a different answer, I know. The solution isn't to shield Hope, but to guide her. The first step on that journey is forgiveness. Susan, I grieve for my family, yet I harbor no remorse over my role in the conflict." He paused, standing in the center of the room. "You protected your family and changed the world. The only thing standing in the way of your happiness is guilt. I cannot forgive you, Susan, you have to forgive yourself."

She took a deep breath, and unfastened the harness. Holding Hope on her lap, she stared at the tiny face, the soft features, and the icy blue eyes so much like her father's. *Everything I did was for you and Will.*

"A good place to start." Giri walked behind her chair, placing a calm hand on her shoulder. "Children have an innocence and joy that makes all other problems melt away. I envy you. Your family loves and supports you. To return home every day and see that face waiting. It is a blessing." He smiled. "I know it's not how you started. However, I'd wager you're the single-most respected Death alive."

"Move into the College with us."

"What?"

"You've nothing here. The other 'Mentals can rebuild Karis. Will and I would be honored if you'd be her godfather. There are plenty of vacant homes around the College."

Giri touched Hope's cheek. The baby smiled, a tiny bubble of spit appearing between her miniature lips.

"For you, Susan. Yes, I think I will do that."

The baby wriggled.

Giri walked back to the other chair and sat again. "I think we're both feeling better."

Indeed, the more she watched Hope, the lighter her burden weighed. At night, she knew the screams of Dragons would return, just before she sank into dreams. For now, however, her mind focused on her family, and all the approaching joys of raising Hope in this new World of Shadows.

"Go on." He gestured to the diary. "Ask the other question. The real reason you came."

"You're a seer. Grym told me that Hope was a Dragon Key, the most powerful one ever created. Yet, when Sindril cut off her…" The words caught in her throat. She glanced at the stub on the end of her baby's left leg. "When he chopped off her foot, he said the Key didn't work."

Giri stared at Hope for a long moment. "I believe Grym was correct. She is far more powerful than Sindril or the Shadow King anticipated. Hope withdrew her power from her foot, a moment before the amputation. The Door shattered and the waterfall collapsed. All of that happened *without* her full power."

"She's only a child. She couldn't know what was happening."

"How does she know to cry or to suckle? How does she recognize your face or Will's? Instinct is a powerful force, Susan."

Hope squirmed in her lap. Susan remembered the souls swarming around her in the Mortal World, and the sound of the word "door" moments before the iron re-sealed.

"What will happen to her? Is she safe? Is she still a Dragon Key?"

Giri frowned. "When a seer looks at someone, a field appears around them. When I stare at you, I see so many possible futures, yet in all of them I see joy. I see you ushering in a generation of female Deaths, and becoming a model of integrity, leadership, and respect. I see you living a long, happy life with Will, who shall love you until he fades. Every soul I encounter holds stories and possibilities, and although I don't always know which path they'll take, I always see *something*."

"So what do you see when you look at Hope?"

"I see a veil. She *is* a Dragon Key, that is clear. I do not know if she retained her powers after the Dragons merged. I don't know anything about her. She sits before me like a shadow, a form I cannot penetrate with my eyes."

"I don't understand. Is she in danger?"

"Susan, I wish I could tell you that she'll be safe. I shall move into Eagle Two and help you and Will keep an eye on her, for now at least. I don't know who she is, or what she'll become."

They lapsed into silence again.

Running a finger along the diary's spine, she stared at the door. "What happened to Lovethar? How did she die?"

"She lived a long and happy life with her husband Orryn, and their son Gesayn. Yes, Gesayn was a Dragon Key as well, and no harm came to him after the first War."

"So history's on our side? Hope's going to be all right?"

Giri smiled, and reached forward, touching Susan's knee. "She has you for a mother, and Will for a father. I can't imagine stronger parents. Hope will be fine."

"One final question. In the fall, they're planning to bring girls here. It'll be their *choice*. Before we start repopulating this world, I need to know. Will their children become Dragon Keys?"

"Frank was clear. He spoke to me through the mind of the Earth Queen, sending a stronger message than I've ever received. Whatever her future, and whatever lies beneath the veil clouding my sight, Hope is the last Dragon Key."

Susan stood. "I should head back. I'm glad you'll be moving nearby."

At the door, Giri grasped her hand. "Protect her, Susan. No matter what happens."

"I will."

# Epilogue

**H**ope threw the ball high into the air.

Agmundria caught it, rolling to her side.

*"Your aim's pathetic."* The icy voice echoed in her mind.

"Hey, no telepathy. It creeps me out."

Betty ran up, slapping Hope on the back. The black girl's face spread into a playful smile. "Kid, your mom's calling you. You too, scary-girl."

"What? Now?" Hope frowned. "They do this every time we start having fun."

Uncle Giri waved them over. His glass eye stared in a lifeless direction. The other burned with green fire. "Come on, you two. This is important."

Walking away from the field, Hope followed her uncle. Agmundria tossed the ball to Betty, who smirked.

Hope spun around, making a fist. "Don't call her scary. You and Sarah are mean."

"Hey, it was just a joke. Lighten up, kid."

*"Ignore them. Come on, I'll race you."*

"Ha ha, very funny." Hope walked as fast as she could. With a wooden foot, she never outran any of her friends.

Agmundria walked beside her, her ponytail bobbing with each step.

*"It's just two weeks until we start getting some new Deaths."*

Hope nodded. "Thanks again for that boskery blade. Mom and Dad were so mad, but it's cool."

Agmundria grinned. *"I caused more mischief than you when I was seven, but don't use it without their permission."*

"Of course not." She winked.

*"Well at least don't get caught."*

They laughed.

A shadow crossed their path, and Hope glanced up at the two Dragons flying overhead, approaching East Tower.

Mom and Dad stood at the Ring of Scythes looking dour. Uncle Giri whispered something in Mom's ear and she nodded.

"Hope, were you having fun?"

"Yeah, until you and Dad made me stop."

"I'm sorry, honey. Today's an important day. We did this last year too, remember?"

"Are we going to visit your friends again? The stone ones?"

"That's right." Dad smiled, and picked her up. He spun her around, so that her arms straddled his neck in a piggyback ride. Though she was *far* too old for it, she humored him.

Dad walked through the Ring, setting her on the ground again. Mom reached into a pot and picked a large clump of small white flowers. Uncle Giri drew a clump of flowers himself. The three adults led the two girls at a slow pace through the College, until they reached the memorial.

Hope liked the monument. Around the giant marble block, four fountains bubbled, and on top of each one, a flame flickered. Fire burning on top of water, that was pretty neat. Mom separated some of the flowers, laying them on top of the golden scythe embedded into the stone's edge, and Uncle Giri did the same.

Dad pointed to the six-foot curvy spike emerging from the back of the enormous memorial. "You remember what that is, Hope?"

"You ask me this every time. It's a miniature version of West Tower, which used to stand here."

"Your mother was one of the strongest fighters in the war." Uncle Giri grinned. "Both your parents, and Agmundria too, all helped change this world forever."

Hope nodded. She touched the cool marble stone with her fingers. "That's when I lost my foot."

"That's right."

"Come on." Mom ran a hand through Hope's hair, resting it on her back.

They walked around the memorial, continuing west through the Ring of Scythes. Silver Lake glistened to their left, beneath the small mound of Lovethar's Peak. A narrow stone road cut through the open fields, turning to the right, and sloping uphill.

They continued in silence, climbing up steps. Clumps of flowerlights, like the ones in Mom and Uncle Giri's hands, stood at the end of each level. At the top, they paused at Silver Pond. The small pool of water reflected the blue sky above, forming a perfect mirror.

"I still get nostalgic here," Mom muttered to Dad. "This was the first spot Cronk brought me to in the World of Shadows. He showed me my reflection."

"It was my first stop in this world as well." Dad smiled. "Ancient history, now."

On the other side of the pond, two life-sized marble statues stood, gazing at the sky.

Hope turned, glancing at the College behind them. Uncle Giri and Agmundria sat on a narrow bench on the bank of Silver Pond, facing the stone figures. Mom and Dad sat on the other bench, beckoning her to join them.

The two marble figures held hands. One was a young man with a serious expression and a square jaw. The other was a soft-featured young woman with long hair. In one hand, she held a butterfly. Both statues reflected perfectly in the still pond waters.

"We've brought you here before, yet never told you the full story." Dad pointed to the statues. "Frank and Michi were our closest friends for a long time."

"They rescued us from villains, and were there the day you were born." Mom patted Hope's knee. "In the end, they sacrificed their lives to protect you."

"Me? Why would they do that?"

Dad, Mom, Agmundria, and Uncle Giri all took turns relaying the tale. Daylight faded. Hope knew parts of their story, but many of the details were new and exciting. She loved hearing about Frank's jump out of a window, with Michi's bugs helping him down.

Finally, Mom and Uncle Giri circled the small pool, laying their flowers at the statue's feet. The sun faded behind the trees, and Hope's stomach rumbled with hunger.

In the dim light, the flowers below Frank and Michi began to shine.

"This is when they look best." Mom smiled. "At dusk, illuminated by the glowing flower lights."

"I agree." Dad took her hand, and the two embraced.

One by one, Mom, Dad, Uncle Giri, and Agmundria started down the steps toward the College. Hope lingered.

The flower lights dimmed around the statues.

*They do look better when they're glowing.*

Hope gestured with a finger, and both statues filled with soft white light, not from the flowers, but emanating out of the stone itself.

*Much better.*

"Come on, Hope." Mom and the others were out of sight, already down the stairs.

She ran to catch up.

# About the Author

Christopher Mannino teaches high school theatre in Greenbelt, Maryland. Mannino holds a Master of Arts in Theatre Education from Catholic University, and has studied mythology and literature both in America and at Oxford University. His time in Oxford provided inspiration for The Scythe Wielder's Secret, and his work with young people helped encourage him to write young adult fantasy. Mannino is currently working on several adult novels. Learn more and discover free content including extra stories at www.ChristopherMannino.com

His wife, Rachel Mannino, is a romance author. Her website: www.RachelMannino.com

\* \* \* \*

*Did you enjoy Daughter of Deaths?*
*If so, please help us spread the word about*
*Christopher Mannino and MuseItUp Publishing.*
*It's as easy as:*

*•Recommend the book to your family and friends*
*•Post a review*
*•Tweet and Facebook about it*

*Thank you*
*MuseItUp Publishing*

MuseItUp
PUBLISHING

# The Scythe Wielder's Secret

*School of Deaths*

*Sword of Deaths*

*Daughter of Deaths*